The Man With
The Golden Torc

The Man With The Golden Torc

Simon Green

GOLLANCZ

LONDON

Copyright © Simon Green 2007
All rights reserved

The right of Simon Green to be identified as the author
of this work has been asserted by him in accordance with
the Copyright, Designs and Patents Act 1988.

First published in Great Britain in 2007 by
Gollancz
An imprint of the Orion Publishing Group
Orion House, 5 Upper St Martin's Lane, London WC2H 9EA

A CIP catalogue record for this book
is available from the British Library

ISBN-13: 978 0 57507 938 0 (cased)
ISBN-10: 0 57507 938 X (cased)
ISBN-13: 978 0 57507 939 7 (trade paperback)
ISBN-10: 0 57507 939 8 (trade paperback)

10 9 8 7 6 5 4 3 2 1

Typset by Input Data Services Ltd, Frome

Printed and bound at Mackays of Chatham plc, Chatham, Kent

The Orion Publishing Group's policy is to use papers that
are natural, renewable and recyclable products and made
from wood grown in sustainable forests. The logging and
manufacturing processes are expected to conform to the
environmental regulations of the country of origin.

www.orionbooks.co.uk

You know what? It's all true. Everything that ever scared you, from conspiracy theories to monsters under the bed to ghosties & ghoulies & long-leggity beasties. The only reason they haven't taken over the world is because my family has always been there to stand in their way. We guard the door, keeping you safe from the big bad wolf, and you never even know our names. Of course, there's a price to be paid. By us, and by you.

The name's Bond. Shaman Bond. Well, no; actually that's just my use-name. When your job description involves going one on one with creatures of the night on a regular basis, you have to find your humour where you can. My real name is Eddie Drood. Licensed to kick supernatural arse. My family is one of the oldest in England, perhaps the oldest, and we've been protecting Humanity from the forces of darkness for more centuries than even we care to remember. There are those who say Drood is just a derivation of Druid, but that's always seemed a bit too obvious for me. The job of a shaman is to protect his tribe from outside threats, and that's what I used to do. I loved my job. Until it all blew up in my face.

CHAPTER ONE
Everything but a bunch of grapes

It started out as just another everyday mission. A certain Very Important Politician, whose face and name you'd recognise, had come, very secretly, to Harley Street in London. Home to some of the most expert, and certainly some of the most expensive, specialised medical care in the whole of the civilised world. This politician, let's call him Mr President, and no not the one you're thinking of, had himself booked into the Hospice of Saint Baphomet under an assumed name, after contracting a supernatural venereal disease during a goodwill tour of Thailand. He was stupid enough to slip his handlers' leash and go looking for a little fun in the back-street bars of Bangkok; and unlucky enough to end up getting it on with an agent of darkness masquerading as a ladything. As a result of which Mr President was now heavily pregnant, with something the very opposite of a lovechild. I had been ordered to terminate this unnatural pregnancy with extreme prejudice. The offspring was not to be born; or if born, not allowed to run loose in the material world.

I'd been supplied with a gun, and I was expected to use it.

(How did we find out about this? My family knows everything. That's its job. And when you've been fighting the good fight for as many centuries as we have, you can't help but accumulate an extensive network of sources and informers.)

I strolled casually down Harley Street, hiding in plain sight. No one looked twice at me; no one ever does. I've been trained to blend in; to be just another face in the crowd. I was wearing a nicely anonymous three-piece suit, expensive enough to fit in but not stylish enough to draw attention. I strode down Harley Street like I had every right to be there, so everyone else assumed I did. It's about attitude, really. You can fit in anywhere with the right attitude. It helps that I have the kind of face that always reminds you of someone else; average, pleasant, nothing to jog your memory afterwards. An agent's face.

It's all in the training. You too could learn to look like nobody in particular, if you wanted to.

It was the lazy end of a summer afternoon in London. Pleasantly warm under a pale blue sky, with a hint of breeze. Traffic roared by in the background, but the street itself was relatively calm and quiet. There were taxis, squat black London cabs, dropping people off and picking them up, men and women of all nationalities, carefully minding their own business. And a large percentage who weren't men or women, or anything like it. You'd be surprised how many monsters walk plainly in open sight every day, hidden from merely mortal gaze by only the flimsiest of illusions. But I'm a Drood, and I wear the golden torc around my throat, so I can use the Sight to see everything; for as long as I can stand it.

An elf lord was getting out of a taxi a few feet away, looking tall and regal in his glowing robes. He had pointed ears, all black eyes, and a look on his face of utter contempt for the whole of human kind. He paid off the taxi driver with a large-denomination note, waving away the change with aristocratic disdain. The driver had better bank that note quickly, before it touched cold iron and turned back into a leaf or something. Elves live to screw over Humanity; it's all they've got left.

Up and down the street, ghosts walked in and out of walls that weren't there when they were alive, trapped in their repetition like insects in amber. Just echoes, in Time. Demons rode unsuspected on people's backs, their spurred heels dug deep into shoulder and back muscles, whispering into their mounts' ears. You could always tell which mounts were listening; their demons were fat and bloated. One man had the beginnings of a halo. He was escorting a friend with stigmata. It's moments like that which give you hope. An alien with grey skin and big black eyes appeared out of nowhere, clutching a London A-Z in a three-fingered hand. Harley Street's reputation stretches further than you'd think.

None of them paid me any attention. I told you; I've been trained.

There are times when I wonder if it might not be nice to live a normal life, with only normal worries and responsibilities, and not have to know all the things I know. Not to have to see the darkness in the world. To be one of the sheep, and not the shepherd. But, on the other hand, I get to know what's really going on, and who the real bad guys are, and I get to kick their nasty arses on a regular basis. Which makes up for a lot.

Harley Street is still mostly a long row of Georgian terraces, with expensively bland anonymous façades. There are hardly any names on display; either you know where you're going, or you don't belong there. The heavy, secretly reinforced doors only open to buzzers when you know the right Words to say, you can't see in through any of the windows, and many of these venerable establishments are guarded and protected in ways you don't even want to think about.

Those were the ones that interested me.

I studied the Hospice of Saint Baphomet from a safe distance, while apparently listening to my mobile phone. Wonderful things; the perfect excuse for standing around with a blank look on your face. There wasn't any point in even approaching the hospice's front door. I could see layer upon layer of seriously hard-core defences set in place. The kind that don't even leave a body to identify. Imagine over-sized magical man-traps, with really big teeth and a built-in mean streak. The sort of defences you'd expect around a hospital that specialised in weird and awful diseases; the kind you really don't want the rest of the world to know about.

So I decided to break into the building next door to Saint Baphomet's: a smaller and even more specialised practice, Dr Dee & Sons & Sons. They dealt strictly with exorcisms; very strictly, by all accounts. (Their motto: We Get The Hell Out.) Their defences were just as strong, but more concerned with keeping things in than keeping people out; on the perfectly logical grounds that only a madman would want to get in. Most people had to be dragged in, kicking and screaming all the way. But then, I'm not most people. I put away my mobile phone and glanced up and down the street, but as always everyone else was far too caught up in their own important business to spare any interest for a nobody like me. So I slipped into the deserted narrow alleyway beside Dr Dee's, and activated my living armour.

Most of the time it lies dormant, as a golden circlet around my throat. A torc, in the old language. Invisible to anyone who's not a member of the Drood family, or at the very least a seventh son of a seventh son. (There don't seem to be many of those around any more. I blame family planning.) I subvocalised my activating Words, and the living metal in the torc spread out to cover my whole body, embracing me in a moment from head to toe. It's a warm, refreshing feeling, like pulling on an old familiar coat. As the golden mask covered my head and face, I could see even more clearly, including the things that are normally hidden from even gifted humans like me. I felt stronger, sharper, more alive; like waking from a pleasant doze into full alertness. I felt like I could take on the whole damned world, and make it cry like a baby.

The armour is the secret weapon of the Drood family. It makes our work possible. The armour is given to each of us, right after we're born, bonded for ever to our nervous systems and our souls, and while we wear the armour we're untouchable, protected from every form of attack, scientific or magical. It also makes us incredibly strong, amazingly fast, and utterly undetectable. Most of the time.

With the armour on I look like a living statue, golden and glorious, with no joints or moving parts, and not a weak spot anywhere in its whole smooth, gleaming surface. There aren't any eye- or breathing-holes in the golden mask that covers my face. I don't need them. While I wear it, the armour is me. It's a second skin, insulating me from a dangerous world.

Looking through the mask I could now clearly see the huge demon dog guarding the back door to Dr Dee's. Night dark, big as a bus and bulging with muscles, it sprawled across the cobbled square, glaring suspiciously about it with a flat, brutal face and flaring hellfire eyes. It was gnawing lazily on a human thigh bone that still had some meat left on it. More bones lay scattered before the dog, broken open to get at the marrow. I had a fleeting but very real temptation to grab one of the bones, throw it and shout Fetch! to see what would happen. But I rose above it. I am, after all, a professional.

I walked up to the demon dog, and it couldn't see or hear or smell me. Which was just as well, really. I wasn't looking for a fight. Not with anything that big and infernally nasty, anyway. I eased past the dog, careful not to touch it. The armour does have its limitations. I studied the locked back door. Very old, very intricate, very secure. Piece of cake. I reached through my golden side with my golden hand, easy as plunging my hand into water, and took out the Hand of Glory I'd been sent by the family Armourer, especially for this mission. The Hand of Glory is a human hand, cut off a hanged man immediately after he's died, and then treated in certain unpleasant ways so that the fingers become candles. Light these candles, in the right way and with the right Words, and the Hand of Glory can open any lock, reveal any secret. The family makes these awful things out of the bodies of our fallen enemies. We do other things with the bodies too, really quite appalling things. Another reason not to get us mad at you.

I lit the candles and subvocalised the Words, and the demon dog raised its blunt head and sniffed suspiciously at the still air. I froze, and the dog slowly lowered its brutal head again. The lock had already opened itself, so I pushed the door gently inwards. The dog didn't even look round. I eased inside, and pulled the door softly shut behind me. It locked itself again, and I relaxed a little. I could probably take a demon dog, with my armour, but I didn't feel like testing that probably unless I absolutely had to. Demon dogs are trained to go for the soul.

I tucked the Hand of Glory away, and studied my new surroundings. Dr Dee's was dark and gloomy, and the bare stone walls of the hallway ran with damp, and other fluids. There were rusted iron grilles in the bare stone floor, to carry them away. I headed forward, and it was like walking into a slaughterhouse of the soul. This was a place where bad things happened, on a regular basis. A place where really bad things happening was just business as usual.

I moved silently down the long stone hallway, reached the blunt corner at the end and emerged into a cavernous hall filled with row upon row of box-like cages, each big enough to hold one man, or woman, or child. The bars of the cages were solid silver, as were the heavy shackles that held their prisoners secure. The only light came from a great iron brazier at the far end of the hall, glowing blood-red in the gloom around the long-handled instruments of instruction the brazier was heating. I moved steadily down the narrow central aisle between the two rows of cages, carefully not looking to the left or to the right. There were no innocents here. These were the possessed, Hell's playthings, brought here to be freed of their burden. One way or another.

Most of them couldn't see me, so they didn't bother to put on an act. But one dark, hulking figure raised its mutilated head and stared right at me with eyes that glowed as golden as my armour. It spoke to me, and I shuddered at the sound. Its voice was like an angel with syphilis, like a rose with a cancer, like a bride with teeth in her vagina. It promised me things, wonderful, awful things, if only I would set it free. I kept on walking. It laughed softly in the darkness behind me, like a small child.

I moved on up a floor into the residential part of the building, where recovering patients were coaxed back to sanity, following the layout I'd memorised earlier. Everywhere I looked I could see ghost images of hidden defence systems, ready to spring into action at the hint of an intruder. Only my armour prevented Dr Dee's security from setting off any number of alarms and retributions. There were cameras everywhere, of course, including infra-red, tied into the holy water sprinkler system, but my armour redefines the word 'stealth'. No one sees me unless I want them to.

Soon enough I came to the wall connecting Dr Dee's to Saint Baphomet's, and all I had to do was take out the portable door the Armourer had sent me, and slap it against the wall. It spread quickly out to form a perfectly normal-looking door, complete with brass handle. I opened it, stepped through into the next building, and then peeled the door off the wall. It shrank quickly back into a small rubbery ball of something far too complicated for me to understand, and I put it back in my pocket. My family has the best toys. All I had to do then was follow the layout of Saint Baphomet's I'd memorised, to take me straight to Mr President's room.

(No, not the one you're thinking of. Definitely not. You must trust me when I tell you these things.)

The hospice was all bright lights, and walls painted in cheerful colours, but the magical protections were just as strong as in Dr Dee's. There were cameras everywhere, whirring officiously to themselves as they turned back and forth, and motion detectors blinked redly at ankle height. But I was walking unseen, the ghost in the machine. No one ever sees the armour! Unless we want them to. The air smelt of disinfectant, and something rotten, not quite buried under expensive flowery scent.

I made my way unchallenged up to the ward on the top floor,

where they kept the really interesting patients, and padded silently down the starkly lit corridor, pausing now and again to peek in through some of the windows in the doors I passed, just out of curiosity. Well; wouldn't you? I'd already been briefed on what everyone was in here for, and I couldn't resist taking a quick look.

A celebrity chef with his own television show was in, to have a tattoo removed the hard way. Seems the tattooist's hand had slipped at the wrong moment while inking an ancient Chinese phrase, turning a simple invocation for good luck into an open invocation for really bad luck. As a result, the chef's famous West End restaurant had burned down during an outbreak of food poisoning. He'd had explosive diarrhoea during his live show, his best recipes had turned up on the Net and he'd been struck by lightning seventeen times. In his own kitchen. You don't shift a tattoo like that with just a laser, so they were flaying his back an inch at a time to get rid of it. The famous chef was currently lying face down on his bed, sobbing like a baby. Next time he'd settle for MUM, or his favourite football team.

Next door to him, a woman was suffering from a severe lack of gravity. The staff had had to strap her to the bed to keep her from floating away. Her long hair streamed upwards. The next room held some poor unfortunate who'd made the mistake of walking into a séance with a really open mind, and now he was possessed by a thousand and one demons. He ricocheted around his room in his straitjacket, screaming in tongues as he bounced off the rubber walls, while the demons fought it out for dominance. They didn't seem to care that they were making a right mess of their host in the process. He really should have gone to Dr Dee's. You get what you pay for.

The next few rooms held a severed hand that was trying to grow itself a new body, a Time agent whose latest regeneration had gone terribly wrong, turning him inside out, and a sorry-looking werewolf with the mange. Takes all sorts, I suppose.

I peered cautiously round the end of the corridor, and there was Mr President's room. An armed guard was sitting outside his door, for the moment concentrating totally on his muscle man magazine. I checked carefully, but that was it. One armed guard. They weren't even trying, really. I walked up to the man, and he didn't know I was there until I squeezed a particular nerve cluster in his neck, and he went straight to sleep. I sat him back in his chair, after moving it away from the door. I peered in through the window, and there was Mr President, sleeping fitfully on his back, his swollen belly pushing up the bedclothes. Pregnancy can be very tiring, or so I'm told. Mr President's wife was snoozing in a chair beside his bed. How very understanding and supportive of her.

I reached under my armour for the gun holstered on my hip. The Armourer has supplied me with many different guns down the years, but this one really was rather special. A needle gun, with a pressurised gas cylinder, firing slivers of frozen holy water. Very quiet, very efficient.

I didn't bother with the Hand of Glory for the locked door, just kicked it in with one golden foot. It crashed open, and Mr President sat up in bed and looked right at me. The baby he was hosting must have boosted his senses. He took one look at me in my golden armour, and started screaming that I was there to assassinate him. I aimed my gun carefully, and shot his wife while she was still half up out of her chair. The ice needle hit her square in the jugular vein, entered her bloodstream and melted down into holy water; and Mr President's wife convulsed as the demon possessing her was forced out.

She'd been my target all along. The demon had hidden itself inside her while her husband was out playing pattycake with the ladything, and then waited undetected for Mr President's baby to be born through a caesarean. The demon could then possess the unnatural baby, and assume a permanent physical form, safe from all attempts at exorcism. Who knows what its plans were, after that? My family hadn't felt like waiting around to find out.

We'd all seen *The Omen*.

The wife went down on all fours, shuddering and convulsing, while her husband looked on, shocked into horrified silence. Black slime burst out of her mouth and nose and ears, and even ran down her face as viscous black tears. More and more of the stuff spilled out of her, faster and faster, forming a widening pool of black tarry stuff on the floor before her. And from this dark ectoplasm the demon made itself a new body, its last desperate attempt to assume a physical form in the material world.

A squat, powerful form thrust up out of the black pool; first long muscular arms, then a broad chest and shoulders, and finally a horned head with coal-red eyes. I shot it with another holy water needle, and it howled horribly but kept on growing. Determined little fellow. It pulled itself up out of the black pool, towering above me now. It grew long claws on its hands, and a wide smile split the dark face to show me row upon row of needle teeth. It looked like what it was; vile and evil and terribly strong. I put away my gun, and grew thick golden spikes on my armoured fists. Some days you have to do things the hard way.

The demon surged forward, lashing out at me with a clawed hand. Sparks flew as the claws skittered harmlessly across my armoured chest. I punched the demon in the head, and thick chunks of black ectoplasm flew away as my spiked knuckles ripped through its pseudoflesh. I hit it again and again, beating it down and driving it back, while all its strongest blows slipped harmlessly off my armoured form. I grabbed hold of one flailing black arm, braced myself and ripped it right off. The demon howled and its body started falling apart, unable to maintain itself in the face of such punishment. The dark form collapsed into thick pools of stinking, rotting ectoplasm, and the demon fell screaming back into Hell.

I shook dripping black slime from my armoured fists, and took a moment to get my breath back. One good thing about beating the crap out of demons from Hell is that you don't have to feel the slightest bit guilty afterwards.

I looked around for Mr President. He was out of his bed and cowering in the furthest corner of the room. He saw me look at him, and whimpered feebly. I took out my needle gun and shot him too. The holy water would ensure that whatever was finally taken out of him would be stillborn, and no threat to anyone. He gasped, his eyes widening as he felt the changes happening within him. He looked away then, and cursed me feebly, but I was used to that.

'Did you really think you could hide this from us, Mr President?' I said. 'Next time, forget your pride and come to us first. Or better yet: stay away from the ladythings.'

CHAPTER TWO
Alarms And Excursions And Getting The Hell Out Of Dodge

The demon's manifesting had set off all kind of alarms. Sirens, flashing lights, the works. I paused long enough to check Mr President's wife was okay (unconscious, covered in black ectoplasmic gunk, but basically okay, poor cow), and then I slammed the door open and charged out into the corridor. The sirens were deafening, and the lights flared rapidly in time to the raucous electronic noise. Whatever happened to pleasant-sounding alarms, with bells? Ambulances are the same. And fire engines. I think about things like that. It worries me sometimes. The moment I appeared in the corridor, concealed gun ports opened up in both walls, and heavy-duty gun barrels slammed out. I started running.

All the guns opened up at once, the roar physically painful at such close quarters, and the muzzle flare was dazzling. The heavy rate of fire chewed up the opposite walls behind me as I raced down the corridor. My armour was still in full stealth mode, so the guns couldn't track me. As far as the security cameras were concerned, the corridor was empty; but the operators knew somebody had to be there, because they'd seen the door open. So they opened up with everything they had, and hoped for the best. The gun barrels swept back and forth, keeping up a murderous rate of fire, but even the occasional lucky hit simply ricocheted off my armour. I didn't even feel the impact.

I rounded the far corner, just in time for a heavy steel grille to slam down from the ceiling, blocking my way. I didn't slow, hitting the grille with my shoulder, only to lurch to a sudden halt as the heavy steel buckled, but held. I grabbed the grille with both golden hands and tore it apart like so much lace, the steel squealing loudly as it sheared. I forced my way through the opening, and raced down

11

the next corridor. The armour makes me supernaturally strong, when I need to be. Wonderful stuff, this living metal. I'd left the guns and the sirens behind me, but now I could hear running footsteps and raised angry voices closing in on me from all directions. Time to hide out in another room, and let the hue and cry run past me.

I ran down the stairs to the next floor, chose a door at random, forced the lock with one push of an armoured hand, and slipped into the darkened room, closing the door carefully behind me. The room was pleasantly quiet, and I stood very still in the gloom, listening as a whole group of people ran past the door, first from one direction and then the other. There was a lot of confused shouting, and I smiled behind my golden mask. First rule of a good agent: always keep them guessing. All I had to do now was wait for things to calm down a little, and then I'd just ease out of here and walk past the security forces in full stealth mode, and they'd never even know I was there. The room's light snapped on, and I spun round, startled. The room's patient was sitting bolt upright in bed and staring straight at me.

Which wasn't supposed to be possible. All right, Mr President saw me, but that was because he had a demon in him. Twice in one afternoon was unprecedented. I moved quickly over to the bed, raising one golden fist in warning, and the patient took his hand away from the call button. I stopped abruptly, as I finally recognised the patient. Behind my golden mask, I was gaping. No wonder he was able to see me. The man in the bed was the Karma Catechist.

A living legend, the Karma Catechist knew all there was to know about magic systems, rituals, and forms of power. He was the living embodiment of every mystic source, every forbidden book, every obscure and secret treatise on how to do terrible things to other people in seven easy steps. He'd been designed that way while still in the womb, shaped by terrible wills, his form and function and fate decided in advance by powerful sorceries and arcane mathematics. He knew it all, from the Kaballah to the Necronomicon, from the Book of Judas to the Herod Canticles. Every spell, every working, every concept.

My family had been trying to get their hands on him for ages, but no one had set eyes on him for decades. He'd been passed back and forth by every group that ever dreamed of power, stolen and abducted and traded, because no one group could hold on to him for long. The problem was, he knew too much; and you had to know the right questions to get the answers you needed. A living encyclopaedia of appalling knowledge, but no index. And now he was in my grasp. If I could get him out of here with me ... No. Too much trouble. His very nature would interfere with my armour's stealth mode. He'd get me noticed, slow me down ... No; I'd just pass on word that he was here, and let the family decide what to do next.

If it was up to me, I'd hit Harley Street with a tactical nuke, to be sure of getting him. There is such a thing as too much knowledge. The Karma Catechist knew a hundred ways to end the world, or disrupt reality itself. But the family would never sanction a hit on such a valuable asset as this. They wanted the information he held within him, like everyone else did.

I would have killed him myself, and to hell with the consequences, but ... he didn't look so terrible, close up. He was just a small, middle-aged man who'd already lost most of his hair. He had a soft, kind face, vague eyes and a diffident smile. He was wearing old-fashioned striped pyjamas, with the jacket drooping open to reveal a tuft of white chest hair. He looked tired and sad and very vulnerable. It was easy to feel sorry for him; he hadn't had much of a life, and hardly any of it his own choice. It wasn't his fault he was a living doomsday device.

'Don't hurt me,' he said, looking at me with almost childlike detachment.

'Hush,' I said. 'You keep quiet, and I'll be on my way in a minute. What are you in here for, anyway?'

'Because I can't keep quiet,' he said sadly. 'I've been conditioned, reprogrammed, my working parameters altered; and it all went hor-ribly wrong. Now if anyone asks me a question, I have to answer them, whether they know the right passwords or not. I've become a security risk.' His eyes widened suddenly, alarm filling his face. 'They'll know I talked to you! They'll think you asked me about what's coming! I won't tell you! I won't!'

He gritted his teeth, and I heard a distinct crunch. He convulsed, his back arching up from the bed, his eyes bulging from their sockets, and then he was limp and still, his last breath a small, sad sigh. I checked for a pulse in his neck, but he was definitely gone. A poison tooth, for God's sake. I thought they went out in the sixties. A man had just killed himself in front of me, and I had no idea why. I don't know what he thought I might ask him. The guilty flee where no man pursueth, and all that.

It occurred to me then that a whole lot of people were going to be really upset that such a valuable resource as the Karma Catechist was dead, because of me. Maybe I wouldn't mention this particular incident in my mission report, after all.

I listened at the door; the sirens were still wailing their little electronic hearts out, but the angry footsteps seemed to have departed. I eased the door open and slipped out into the corridor. More guns thrust out of the walls, opening up immediately they saw the door open. I sprinted down the corridor, my armour giving me supernatural speed, running laughing through the bullets like so much rain.

I reached the end of the corridor and jumped down the stairs to the next floor, sailing through the air from top to bottom in one go. My armoured legs bent to absorb the impact as I landed, and I couldn't help grinning. Sometimes my job is so damned cool. I sprinted down the next corridor, moving so fast now the guns in the walls didn't have time to react. I reached the end and then skidded to a halt at the top of the next stairway. A whole company of heavily armed and armoured security guards was already halfway up the stairs. I turned and ran back the way I came. I could have fought my way through them. They wouldn't have known what hit them till it was too late. I could have killed them all, without breaking a sweat; but that's not what I do. I'm an agent, not an assassin. Those guards weren't the real bad guys here. Just hired help. Probably didn't even know what went on, up on the restricted top floors. Probably thought Saint Baphomet's was just another hospital for rich weirdos.

I do kill, when I have to. But mostly I don't have to. So I don't.

I found the elevators, forced the protesting doors open with my armoured hands, and jumped down the empty shaft. I dropped all the way to the bottom, one golden hand tightly gripping the steel cable to guide my descent. Fat sparks from the cable filled the shaft's gloom like fireworks. I hit the bottom of the shaft with one Hell of a bang, and didn't feel a thing. I forced the elevator doors open, stepped out into the lobby . . . and there was Saint Baphomet's Head of Security, waiting for me. I'd been hoping I wouldn't run into him, ever since I saw his name in the mission briefing. We had history.

I allowed myself a few mental curses. Not out loud, of course. That might be taken as a sign of weakness, and the Droods are never weak. It's all about attitude, remember?

So I ostentatiously relaxed, and nodded casually to the Head of Security. I knew who it was, who it had to be, even though the face and body were new to me. This was my old adversary Archie Leech, breaking in a new body: big and muscular and loaded down with weapons. I only recognised him by the Kandarian amulet hanging round his throat. An ugly lump of carved stone, relic of a race wiped out millennia ago and quite rightly too, it allowed Archie to jump his soul from one body to another, at will. Rumour had it he always kept a dozen or so in reserve, in some kind of suspended animation, in case the one he was wearing took too much damage to continue.

Archie was a serial possessor, a spiritual rapist, and he never gave a damn what happened to his bodies after he abandoned them. I tried to, but it wasn't always possible. I'd killed Archie before, when I absolutely had to, but it had never taken. I don't know what he looked like, originally. I suppose it's possible even he doesn't remember any more, after so many faces. He scowled at me, seeing me clearly thanks to his damned amulet. Three times in one afternoon . . . I was starting to feel a bit conspicuous.

'This place is off limits to everyone,' Archie said flatly. 'Even to the high and mighty Droods.'

I had to smile, behind my golden mask. 'Nowhere is off limits to us, Archie. You know that.'

'Why here, Drood? Aren't even hospitals safe from you and your kind?'

'That's rich, coming from you, Archie. When have you ever cared about putting innocents at risk? Droods go where we have to, to do what we have to do. That's a new look for you, isn't it, Archie? All big and brutal and steroid abuse. You usually like them younger . . . and prettier.'

He shrugged. 'It's a bit long in the arm, but it's good for heavy lifting. And they've been wearing out so quickly recently . . .'

I took a deliberate step forward. He didn't budge. 'Stand aside,

Archie,' I said. 'My mission's completed. No need for this to get nasty.'

'You worry about the bodies I wear,' he said, smiling with his stolen mouth. 'That's always been your weakness.'

'Step aside,' I said. 'Or I'll damage you.'

'Not a chance in Hell. I've always wanted to kill a Drood.'

He opened fire with a machine pistol, spraying me with bullets. They ricocheted away from my armoured chest and face, and I walked right into the hail of bullets and slapped the gun out of his hand. He cut at me with a glowing dagger, but the spells enchancing its edge still weren't enough to do more than raise a shower of sparks as the blade skidded across my throat. I grabbed for the amulet around Archie's neck, but at the last moment my hand slipped aside. The amulet had serious protections.

Archie punched me in the head, with all his body's strength behind it. I heard the knuckles crack and break. I didn't even flinch. I grabbed his shoulders and threw him against the nearest wall. He hit hard enough to crack the plaster, and slam the breath out of him. I started past him, hoping it was over, but he surged to his feet again, drawing dangerously on his body's reserves, one hand full of plastique explosive. He slapped it against my armoured chest, and it stuck fast. He laughed hoarsely as I tried to pull the sticky stuff off, but it wouldn't budge. Archie held up the detonator before me, brandishing it mockingly.

There was enough plastique on my chest to blow out most of this floor. My armour would withstand it . . . but the blast radius would almost certainly take out half of Saint Baphomet's underpinnings, and bring the upper floors crashing down. Hundreds dead, maybe more, most of them probably innocents. Archie didn't care; he'd just jump to another body. Hundreds could die, if it meant he could boast of killing a Drood. He didn't care. But I did.

I grabbed Archie by the shoulders again and pulled him to me, slamming his chest against mine with the plastique crushed between us. He struggled fiercely, but I held him easily with one golden arm. He cried out in a pettish fury as he realised what I intended, and then my free hand closed over his, and activated the detonator.

My mask darkened briefly to protect my eyes from the glare of the explosion, and my ears from the blast, and when I could see and hear again, I was surrounded by smoke and rubble and small bloody gobbets of what had been Archie Leech's stolen body. My armour and his body had absorbed most of the explosion, and the walls around me looked scarred but still solid. The hospice would stand. Archie was gone, of course, his soul wafted away to his next bolt-hole, along with the amulet. I had no doubt I'd see them both again, some day.

Once again, there was the sound of a Hell of a lot of running feet approaching fast from above. The security guards here were nothing if not persistent. I took the portable door out of my pocket and slapped it against the floor, where it immediately became a nice new trapdoor. I opened it, dropped through into the basement and pulled the portable door away from what was now my ceiling. Let them search the rubble for my body, while I calmly and quietly made my way up the stairs, and walked past them to the nearest exit.

This proved to be the back door, and I slipped silently out into the back square, where Dr Dee's dog from Hell was lying in wait for me. Next door's alarms and excursions had clearly attracted its attention. It was growling steadily, like a long rumble of thunder, up close and threatening, and its huge jaws opened, revealing more teeth than seemed physically possible. It glared at the door that had just opened before it, but still it couldn't see or hear or smell me . . . So I held the door open, and let the demon dog charge straight past me and on into the hospice. Where no doubt the security guards would think of something to do to keep it occupied. I do my best, but I'm really not a very nice person sometimes. I closed the door quietly behind the demon dog, and strolled away.

I powered down my armour, and in a moment it was only a golden collar round my throat. And I was just a man again, with a man's limitations. Sometimes that's a relief. I left the side alley and walked unhurriedly out into Harley Street. The same people were walking up and down, with no idea that the whole history of the world had been changed behind their backs. None of them paid me any attention. I was my old anonymous self again. No one ever sees a Drood's face, just occasionally the golden armour. It's enough that the world is protected; they don't need to know by whom.

They might not approve of some of our methods.

CHAPTER THREE
Chilling At The Wulfshead

I disappeared into the Underground, mixing in with the crowds, and took the next train to Tottenham Court Station. I joined the army of people bustling up and down Oxford Street, another face among many, and browsed shop windows until I was sure I hadn't been followed. Because when you work for the Drood family, the rest of the world is usually out to get you. I headed down into Soho. The city's gentrified the Hell out of what used to be the last truly wild part of London, but there's still plenty of sin, sleaze and secrets to be found there, if you know where to look.

A little off the beaten track, down a side street that never gets any sunlight, lies my very favourite internet café. It's a part of the Electronic Village chain, but I like it because it's open twenty-four hours a day, serving twilight people like me. The single window in the shopfront is whitewashed over, and the neon sign above the door hasn't worked in years. The people who come here like their privacy, while they do strange, illegal and possibly unnatural things with their computers. I entered the café and stopped just inside the doorway to let my eyes adjust to the gloom. There were chairs and tables and computers and absolutely nothing else. The surprisingly large area had an air of quiet reverence not unlike that of a church. The customers sat huddled over their glowing screens, deaf and dumb to those around them. The only sounds in the room were the swift tapping of keys and the quiet chirping of working machines.

The café's manager came forward to greet me. Willy Fleagal was a tall gangling sort with bifocals, a high forehead and a ponytail, wearing a T-shirt saying *Information Wants To Be Free*™. He gave me a big smile and a limp handshake. He knew me as a regular customer, with special privileges guaranteed by the chain's owners, but that

18

was all he knew. I've dropped him the occasional hint that I might be an investigative journalist chasing the corporate bad guys, and he loved that.

'Wow, hello again, Mr Bond,' he said, trying hard for cheerfulness, but not quite making it. Willy was a conspiracy theory freak of long standing, and therefore tended towards depression, misery and gloom as natural default positions. 'Always a pleasure to see you in here, man. Are you sure you weren't followed? Of course you are, 'course you are.' He produced a hand-held scanner and checked my clothing for any planted bugs. All part of the service, for Willy.

'You seem busy enough, Willy,' I said. 'Turned up anything juicy recently?'

He nodded quickly, and lowered his voice as he filled me in on the latest conspiracy gossip. Most of which I already knew, but I didn't have the heart to tell him. His watery eyes glowed behind the bifocals as he solemnly assured me that the British Royal family is actually descended from ancient lizard gods who had their awful genesis in the German Black Forest; that the US Pentagon has a secret sixth side, invisible to all but the chosen few, where the really important decisions are made; and that a certain Hollywood actress is actually a shape-changing alien, which is why she can put on and take off weight so easily, while never seeming to age. That last one was new to me, and I made a mental note to check it out later. The family knows of four shape-changing alien species currently busy on our world, and part of the agreement is that they're supposed to stay out of the public eye.

Willy finally ran down, and led me past his oblivious customers to the back room reserved for my use. He unlocked the door, ushered me in with a last dismal sniff, and left me alone. I waited till I heard him lock the door again, and then sat down before the waiting computer. I didn't need to check whether Willy or anyone else had tampered with it; if anyone but me even approached it, the whole thing would self-destruct in a quiet impressively nasty manner. Willy didn't know that, of course. He didn't need to. He also didn't need to know that inside the standard computer shell was nothing more than a properly prepared crystal ball. Far more powerful than any computer, and a damned sight harder to hack.

I said my real name out loud, and the monitor screen turned itself on, showing me an image of my usual contact, Penny Drood. A cool blonde in a tight white sweater, sweet and smart and sexy enough, in a distant sort of way. I like Penny. She doesn't take any shit from me.

'You're late,' she said. 'Agents in the field are required to report in exactly on the hour.'

'Yes, I did manage to avoid being killed or severely injured, thank you for asking, Penny. May I enquire why the mission briefing didn't inform me about the bloody big demon dog standing guard outside Dr Dee's?'

Penny sniffed. 'Demon dogs come as standard these days, Eddie. As you'd know if you actually bothered to read the updates I send you.'

'If I read everything the family sends me, I'd never get anything done. And this was a really big bastard.'

Penny smiled briefly. 'The day you can't handle a demon dog, Eddie, we'll retire you. Now make your report, please. I do have other agents on my watch, you know.'

'Ah, but they don't worship your very existence, like I do.'

'Idolatry will get you nowhere. Make your report.'

I launched straight into it, fluent and precise with the ease of long practice. Just the relevant details; the family don't need to know everything, as long as the mission is completed successfully. I didn't mention my brief, unfortunate meeting with the Karma Catechist. But when I got to the end of my report, and sat back in my chair, the very first thing Penny said was: 'Tell me about the Karma Catechist.' I sighed, deeply, but I wasn't really surprised. The family knows everything, remember? That's the way it is. So I told Penny what happened, being very careful to emphasise that none of it was in any way my fault, and at the end she just nodded, and broke contact. The screen went dead, and I stood up, stretching slowly, feeling rather relieved. If I'd been in any trouble, she would have told me to wait while she kicked it upstairs.

So, report over, mission concluded. Time to repair to a civilised hostelry, and get utterly rat-arsed.

I left the internet café, nodding goodbye to Willy, who was busy sending anonymous hate e-mail to Bill Gates. I shut the door firmly behind me and looked casually up and down the side street to make sure no one was about. The afternoon was shading into evening now, the shadows growing darker and deeper. The side street ended in a grimy brick wall, covered with faded graffiti. I stood before the wall, said certain Words, and a door appeared in the brickwork before me. A door of solid silver, deeply etched with threats and warnings in angelic and demonic script, and absolutely no trace of a handle. I placed my left hand on the silver, and the door swung open. Try that when your name isn't on the approved list and the door will bite your hand off; but one of the things I like most about the Wulfshead Club is how jealously it guards its privacy, and that of its patrons.

The Club isn't actually in London, but you can enter it from any city in the world, as long as you're a member in good standing, and know the current passWords. I'm not sure if anyone knows exactly where (or indeed when) the Wulfshead is really located. Which makes it the best of all possible places to go, when you need to get away from the world and its demands.

I stepped through the door into dazzling light, pounding music and the roar of people determined to have a good time, no matter what. The Wulfshead is very up to the moment, very high tech. All neon strip lighting, and furniture so modern half the time you can't even tell what it's supposed to be. The walls are giant plasma screens, showing dramatic views from around the world, constantly changing. Every now and again they flash up the bedroom secrets of famous and important people, secretly recorded by peeping Toms with access to far too much technology for their own good. The music slammed and pounded, while girls in hardly any clothing stomped and strutted on the spotlit miniature stages, dancing their hearts out till the sweat flew from their flailing bodies, and the bass lines shuddered up through the floor.

The Club was crowded, as always, full to the brim with the most interesting people you'll find anywhere. The Wulfshead is where the weird people go to relax, and enjoy a drink and a chat with their own kind. The Club's membership includes the supernatural, the superluminal, the super-scientific and all the rest of the superhuman crew. It's a cosmopolitan mixture, embracing good guys and bad guys and the strange people in between. Deals are made, people and others get laid, there's the odd murder or transformation, and a good time is had by all. Got a hell of an atmosphere.

The Club is neutral ground, by long tradition, but the occasional brawl is only to be expected. It's just high spirits. The bartender keeps order with a steamhammer, and the bouncers are golems so they can't be bribed or intimidated.

I made my way to the long bar at the back of the Club, a gleaming high-tech structure that looked more like a piece of modern art than anything functional. The Club prides itself on having anything you can name on tap; everything from absinthe to human blood to steaming nitric acid with an LSD chaser. In fact the choice is so wide that most of us believe the Club keeps its stock in a pocket dimension, attached to the bar by a hyperdimensional link. It's still best to avoid the house wines, unless you're already on your third stomach.

The bar snacks are appalling, but then bar snacks always are.

I nodded and smiled to old friends and familiar faces as I eased my way through the press of bodies. They know me only as Shaman Bond: another face on the scene. None of them even suspected I might be a Drood, and I was determined to keep it that way. We protect the world, but no one ever said we were popular. I ordered a chilled bottle of Beck's from the bar, and looked around me. To my left, Charlatan Joe was holding forth to a select group, and I wandered over to listen. Joe was a city slicker and confidence trickster; a shark on legs in an Armani suit. Listening more or less patiently to his boasting and preening was another familiar face: Janissary Jane. She nodded briskly to me as I joined the group. Her army fatigues were stiff with black blood, and up close she smelled of smoke and brimstone.

'Just back from the battlefield?' I said, raising my voice to be heard above the din. 'Where did you end up this time?'

Jane shrugged, gulping her whisky straight from the bottle. She wore her black hair cropped short so no one could grab it during a fight, and if her scarred face had ever been pretty that was a long time ago. She was a good drinking companion, as long as you kept her off the gin. Gin made her maudlin, and then she tended to shoot people.

'Some demon war, in another dimension,' she said finally. 'Some damned fool necromancer opened up a Hellgate, and the call went out for all good mercenaries to rally to the flag. Pay was good, but I'd have gone anyway, for the fight. Hate bloody demons.'

'Who doesn't?' said the Indigo Spirit, splendid as always in his midnight blue leathers, cape and mask, sipping his Manhattan cocktail with his little finger carefully extended. 'Damned things are worse than cockroaches.'

I raised my bottle to him briefly. 'Good to see you again, Indigo. How goes the War on Crime? Killed any interesting super-villains recently?'

'Only the usual scum, dear boy. Nothing wrong with them that two bullets in the head won't cure. I have to say the current breed of diabolical masterminds and deadly fiends is really very disappointing ... No style, do you see, no sense of occasion. Sometimes it's hardly worth dressing up in the outfit. I mean, is it really too much trouble for a villain to at least wear a domino mask in his secret lair?'

Charlatan Joe had given up on his story now, since no one was listening, and sipped sulkily at his port and lemon. Beside him, the Blue Fairy was pissed as a fart, bemoaning the approaches of middle age and complaining that his wand didn't work as well as it used to.

'So,' I said, loud enough to drown out the Blue Fairy, 'what's the latest gossip, people?'

There's always someone trying to take over the world, or blow it up, or make it A Better Place; all equally dangerous, and disturbed.

'Dr Delirium is up to something nasty again,' said the Indigo Spirit. 'Swanning around in the depths of the Amazon jungle. Thinks he's so big, just because he has his own private army. The only reason he's got an army is because his uncle left it to him.'

'Right,' said Janissary Jane, gesturing a little too wildly with her whisky bottle. 'Never trust private soldiers. Nice uniforms, but no real guts. No fire in their bellies. If they can't outnumber you ten to one, they don't want to know. Delirium tried to get me to sign up a few years back, but of course I said no. The pay offer was really lousy.'

'Delirium,' said Charlatan Joe. 'Isn't he the one who collects new plagues, and then threatens to turn them loose on the civilised world unless he's paid off?'

'That's the one,' I said. 'Always wants to be paid in rare postage stamps. I guess once a collector, always a collector.'

'There's a rumour going round that one of the Old Ones is slowly waking from its long sleep under the Arctic Circle,' said Charlatan Joe. 'And that's why the polar ice pack is melting so much faster than it should be.'

Janissary Jane sniffed loudly. 'Every time there's a blip in the weather, someone thinks the Old Ones are coming back. Not gonna happen. They've been asleep so long now you couldn't wake one if you stuffed a nuke up its backside and detonated it.'

'I did hear that the troll problem's getting worse in the Underground train tunnels,' said the Indigo Spirit. 'Nasty things; all teeth and appetite and no manners. Word is, they could be getting close to swarming again.'

Janissary Jane brightened. 'Always good money to be made during a cull. I'll contact my agent, see if anyone's hiring. The city better not have tendered it out to Group Forty-Two again; those bastards always want to see the heads as proof of kill. Last time I came up out of the Underground like Santa Claus with a sack full of goodies.'

'Got some new videos in, if any of you are interested,' said Charlatan Joe. 'I know this guy who knows this guy who claims his television set is receiving transmissions from the future. He's selling best-of compilations on VHS and DVD, and I can get my hands on some for a really reasonable price . . .'

'I wouldn't,' I said. 'I've seen that tape. A bunch of guys in weird clothes showing their bums to the camera and giggling a lot. Technology is wasted on some people.'

So we drank and talked and drank some more, and the evening passed pleasantly enough. Charlatan Joe put it all on his tab, since he was still flush from his latest sting. Janissary Jane tried to chat up some guy in chain-mail, and then shot him in the arse when he turned his back on her. The Indigo Spirit offered to show me his secret cave, but I politely declined. The Blue Fairy passed out cold, and lay snoring on the floor at our feet. '*Don't step on him*,' Charlatan Joe said wisely, '*or it'll rain for forty days and forty nights*.'

At some point, the conversation got around to the latest sightings of the infamous Drood family and their golden agents, and I shut up and paid attention. Never know when you might learn something useful. There are always sightings of my family at work, most of them apocryphal or wishful thinking. If a Drood agent's done his job properly, no one but the victims should even know he was there. But we're a bit like crop circles and cattle mutilations; we get blamed for all kind of things that are nothing to do with us. The current sightings included action in Moscow, Las Vegas and Venice. That last one was particularly nasty; no one seemed to know precisely what happened, but the city was fishing bodies out of the canals for hours afterwards. I made a mental note to check up on that, though it sounded rather sloppy for us.

My family gets a lot of credit (or blame) for things we haven't actually done, but we never confirm or deny anything. It's enough that the world is protected; they don't need to know family business. Besides, it's all good for the reputation.

The company is usually good at the Wulfshead, but there's always one in every crowd. A large figure loomed suddenly over us, brandishing a pint of lager and insisting on joining our conversation. He had to be seven feet tall, with shoulders to match, in a battered oversized biker's jacket and scuffed leather trousers. This, it turned out, was Boyd, Bodyguard to the Stars. A newcomer to the Wulfshead, young and strong and stupid enough to believe the Club's rules didn't apply to him. He was obviously a Hyde; using a distillation of Dr Jekyll's old formula, potent enough to keep him big and brutal while diluted enough that he was able to maintain control.

He talked right over us, insisting on telling us all about his new job as bodyguard to a major Hollywood actress. Who, if Boyd was to be believed, couldn't do a thing without him there to supervise it. He also dropped heavy hints that he'd sampled her famous body, when he wasn't guarding it.

'Really?' said the Indigo Spirit. 'I always thought she was a Friend of Dorothy.'

'Don't know if I'd go that far,' I said. 'But if they were short-handed, she'd probably help out.'

Boyd glared at me. 'That's tabloid trash. Gossip and spite. She's all woman, and I should know. Right?'

He glared round at us, but I must not have looked convinced enough, because Boyd decided he needed to push me about a bit, just to show he wasn't to be contradicted. He jabbed me hard in the chest with one large finger, and I looked at him thoughtfully as he raised his voice to me.

He was twice my size and more, most of it muscle. I could have taken him easily if I armoured up, but I couldn't do that. Strict family rule: the armour is only ever to be used for family business. More importantly, the armour would have given away to everyone that I was a Drood, and then I'd never be able to come here again. I liked being just Shaman Bond, and I wasn't about to give it up.

The bartender was already looking meaningfully in our direction, getting ready to intervene, and I really did consider letting him handle it. For about a second or two. But I didn't spend most of my life being trained to fight the good fight, just so I could let a mere Hyde push me around. Besides, if I let him get away with this, I'd never be able to drink here in peace again. Even the weird and terminally strange have their pecking order. Still, given that Boyd was a Hyde and big with it, I sure as Hell wasn't going to fight fair.

So I held his gaze with mine, quietly retrieved the portable door from my pocket, activated it and flipped the door neatly under the Hyde's feet. Boyd had enough time to look startled before he fell through the new opening and into the cellars underneath the Club. He landed with a satisfyingly loud crash, followed by a series of low moans. I picked up my portable door and the floor returned, sealing Boyd in the cellars until someone could be bothered to go down and rescue him. The bartender nodded his thanks, glad he hadn't had to get involved, and the watching crowd gave me a round of applause. Janissary Jane and I shared a high five, while Charlatan Joe considered me thoughtfully.

'Where did you get your hands on a restricted device like a portable door, Shaman?'

'Found it on e-bay,' I said.

Time continued to pass pleasantly, and by the early hours of the morning I was drifting through a drunken haze and chatting up a giggly sex droid who'd dropped in from the twenty-third century to do some research for her dissertation on strange sexual hang-ups of the rich and famous. She was tall and buxom and one hundred per cent artificial, sweetly turned out in a classic little black dress, cut high enough at the back to show off the bar code and copyright notice stamped on her magnificent left buttock. Her fizzing steel hair was full of sparking static, her eyes were silver, and she smelled of pure musk. She ran off a nuclear power cell located in her lower abdomen, which was a tad worrying, but then no one's perfect.

'So, what brings you to the Wulfshead?' I asked.

'Just playing tourist,' she said, with a smile so wide even Julia Roberts couldn't have matched it. 'I've so much more spare time, since we finally got unionised. Let's hear it, for Rossum's Unionised Robots!'

'Down with the bosses!' I said solemnly. 'Work is the curse of the drinking classes.'

'Oh I love my work,' she said, batting her huge eyelashes at me. 'It took more than one man to change my name to Silicon Lily.'

And that was when my mobile phone rang. I was not pleased. The only people who have that number are my family, and I shouldn't have been hearing from them so soon after a completed mission. It had to be some kind of bad news, and almost certainly more mine than theirs. People around me scowled at the phone in my hand, and gave me significant looks; you're supposed to turn off all communication devices before entering the Wulfshead. I hadn't thought to, because the family so rarely bothers me when I'm on downtime. I smiled weakly, shrugged apologetically, blew a quick kiss to the sex droid, and retired to a more or less private corner to take the call.

'I thought I told you never to call me here,' I said coldly.

'*Come home*,' said an unfamiliar voice. '*Come home now. You are needed for a personal briefing on an urgent mission.*'

And that was it. The phone went dead, and I slowly put it away, my mind racing. Another mission, already? It was unheard of. I was guaranteed at least a week between missions. Too much work in the field, and you burn out fast. The family knows that. And why did I have to go home to be briefed? Ordinarily they send me my mission brief, and whatever hardware I might need, via a blind postal drop that I rotate on a regular basis; and then I go off and do whatever needs to be done and try my best not to get killed in the process. Make my report to Penny afterwards, and then go to ground till I'm needed again. The family and I maintain a civilised distance, and that's the way I like it.

I scowled into what remained of my drink. The phone call had shocked me sober again. I really didn't want to go home. Back to The Hall, ancestral home of the extended Drood family. I hadn't set eyes on the place in ten years. I left right after my eighteenth birthday, to our mutual relief, and the family sent me a regular and (fairly) generous stipend guaranteed as long as I continued to work in the field. If I ever chose to give up my career as an agent, I could either go home or be hunted down and killed as a dangerous rogue. That was understood. They allowed me a short leash, but that was all. I was a Drood.

I left home because I found the weight of family duty and history more than a little suffocating, and they let me go because they found my attitude a pain in the arse. I'd kept myself busy, down the years, accepting assignment after assignment just to avoid having to go home again and submit to family authority and discipline. I liked the illusion of being my own man.

But when the family calls, you answer; if you know what's good for you. I was going home again, damn it to hell.

In the morning. Tonight, there was Silicon Lily . . .

CHAPTER FOUR
Home Is Where The Heart Is

The sun had only been up an hour or so when I finally left my comfortable little flat, tucked away in an enclosed square in one of the better parts of Knightsbridge. The place cost more in rent every week than the family sent me in a year, but I once did the owner a favour and now he picks up the tab. And in return I keep very quiet about exactly what the succubus had been doing in that flat, before I exorcised her. (Let's just say I had to burn the bed and scrub down the walls with a mixture of holy water and Lysol.) The brightening sky still had streaks of crimson in it, the birds were singing their tiny hearts out, the noisy bastards, and the day felt fresh and sharp with the anticipation of things to come.

I'm not normally a morning person, but it had been a really good night, thanks to Silicon Lily. She'd vanished from my bed in a crackle of discharging tachyons about an hour ago, leaving me with the memory of a wink and a smile, and the scent of her perfumed sweat on my sheets. Damn, they know how to live in the twenty-third century. I took a few deep breaths of crisp morning air, yawned abruptly, and brushed vaguely at my blue jeans, white shirt and battered black leather jacket. Good enough for the family. I don't normally believe in getting up at the same time as everyone else, people who actually have to earn a living, but I had a long day ahead of me. I unlocked the garage under my flat with a Word and a gesture, and then backed my car out into the cobbled courtyard. I revved the engine and it roared cheerfully, and I had to grin as I thought of heads jerking up off pillows in flats all around the square. I have to get up early, everyone gets up early.

I swept through the almost empty streets of London, ignoring red lights and speed limits, and marvelling at the empty parking spaces.

London just after dawn is a whole different place. A few party-goers were still stumbling home, clutching empty champagne bottles and the occasional traffic cone, and I waved cheerfully to them as I passed. We twilight people have to stick together.

I was driving my Hirondel sports car, the powder blue convertible model with the top down, and the wind ruffled my hair affectionately as I headed out of London and aimed for the south-west countryside; going home to meet the family. I'd had hardly any sleep and only a rushed breakfast of milky cereal and burnt toast, but there's nothing like a night of really good sex to stave off a hangover. I powered down the M4 motorway, through grasslands and open fields and cultivated countryside, enjoying the run. I sang lustily along to the Eurythmics' *Greatest Hits* on the CD player, doing harmonies when I couldn't hit the high notes. That Annie Lennox has got a hell of a range.

The Hirondel is a 1930s model, perfectly restored, but it also has many modern extras and some extraordinary options, courtesy of the family Armourer. Who firmly believes in every member of the family being prepared for enemy attack at all times. He also believes in doing unto others before they get the chance to do it unto you. As a result of his very talented work, speed cameras can't see me, my number plate is Corps Diplomatique so the cops don't bother me, and any car that makes the mistake of getting too close can suddenly find itself experiencing severe engine problems. For those who insist on getting too close, I have fore and aft electronic cannon capable of firing two thousand explosive flechettes a second, flame-throwers, and an EMP generator. If you ask me, the Armourer's seen too many spy movies. I prefer to put my faith in driving like a bat out of Hell and leaving my enemies behind to eat my exhaust.

I turned off the M4 near Bristol, by now crooning along to Leonard Cohen's *I'm Your Man*, and quickly left the main roads behind me as I headed deep into the countryside. I drove down increasingly narrow roads until I was well off the beaten track, and the roads became lanes, without even any road markings or cat's eyes down the middle. The morning air was sharp and fresh, cut with the scents of recently cut grass and the unmistakable presence of cows. The south-west is dairy country. Small towns gave way to even smaller villages and hamlets, until finally the lane I was following petered out into a dirt track, deeply churned by heavy farm vehicles. I kept going, slower now, following a winding way through dark and brooding woods, golden shafts of sunlight forcing their way through the general gloom like spotlights full of dancing dust motes. I braked sharply to avoid hitting a badger the size of a pig as it wandered across the road, and it actually had the nerve to give me the evil eye before scurrying off into the undergrowth. Deer watched me silently from the sides, their eyes gleaming in the shadows.

I rounded a sharp corner, and the track ended abruptly in a high stone wall, buried under centuries' growth of creeping ivy. Anyone else would have slammed on their anchors and prayed for their souls, but I kept going. The stone wall loomed up before me, terribly solid and unforgiving, filling my view, and then I was upon it and through it, the illusion dissipating harmlessly around me, trailing wisps of ghostly stonework across my face like chilly fingertips.

(To a Drood, it's an illusion. To everyone else, it's a solid stone wall. And if you crash into it, don't come crying to us. Serves you right for trying to find us.)

Bright sunlight splashed over the car as I left the illusion behind me and followed the gravel drive between two long rows of elm trees, and on into the extensive grounds of The Hall. There were perfectly laid out lawns, expertly trimmed and long enough to land a plane on. Sprinklers tossed their liquid bounty around, filling the summer air with a moist haze. Beyond the lawns there were hedge mazes and flower gardens, ornamental fountains in the grand Victorian style, with water gushing tastefully from classical statues, and even our own lake with swans drifting on it.

As I approached The Hall, peacocks paraded across the manicured lawns, announcing my arrival with their harsh and raucous cries. An old wishing well stood to one side, its red roof rusting and flaking away. We filled it in with concrete for getting too cocky. Winged unicorns grazed outside the adjoining stables, tossing their noble heads at me, their coats so perfect a white they seemed almost to glow. Watchful gryphons patrolled around The Hall, keeping an eye on the near future, ready for any attack. The perfect guardians and watchdogs. Unfortunately they only eat carrion and they like to roll in it first, so no one ever pets them and they are never allowed inside.

My family home has always been colourful as all hell. The

31

waterfall feature has an undine in it, the old chapel has a ghost (though my family isn't on speaking terms with it), and there are occasionally faeries at the bottom of our garden. Though if you're wise you'll give them plenty of space.

The Hall loomed up before me like a dentist's appointment; it might be necessary, but you just know it's going to end in tears. My feelings on seeing the old homestead again after this long were so mixed I didn't know where to start. Everywhere I looked, familiar sights leapt to my eyes, assaulting me with nostalgia for times past, when the world seemed so much simpler. This was the place of my childhood, my formative years. I remembered sailing across the lake in a boat made of cobwebs and sealing magics, under the kind of blue sky and brilliant sun you only get in memories of childhood summers. I remembered being four years old, chasing the peacocks on my stubby legs and crying because I couldn't catch them. I remembered dancing on the roof in elfin boots, and flying on the unicorns, and ... just lying on the lawns with a good book, dozing through endless summer afternoons ...

I also remembered endless lessons in crowded schoolrooms, endless harsh discipline and cold courtesy, and the silent, sullen resistance of my teenage years as I stubbornly refused to be led and moulded and dictated to. The never-ending arguments with increasingly senior members of the family over the way my life should go, and the terrible feeling of being crushed and limited by their rigid expectations of who and what a Drood should be. My need to be my own man, in a family where that could never be permitted. In the end I didn't so much leave as run away, and to the Matriarch's credit, she let me go.

I remembered the beatings, the angry raised voices and worse: the cutting, cold words of disappointment. The withholding of treats and privileges and affection; until I learned to do without them, just to spite the family. I learned to be self-sufficient the hard way. You temper a sword by beating the crap out of the steel; and I have one Hell of a temper.

Now I'd been summoned back, without explanation or warning, and a cold knot of alarm and paranoia twisted in the pit of my stomach. Nothing good could come of this. Nothing good for me, anyway. Part of me wanted to crash the car to a halt, turn it around and drive back out. Keep driving and driving, leave England and lose myself in the darker parts of the world, forget I ever was a Drood. But I couldn't do that. The family wouldn't forget. They would declare me rogue, apostate, security risk, and they would never stop until they had hunted me down.

And besides, even after all the arguments and disagreements, I still believed in what the family stood for. I still believed in fighting the good fight.

I turned the car through a long drawn-out curve, and The Hall itself swung into place before me, dominating the scene. A huge sprawling old manor house, The Hall dated back to Tudor times originally, but had been much added to down the centuries. The central building still had the traditional black and white boarded frontage, with heavy leaded-glass windows and a jutting gabled roof. Surrounding it were the four great wings, massive and solid in the Regency style, containing some fifteen hundred bedrooms, all of them currently occupied by family members. Everyone here is a Drood. The roof rose and fell like a grey tiled sea, complete with gables, gargoyles and ornamental guttering. Not forgetting the observatory, the eyrie, the landing pad and more aerials and antennae than you could shake a gremlin at. There are many rooms in my family's mansion, and there's room for everyone. As long as you toe the line.

The Hall is also a real swine to heat, draughty as Hell in the winter, and the family doesn't believe in central heating because they think it makes you soft. I grew up believing wearing long underwear half the year was normal.

And in The Hall's most secret chambers, my family decides the fate of the world. Seven days a week, no time off for good behaviour.

This isn't my family's first home, of course. The Droods were an old, old family even back in Tudor times. We moved on and moved up as we grew in size and status and influence. But The Hall has been our home and centre of operations for so long now it's hard to think of us anywhere else. You won't find The Hall on any official map, or any of the routes that lead to it. I'd felt the many layers of scientific and magical defences sliding aside to let me pass as I drove down the long gravelled drive, rising and falling before me like a series of shifting veils, and then sealing themselves behind me again. Someone was watching me from the moment I passed through the stone wall, and would continue to watch until I left again. Robot guns actually rose up out of the lawns to track my car at one point, before reluctantly burying themselves again. They were new. But, of course, it's always the defences you can't see or sense that will really screw you over. Anyone who comes looking for us, uninvited and unexpected, risks being killed in any number of increasingly distressing ways.

The family has always taken its privacy very seriously. When you've been protecting and policing the world for as long as we have, you can't help but accumulate serious enemies. The Hall and its extensive grounds are surrounded and suffused with layer upon layer of protections, including a whole bunch of scarecrows. We make them out of old enemies. If you listen in on the right supernatural frequency, you can hear them screaming. Don't mess with the Droods. We take it personally. We get mad and we get even.

I brought the Hirondel to a crashing halt before the front door, in a swirl and a spray of churned-up gravel, and parked right there because I knew I wasn't supposed to. I turned off the engine, and then sat there for a while, staring at nothing and tapping my fingertips on the steering wheel, listening to the cries of the peacocks and the slow ticking of the cooling engine. I didn't want to do this. By not leaving the car I was putting off the moment when I would have to enter my old home, and walk back into the cold, distant embrace of my family. But . . . sooner or later you have to walk into the dentist's surgery and get it over with.

I slammed the car door loudly, enjoying the echoes, and locked it. Not because it was necessary, or even because it would stop whoever they sent to move it. I just wanted to make it clear to everyone that I didn't trust anyone here. The Hall rose up before me like a tidal wave cast in stone. It looked even bigger than I remembered, up close; and even more forbidding. I could feel its mass, its centuries of accumulated duty and responsibility, trying to suck me in like a black hole, but I balked at the front door. I was supposed to walk straight in and present myself to the Matriarch, as custom and tradition demanded . . . but I've never been big on doing what I'm supposed to do. And since I was still more than a bit resentful at being summoned back so abruptly, I decided that the Matriarch could wait while I went for a little walk.

I turned my back on the front door, humming aloud in an unconcerned sort of way, and strolled past the many arched and stained-glass windows at the front of the house. I could feel their presence, like the pressure of so many watching eyes, so I kept my own gaze resolutely straight ahead. The gravel crunched loudly under my feet as I headed past the East Wing, rounded the corner, and smiled for the first time as I beheld the old family chapel. Tucked away out of sight, and set firmly apart, the chapel was a squat stone structure with crucifix windows. It looked Saxon, but was actually an eighteenth-century folly. The family had its own chapel inside The Hall now, pleasant and peaceful and graciously multi-denominational, and the old building had been left to rot. It is currently occupied by the family ghost, Jacob Drood, cantankerous old goat that he is. He's my great-great-great-grandfather, I think. Genealogy never was my strong point.

On the whole, my family discourages ghosts, otherwise we'd be hip deep in the things. If any do come bleating back to The Hall after being killed in the field, they get dispatched on to the Hereafter pretty damned sharply. The family looks strictly forward, never back, and there isn't room in The Hall for anyone to be sentimental. Jacob is allowed to linger on in the chapel through some technicality I've never really understood, mostly because the few people who do know are too embarrassed to talk about it. All families have the odd skeleton in the closet, and ours is Jacob. The family ostentatiously hasn't been on speaking terms with him for years, and he couldn't care less. Mostly he sits around in his ghostly underwear, watching the memories of old television shows on a set with no insides in it. Now and again he keeps a spectral eye on what the family's up to; just because he knows he's not supposed to.

Jacob and I have always got along fine.

I first found out about him when I was eight. Cousin Georgie dared me to go and peek in the window of the forbidden chapel, and I never could resist a dare. I was caught (of course) and punished (of course), and told that the chapel and its occupant were strictly off limits. After that, I couldn't wait to meet him. I knew we'd be kindred spirits. So I sneaked out that night, and basically ambushed the old ghost in his den. He made a few half-hearted attempts to scare me off, but his heart wasn't in it. He'd waited a long time for the family to throw up another black sheep like him. We quickly warmed to each other, and after that no one could keep us apart. The family did try, but Jacob came striding out of the chapel and into the Matriarch's private chambers, and whatever was said there after that the two of us were left strictly to ourselves.

Jacob was perhaps the only real friend I had, then. Certainly the only one I could trust. He encouraged my early rebellions, and was the only one who was always on my side. He was the one who told me to get out, first chance I got. He approved of me; said I reminded him of himself as a teenager. Which was rather worrying, actually.

The chapel looked as squat and ugly as ever: rough stone buried under thick mats of ivy that stirred and twisted threateningly as I approached the door. Part of Jacob's early warning system. I patted the ivy and spoke to it in a friendly fashion, and it relaxed again as it remembered and recognised my voice. The door was stuck halfway open, as always, and I put my shoulder to it. The heavy wood scraped loudly across the bare stone floor, raising a cloud of dust. I coughed and sneezed a few times, and peered into the gloom. Nothing had changed.

The pews were still stacked up against the far wall, to make room for Jacob's giant black leather reclining chair, and beside it an old-fashioned refrigerator that was somehow always full of ethereal booze. A massive old television stood before the chair, with real rabbits' ears piled on top to help with the reception. Jacob didn't look around as I approached. He sprawled bonelessly in his great chair, a grey wispy figure who flickered in and out as his concentration wavered. He looked older than death, his face a mass of wrinkles, his bony skull graced with just a few long flyaway hairs. He was currently wearing faded Bermuda shorts and a T-shirt bearing the legend *Ghosts Do It From Beyond*. He chugged down the last of his beer and threw the can away. It disappeared before it hit the floor. Jacob waved a grey hand jerkily in my direction, leaving thin trails of ectoplasm on the air.

'Come in, Eddie, come in! And shut the door behind you. The draughts play havoc with my old bones.'

I stood my ground beside his chair, my arms folded across my chest. 'And what bones would those be, you disgusting old revenant?'

He scowled at me from under bushy white eyebrows. 'You get to be as ancient as me, lad, you'll suffer a few aches and pains too. It's not easy, being this old. Or everybody would be doing it.'

'How can you have aches and pains? You're dead. You don't have an actual body any more.'

'That's right! Rub it in! Just because I'm dead, it doesn't mean I don't have feelings. The way the family treats me these days makes me spin in my grave.'

'You were cremated, Jacob.'

'All right, I'll turn in my urn!' He turned off his ghostly television set with a snap of his fingers, and finally turned to smile at me. 'Damn, it's good to have you back, lad. None of the current generation have the spunk to come out and talk to me. How long has it been, Eddie? I lose track in here.'

'Ten years,' I said.

He nodded slowly. 'You've filled out nicely, lad. Good outfit, rotten attitude, and you look like you could punch your weight. A credit to my teachings. But what the Hell are you doing back here, Eddie? You did the one thing even I couldn't do; you escaped.'

'The family called me home,' I said, trying hard to keep my voice light and unconcerned. 'I was kind of hoping you might know why.'

Jacob sniffed and settled back in his reclining chair. The ghost of a pipe appeared in his hand, and he sucked thoughtfully on the stem, releasing thick puffs of ectoplasm that drifted up to the cobwebbed ceiling. 'Not much point in asking me, lad. The family's been keeping me at even more arm's length than usual, of late. Of course, that doesn't stop me from keeping a watchful eye on them . . .' He grinned nastily at me. 'You want the latest gossip, Eddie lad? You want to know who's having who, who messed up in the field again, and who came back stoned out of her mind and crashed the autogryro on the roof landing pad?'

'Tell me everything,' I said. 'I think I need to know everything.'

Jacob waved his pipe away, and it disintegrated into drifting streams of ectoplasm. He sat up straight in his chair and fixed me with a steady gaze, his ancient eyes pinning me where I stood. 'To start with, there's a new faction in the family. Gaining a lot of support, especially among the youngsters. Basically, it boils down to a *Let's get them before they get us* strategy. This new faction is talking very loudly about the virtues of pre-emptive strikes and a zero tolerance for all identified bad guys. No more dealing with problems as they arise; stick it to the bad guys with extreme prejudice, whether we can prove anything or not.'

'If we were to declare open war,' I said slowly, 'our enemies would simply band together for protection against a common threat, and we'd be vastly outnumbered. We've only survived as long as we have because we understand the virtues of divide and conquer.'

Jacob shrugged. 'Youngsters today; no patience. No taking the long view. It's all instant gratification now. I blame MTV and video games. So far, older and wiser heads in the family are keeping the new faction firmly in its place, but everyone's talking about it ... Also, your cousin William's been stirring things, so he can get plenty of good footage for the documentary he's been making about the family. Though God alone knows who he thinks is going to see it. Could be a big hit, mind, with all those people who watched *The Osbournes*. Meet the Droods; an even more dysfunctional family, only far more dangerous ...

'The Matriarch's stepped up security around The Hall. Again. You probably noticed the extra measures on your way in. Of course, they can't keep me out. It's hard to keep secrets from the dead. We're natural voyeurs. Shall we take a look at what our beloved leader is up to at the moment?'

He snapped his fingers at the empty television set before him, and the screen came up with an impressively sharp image of the family Matriarch in her study, talking with her husband, Alistair. He was pacing up and down, looking distinctly worried, while she sat straight-backed in her chair, all icy calm and dignity.

'He'll be here soon,' said Alistair. 'What are we going to tell him?'

'We'll tell him what he needs to know, and no more,' said the Matriarch. 'That's always been the family way.'

'But if he even suspects ...'

'He won't.'

'We could tell him the truth.' Alistair stopped pacing and looked directly at the Matriarch. 'We could appeal to his better nature. To his duty, to his love of the family ...'

The Matriarch sniffed loudly. 'Don't be a fool. He's far too dangerous. I have determined what needs to be done, and that's all there is to it. I have always understood what's best for the family. Wait ... Someone's listening! Is that you, Jacob?'

She turned abruptly and stared right out of the screen at us. Jacob gestured quickly and the picture disappeared, replaced by an old episode of *The Addams Family*.

'Told you she'd stepped up security,' said Jacob. 'What do you suppose that was all about?'

'I don't know,' I said. 'But I don't like the sound of it.'

'Something's going on,' Jacob said darkly. 'Something the Matriarch and her precious inner circle don't want the rank and file to know about. There's something in the air ... Something big is coming. I can feel it, gathering like stormclouds in the future. And when it finally breaks, it's going to be a monster ... There have been several direct attacks on The Hall, just recently.'

'Hold it,' I said. 'Attacks? No one's told me anything about any attacks. What kind of attacks?'

'Powerful ones.' Jacob stirred uncomfortably in his chair. 'Even I didn't see them coming, and that's not like me. Nothing got through, of course; but the mere fact that someone or something felt confident enough to launch a direct attack on where we live speaks volumes. In my day, no one would have dared. We'd have tracked them down, ripped their souls out and nailed them to our outer walls. But it's all politics now; agreements and pacts and truces. The family isn't what it was ... I don't know why they've called you back, Eddie; but it sure as Hell isn't to pin a medal on your chest. Watch your back, lad.'

'Always,' I said. 'Anything I can do for you, Jacob?'

He leered at me in a frankly unsettling way. 'If that headless nun is still haunting the North Wing, tell her to get her ectoplasmic arse down here, and I'll teach her a whole new way to manifest.'

'But ... she hasn't got a head!'

'It's not her head I'm interested in!'

And he wonders why the rest of the family won't talk to him.

Out in the bright sunlight again, under a perfect blue sky, with gryphons prowling watchfully on the perfect lawns, while butterflies big as my hand fluttered through the flower gardens, it was hard to believe that the family could be in any real danger. Or that I might be. I might not have been happy here, but I always felt safe in The Hall. The power of the Droods depended on the fact that no one could touch us. I looked up at The Hall, towering over me, ancient and powerful, just like us. How could anything be wrong, in such a perfect place, on such a perfect day?

I walked in through the main entrance, and there in the vestibule was the Serjeant-At-Arms, waiting to meet me. Of course he was waiting; the gryphons would have told him the exact moment I'd arrive, hours before. The Serjeant was never surprised by anything or anyone. That was his job. He inclined his head stiffly to me, which was about as much welcome as I'd expected. In the Drood family, the prodigal son was always going to be in for a rough ride. The Serjeant-At-Arms wore the stark black and white formal outfit of a Victorian butler, right down to the stiff and starched high collar, even though he had the build and manner of an army serjeant major. I knew for a fact he always carried half a dozen concealed weapons of increasing power and viciousness somewhere about his person. If The Hall ever was attacked and breached, he'd be the first line of defence, and very likely the last thing the attackers ever saw.

He had a face that might have been chiselled out of stone. He didn't look at all pleased to see me, but then he never looked pleased about anything. Gossip had it smiling was against his religion.

'Hi there, Jeeves,' I said, just to wind him up, because we both knew he was far more than just a butler. (There are no servants, as such, in The Hall. We all serve the family, in our own way.) (Or at least, that's the official line . . .)

'Good morning, Edwin,' said the Serjeant, in his voice like grinding gravel. 'The Matriarch is expecting you.'

'I know,' I said. 'I wish I could say I was glad to be home again.'

'Indeed,' said the Serjeant. 'I wish I could say I was glad to see you again, boy.'

We sneered at each other for a moment, and then, honour satisfied, I allowed him to lead the way through the shadowy vestibule and on into the great hallway. Light streamed in through hundreds of stained-glass windows, filling the extended hallway with all the colours of the rainbow. Old paintings and portraits showed honoured members of the family: Drood men and women sitting and standing in fixed and formal poses, in the dress and fashions of centuries past, staring out at their descendants with stern, unwavering eyes.

Drood service and tradition goes back a long way, and none of us is ever permitted to forget it. By the time we got to the end of the hallway, the paintings had given way to photographs. From the first shadowy images to sepia tones to the garish colours of modern times, the fallen dead stared proudly out at the world they made.

I stopped to consider one photo in its silver frame, and the Serjeant stopped reluctantly beside me. The photo held two faces I knew like my own. A man and a woman stood together, proudly erect as befitting Droods, but there was a clear warmth and affection in their smiles and in their eyes. He was tall and elegant and handsome, and so was she, and they looked every inch the roistering adventurers everyone said they were. Charles and Emily Drood; my father and my mother. Murdered on a family mission in the Basque region, while I was still a small child. Looking at them, so young and full of life, it felt strange to realise that I was older now than they were when they died.

The Serjeant-At-Arms hovered silently close beside me, making me aware of his impatience with his proximity, but I wouldn't let myself be hurried. *Hello, Dad*, I thought. *Hello, Mum. I've come back.* But I couldn't think of anything else to say, so I nodded to them, and moved on.

The Serjeant-At-Arms finally ushered me into the Library, to wait there until the Matriarch was prepared to see me. He inclined his head again, very stiffly, and withdrew, shutting the door firmly behind him. I pulled a face at the closed door, and relaxed a little. Walking with the Serjeant always felt like you were being marched with a gun at your back. I wandered slowly through the many towering stacks and shelves of the family Library, inhaling the old familiar smells of leather bindings, paper and ink and dust. On these shelves, in these books, is recorded the true history of the world. The secret deals and treaties, the private promises and betrayals, and the secret wars that take place behind the scenes that normal people never get to hear about. The subtle moves on the invisible board, in the greatest game of all.

I was born, raised and educated here in The Hall, like every other Drood son and daughter, but I was one of the very few who ever bothered to read any book that wasn't part of the official curriculum. I discovered the Library when I was ten, and after that they couldn't keep me out. The family teaches you what it thinks you need to know, and nothing more. I, on the other hand, ploughed through books like others devoured junk food, and what the family called education I came to see as indoctrination. I wanted to know it all, the context as well as the bare facts. And the more I read, the more I wanted to get out into the real world, and see it as it really was.

For a long time, I couldn't see why this was such a problem for my teachers. I was being trained to fight evil, to know who Humanity's real enemies were and how to defeat them; so surely the more I knew about them, the better. Whenever I challenged anything, I was always told to shut up and go along, like everyone else, because only my elders and betters could see the Big Picture. So I kept reading, trying to see it too.

The problem with the Drood family Library is the sheer bloody size of the thing. Miles and miles of stacks and shelves, taking up the whole lower floor of the South Wing, every shelf packed tight to bursting with the accumulated knowledge and wisdom of centuries. Written in every language under the sun, and some from darker places, including a few so arcane that human vocal chords can't pronounce them out loud. So I read what I could in the original, and badgered the librarian endlessly to find translations for those I couldn't. A decent old stick, the librarian. Wore gaudy pullovers, even in the summer, and went motorbike scrambling every weekend. He disappeared suddenly, years before I left. We never did find out what happened to him.

I wandered aimlessly through the racks, trailing my fingertips lightly along the leather spines. We believe in books. Computer files can be hacked; paper can't. The only way to access the information in this Library is to come here in person. And the only way to do that is to be part of the family.

'Hello, Eddie. It's good to see you again.'

I turned around, already smiling. Uncle James strode forward to greet me, one hand outstretched to give me a firm, manly handshake. He looked great, as always, perfectly outfitted in the most stylish three-piece suit money could buy, looking every inch the rakish gentleman adventurer he was. Uncle James was tall, darkly handsome, effortlessly elegant and sardonic, and in really good shape for a man in his late fifties. His striking face had more than its fair share of character lines, but his hair was still jet black. His welcoming smile was broad and genuine, but even with me there was a touch of the ingrained iciness that never left his eyes.

James had always been my favourite member of the family. After my father and mother were killed, James became the closest thing to a parent I had. He took a sullen, silent, lost and introverted boy, and gave him a reason to live. He found things to interest and challenge me, encouraged my rebellions and gave me a purpose, in learning to fight all the evil people in the world, responsible for orphaning so many children. He brought me back out of myself, and made it possible for me to be happy again. If I ever had a hero, it was Uncle James. The last of the great adventurers, he went to the good war like a starving man to a feast. He had the most experience, and the most successful missions to his credit, of any member of the family. His use-name was a curse on the lips of the ungodly, and you could stop conversations with it in bars and dives all across the world. They called him the Grey Fox, and he was everything I ever aspired to be.

He was also the first one to advise me to leave and strike out on my own, before the family's insistence on duty and tradition crushed my spirit. I've always believed that the only reason I was ever allowed to operate at such a distance was because Uncle James went in to bat for me with the Matriarch. Not that I've ever mentioned it, of course. It would only have embarrassed him.

'It's good to see you again, Uncle James,' I said. 'Ten years it's been and yet, strangely, there's not even a hint of grey at your temples ...'

'Clean living and heavy drinking,' he said easily.

'Do you know why I've been summoned back here?' I said bluntly.

'Haven't a clue, Eddie. I'm only looking in between missions. A soft bed, a good meal and a wander through the wine cellars before they pack me off again. I'm just back from giving Dr Delirium a bloody nose in the Amazon jungle, and as soon as I've done a little research here, I'm off to sort out the Shadow Boxers of Shanghai. You know how it is; one damned thing after another.'

'I am so jealous,' I said, grinning despite myself. 'You get all the most glamorous assignments. I've never even been allowed out of the country.'

He raised a single eyebrow as he lit a black Russian cigarette with his monogrammed gold lighter. 'Now you know why that is, Eddie. But you do good work. People notice. The more missions you complete successfully, the more trust you'll earn and the more leash they'll give you.'

'But they'll never take the leash off, will they? I'll never be free of the family.'

'Why would you want to be? You're part of the most important heritage in the world.' James looked me in the eyes, very seriously. 'To be born a Drood is a privilege as well as a responsibility. We get to know the truth about the way things really are, and we get to fight the battles that really matter. And if in return we get the best of everything, it's because we've earned it. And all the family has ever asked for in return is loyalty.'

'We're born drafted into a war that never ends,' I said, meeting his gaze squarely. 'And most of us die fighting that war, far from home and family. Some of us never get to know our parents, and some parents never get to know their sons. I understand: it's an honour to serve. But I would have liked to be asked.'

And that was when the general alarm sounded, like every bell and siren in the world going off at once. James and I turned as one and ran back through the Library. We charged out into the corridor and almost ran over the Serjeant-At-Arms as he ran past, a gun in each hand. James grabbed him by the shoulder and hauled him to a halt, as family members came running from every direction.

'It's the Heart!' yelled the Serjeant, pulling away and racing off down the corridor. 'It's an attack on the Sanctity!'

He didn't need to say any more. James and I were already full pelt after him. James had a gun in each hand too now. And all I had was my needle gun. I didn't draw it. I was pretty sure frozen holy water wasn't going to be enough this time. The Heart was the source of the family's power. Its stored energies made our magics and super sciences possible, including the living armour we depended on. But the Sanctity, the great chamber that holds the Heart, was the single most heavily defended and protected part of The Hall. It's supposed to be invulnerable, inviolate. A direct attack on The

Hall was rare enough; an attack on the Heart was unprecedented, unthinkable.

James and I ran on, plunging through corridor after corridor at breakneck speed, both of us breathing steadily to conserve our wind, as we'd been trained. More and more members of the family came from everywhere to join us, men and women with shocked, strained faces and all kinds of weapons in their hands. Young and old, fighters and researchers and even duty staff; unheard of in the guaranteed safety of The Hall.

We were closing in on the Sanctity now, at the very centre of The Hall. I could feel the hair standing up on the back of my neck. There was a pressure, a presence, on the air; like the cold shadow of a place where bad things had happened. *Something big is coming*, that's what old Jacob had said. Something big ... Something bad. And it was close now. Very close.

Uncle James and I caught up with the Serjeant-At-Arms just as he slammed through the great double doors into the Sanctity, and there was the Heart: a single huge diamond shining like the sun, so big it filled the massive chamber the family had built to contain and protect it. A diamond bigger than a bus, a million facets shining and shimmering so brightly none of us could bear to look at it directly. The room was full of its light, and entering the Sanctity was like diving into ice-cold water. It took your breath away, like a shock to the soul. The Heart blazed with an otherworldly light, holding and harnessing the power that made our family's job possible. A light or an energy, a science or a magic; even after all the centuries it had been with us, we were no nearer understanding it.

The Heart was surrounded by powerful protections. I could feel them as I edged into the Sanctity, hammering on the shimmering air. Some of the family couldn't bring themselves to enter the room. But still the bells and sirens were shrieking, summoning the family to defend the Heart from an attack by someone or something unbelievably powerful. Only the most terrible of our enemies would dare launch so blatant an assault. I circled slowly round the gigantic diamond, one arm raised before my eyes to shield me from its overwhelming glare. The light seemed to blaze right through my fragile flesh, like an X-ray. James was there with me, and the Serjeant-At-Arms, and I sensed as much as saw other members of the family

45

moving slowly round the Heart, searching desperately for some sign of the enemy.

I had my needle gun in my hand. I didn't have a lot of faith in it, but its presence made me feel better. I hadn't armoured up. None of us had. We were all still thinking in terms of threats to the safety of the Heart. It never even occurred to us that we might be in danger. This was The Hall, and we had always been safe here.

I felt something approaching, from a direction I could sense but not name. It was a presence, something so vast and alien and utterly Other that its terrible nature actually eclipsed and overwhelmed the Heart. It drew closer and closer, straining to materialise inside the Sanctity, trying to force its way in from some other dimension of reality. It seemed to be closing in on us from every direction at once, and just the sense of it was like shit smeared across my soul. Like a mountain of maggots, or the smile the razor blade leaves as it slices through a suicide's wrists. It was almost upon us, and it hated us, just for being human.

The wood-panelled wall to my left groaned loudly as it bulged inwards, the old wood stretching impossibly, forced out of shape by some unnameable pressure from outside our three-dimensional reality. The floor rose up at its centre like some monstrous boil, and the ceiling bulged down. All the walls were crying out now, straining inwards towards the Heart. Something was forcing its way into the Sanctity, from some higher or lower dimension, from some place we couldn't even hope to comprehend. And one by one, the many layers of protection the family had set in place around the Heart shattered and blew apart, like so many cheap firecrackers.

Family magicians were in the room now, crowding round the Heart, chanting spells and brandishing ancient talismans, trying to set up new defensive parameters. Family scientists worked beside them, operating esoteric constructions of weird technology, some of which looked like they'd been dragged in from the testing labs. All kinds of energy fields crackled on the air, but still the awful presence surrounded us, descending on us from everywhere at once.

And finally, it broke through. Something was suddenly there in the room with us; or rather, nothing was. There was a gap, an absence, a horrible void hanging on the air before the Heart. I couldn't see or hear it, but I could feel it, on a level that had nothing to do with senses. It was as though some terribly old, perhaps even pre-human, part of me recognised it. A sucking pit of the spirit; a hole in reality itself. It pulsed, like some great malignant heart, and then it reached out and sucked the flesh off those members of the family nearest it.

We lost a dozen men and women in a moment, meat and blood torn from their bones, whole organs flying through the air and into the void, to make it a body, to give it shape and form in this world. The bloody pulp of organs and muscles slammed together, flesh slapping upon flesh, building a body whose shape made no sense, to house and hold the awful thing that had forced its way in. Bloody bones lay scattered across the floor, unwanted, along with a dozen golden torcs. People were puking and retching everywhere, even as they backed away.

'Armour up!' James yelled. 'Everyone! Now!'

We subvocalised the Words, and living armour encased us, glorious and golden, sealing us off from the pull of the void. For the first time I felt sane and human again, able to think clearly, my spirit no longer soiled by the presence of the thing before us. Where the void had been, a huge new thing had taken shape. It looked like it was made out of cancers, like sickness and death made solid and vicious. It was scarlet and purple with bulging dark veins, and it glistened wetly. Uneven rows of human eyes stared unblinkingly out of a pulpy mass that might have been meant as a face. It rose up to the bowed ceiling, big as ten men, limbs of a sort radiating from its central mass, but its shape and dimensions and attributes made no sense at all. I felt its attention turn away from the family, towards the Heart, and I sensed a terrible emotion in the shape that might have been rage, or hunger, or a need to violate. It moved towards the Heart, surging forward like a snail, and the great diamond's light seemed to flicker and diminish, just from the thing's proximity.

'Stop it!' James yelled. 'Don't let it touch the Heart!'

The Serjeant-At-Arms had already opened fire, blazing away with both guns at once. James strode forward, pouring bullets into the bloody shape from close range, and I was there with him, firing my needle gun. Everyone else in the Sanctity opened fire on the mass with whatever weapons they had, crowding forward, ignoring their own safety to protect the Heart. Magicians unleashed curses and damnations, and scientists fired strange energies from stranger weapons . . . and none of it did any good. The bloody shape absorbed our bullets, and everything else, with equal indifference, pressing slowly but inexorably towards the Heart. Golden armoured hands that could punch through walls or shatter steel flailed at the pulpy mass, and it ignored us. One armoured man stood defiantly in its path. The scarlet shape sucked him in and spat him out the other side. He thrashed weakly on the floor, screaming like the newly damned.

I grabbed James by the arm and made him look at me. 'Call them off! They'll listen to you. I've got an idea!'

He looked at me, and then nodded curtly and ordered the family to disengage. Everyone fell back immediately. They trusted James, where they most certainly wouldn't have trusted me. James looked at me expectantly. I reached through the armour on my side, drew the portable door from my pocket, activated it and tossed it into the path of the bloody shape as it surged forward, as I had with the Hyde at the Wulfshead. The portable door slid neatly into position, sparked and sputtered a few times, and then lay there, inert. I'd used it too often. The batteries were dead.

James was still looking at me. I couldn't see his face behind the gleaming golden mask, but I could guess his expression. He'd trusted me, and I'd let him down. I looked back at the shape. It was almost upon the Heart. I thought hard, glaring desperately about the Sanctity in search of inspiration, and then my gaze fell upon the dozen torcs lying discarded on the floor, left behind when their owners were stripped of flesh to make the bloody shape. I lurched forward, grabbed a handful of the golden collars, raised my golden fist and punched the torcs right through the dark-veined cancerous side of the thing. I forced them deep into the mass, let go of the torcs, and then tried to pull my hand out again; but it was stuck.

A terrible coldness, as much of the spirit as the body, crept up my arm. I think I cried out. And then James was there beside me, pulling at my trapped arm with all his strength. For a terrifyingly long moment even our combined strength wasn't enough, and then my hand jerked out of the bloody mass, and we both staggered backwards. I yelled aloud the Words that activated the living armour, the Words we normally only ever subvocalised, and the five torcs within the bloody shape activated. All at once.

48

Inside the cancerous fleshy mass, the torcs did what they were programmed to do. They identified their owners, or in this case what was left of them, and encased them in living armour. Golden shards erupted out of the red and purple shape, slicing it apart. The bloody mass fought back, struggling to maintain the integrity of the form it had taken, but the torcs' progress was inexorable. Once started, their transformation could not be stopped by anyone or anything. The bloody shape collapsed, and a soundless howl of fury filled all our heads for a moment, as the thing snapped out of existence, its hold on our reality broken. Lying on the floor before the Heart, in awful unnatural attitudes, were five suits of golden armour surrounded by pieces of bloody meat. I didn't want to think about what those suits contained.

The oppressive sense of the invading presence was gone. The bells and sirens snapped off, and a blessed silence filled the Sanctity. One by one we armoured down, golden forms giving way to men and women with shocked, traumatised faces. James clapped me on the shoulder.

'Well done, Eddie. Good thinking.'

People began slowly filing out of the room. The Heart was safe. Everyone went back to their normal, everyday duties. Some were in shock, some had to be helped. Some were openly angry, or scared; because The Hall was no longer the safe place it had always been before. Some were crying over the loss of friends or loved ones. You couldn't blame them. Most of the family never see fieldwork, never see any kind of action, never see the blood and suffering and death that lies at the heart of what the Droods do and are. There'd be a lot of sleeping pills and bad dreams in the four wings tonight.

The Serjeant-At-Arms had already collared a few of the harder-hearted souls and set them to work, and the clearing up had begun. He didn't even look at me. I might have saved the day, and the Heart, and maybe the whole family, but he still didn't trust me. And none of the others congratulated me as they left. Most also didn't look at me. None of them wanted to be seen talking to me, didn't want to get too close to the man who'd turned his back on family tradition and responsibility, in case some of my independence rubbed off on them. James made a point of standing next to me, his hand still on my shoulder.

Everyone respected the Grey Fox.

Finally, we left the Sanctity together, and went out into the corridor. Away from the stench of spilled blood and meat and guts, the old familiar smells of wood and polish and fresh flowers was immediately restorative. I breathed deeply, and my head cleared. The old solid walls, with their sense of long history and service, were actually reassuring for once.

'This assault is unprecedented,' said James. He kept his voice low as we walked, but it held a cold anger that was disturbingly near the surface. 'Not only did something hammer its way through The Hall's defences, and the Heart's; it actually killed Droods! Right here in the midst of the family! That's never happened before. We're supposed to be safe here, protected from all threats and dangers.'

'This has never happened before?' I said. 'I mean, ever?'

James looked at me for a long moment, as though deciding how much he trusted me. 'There have been two previous attacks on the Heart,' he said finally, in a voice so low I had to strain to hear it. 'No one was hurt, and neither of them got this close, but still ...'

'Jesus ... No wonder the Matriarch's been busy punching up The Hall's defences ...'

James looked at me oddly. 'How did you know that, Eddie?'

'I had a word with old Jacob. He doesn't miss much.'

'Oh, yes. Of course. You always were fond of that disgusting old reprobate. You must understand, Eddie ... The Hall has been inviolate ever since we first moved in here. No one's ever been able to crack our defences, let alone actually threaten the Heart. There can only be one answer ... an inside man. A traitor in the family, giving up the secrets of our protections.'

I was so shocked I actually stopped in my tracks and stared at him with my mouth hanging open. Members of the family had left in the past, or been declared rogue and forced out, but no one had ever turned traitor, working from within to betray us to our enemies ... It was unthinkable.

'Is that why everyone's been so conspicuously giving me the cold shoulder?' I said eventually. 'Is that why I've been called back?'

'I don't know, Eddie. The Matriarch ... hasn't been taking me into her confidence like she used to. So watch your back while you're here. Paranoia breeds suspicion. Because if the family can't identify their traitor, they might just choose one . . .'

We walked on together, back through the many rooms and passageways of The Hall, past magnificent works of art that we all simply took for granted. Rembrandts. Goyas. Schalckens. The Hall is stuffed with priceless paintings and sculptures and precious items, donated by princes and powers and governments down the centuries. They've always been very grateful for everything the family does for them. And then there were the displays of weapons, and the other spoils of war we've accumulated. The family might not be very sentimental about its past, but it never throws away anything useful.

'Someone is testing us,' said James after a while. 'Testing their traitor's information, seeing how far they can get before we stop them. But who? The Stalking Shrouds? The Loathly Ones? The Cold Eidolon? The Mandrake Recorporation?' He shook his head slowly. 'There are so many of them, and so few of us.' And then he smiled at me, his old damn-them-all-to-Hell smile, and clapped me on the shoulder again. 'Let them come. Let them all come. We're Droods, and we were born to kick supernatural arse. Right?'

'Damn right,' I said.

CHAPTER FIVE
Remote viewing

When the Serjeant-At-Arms finally came looking for me, Uncle James and I were standing before a caricature by Boz of good old Jacob in his prime, sharing a conversation with Gladstone and Disraeli outside Parliament. (One of those revered Prime Ministers was actually a Drood, on his mother's side, but I can never remember which.) God alone knows what the three of them were discussing, but given the expressions on Disraeli and Gladstone's faces, Jacob was almost certainly telling them one of his famously filthy jokes. Jacob could shock the knickers off a nun at forty paces. Both James and I heard the Serjeant approaching, but we deliberately kept our attention fixed on the piece of art until the Serjeant was obliged to announce his presence with a somewhat undignified cough. James and I turned unhurriedly, and looked down our noses at him.

'Well?' James drawled, in that infuriatingly snotty polite voice of his. He'd been known to start bar fights with less. He even threw in a raised eyebrow. 'Do you have any information yet, as to how such an appalling assault was able to get past all our legendary security systems, to attack the Heart?'

Give the man his due, the Serjeant just stared impassively back. 'An investigation into the security breach is ongoing, sir.'

'That'll be a No, then. Anything else?'

The Serjeant-At-Arms gave James a meaningful look, and James nodded, knowing he'd pushed the situation as far as he could. He turned his back on the Serjeant and smiled warmly at me. 'It's time I was on my way, Eddie. The ungodly await, and there shall be beatings. Another exciting adventure lies ahead, in the scurrilous back streets and bars of fabulous Shanghai.'

'I could spit,' I said feelingly. 'I never get missions like that. I suppose it's going to be all good booze, bad women and lots of gratuitous violence?'

'Ah yes,' said James. 'The same old, same old . . .'

We laughed, he crushed my hand in his and off he went, striding grandly down the gallery in search of danger and diversion like the accomplished adventurer he was. The Grey Fox always was the best of us. The Serjeant-At-Arms reminded me of his presence with another of his weighty coughs, and reluctantly I allowed him to lead me back through The Hall to meet the family Matriarch.

It turned out she was down in the War Room, deciding the fate of the world again, so we had to tramp through most of the North Wing to reach the heavily reinforced steel door at the back of what used to be the old ballroom. It took us three passwords, a retina scan and a not entirely unfriendly frisking before the Serjeant and I were even allowed to approach the door, but eventually it opened and we descended a very basic stairway cut into the stone wall itself, with no railing and a frankly intimidating open drop on the other side. The electric lighting was almost painfully bright, and extra security measures were already in place, so that glowing force fields and shimmering mystical screens opened before us as they acknowledged our torcs, and then sealed firmly behind us. The usual guard goblins were in place, sitting in their stone recesses; squat and ugly things with a face like a bulldog chewing on a wasp. They weren't much bigger than a football, with long spindly arms and legs, but they could be quite spectacularly vicious when roused. I'd once seen a goblin run down a werewolf and eat it alive; and you don't forget things like that in a hurry.

While waiting for a chance to express their utterly vile and nasty natures, the goblins whiled away the time by working on crossword puzzles from *The Times*. Goblins love word games. One of them stopped me to ask for a seventeen letter word for bad government beginning with an m, and got really quite upset when I came straight back with *maladministration*. The poor thing didn't realise he was doing yesterday's crossword.

At the bottom of the stairs, we both had to place our hands on an electronic scanner before we were allowed into the great vault that held the family War Room. The Serjeant led me inside and then insisted I stay put by the door, while he went to inform the Matriarch that I'd arrived. I folded my arms stiffly across my chest and sneered after him, but I didn't push the point. There was a gorgon squatting next to the door, head down, wrapped in leathery wings like an enveloping cloak. She looked like she was sleeping, but I knew she wasn't. Even though several of the snakes were making a game attempt at snoring. Entering the War Room without following exact rules of procedure would lead to the gorgon opening her eyes and looking at you, and then the family would have another surprised-looking statue for the back gardens.

The War Room was a vast auditorium carved from solid stone. In here we saw everything, or at least everything that mattered. All four walls were covered with state-of-the-art display screens, showing every country of the world, with little lights blinking to indicate cities and other places where members of the family were currently at work. Green lights for a successfully completed mission, blue for certain individuals currently on the family Hit List, and the occasional purple signifying a major cock-up and its equally large cover-up operation. Potential trouble spots were marked with amber lights, current threats with red. There was a hell of a lot of amber and red showing all across the world, and a lot more red than amber compared to ten years ago. Hell, even Lithuania had a red light.

The family sat in long rows, concentrating on their work stations despite the hustle and bustle around them. Dozens of farcasters caressed crystal balls or peered into scrying pools, studying the world's problems from afar, while softly murmuring their findings into hands-free headsets. Technicians worked their computers, worrying out useful data, fingers darting across keyboards with dazzling speed. Agents may operate alone in the field, but each and every one of us is backed up by a staff of hundreds. And not just in the War Room. Information retrieval experts are constantly at work in the newsroom (usually referred to by those who work their eight-hours shifts in that windowless hole as the Pit) sifting through the world's media and cross-referencing the official version with the mountain of information that comes in every day from our worldwide web of spies and informers. The family relies on these dedicated researchers to spot trouble forming before it gets out of hand, as well as keep to track of certain individuals who like to think they can pass through the world without leaving a trace. These researchers could tell you exactly where to find a needle in a haystack, and make a pretty good guess about which way it would be pointing. They knew everything there was to know about the world, except what it was like to live in it. They were far too valuable to be ever allowed to leave The Hall.

At any given moment, hundreds of Droods are operating in hot spots all across the world. And they work alone, because agents in the field can't be viewed from afar. Their torcs hide them from us, as well as our enemies. That's why only the most trusted in the family are allowed to become field agents. And why I'm always kept on such a short leash. The War Room has to wait for field agents to report in by traditional means, often on the run, and then provide them with as much information and back-up as possible. Every agent is supported by thousands of researchers, advisors, experts in the more arcane areas of science and magic and round-the-clock communications staff.

Field agents gather information, defuse pressure points, and take direct action when necessary. (We prefer to work with a quiet word and a subtle threat, but the family's never been afraid to get its hands dirty.) But every one of us knows that it's the back-up people at The Hall who make our job possible.

The family has raised remote viewing, in all its forms, to something of an art. And since we've always seen both science and magic as two sides of the same useful coin, we work hard to stay in the forefront of all the latest advances. In fact, our research labs make damned sure we're always one step ahead. We've turned out weapons, and answers to weapons, that most of the world doesn't even dream exist yet. We use whatever we have to, to keep the world safe.

I was surprised, and a little alarmed, to see how many Red Alerts were showing: warnings of major threats not as yet narrowed down to any particular country or group or individual. And when I say major threat, I mean a clear and present danger to the world. I'd never known the War Room to seem so busy, with people crowded round every display, every computer, every paper-strewn table. There was a general susurrus of combined murmured voices, almost like being in a church. (Raised voices are discouraged; they breed agitation.) Messengers were constantly hurrying in and out, bearing notes and reports and vital updates. And fresh pots of tea. The family runs on tea. And Jaffa cakes.

No one even glanced in my direction.

The Matriarch was sitting at the main mission table, stiff-backed and coldly attentive as always, studying an endless series of urgent reports as they were handed to her. Some she initialled, approving an action, others she sent back for more detail. Messengers waited in line for a chance to push a paper in front of her, or murmur confidentially in her ear, before hurrying off with new instructions. The Matriarch never allowed herself to seem hurried or worried, and she never raised her voice. If some especially harried messenger did overstep the mark, by questioning a detail or insisting on the importance of his message, one look from the Matriarch's cold grey eyes was all it took, and the messengers would practically break their backs bowing and scraping as they hurried away from her.

The Serjeant-At-Arms advised the Matriarch of my arrival, and she turned immediately to look at me. I stared calmly back, not even bothering to unfold my arms. She beckoned imperiously, and I ambled across the War Room to join her, deliberately not hurrying myself. The Matriarch gestured sharply for everyone to withdraw, and they fell back a decent distance so she and I could talk in private. The Serjeant looked outraged at being lumped in with everyone else, but he went. One didn't argue with the Matriarch. She stood up to greet me, wearing her usual cold and disapproving expression.

The family Matriarch. Martha Drood. Tall, elegant, and more royal than any queen. In her mid-sixties now, she dressed like country aristocracy: twin-set, tweeds and pearls and understated make-up. She wore her long grey hair piled in a sculpture on top of her head. She'd been beautiful in her day, and her strong bone structure ensured she was striking, even now. Like the Ice Queen of fable, who drives a splinter of her ice into your heart while you're young and helpless, so you have no choice but to love her for ever. She didn't offer me a hand to shake, and I didn't offer to kiss her on the cheek. Honours even. I nodded to her.

'Hello, Grandmother.'

The family has always been led by a Matriarch; it's a holdover from our Druidic heritage. Martha is descended from a long line of warrior queens; and it shows. Her word is law. When I was a child, in family history class, I pointed out to the teacher that if she was our queen the rest of us were her drones. I got shouted at a lot for that. Technically, the Matriarch has absolute power over the family. In practice, she is very firmly advised by the Council of Twelve, drawn from the foremost members of the family. You have to achieve something quite remarkable, even to make the short list. Matriarchs who don't or won't listen to their councils don't tend to last long. In extreme cases, accidents have been known to happen, and a new Matriarch takes over. The family can be extremely ruthless, when it has to.

Martha's second husband, Alistair, stood diffidently at her side, as always, ready for whatever she might need him to do. Tall and sturdy, he dressed like a gentleman farmer, the kind that never ever gets their expensive boots dirty. He was ten years younger than Martha, and handsome enough, I suppose, in a weak and unfinished sort of way, like the investment broker who assures you that the deal he's proposing is absolutely guaranteed to make you rich. I nodded briefly to him.

'Hello, Alistair.'

He was Principal Consort of the family, by long tradition, but I was damned if I'd call him 'Grandfather'. My real grandfather, Martha's first husband, Arthur, died fighting the Kiev Conspiracy in 1957. I never knew him.

Alistair and I never did get along. Officially, his function in the family was as personal advisor to the Matriarch, but that was something to keep him busy so he wouldn't realise he was just a glorified gopher. He'd never been on a field mission in his life, to his and everyone else's relief. Before he married Martha he was something in the City, but only because he inherited it. Word was, the City was glad to be rid of him. The whole family knew he was useless, but Grandmother loved him, so out of respect for her no one ever said anything. While making very sure Alistair was never allowed near anything important. Or breakable. There's one like Alistair in every family.

Martha studied me coldly. 'It's been quite a while since you graced us with your presence, Edwin.'

I shrugged. 'I like to keep busy. And it's not as if there's anything here I miss.'

'After all this time, you still blame the family for the deaths of your mother and father,' said Martha. 'You should be proud of their sacrifice.'

'I am,' I said. 'But no one's ever going to send me to my death on an operation that wasn't planned properly. I run my own missions.'

'You serve the family,' Alistair said, trying for Martha's frosty tone and not bringing it off.

'I serve the family,' I said. 'In my own way.'

'The people responsible for the inadequate planning of that mission were punished long ago,' said Martha. 'You have to let it go, Edwin. She was my daughter too.' She made a deliberate effort to change the subject. 'What is that you're wearing, Edwin? Is this really the best you could do, on your first visit to The Hall in ten years?'

'Sorry,' I said. 'But I've been recently diagnosed as fashion intolerant. I can't wear anything good, in case I develop style.'

She looked at me. 'You know I don't find humour funny, Edwin. And stand up straight. Do you want to develop round shoulders? And when are you going to get married, and give the family children? Like everyone else, you have a duty to provide the family with fresh blood, to keep us strong and vital. We have provided you with several lists of perfectly respectable candidates from suitable families. Any one of whom would make you a good match. You're getting a little too old to be so choosy.'

'That is something else I'll decide for myself,' I said firmly.

'What was wrong with dear Stephanie Mainwearing?' said Martha. 'Delightful creature, I thought.'

'Oh come on, Grandmother. If she was any more inbred, she'd be her own sister.'

'Alice Little?'

'Lives in a world of her own and only comes out for mealtimes. Lots of mealtimes.'

'Penelope Creighton?'

'You have got to be kidding! She's slept with more women than I have! Don't your people do even basic research any more?'

'Well . . . are you at least seeing anyone at the moment, Edwin?'

I considered telling her about Silicon Lily, but rose above the temptation. 'No one special, Grandmother,' I said.

'I hope you're being . . . careful, Edwin,' said Alistair, in an even more snotty voice than usual. 'You know how the family feels about bastards.'

I looked at him for a moment, and then said, 'I'm always careful, Alistair.'

'After all,' said Alistair, 'whoever you eventually settle on, she has to be acceptable to the family.'

'Like you, Alistair?' I said.

Martha decided to change the subject again. 'You have been summoned back to The Hall, Edwin, because I have a very important and very urgent mission for you.'

'I had sort of gathered that,' I said. 'But can I ask what could be so important that I had to be dragged all the way here, just to discuss it? What was wrong with the usual channels?'

'It's a matter of security,' said Martha. 'It has to be you, because everyone else is busy. Busier than ever before. You can see the boards; we are stretched to our limits. And you saw what happened in the Sanctity. Once such an attack would have been unthinkable, but now the whole family is under threat. Our best efforts have to go into defending ourselves and identifying our attackers. The mission I have for you now, Edwin, is your chance to prove your worth at last, and come back to the bosom of the family. Carry out this mission successfully, and you will have earned a seat on the Council.' She paused, considering her words carefully. 'Some of us have come to believe that there is a traitor, perhaps at the very heart of the family. I am no longer sure who I can trust. Even my own Council has become . . . divided, and quarrelsome, of late. As an outsider, you might see things the rest of us cannot. Prove yourself with this mission, Edwin. I would value your voice in my Council.'

I just stood there and looked at her. I really hadn't expected that. The Council was where policy was decided. Where the decisions that mattered were made. It had honestly never occurred to me that I might end up on it some day. I wasn't even sure I wanted such an honour, or such responsibility; but I had to admit I was tempted. If only so I could use my new exalted position to identify and help others like myself in the family.

'What's the mission?' I said flatly. 'And what's the catch?'

The Matriarch smiled briefly for the first time. 'Your mission is to take the Soul of Albion back to Stonehenge and rebury it under the main sacrificial altar, where it belongs. Once it is in place, the Soul will be safe again. The Stones will protect it. And the catch, as you put it, is that if word should get out about what you're carrying ... all the forces of darkness will come after you. In the wrong hands ... the Soul could bring down England, and perhaps even the Droods.'

I was nodding even as she spoke. This had to be what Jacob and I had overheard them discussing, on his dead television.

Martha called to armed guards, who brought forward a great oaken chest sealed with solid silver bars and half a dozen cold iron padlocks. On top of which, the whole casket practically crackled with protective spells. The guards couldn't have handled it more respectfully if it had been filled to the brim with nitroglycerine. They placed the casket very carefully at Martha's feet, and then almost tripped over each other as they backed away from it at speed. Martha gave them one of her best icy looks, and undid the bands and padlocks with a Word. They snapped open, one after the other, and the defence spells immediately started warming up, until Martha shut them down with a quick gesture. The casket lid opened by itself and Martha reached in and drew out a small silver jewel box, no bigger than her hand.

She turned the delicate key in its lock, and the box opened to reveal a bed of red plush velvet, and on it the Soul of Albion. A polished crystal sphere, no bigger than my thumb, it blazed with unearthly fires. It was impossibly, heartstoppingly beautiful, almost painful to the eyes, like the platonic ideal of every gem or jewel or precious stone that ever was. All across the War Room people stopped what they were doing, and looked around, sensing the presence of something new and wonderful in their midst.

The Soul is supposed to have fallen to earth from the stars, some three thousand years ago, but there are more legends about it than you can shake a grimoire at. Terribly beautiful, impossibly powerful, linked for ever to the land in which it fell. Martha snapped the lid of the jewel box shut, cutting off the brilliant light, and we all breathed a little more easily again. While its light blazed, it was almost impossible to think of anything but the Soul. Martha glared around her, and everyone quickly got back to work. She locked the box and handed it to me. I accepted it gingerly. It felt strangely light, almost insubstantial in my hand. I slipped it into my jacket pocket, taking my hand away from the box as quickly as possibly. On the whole, I think I'd have felt safer carrying a backpack nuke with the timer already running.

'As long as the Soul of Albion remains in that box, it is protected by powerful masking spells,' said Martha. 'And the lead lining should shield you from most of the Soul's destructive radiation.'

'Oh good,' I said. 'I feel so much safer now.'

Long and long ago, so far back that history becomes legend and myth, someone used the Soul to perform a mighty magic, and now as long as the Soul of Albion rests in its appointed place within the great circle of standing stones that is Stonehenge, England is safe from threats of invasion. (There is another legend, about three royal Crowns of Anglia, but that was always just a diversion.) King Harold unearthed the Soul and took it with him to Hastings in 1066, thinking it would help him stand off William of Normandy, the fool. After the battle, William the Conqueror personally oversaw the returning of the Soul to Stonehenge, and no one had moved it since.

Until now.

'I have to ask,' I said. 'Who the Hell thought it was a good idea to bring the Soul of Albion here in the first place? And have they been given a really good slapping?'

Alistair sniffed, and did his best to look down his nose at me. 'That concerns policy, Edwin. You don't need to know. Suffice to say ... there were security issues involved.'

'However,' Martha said quickly, 'given the recent attacks on The Hall, and now the Heart itself, it has been decided that the Soul should be returned to its rightful place, and the sooner the better. Originally, your Uncle James was to have performed this mission. That's why we called him back from the Amazon jungles. But, we feel that under ... current circumstances, the movements of a major agent like the Grey Fox are bound to be more clearly monitored than usual. If any of our enemies discovered he was heading for Stonehenge, they might draw some very accurate conclusions. On the other hand, a fairly minor, semi-rogue operative such as yourself might well slip under their radar and go unnoticed.'

'Spell out the catch for me,' I said, 'so I can be sure I've got it right.'

'I would have thought it was obvious,' said Martha, meeting my gaze unflinchingly. 'If you are noticed, and your mission deduced, the odds are that every bad thing in the world will come for you, desperate for a chance to get their hands on the legendary Soul of Albion.'

'And then my mission turns into a suicide run,' I said, nodding slowly. 'No wonder you felt the need to bribe me with the offer of a place on the Council. The odds are you're sending me to my death.'

'But will you do it?' said the Matriarch. 'For the family, and for England?'

'Of course,' I said. 'Anything, for England.'

CHAPTER SIX

Dangerous lab interns

So, I went to pay a visit to the family Armourer. Bit of a dry old stick, but there's nothing he doesn't know about weapons, devices and things that go boom; whether scientific or magical in nature. In the more than likely event of something going horribly wrong on my new mission, it was clear I was going to need all the serious weaponry I could get my hands on if I was to protect the Soul of Albion on its journey.

I wanted a new gun. A big gun. A really, really big gun. With atomic bullets.

The family Armoury is situated a decent distance beneath the West Wing, set even deeper in the bedrock than the War Room. That way when (rather than if) the whole Armoury finally blows itself to Hell, it won't take the rest of The Hall with it. The Armourer and his staff, geniuses though they may be, and enthusiastic to a fault, have always had a tendency towards the *kick it and see what happens* school of scientific enquiry. They also have unlimited access to guns, grimoires and unstable chemicals. I'm amazed this part of England is still here.

The present Armoury is set up in what used to be the old wine cellars, behind vast and heavy blast-proof doors. Designed to keep things in, rather than out. The cellars are basically a long series of connected stone chambers, with bare plastered walls and curving ceilings, all but buried under a multi-coloured spaghetti of tacked-up electrical wiring. The fluorescent lighting was a sometime thing, and the huge air-conditioning system grumbled constantly to itself. The stone chambers were full to bursting with the Armourer's extended staff: researchers, expediters, mechanics, weaponeers and human guinea pigs. (Someone had to test each new device. This was decided by a lottery among the staff, and the loser was the one who wasn't smart enough to fix the outcome in advance.)

The Armoury is always coming up with new weapons, devised, constructed and tested right here in the labs. Which is why the place is always so appallingly noisy. I stood by the closed blast-proof doors a while, waiting for my ears to adjust to the din. Men and women with earnest, preoccupied faces bustled back and forth, giving their whole attention to the latest generation of deadly devices they were producing for agents to use in the field. And hopefully getting all the bugs out in advance. I could still remember the explosive whoopee cushion, which didn't, and the utterly impenetrable arm-mounted force shield, which wasn't.

Lights flared brightly, shadows danced, and lighting crawled over one wall like electric ivy. Sharp chemical stinks fought it out with the gentler aromas of crushed herbs, while molten metal flowed sluggishly into ceramic moulds, and smoke drifted gently on the air from the latest unfortunate incident. The Armoury didn't have a first-aid box; it had its own adjoining hospital ward. A hell of a lot of people crowded around test benches and futuristic lab equipment, alchemical retorts and silver bullet moulds, and of course the ubiquitous computers and chalked pentagrams. Most of these very busy people were cursing loudly and emphatically as they tried to persuade their latest projects to do what they were supposed to without exploding, melting down or turning the experimenter into something small and fluffy. Somebody close to me reached for a handy lump hammer, and I decided to go somewhere else.

I strolled through the labs, keeping an eye out for the Armourer. Doorways opened in mid air, giving brief glimpses of faraway places, and a test animal imploded. A desperate young intern chased through the labs, flailing away with a butterfly net, trying to catch an oversized eyeball with its own fluttering bat wings. I'm sure it looked perfectly reasonable at the drafting stage. No one paid any attention to these disruptions, except to jump a little, absent-mindedly, at the latest bang. Just another day in the Armoury. You have to expect and allow for the occasional setback when you're working at the cutting edges of devious thinking; along with regular stinks, spatial inversions, and the odd unexpected transformation. Everyone who worked in the Armoury was a volunteer, drawn from a long list of applications,

64

carefully selected from those in the family who had clearly dem-
onstrated they had far more brains than was good for them. (Often
accompanied by an unhealthy curiosity and a complete lack of self-
preservation instincts.)

(The really dangerous thinkers were either rapidly promoted to
purely theoretical projects, or sent to alternate dimensions and told
not to come back till they'd calmed down.)

The current crop of interns looked like science nerds everywhere,
all heavy spectacles and plastic pocket protectors, except that some
of them wore pointy wizard's hats as well. A lot of them were
wearing T-shirts under their lab coats bearing the legend, *I Blow
Things Up, Therefore I Am, Even If Someone Else Suddenly Isn't*. Science
nerd humour. They seemed very earnest and very committed, and if
they survived long enough would eventually be promoted to the
somewhat safer environs of the Research and Development labs. It
did seem to me, though, as I wandered through the chaos in search
of the Armourer, that the old place held a lot more people and
projects, along with a greater general sense of urgency, than I remembered from my last visit ten years ago.

Two of the more brawny types were sparring with electrified brass
knuckles, sparks crackling and spitting fiercely on the air as they
swung and parried. One girl had her head stuck deep in a fish tank,
proving she could breathe underwater. Impressive, but I couldn't
help thinking the gaping rows of gills on her neck would be a bit of
a giveaway in polite society. Not far away, an unfortunate young man
had stopped proving he could now breathe fire, because it had given
him hiccoughs. Unpredictable and highly inflammable hiccoughs.
Someone led him away to put an asbestos bag over his head. I didn't
see why they couldn't stick his head in the fish tank, next to the girl.

And someone had blown up the firing range again. There's always
someone trying to break the record for biggest and most powerful
handgun.

I finally spotted the Armourer up ahead, striding back and forth
through the caverns, keeping a stern eye on everyone and everything.
He paused here and there to dispense advice, encouragement, and
the occasional clip round the ear, where necessary. The Armourer
was strict but fair, but strict. I waited until he came back and settled
at his usual testing bench, and then slipped in beside him. He glanced

65

briefly at me, sniffed loudly, and went back to what he was working on. It takes a lot to surprise the Armourer.

A tall, middle-aged man with far too much nervous energy, he wore a permanently stained white lab coat over a T-shirt saying, *Guns Don't Kill People; I Kill People.* Two shocks of tufty white hair jutted out over his ears below a bulging bald pate, and under bushy white eyebrows his eyes were a steely grey. His expression rarely changed from a habitual scowl, and while he had once been tall and imposing he was now bent by a pronounced stoop, legacy of so many years spent leaning over work benches and lab projects that always needed fixing in a hurry. Or maybe just from ducking a lot. I sat beside him for a while, waiting for him to say something, but as always it was up to me to tear his attention away from his latest project.

'Hello, Armourer. Good to see you again. The old place seems very busy, at the moment. Are we preparing for a war?'

He sniffed loudly. 'Always, boy. Always.'

He plugged a thick electrical cable into a socket, tripped half a dozen switches and then looked expectantly at a computer monitor wrapped in mistletoe and strings of garlic. Nothing happened. The Armourer hit the computer with a hammer, and I quickly took it away from him.

'Give that back!' he said, scowling fiercely. 'That's my lucky hammer!'

'Lucky?' I said, holding it carefully out of reach.

'I'm still here, aren't I?'

I put the hammer down at the opposite end of the bench. 'What's the problem, Armourer?'

He sighed, as he realised he was going to have to talk to me. 'Seems everyone in The Hall is trying to draw power from the Heart at the same time. Every damned department at once. I'm supposed to have priority, but it's all I can do to elbow my way into the queue. If I have to go upstairs and complain, there'll be tear gas and shrapnel flying through the common rooms ...'

'Why is there so much demand for power?'

'Don't ask me. Ask bloody Alistair!'

I recognised the tone. 'All right; what's Alistair done now?'

The Armourer gave me his best put-upon expression. 'First the

Matriarch increases my budget, and my workload, and tells me my projects have top priority until further notice; and then bloody Alistair comes poncing in here and announces he's chosen the Armoury as the best place to start his latest efficiency drive. So now not only has my workload gone through the roof, but I have to account for everything we do and use, in triplicate! If I'd wanted to spend half my life up to my elbows in paperwork, I'd have shot myself in the head. Better yet, I'd have shot bloody Alistair in the head, and it may yet come to that. So far I've taken to ignoring the paperwork, and using his increasingly distraught memos as toilet paper. And then sending them back to him.'

I couldn't help smiling and nodding. Typical Alistair; penny wise and pound foolish. Always trying to be useful in the worst possible way. Someone once suggested, well out of Grandmother's hearing, that the best way to bring down our enemies would be to send them Alistair as a gift. I suddenly stopped smiling. Someone in the family was a traitor ... And what better way to handicap the family than by undermining and disrupting the work in the Armoury? I shook my head reluctantly. I really liked the idea of nailing Alistair as the traitor, but I knew for a fact he'd had to go through all kinds of security checks before the family would allow Martha to marry him. If there'd been even a hint of anything suspicious about him, they'd have found it. I looked round abruptly as the Armourer jabbed me warningly in the ribs, and there was Alexandra Drood bearing down on me like a heat-seeking missile.

'What the hell are you doing down here, Eddie?'

'Hello, Alex,' I said easily. 'Good to see you again too. You're looking deliciously stern, but then you usually do. Especially in certain dreams I've been having, involving you in leathers in a dungeon ... Don't look at me like that. I'm here to pick up something in the small but deadly line, for my next mission. What are you doing here?'

She stood squarely before me, fists planted on her hips. 'I run this place now. I'm in training to take over from the Armourer when he retires.'

I looked at the Armourer. 'Retiring? You? Really?'

He shrugged uncomfortably. 'Comes to us all, Eddie. I'm not getting any younger, despite my experimenting in that area, and the family depends on the Armoury for new ideas and new approaches, as well as new weapons. Maybe it is time for a change. I just oversee things, these days. Paperwork, remember? Alexandra takes care of the day-to-day business. And does it very well.'

He actually managed a real smile for her, which she ignored, her fierce glare fixed on me. I considered Alexandra thoughtfully. She was a cousin of mine, from the same year as me. We'd attended a lot of classes together, and she always was teacher's pet. A first-class student, and the first to tell you so. Alexandra was tall and blonde, with a balcony you could do Shakespeare from. Every inch the Aryan ideal, and twice as scary. Her white lab coat had been starched to within an inch of its life, and was dazzlingly white. She was pretty enough, in a totally intimidating sort of way, but she always gave the impression that she was about to lunge forward and bite you. And not necessarily in a good way. She glared at me with more than her usual ferocity, and I instinctively looked around for some raw meat to throw her. She prodded me hard in the chest with a forefinger.

'Careful, dear,' I said. 'In some cultures, that means we're engaged.'

'I am not your dear!'

'You have no idea how safe and secure that makes me feel, Alex.'

She took a few deep breaths to steady herself, which did very interesting things to her balcony. I had to look away for a moment. When Alexandra spoke again, her voice was icily calm and controlled.

'I'd heard you were home, Eddie. I don't know how you have the nerve to show your face in The Hall. You turned your back on the family, after everything they did for you.'

'Because of everything they did to me. I still serve, but in my own way.'

'There can only be one way! You betrayed the family trust; the old traditions of duty and responsibility. You ran away from The Hall. Away from me.'

'I'd have died by inches if I stayed here, Alex. You know that.'

'You should have stayed away. You have no place here any more. No one in the family wants you here. No one. Now get the hell out of my Armoury, before I have security throw you out.'

'Ah, Alex; it's good to see position and authority hasn't mellowed you. How's the work here going? Bitten the heads off any more white mice recently?'

'That was just the once! And it was a perfectly reasonable scientific experiment!'

'Of course it was, dear. You still cried like a girly when I had to give you those rabies shots afterwards.'

I couldn't say I was that surprised to discover Alexandra was the new Armourer in training. She always was ambitious. Not to mention almost viciously focused and driven to excel. Alexandra was hard-core family, utterly dedicated to the good fight, with no time for people on the edge, like me.

'I'm here to pick up some new weapons for my mission,' I said, putting on my best let's-all-be-calm-and-reasonable face. 'I have a chitty, from the Matriarch.'

Alexandra gave me a look that plainly said she didn't believe a word of it, and stuck out a hand for the paperwork. I handed it over, and she made a point of scrutinising it very thoroughly, line by line, looking for some sub-clause she could use to turn me down. I favoured her with my most confident and beneficent smile, which made her scowl harder. She'd give herself a headache soon, if she wasn't careful. In the end, she had no choice but to approve my chitty. It came direct from the Matriarch, with her seal and signature. Alexandra reluctantly put her initials in the space provided and thrust the papers ungraciously back at me.

'It seems valid enough,' she growled. 'But I don't want you in my Armoury one moment longer than necessary, Eddie. You're a troublemaker. You breed dissent, and you undermine proper author-ity. You stand for everything I disapprove of in the family. We should have eliminated you years ago. You're a security risk, and you always will be.'

I had to smile. 'And to think I sent you a Valentine's card when we were both fourteen.'

Her mouth twitched briefly. 'So it was you. I did wonder.'

At which interesting point, we were interrupted by the arrival of another field agent. It was Matthew Drood and Alexandra was sud-denly all smiles, Matthew was another cousin from my year, and everything the family had wanted me to be. He'd grown up to be everything I'd always thought he would: very slick, very smart, very smooth. And not half as good in the field as he liked to make out. I'd worked a few cases with him in London, and somehow he ended up with the credit after I'd done all the real work. He stood casually before me, in his expensively cut suit, everything a field agent shouldn't be; tall, dark and handsome, and effortlessly charming when he chose to be. Good luck trying to hide him in a crowd. (All right, Uncle James was those things too, but James had style.)

Matthew worked mainly in business circles, keeping the City . . . if not actually honest, at least a lot more cautious. He also tended towards scorched-earth solutions to most problems, in which there was no such thing as an innocent bystander. Hard-core family, of course, which was why he and Alexandra got on so famously together. Matthew finally broke off being charming to her long enough to notice me.

'Ah, Eddie . . . Super to see you again, old thing. You're looking very . . . urban. Back from exile so soon? What happened, old boy? Run into something you couldn't handle? You should have called me; you know I'm always ready to sail in and save the day.'

'Yeah,' I said. 'That'll happen. Actually, the Matriarch summoned me here, to personally brief me on my next mission.' I don't normally stoop to one-upmanship, but Matthew always did bring out the worst in me. His pleasant smile started to look a bit forced, so I pushed things a little further. 'I'm surprised you didn't hear, Matthew. I always thought you were cleared for top-level discussions.'

'Really?' he murmured. 'A secret mission, you say? Do tell . . . I'm dying to know what kind of top-level mission would demand someone of your . . . particular talents.'

'Sorry,' I said. 'But it would appear you don't have high enough clearance.'

He stiffened perceptibly, and turned abruptly away to bestow his most charming smile on Alexandra. 'Lexxy, darling, I come to you in need. I'm afraid I have to have another truth field generator. I absolutely wore the last one out, following paper trails through the City on that big Brazilian fraud case . . .'

'Of course, Matthew. Nothing but the best for the family's golden boy. Come with me, and I'll fix you up.'

They both turned their backs on me and strolled away arm in

arm, laughing easily together. The Armourer and I looked after them.

'What that girl needs,' said the Armourer, 'is a right good ... '

I quickly dropped my clapped-out portable door on the bench in front of him. 'I need this recharging. And as soon as possible.'

'I know, I know, I've read the chitty. Matriarch wants you fully equipped with the best we've got and out of here, on the double. Business as usual, these days.' He called for one of his interns, who came and took the portable door away, holding it at arm's length like a dead mouse. The Armourer lurched to his feet, and fixed me with a penetrating stare. 'You come with me, Eddie, and I'll show you a few things that might just keep you alive when everyone else wants you dead.'

He led me over to another testing bench, shooing away half a dozen interns, and picked up a large silver handgun. He weighed it thoughtfully in his hand, and then passed it over to me. I raised an eyebrow at how heavy it was, and he smiled proudly.

'That is a Colt Repeater. It never runs out of bullets, and it aims itself. All you have to do is point it in the right general direction, and the gun will take care of the rest. Even you should be able to manage that, Eddie.'

'What about recoil?' I said, just to be picky.

'Since I made it with people like you in mind, none worth the mention. Try not to use it for too long at one time, or the binding spells will overheat and the replacement bullets might not be able to find the gun.'

'Why is it so heavy?'

He grinned nastily. 'So if you do run out of bullets, you can club the buggers to death with it.'

He tossed me a shoulder holster, and I struggled into it as he led me over to another bench. I hate shoulder holsters. How women manage with brassieres, I'll never know. I'd got it more or less into place by the time the Armourer was ready to show me his next creation. It looked a whole lot like an ordinary wristwatch.

'It looks a whole lot like an ordinary wristwatch,' I said.

'Well you wouldn't want one that shouted, *Look at me! I belong to a field agent!* would you? This is a reverse watch. Looks and works as normal, except for this button here. *Don't touch it*, except when you mean to use it. Push it down hard, and the watch will reverse time, rewinding the last thirty seconds of your life. This will give you a second chance to undo your more serious mistakes. But be warned: any attempt to meddle with Time is dangerous. Don't use the reverse function too often; it might attract the attention of certain beings who take Time Disruption very seriously.'

I accepted the watch gingerly. 'How does it work?'

'You wouldn't understand if I told you, so put it on and pay attention to this.'

I put the watch on, slipped my old Rolex into my jacket pocket and looked at the compass the Armourer was holding. It appeared to be an ordinary compass. The Armourer raised an eyebrow and I smiled politely. I hate to be predictable. He gave in.

'This compass will show you the best way out of any situation, no matter how turned around you've got yourself. It's pre-programmed to lock on to the nearest viable exit, and take you there. Just follow where the needle points. The Matriarch specifically asked for something simple in this line, and this is so simple a dog could use it. Keep it away from strong magnetic forces, or it gets confused. If it starts sticking, grease the works with a little butter. Only the best butter, of course.'

'Oh, of course.'

'Now then, what else have I got for you? I had a really nice aboriginal pointing bone, but someone stirred their coffee with it and it was never the same after that. Then there was the personality enhancer ... Looked really good on the drawing board. The idea behind that one was that you'd use it to bring to the fore whatever part of your personality was best suited to deal with the situation you found yourself in.'

'Do I gather something went wrong?'

'The enhancing part went fine. It was shutting the bloody things down afterwards that was the problem. So far we're dealing with six cases of multiple personality disorder and two cases of people refus-ing to talk to themselves. Further testing has been suspended. Ah! Yes; this is what I was looking for.'

He presented me with a small, blue-black lacquered box, not much bigger than a matchbox, with a big red button on top. I shook it to see if it would rattle, and the Armourer winced.

'Please don't do that. What you're holding is actually a prototype we haven't finished testing yet, but the Matriarch said she wanted you supplied with the very best we could offer, so . . . That is a random teleport generator. Press the button, and the box will instantly send you somewhere else. And because it chooses each destination at random, no one will be able to trail you. Use it to escape from prison cells, blind alleys, death traps, that sort of thing. It works perfectly, except for the times when it doesn't.'

'What?'

'Which part of the word *random* do you need explained to you, Eddie? This box could send you *anywhere*, theoretically. It's pre-programmed not to rematerialise you inside anything solid, but apart from that all bets are off. You could end up at the North Pole. Or Death Valley. Or the Mariana Trench . . .'

'I get the idea. Think I'll pass on this one.'

I handed the box back to him, very carefully. He shrugged, and put it down on the bench. 'Suit yourself, boy.'

'Maybe Matthew would like to test it.'

'Now you're just being nasty.'

I grinned, and nodded my thanks to the Armourer. He looked at me for a moment.

'You watch yourself out there, Eddie,' he said gruffly. 'It's a lot scarier in the world now than it was in my day.'

The Armourer had spent twenty years as a field agent. That was what made him such a fine Armourer. He always understood that his clever devices had to work in the real world, not just in the labs. Alexandra, on the other hand, had never been out in the field in her life.

'Don't worry,' I said. 'I'll be careful, Uncle Jack.'

But he was already hard at work on something else. Two of his interns had brought him a large wooden case, held together by faded leather straps with heavy black iron buckles. He undid each one, opened the lid and rooted around in the packing material, before bringing out a large old-fashioned chestplate. He held it up to the light to study it, and I leaned over his shoulder. The dark scarlet metal was wafer thin, and deeply scored with long lines of writing in Sanskrit. The Armourer placed the chestplate gently on the bench before him, and screwed a jeweller's loupe into one eye to study it close up. I was puzzled. If this piece of armour was as old as it seemed to be, it ought to be part of family history and I ought to recognise it. But I'd never seen anything like this before.

'What is it?' I said, trying to sound casually curious.

He grunted, not looking up, and not fooled for a moment. 'This is part of a juggernaut jumpsuit. Not dissimilar to the armour we wear, except on a much higher level. This is the kind of thing you wear when you want to push a mountain on to its side with one hand. And the reason you've never seen it before is because it's a part of the Armageddon Codex.'

I stood there and gaped at him for a moment. 'But ... but ... Those are the forbidden weapons! The weapons too dangerous to be used, except when reality itself is threatened!'

'I do know that, Eddie.'

'Then what the Hell is something like that doing outside the Codex?'

'Matriarch's orders. She wants the forbidden weapons removed and examined, one at a time, and checked to make sure they're operating at peak efficiency. Just in case they should be needed. She hasn't actually ordered any testing yet; I don't think the Council would stand for that. But how bad must things be, if we're opening the Codex for the first time in centuries?'

I leaned in close for a better look at the scarlet metal chestplate. I'd never seen anything from the Armageddon Codex. I don't think half a dozen people in the family have.

'No one else is supposed to know what this is,' the Armourer said quietly. 'It's here under a codename. But I wanted someone to know. Someone I trusted.'

'Not Alexandra?' I said, just as quietly.

'The Matriarch specifically said not to tell her. Not tell the Armourer in training? What does that say to you?'

'She thinks there's a traitor in the family, Uncle Jack. And she's not the only one ...'

'A traitor? In the family? Dear God, what have we come to?' The Armourer shook his head slowly. 'There was a time I would have said such a thing was unthinkable. Now ... I just don't know, any more.'

'Do you know what my mission is?' I said. 'What I'm carrying, and where I have to take it?'

'Of course. One of the few who do. You put it back, Eddie. It should never have been brought here in the first place.'

'You didn't ask for it?'

'Hell, no! That was the Matriarch's orders again.'

'This opening of the Codex,' I said slowly. 'Could it have something to do with the recent attacks on The Hall? And the Heart?'

The Armourer looked away, his shoulders sagging even further than usual. And for the first time, he sounded . . . old. 'I don't know, Eddie. I don't know what's happening, any more.'

CHAPTER SEVEN
Hellhounds on my trail

There are moments in every field agent's life when he becomes convinced that his cover has been blown and the eyes of the world are suddenly upon him. Usually because someone is shooting at him. I felt that way from the moment I left The Hall and its many protections behind me. Having the Soul of Albion in its lead-lined container tucked away in my dashboard compartment made me feel as though someone had painted a target on my car; or maybe even added a flashing neon sign saying, *Rob This Idiot Now*. I drove the Hirondel back through the winding country lanes, and on to proper roads again. Cows in fields watched me pass, following me with their heads as though even they knew what I was carrying. I'd never couriered anything this important in my life. It felt as though there was someone else in the car with me. Hamlets gave way to villages, which gave way to towns, and soon enough I was back on the M4 motorway.

The afternoon was pleasantly warm as I motored along, and the breeze was refreshingly cool as it ruffled my hair. There's a lot to be said for a convertible. Traffic was light for a summer afternoon, and I cruised along, listening to a Mary Hopkin compilation on the CD player. I hadn't been to Stonehenge in years, since I went as part of an organised school trip. Apparently these days the ancient stone circle was sealed off behind perimeter fences and barbed wire, to keep the public at a respectful distance from such an important national monument. (Not so unreasonable; in Victorian times they'd sell you a hammer and chisel on the way in, so you could gouge out your own personal souvenir to take home with you.) Still, I doubted they had anything that could keep me out. And no one sees me unless I want them to; remember?

It suddenly occurred to me that I hadn't passed a car coming the other way in quite a while. There wasn't any traffic in front of me, and a quick glance in the rear-view mirror confirmed that there was nothing behind me for as far as I could see. It seemed I had this whole stretch of the motorway all to myself. And the chances of that happening at this time of the day, on such a busy route, were ... fantastically low. I shut off the CD player, and tapped my fingers thoughtfully on the steering wheel. I was being set up for an ambush.

Question was; were they just after a Drood agent, or did someone know what I was carrying?

I subvocalised the Words, and the living metal swept over me in a moment, sealing me off from danger behind my golden armour. I checked the Colt Repeater was comfortably loose in its shoulder holster under the armour, and looked around me. Still nothing ahead and nothing behind, and only empty fields on either side of the road. An alarm blared suddenly inside the car, making me jump, and a flashing red arrow appeared on my dashboard, pointing straight up. I looked up, and there were six black helicopters flying in close formation right above me, in complete silence. If it hadn't been for my car's detection system, I'd never have known they were there until it was too late. I hadn't actually known my car could do that. Score one for the Armourer and thank you, Uncle Jack.

I braked hard, and the black helicopters shot ahead, caught off guard. They spun round in a wide circle, still utterly silent, and headed straight for me. They looked like nasty, ungainly insects. Two of the leading helicopters opened up with machine guns, raking the road on either side of the Hirondel, throwing up debris, trying to frighten me into stopping. I put my foot down again, and the Hirondel responded eagerly, surging forward. The helicopters were behind me now as I raced along, but already they were circling round to follow me, still holding perfect attack formation. One launched a missile, and it swept past me to explode on the road ahead. I snapped the wheel around to avoid the crater, and the car punched through the smoke and flames and out the other side. The armour protected me from the heat and from smoke inhalation, but that was all it could do for the moment. The armour's strengths were mostly defensive in nature. Unless and until I got my hands on someone.

I pressed the pedal to the metal so hard my foot ached, and

the Hirondel hammered down the motorway, the engine roaring joyously. More missiles exploded on either side of me, the blasts rocking the car, but I refused to be bluffed. They couldn't afford to blow up the car, in case they damaged the Soul. The black helicopters kept up with me easily, taking up formation all around me. My thoughts were racing, trying to find a way out of this trap, but mostly I couldn't help thinking, *Why are the bloody Men In Black after me?* It was more than three years since I'd burgled Area 52 on the family's behalf. And I only took a few things . . . Could it be that Mr President was still mad over the Harley Street affair, and had called in a favour from his American counterpart? How very small-minded of him. You try to do someone a favour . . .

Bullets raked along one side of the Hirondel, punching through the thick metal, slamming me back and forth in the driving seat, and driving the car right across into the other lane. I had to fight the wheel for control, all the time screaming obscenities at the helicopter pilots. Didn't they realise the Hirondel was a classic car, a genuine antique and a work of art in its own right? You don't put bullet holes in a work of art! Bloody philistines. Right. Enough was enough. I was angry now. Who the hell did they think they were messing with? I hit one of the Armourer's concealed switches, and a panel flipped open, revealing a big red button. I pressed my thumb down firmly, and an electromagnetic pulse radiated out from the car, swatting all six black helicopters from the sky like the hand of God.

They plummeted to the ground as their electrical systems crashed and fried, and it was a credit to their pilots that only two of them exploded on impact. Thick black smoke curled up into the pale blue sky as I hammered on down the motorway, punching the air with one golden fist. I don't normally celebrate my kills, but they had got me seriously angry. Killing me was one thing, stealing the Soul of Albion another; but vandalising a classic like the Hirondel . . . Hell was too good for them.

(Do I really need to explain that the car was shielded from its own EM pulse? The Armourer's not an idiot, you know.)

Half a dozen cars came shooting on to the motorway from a slip road, and I actually relaxed a little, assuming their presence meant the attack was over and normal traffic was resuming. I should have known better. I noticed almost immediately that each of the cars was a sharp scarlet in colour, glistening like lipstick, and none of them was any make or model I was familiar with. There was something odd, something off, about the six scarlet cars as they crept up behind me. I was still driving the Hirondel flat out, but they had no trouble catching up. They were long limousines with old-fashioned high tail fins, and they moved smoothly up and alongside me, pacing me effortlessly like hunting cats. For the first time I got a good look at them, close up, and my skin crawled. The hackles stood up on the back of my neck. I could see the driver of the car on my right, and the car was being driven by a dead man. He'd been dead for some time, his grey face shrunken and desiccated, almost a mummy. His shrivelled hands had been nailed to the steering wheel, which moved by itself.

These weren't cars. None of them was a car. These were CARnivores.

I'd read about them, heard about them from other agents, but I'd never seen one close up before, and never wanted to. CARnivores are sentient, meat-eating cars with attitude. Some say they came originally from some other dimension, where cars evolved to replace humans, and some say they evolved right here, ancient predators who'd learned to look like cars so they could prey on humans unnoticed. They stalk the motorways, following tired souls who drive alone in the early hours of the morning. The CARnivores close in, cut them off from the pack, and then choose a secluded spot and force their prey off the road. And then they feed . . .

But what the Hell were this many CARnivores doing travelling together in bright sunlight in the middle of the day? I supposed even demon cars could be tempted by a prize like the Soul of Albion. My mission wasn't a secret any longer; there was a traitor in the family, and he had sold us out.

The CARnivores pressed in on either side, bumping me hard, first from the left and then from the right. The Hirondel absorbed the impact and kept going. Sturdy old car. I could see dead men swaying in their driving seats, their eyeless heads lolling back and forth. Another CARnivore rammed the Hirondel from behind, jolting me forward in my seat. Two more bumps, left and right, harder now. CARnivores like to play with their food. The one on my left slowly opened its bonnet, the blood-red steel rising tauntingly to show me a pink glistening maw within, and rows of churning steel teeth. It was hungry, and it was laughing at me.

Underneath the protection of my golden armour, I was sweating. I could feel it running down my face. I was pretty sure the living metal would be a match for the CARnivores, but it couldn't do anything to protect the Hirondel. And I needed the car if I was to get the Soul safely to Stonehenge, still a good hour's hard driving away. I could see the effects of the CARnivores' proximity already manifesting in the Hirondel. Every part of the car looked older, dimmed, even shabby. CARnivores could leech the vitality out of any car, aging it at an accelerated rate until it malfunctioned or fell apart from metal fatigue. And then the CARnivores would drive it off the road and feed on the driver and any passengers. CARnivores exist by draining other cars dry, but even more than that, they love their human prey.

They're meat junkies.

The Hirondel had a lot of extra options built in, but at the end of the day it was still just a car and as vulnerable as any other. And the CARnivores were getting awfully close. They bumped and barged me from both sides almost constantly now, jostling me like bullies in a playground, just for the fun of it. Time to show them who was the eight-hundred-pound gorilla around here. I let my left hand drift over the Armourer's special control panel. I doubted the EMP would work on the CARnivores, even if it had recharged itself yet; they were too different, too alien, too alive. So I used the rear-mounted flame-throwers instead. Twin streams of raging fire blasted out of the back of the Hirondel, and a thick rush of flames enveloped the CARnivore behind me. The demon car screamed shrilly, thrashing wildly from side to side as it fell back. The fires had taken hold, and the CARnivore blazed brightly, flames and smoke leaping up into the sky.

I hit my brakes hard, the Hirondel's tyres screeching as my speed dropped by half. The two CARnivores on either side of me shot forwards, caught unawares, And I opened up on them with the electric cannon mounted above the front bumper. Explosive flechettes raked both cars, chewing up the demon metal, pumped out at two thousand rounds a second. One CARnivore exploded, flipping end over end down the motorway before finally skidding to a halt.

The other surged back and forth across the lanes, leaking long trails of blood and oil. I kept tracking it with both cannon until it exploded, shooting off over the hard shoulder and embedding itself in the grass verge beyond.

Three down, three to go.

But the other CARnivores had had enough. They slowed down and took the next exit, not used to prey who fought back. I swept on, checking my inventory. The flamethrowers had exhausted most of their fuel, the cannon were almost out of ammunition, but the EMP was fully recharged and ready to go again. I rummaged in my glove compartment for my maps. Now that my cover was blown I needed to get off the motorway as quickly as possible. Use the side roads and the round-about routes that an enemy might not know. And I needed to stop and find a land-line phone so I could contact my family, let them know what was happening. I couldn't trust my mobile. My enemies might tap into the GPS. In an almighty cock-up situation like this, I wasn't too proud to beg for reinforcements. And then the car's alarms went off again, and I looked up to see elf lords flying towards me on their dragon mounts.

I should have expected elves. They'd sell the souls they didn't have to get their hands on the Soul of Albion, so they could use it to destroy the humans who'd driven them from their ancient ancestral holdings. Not through war or attrition, but by outbreeding them. The elves hate us, and they always will, because we won by cheating. I could hear their laughter on the wind, cold and cruel and capricious.

There were twenty dragons, and none of them was the graceful, romantic beasts of myth and legend. These were great worms, thirty to forty feet long, with wet glistening segmented bodies and vast membranous batwings. They forced themselves through the sky by brute effort, ugly and inglorious, their flat faces made up of a ring of dark unblinking eyes surrounding a sucking mouth like a lamprey. Sat astride their thick necks, on ancient saddles upholstered in tanned human skin, sat the elf lords and ladies. Beautiful and magnificent, vicious and vile, human in shape but not in thought, they rode to the slaughter with laughter on their colourless lips, singing ancient hunting songs on the glories of suffering and the kill.

They came straight at me, moving so fast they were over me and then behind me before I even had time to react. They swooped

81

around, the hunting pack in full cry, and the lords and ladies threw lightning bolts at me with their bare hands. The bolts exploded in the road ahead of me, blasting out craters and cracking the surface. I put my foot down and kept going, swerving the car back and forth to avoid the larger holes. The dragons pounded through the air above and beside me, taking their time, enjoying the hunt. Seeing how close they could get to the car without actually touching it. The continuous explosions of the lightning bolts were deafening, and the flaring lights were bright enough to dazzle me momentarily, even through the armour's protection. I could hear the Hirondel's engine straining. I tried to think what I had that could reach the elves and their dragons, safe up in the sky. A lightning bolt hit the bonnet of the Hirondel, blasting the paint away in a moment, and the car slammed this way and that under the impact, swerving blindly across the lane divider and back again. Only the armoured strength in my hands kept the steering wheel under control, even as the wheel itself crumpled slowly out of shape.

A dragon and its rider came flying straight at me, only a few feet above the road. I wondered at first if he was planning to ram me, but then I saw him fitting an arrow to his bow, and I smiled despite myself. An arrow against my armour. Yeah, right. I reached for the switch to activate the electric cannon, and blow him out of my way. The elf lord loosed his arrow. And while I was still reaching for the switch, the arrow punched through my windshield, through my glorious golden armour and buried itself in my left shoulder. I slammed back in my seat, crying out in shock and pain, and actually let go of the wheel for a moment to grab at the arrow shaft with both hands. It wouldn't budge. The car skidded across the lanes. I tugged at the arrow again, crying out in agony, but I couldn't move it. The extra pain cleared my head like a shock of cold water in the face, and I grabbed the steering wheel and brought the Hirondel under control again.

I was panting harshly, and sweat poured down my face under my golden mask. I could feel blood coursing down my arm and chest, under my armour. Every movement, every breath, brought me a new pulse of pain. I gritted my teeth until my jaws ached. I was still in shock, and not just from the pain. My armour was invulnerable. Impregnable. Everyone knew that. The strength of the living armour was the strength of the family. It made our work possible, because none of our enemies could touch us while we wore the living metal. Only the silver shaft sticking out of my shoulder was a pretty convincing argument to the contrary. Trust the elves to find a way to hurt us. The pain beat in my head, interfering with my thoughts, and it took all my self-control to push it aside and concentrate. There had to be a way out of this. I couldn't surrender the Soul of Albion. And anyway, I was damned if I'd be beaten by a bunch of snotty, arrogant elves.

I kept driving, foot hard down, blinking sweat out of my eyes. I'd lost all feeling in my left arm, and it hung limply at my side. I studied the arrow shaft protruding from my armoured shoulder. It was a strange silvery metal, glowing faintly. God alone knew from what far dimension the elves had plundered it, desperate to find the one thing that would pierce Drood armour. I looked up and around. The dragons were still keeping up with me, flailing their vast wings into a blur, even though the Hirondel was pushing its top speed. I couldn't outrun them, couldn't shake them off. So I stamped both feet down on the brake and clutch and brought the car to a screeching halt, leaving long smoking trails of burned rubber behind me. The dragons and their riders swept on, caught off guard, but quickly circled round to come back at me again. Some of them were already stringing arrows to their bows.

I forced the bullet-holed door open and stumbled out of the car, crying out despite myself as every new jolt of movement brought me fresh pain. I strode out into the middle of the road, facing the oncoming dragons, my left arm useless at my side. I could see the elves' faces now, their cold, cruel smiles. They were laughing at me. I reached through my golden armour with my golden hand and drew the Colt Repeater from its holster. There was blood on it from my shoulder wound, and I shook a few drops off. I aimed the Colt at the nearest dragon rider, and the gun took care of the rest.

The cold lead bullet hit the elf lord right between the eyes and blew the back of his head off. For good measure I shot the dragon in its ugly head too, and it crashed to the motorway in an ungainly sprawl of flapping wings. I shot all the elves and all the dragons, all the vicious lords and vile ladies and their ugly mounts, and they didn't have the time to fire off a single arrow at me. I just fired the

Colt Repeater again and again and again, and the bullets kept coming and the gun never missed. A triumph of the Armourer's art. The dead dragons piled up before me, twitching and shuddering as the last of their unnatural life leaked out of them, and not a single elf escaped my cold anger. God bless you, Uncle Jack.

I sat down carefully on the Hirondel's bonnet, and got my breath back. The arrow in my shoulder hurt like hell. I had to contact the family. Get them to send a clean-up crew, to remove the dragons and elves before Joe Public turned up to see them. And then the Matriarch would have to send a stiff and very formal complaint to the Fae Court, telling them to keep their arrogant noses out of Drood business, or else. It slowly occurred to me that I'd been driving for some time while fighting for my life, and I still hadn't seen any traffic. Someone had to have arranged for this whole section of the motorway to be sealed off. To close the exits and shut down the CCTV coverage would take serious clout. How high up was this traitor in the family, that they could arrange something like this? Yes, I had to get to a safe phone. Tell the family. About the traitor ...

My head was actually nodding, my thoughts fading in and out, when the car's alarms went off again. My head jerked and I slid off the bonnet and looked around. A thick fog covered the motorway, a dirty grey mist that churned and boiled, with nothing natural about it. I climbed back into the driving seat, gritting my teeth against the pain, and then pounded my left arm with my right fist until some sensation returned, so I could slam the car into first gear. I took off again, and out of the mists behind me came the phantom fleet.

My first thought was, *This isn't fair. Not after everything I've already been though* ... But I was too tired even to maintain a good sulk, so I concentrated on building up some speed. My injured arm shrieked at me as I raced through the gears, but that was better than the scary numbness. The pain cleared my head and kept me angry. I was going to have to be sharp, on top form, to take out the phantom fleet.

They swept down the deserted motorway after me, ghosts of crashed vehicles driven and possessed by spirits from the vasty deeps. Half-transparent cars and trucks and articulateds, and everything else that ever came to a nasty end on a motorway. Some looked real as real could be, while others were just misty shapes, all of them still bearing the damage and burn marks of their previous ends. Too many to count, they came howling after me in a vicious pack, their ghostly engines supernaturally loud. Black brimstone smoke issued from their exhausts, and hellfire burned around their squealing tyres. The phantom fleet, the wild hunt of modern times; hungry for souls.

The lead car drew up alongside me, matching my speed effortlessly. It was a Hillman Minx from the sixties, the front smashed in, the long bonnet concertinaed. Through the cracked side windows, I could see the car was packed to bursting with grinning ghouls and demons and mutant creatures. They writhed together like maggots infesting a wound, churning and shifting and pressing their awful faces against the windows to laugh at me. None of the Hirondel's weapons would touch these things, because they weren't really there. Just memories of vehicles that once were, and the things from beyond that had repossessed them.

Another car came forward, filling my rear-view mirror. Some big boxy foreign job, driven by a hunched-over demon with huge bulging eyes and a mouth full of needle teeth. It hit the horn again and again, and the dead car howled like something in pain. The demon pounded on the steering wheel with its thorny hands, caught up in the excitement of the chase. And then the ghost car surged forward, passing through the back of the Hirondel, penetrating my space with its dead shape. A wave of supernatural cold preceded its progress, freezing the blood in my veins. The dead car drew level, its ghostly outline superimposed on mine, and then the demon driver dropped a thorny hand on my shoulder, ghosted right through my armour, and grabbed hold of my soul. I screamed, just at the touch of it. The demon *pulled*, trying to haul my soul out of my body to be prey for the pack, for the phantom fleet. Another stolen soul, to drive the engines of the cars.

But my soul was linked to my armour, from the moment I was born. You couldn't have one without the other. And together they were stronger than any damned dead thing. The gripping ghostly fingers slipped slowly away, unable to maintain their grip. I goosed the accelerator, and the Hirondel jumped forward. The ghost car fell back, the demon howling in outrage at being cheated out of its prey. Pain surged up in my left arm again, and I embraced it. It meant I was alive. I forced my left hand forward and hit the emergency default button on the CD player. The system immediately began broadcasting a recording of the ritual of exorcism, read by the last Pope in the original Latin. The sonorous words boomed out of the car's speakers, and the ghost car was driven right out of the Hirondel. Around and behind me, the phantom fleet shrieked horribly, and fell back. Some were already breaking up under the impact of the holy words, drifting away in long ghostly streamers. The thick curling mists reappeared in my rear-view mirror, and the phantom fleet vanished back into them.

I drove on, half dead behind the wheel myself, and for a while I had the motorway to myself.

And then, from up ahead came the Flying Saucerers. And I was so hurt and tired and generally pissed off that I didn't even slow down. Let them come. Let them all come, every damned thing from above and below and in between. I was on a roll, and mad enough to take on the whole bloody world. The Flying Saucerers are high-level magic-users who swan around in flying saucer-shaped artefacts made up of ionised plasma energies; for reasons best known to themselves. Personally, I think they just like to show off. They're the vultures of the paranormal world, darting down to pick up the spoils of other people's battles, and carry off whatever isn't actually nailed down. Which is actually pretty pathetic behaviour, if you ask me, for a group who claim they're out to rule the world.

I peered wearily through my cracked windscreen, and scowled at the saucers shooting through the sky towards me. There had to be a whole fleet of the bloody things. Twenty, maybe thirty, their wide saucer shapes as insubstantial as soap bubbles, condensing into weird rainbow colours around the pilots sitting cross-legged in the centre of the craft. A whole fleet, slamming towards me in broad daylight. Made bold at the prospect of a prize like the Soul of Albion. And knowing them, they'd waited for everyone else to take a crack at me, and weaken me, before they tried for the Soul themselves. I could feel my smile widening into a death's-head grin under my golden mask. I might be down, but I wasn't out. And I had weapons and tactics and dirty tricks I hadn't even tried yet.

The Flying Saucerers are dangerous because, like the family, they take science and magic equally seriously. They embrace both schools of knowledge, two very different doctrines, and combine them in unnatural and unexpected ways to produce a whole that is far greater than the sum of its parts. Like the plasma saucers: science devised, magic driven. They came howling in, one after the other, targeting computers zeroing in on my car. Energy bolts cracked and exploded on the road ahead of me, and I threw the Hirondel this way and that, ducking and dodging as best I could. Fierce energies crackled around me, chewing up the road in long, ragged runs. One whole grass verge was on fire, and I had to jump the Hirondel over a wide crevice that opened up in front of me.

Anywhen else, I would probably have been scared shitless in the face of so much superior firepower, but after everything I'd already been through the saucers were more annoying than anything.

The road blew up, right in front of me. I punched the Hirondel through the smoke and flames, but the left front wheel dipped into a crack, and snatched the steering wheel out of my hands. The car spun round and round, spiralling down the motorway at sickening speed, before finally skidding to a halt. I sat limply in my seat while my spinning head settled, feeling really grateful I'd had seat-belts installed, even though it was a classic car. My armour had protected me from the sudden deceleration, and probably a really nasty case of whiplash, but I was still pretty dazed. And my wounded arm felt worse than ever. God alone knew what damage the faerie arrow was doing to my system.

I checked the car over. Smoke was rising from under the bonnet, which is never a good sign, but everything seemed still to be working. I considered using the EMP generator, but I was pretty sure the Flying Saucerers would have shielded their craft against that. I would have. Which just left . . . taking out the trash the old-fashioned way.

I undid my seat belt, forced open the door, and half crawled, half fell out of the car. I levered myself upright by leaning most of my weight on the car door, and the heavy metal crumpled under the strain of my golden fingers. I winced. That was going to be Hell to beat out later. I stood up, straight and tall, using all the armour's support, and strode off down the motorway towards the approaching saucers. The first dropped towards me, and opened up a strafing run with its energy weapons. And I drew my Colt Repeater and shot the Flying Saucerer in the head. He'd protected his craft against EMPs, energy weapons and magic attacks, but he'd never expected to face a simple cold lead bullet. Guided by the gun's unnatural nature, the bullet punched through all the pilot's shields and blew his head apart before he even knew what was happening. The saucer dropped like a stone, skidded across the motorway, leaving deep scars in the road behind it, and finally exploded in a rainbow of dissipating energies. I turned slowly, and then shot every other Flying Saucerer out of the sky, one at a time. Even the ones that turned and ran.

I aimed carefully, and the Colt shot the pilot in the gut. His Saucer came down in swoops and rolls and finally crashed a few yards away from me. The saucer shape flickered on and off, colours whorling round and round its surface like an oily film, and then the shape collapsed, no longer held together by the pilot's will. And all that was left was a surprisingly ordinary looking man, lying crumpled on the verge, soaked in blood and curled around his wound.

I walked over to him, grabbed him by the shoulder and slammed him over on to his back. He cried out miserably at the pain, and then cried out again in shock and horror as he saw the golden armoured form standing over him. I'd overridden the stealth function. I wanted him to see me. The whole of the front of his tunic was soaked in his blood. I placed one armoured foot on his stomach, just lightly. Not pressing, not yet. He lay very still, looking up at me with wide, frightened eyes. Like a deer brought down at the end of the chase.

'Talk,' I said. 'And I'll let you call for help.'

'I can't . . .'

'Talk. You don't have to die here. You don't have to die slowly and horribly . . .'

'What do you want to know?'

I'm pretty sure I was bluffing. Pretty sure. But the Drood reputation goes a long way. I pressed my foot down a little, and he yelled, blood spurting from his mouth.

'What the Hell do you think I want to know?' I said.

'All right, all right! Jesus, take it easy, man. Fight's over, okay? Look, we just wanted the Soul of Albion, you know? We got directions, all the details, everything we needed on where to find you, and a guarantee that no one would come to help you. The information came from . . . inside the Drood family. Don't hurt me! I'm telling the truth, I swear I am! We got the word from someone high up in the family. I don't know why, exactly; I'm not high enough in the organisation to be trusted with information like that. I'm just a pilot!'

I considered this, while the pilot lay very still under my armoured foot. He was breathing heavily, sweat soaking his colourless face. Too terrified to lie. Someone in my family wanted me dead, wanted it badly enough to sacrifice the Soul of Albion itself . . . Why? I'm not that important. I looked down at the pilot, ready to question him some more, but he was dead. I looked at him for a long moment, but I couldn't bring myself to feel bad about it. He would have seen me dead without a second thought.

I went back to the Hirondel. It was scorched and blackened from fire and smoke, riddled with bullet holes, and most of the paint was gone from the bonnet . . . but she still seemed basically intact. Much like me, really. I leaned in through the open door, and retrieved the Soul's lead-lined container. So much death and destruction, over such a small thing. I opened the box to check it was okay; and the Soul wasn't there. Lying in the red plush velvet was a simple homing device, broadcasting my location to one and all. I took it out, and crushed it in my golden fist.

I'd never had the Soul of Albion. Somewhere along the line, someone had worked a switch. And the only way that could have happened . . . was with the Matriarch's sanction. She would have known immediately if anything had happened to the Soul. And if she knew about the homing device, she knew about everything. It all made sense now. Only the Matriarch could have arranged for this much motorway to be sealed off, and be sure of clearing up the mess afterwards. The Matriarch had sent me off on a wild goose chase, sent me out here to die. My own grandmother had thrown me to the wolves. But why? Why would she do that?

I armoured down, and gasped as the smoky air hit my bare face. I looked at my left arm, hanging limp at my side. Blood soaked the whole length of my sleeve, and dripped from my numb fingertips. I studied the arrow shaft protruding from the meat of my shoulder. The metal was a brilliant silver, shimmering and shining even in the bright sunlight. There were no feathers; an arrow like this wouldn't need them to fly true. I had to tell the family: the Fae had found a weapon that could pierce our armour. Only I couldn't tell them. The moment I called home, the Matriarch would know I was still alive and send more people to kill me. I looked at the arrow shaft again. Strange matter, from some other dimension. Probably poisonous. Had to come out. Oh shit, this was going to hurt.

I pulled a handkerchief out of my pocket, wadded it up, and bit down hard. Then I gripped the shaft firmly, and pushed it further in, so that the barbed head punched out of my back. The handkerchief muffled my scream, but I still nearly fainted at the pain. I reached up and around, and awkwardly pulled the shaft all the way through and out. Blood was pouring down my chest and back by the time I'd finished. My face ran with sweat, and my hands were shaking. It had been a long time since I was hurt this badly. I spat out the hand-kerchief, and took the arrow shaft in both hands. It seemed to squirm in my grasp. I broke it in two, and it screamed inside my head. I dropped the pieces on the ground and they tried to turn into some-thing else before falling apart into sticky smears of something that couldn't survive in this world.

I sat down in the driver's seat, before my legs collapsed under me. After a while I pulled out the first-aid box, opened it and took out a basic healer. Just a blob of pre-programmed simple matter, full of all kinds of things that were good for me. I said the activating Word, and slapped it against the wound in my shoulder. The blob sealed it off immediately, and pumped all kinds of wonderful drugs into me, cutting off the pain like a switch. I groaned aloud at the sudden relief. The blob penetrated the wound with a narrow tendril, repairing as it went, and emerged to seal off the wound in my back. I could feel all this, but only in a vague and distanced way. I was sort of interested. I'd never had to use one before. But I had other things on my mind.

I needed to know why my own grandmother had betrayed me. Why she'd sent me to my death with a lie on her lips. I couldn't go back to The Hall for answers. Even if I did get past the defences, she'd call me a liar, declare me rogue and apostate, and order the family to kill me. And everyone would believe her and no one would believe me, because she was the Matriarch and I was . . . Eddie Drood. Who could I still talk to, who could I still trust, after everything that had happened? Maybe just one man. I took out my mobile phone and called Uncle James on his very private number. He cut me off the moment he recognised my voice.

'Stay where you are. I'll be right with you.'

And just like that, he was standing before me, his mobile phone still in his hand. The air rippled around him, displaced by the teleport spell. We put away our phones, and looked at each other. Concern filled his face as he took in my condition, and the blood still soaking my left arm. He started towards me, but I stopped him with a raised hand. He nodded slowly.

'I know, Eddie. It's always hard to learn you can't trust anyone. You look like shit, by the way.'

'You should see the other guys, Uncle James.'

He looked beyond me, at the carnage and wreckage I'd left stretched down the length of the motorway, and he actually smiled a little.

'You did all that? I'm impressed, Eddie. Really.'

'How did you get here so quickly, Uncle James?' I said slowly. 'Teleport spells need exact coordinates. How did you know exactly where to find me on this long stretch of motorway, when even I'm not entirely sure exactly where I am? What's going on, Uncle James?'

'The homing device told us where you were, before you destroyed it.' Uncle James's voice was calm, conversational. 'The Matriarch sent me here, Eddie. She gave me specific orders ... said that if somehow you had survived the ambushes, I was to kill you myself. No warnings, not a word; just shoot you down in cold blood. Why would she tell me to do that, Eddie? What have you done?'

'I don't know! I haven't done anything! None of this makes any sense, Uncle James ...'

'You've been officially declared rogue,' he said. 'A clear and present danger to the whole family. Every Drood is authorised to kill you on sight. For the good of the family.'

We stood looking at each other. Neither of us wore our armour. Neither of us had a weapon. His face was cold, even calm, but in his eyes I could see a torment I'd never seen before. For perhaps the first time in his life, James Drood didn't know what to do for the best. He was torn between what he'd been ordered to do, and what was in his heart. Remember, this was the Grey Fox, the most loyal and dependable agent the family had ever had. Uncle James. Who'd been like a father to me. Who in the end wouldn't, couldn't, kill me.

We both sensed that at the same moment, and we both relaxed a little.

'So,' I said. 'What do we do now?'

'I go back to the Matriarch. Tell her you were already gone when I got here,' Uncle James said flatly. 'You ... you run. Run, and keep running. Hide yourself so deep that even I won't be able to find you. Because if we meet again, I will kill you, Eddie. I'll have to. For the good of the family.'

CHAPTER EIGHT
Seduction of the not entirely innocent

Uncle James disappeared without even saying goodbye, air rushing in to fill the space where he'd been. I should have told him about the faerie arrow that pierced my armour, but he hadn't given me a chance and anyway I was still in shock. My family wanted me dead. After everything I'd done for them, after ten long years of fighting the good fight on their behalf, this was my reward; to be declared rogue. Traitor. Outcast. I might have had my disagreements with them, but they were still my family. I would never have betrayed them. It's one thing to run away from home; quite another to be told you can't go back because if you do they'll kill you on sight. I looked at the lead-lined container that should have held the Soul of Albion, staring into its empty red plush interior as though it might have some answers for me. It didn't, so I threw it away.

I slid behind the wheel of the Hirondel again. I might be hurting in all kinds of ways, but I was still a professional; so I had the car's defence systems run a complete diagnostic, to make sure there weren't any more bugs or tracking devices anywhere on board. Or indeed, any other nasty and possibly fatal surprises. The car muttered to itself for a bit, and then gave itself a clean bill of health. I relaxed a little, and started up the engine. Even after all she'd been through, the Hirondel roared smoothly and immediately to life, ready to take me anywhere I wanted. It was good to know there were still a few things left in my life that wouldn't let me down.

I headed the Hirondel towards London. My home territory. If they were going to come for me, I wanted it to be on home ground. I passed dead bodies and crashed vehicles, blazing fires and black smoke and all the other damage I'd done. There seemed to be quite a lot of it. Poor damned fools, dying for nothing over a prize that was never there. And if there were similarities in that to how my life had turned out, I tried not to think about it. The Hirondel laboured along, reluctant to hit high speeds any more, but I was in no hurry anyway. The family's remote viewers couldn't see or find me as long as I wore the torc. Slowly my shock crystallised into anger, and then into something colder and more determined. I wanted answers. My whole world had been turned upside down, and I needed to know why. According to James I had been officially declared a rogue, so none of the other family out in the world would talk to me. Hell, most of them would try to kill me the moment they set eyes on me. Droods have no mercy for traitors.

Which meant there was only one place left I could go for answers, for the truth; the people I'd been fighting all my life. The Bad Guys.

I left the M4 by the first exit I came to. I needed to lose myself in country roads and back lanes before the family's search hounds came sniffing up the motorway after me. I hadn't gone half a mile down the exit before I was forced to slow down and stop by a police barricade. It wasn't a particularly impressive barricade: a few rows of plastic cones backed up by the presence of two uniformed officers and a squad car. A long line of stationary vehicles faced me in the other lane, and a small crowd of drivers had gathered on the other side of the cones, taking it in turns to loudly berate the police officers. They looked round as I approached in the Hirondel, and they seemed pretty surprised to see me. I stopped the car a respectful distance away, and the police officers came over to talk to me. I think they were quite pleased for an excuse to get away from the drivers. They both did distinct double-takes as they took in the condition of my car, and they stopped walking and ordered me to turn off my engine and get out of my car. I smiled, and did as I was told. They had answers, whether they knew it or not.

I sat on the bonnet of the Hirondel, and waited for them to come to me. They approached cautiously, pointing out the bullet holes and the shattered windscreen to each other. They hadn't expected to see anything like that on traffic duty. One of them started writing down my number in his little notebook, for all the good that would do him, while his colleague came forward to interrogate me. I gave him a nice friendly smile.

'Why is this section of the motorway sealed off?' I said innocently, getting my question in before he could ask me for ID that I had absolutely no intention of providing.

'Seems there's been a chemical spill, sir. Very serious, so they tell me. Are you sure you haven't seen anything, sir? This whole section of the M4 has been officially declared a hazardous area.'

'Well yes,' I said, allowing myself another smile. 'I did find it rather hazardous, in places . . .'

The police officer didn't like the smile at all. 'I think you'd better stay here with us for a while, sir. I'm sure my superiors will want to ask you some more detailed questions, down at the station. And the Hazmat people will want to make sure you haven't been exposed to anything dangerous.' He stopped. I was smiling again. He looked at me coldly. 'This is a very serious matter, sir. Please move away from your vehicle. I need to see some identification.'

'No, you don't,' I said. I drew my Colt Repeater from its shoulder holster. The police officer put his hands in the air immediately, palms out to show they were empty. His colleague started forward, and I raised the gun a little.

'Stay where you are, Les, and don't be a fool!' said the other officer. 'Remember your training!'

'It could be a replica,' said Les, staying back but still scowling at me.

I aimed casually at the squad car and the Colt shot out all four of the tyres. The small crowd of drivers by the cones cried out in shock and alarm. People aren't used to guns in England, which on the whole I approve of. I gestured for both police officers to remove the cones from the road, and they did so slowly and reluctantly. I kept a careful eye on them, making sure they stuck together so I could cover both of them with the Colt. I had no intention of shooting anyone, but they didn't need to know that. The crowd of drivers was starting to get restive. I needed to get under way before one of them decided he was a hero type, and did something stupid. Innocent bystanders can be a real pain in the arse sometimes. I backed away, and slid behind the wheel of the Hirondel. I was breaking the first rule of the field agent: being noticed. So, when in doubt, confuse the issue.

'Tell your decadent government that the Tasmanian Separatist Alliance is on the move!' I announced grandly. 'The oppressor will be forced to bow down before our superior dogma! All dolphins shall be freed, and no more penguins will be forced to smoke cigarettes!'

Which should give them something to think about. By the time they'd picked the bones out of that, and wasted even more time trying to track down a terrorist group (and a number plate) that didn't actually exist, I should have had plenty of time to go to ground. I was going to have to lose the Hirondel. It had become too visible, too noticeable. I gunned the engine, annoyed, and roared past the police officers, the crowd of drivers and the long queue of waiting vehicles. I had to get to London, and fast. Some people leaned out of their car windows to try and photograph me with their mobile phones. I smiled obliging at them, secure in the knowledge that my torc hid me from all forms of surveillance, scientific and magical. How else could field agents like me operate, in a world where someone is always watching you?

I left the queue behind and quickly disappeared into side roads and bypasses. I had a secret hideout on the outskirts of London, one of several I maintained for emergencies. The one I was thinking of was nothing special, just a rented garage in a perfectly respectable residential area. But it had everything I needed to go underground. To become invisible. I always kept my hideouts up to date, and stocked with useful items, for those rare but inevitable occasions when my cover was blown and I had to disappear in a hurry. I could go into any of my bolt-holes as one man and come out as someone entirely different, complete with totally new look and ID. The family didn't know about these places. They knew nothing about the way I operated. They'd never wanted to know.

I reached the outskirts of London without incident, though I sat tense and hunched behind the wheel most of the way, in anticipation of a challenge or attack that never actually materialised. The battered and bullet-holed Hirondel drew many stares, but no one said or did anything. This was England, after all. I headed into the respected residential area, and my very respectable neighbours watched open-mouthed as I brought the car to a halt before my rented garage. I nodded and smiled to one and all, and they quickly looked the other way. I'd ruined my reputation here, but it didn't matter. I'd never be coming back. I opened the garage door with a palmprint, retina scan and a muttered Word, and drove the Hirondel inside. I got out and sealed the door behind me, and only then finally allowed myself to relax.

I spent a good ten minutes just sitting on the bonnet, hugging myself tightly, too worn out even to move. I was tired, bone-deep tired, and weary of spirit. So much had happened in such a short time, and nearly all of it bad. But in the end I forced myself up and on to my feet again. I couldn't allow myself the luxury of a rest, or even a good brood. My family would already have people out looking for me. Clever people, talented people. Dangerous people. I was the enemy now, and I had good reason to know how the Droods treat their enemies.

I took off my bloodstained jacket and shirt, to check my shoulder wound. The first-aid blob had almost dried up, a shrivelled and puckered thing that only just covered the wound. I peeled it carefully away, and found the hole was now sealed behind a new knot of scar tissue. The blob had used up its pseudolife to heal and repair me, and now it was just a lump of undifferentiated protoplasm. I dropped it on the floor, said the right Word, and it dissolved into a greasy stain on the bare concrete. First rule of an agent: leave no evidence behind. Useful things, those blobs. I'd have felt easier if I'd had a few more, but if you're going to start wishing for things ... I flexed my shoulder cautiously. It was stiff, and it still ached dully, but it seemed sound enough. My hands drifted up to touch the golden collar round my throat. My armour was no longer invulnerable. The protection and security I had taken for granted so casually all my life had been stripped away from me, all in a moment. I wondered if I'd ever feel safe and confident again.

I sat down before the computer in the corner, fired it up and put together a list of addresses and general locations of various old enemies who might know something about what was happening. Some of them might agree to help me, for the right consideration. Or intimidation. There's never any shortage of Bad Guys in and around London, but only a select few would have access to the kind of information I was after. And most of them were very powerful people, often with good reason to kill me on sight, once I revealed who I was. I worked on the list, crossing out a name here and there where the risk was just too great, and finally ended up with a dozen possibles. I printed out the revised list, shut down the computer and then sat there for a while, gathering my courage. Even with my armour operating at full strength, these were still very dangerous people. Daniel walking into the lions' den had nothing on what I was going to have to do.

But I had to get moving. My very respectable neighbours were bound to have contacted the police by now. So I called a certain notorious taxi firm on my mobile phone: black cabs whose drivers would take anyone anywhere, and never ask awkward questions. You learn how to find firms like that, in my game. They were reliable but expensive, and I realised for the first time that money was going to be a problem. The family would have put a stop on all my credit by now, and flagged my name everywhere else. All I had was the cash in my wallet. Fortunately, I've always been paranoid, and I think ahead. A small metal safe at the back of the garage held half a dozen fake IDs, and ten thousand pounds in used notes. Enough to keep me going for a while.

I changed into a new set of clothes. They smelled a bit musty from hanging in the garage for so long, but they were nicely anonymous. So typical and average, in fact, that any witnesses would be hard pressed to find anything specific about them to describe. I piled my old bloodstained clothes on the floor and broke an acid capsule over them. Shame. I'd really liked that jacket. One more stain on the floor.

I looked sadly at the Hirondel. I could never drive that marvellous old car again. It had become too visible, too remembered; and I couldn't let such a car, with all the Armourer's additions, fall into mundane hands. I smiled grimly. Even after all that had happened, I was still protecting family security. Saying goodbye to the Hirondel was like leaving an old friend, or a faithful steed, but it had to be done. I patted the discoloured bonnet once, and then said the Words that would trigger the car's auto-destruct. Nothing so blunt and capricious as an explosion, of course: a controlled elemental incendiary that would leave nothing useful behind, and scour the garage clean of all evidence. Police forensics could work their fingers to the bone, and still find nothing they could trace back to me.

I'm paranoid, I think ahead, and I'm very thorough.

I left the garage, locking the door behind me, and sure enough the taxi with no name was already there waiting for me. I walked over to it and got in, and never once looked back. It's an important part of a field agent's job; to be able to walk away from anyone or anything at a moment's notice, and never look back.

The taxi took me into London proper, and dropped me off at the first Underground Tube station we came to. I rode up and down on the trains, switching from one line to another at random, until I was sure no one was following me. There was no way my family, or anyone else, could have tracked me down so quickly, but I needed to be sure. I got off at Oxford Street, and went up and out into the open air. It was early evening now, and crowds of people surged up and down the street, in the course of their everyday lives, as though this was just another day. No one paid me any attention. That at least was normal, and reassuring.

The first name on my list was the Chelsea Lovers. Very secretive, and very hard to find. They changed their location every twenty-four hours, and with good reason. The Chelsea Lovers were hated and feared, worshipped and adored, petitioned and despised. And the only way to find them was to read the cards. So I walked casually down Oxford Street till I reached the rows of public phone kiosks, and checked out the display of tart cards plastering the interiors. Tart cards are business cards left in the kiosks by prostitutes advertising their services. Sometimes there's a photo, (which you can be sure will bear little or no resemblance to the real woman), more often a piece of suggestive art accompanied by a brief jaunty message and a phone number.

The cards have a long history, dating back to Victorian times, and down the years have developed a language all of their own. A girl who boasts an excellent knowledge of Greek, for example, will not possess actual academic qualifications; though a visit to her would almost certainly be an education in itself. But underneath all the euphemisms and double entendres, there is another more secret language, for those who can read it. A wholly different message, to be read in the placement of certain words and letters, telling you how to find the current locations for darker and more dangerous pleasures. I worked out that day's message and phoned the indicated number and a voice at the other end, which might have been male or female, both or neither, gave me an address beyond Covent Garden, and told me to ask for the Kit Kat Club. Nice to know someone still had a sense of humour.

The place wasn't hard to find. From the outside it looked like just another building, behind a bland anonymous front. No advertising, no clues. Either you knew exactly what the place was, or you had no business being there. I studied the exterior thoughtfully, while people passed me by, unknowing. The Kit Kat Club wasn't the sort of place you rushed into. You needed to gird up your spiritual loins first.

The Chelsea Lovers were a group marriage of assorted mystical head-cases, dedicated to the darker areas of tantric sex magic, channelled through cutting-edge computer technology. They organised orgies that ran twenty-four hours a day, with participants constantly coming and going. With the kind of mystical power they were capable of generating, they could have picked up the whole of London and spun it around a few times before dropping it again. Only they never did, because ... well, apparently because they were concerned with something far more important. What that might be, no one knew for sure, and most were afraid to ask. The Chelsea Lovers had links to every necrotech, psycho fetish and ceremonial sex club in the city, and were famous for knowing things no one else knew, or would want to. They supported themselves by practising entrapment and blackmail on significant people: celebrities, politicians and the like.

Which was why the Chelsea Lovers had good reason to want Edwin Drood dead. A year or so back the family had sent me in to destroy the Chelsea Lovers' main computers and all their files, after they'd made the mistake of trying to pressure someone sheltering under the family's protection. So I'd armoured up, forced my way in, and taken out their computers with a tailored logic bomb fired from one of the Armourer's special guns. The computers melted down so fast there was nothing left but a puddle of silicon on the floor.

They never saw my real face, only the golden mask. So they had no reason to suspect Shaman Bond. Except, of course, that the Chelsea Lovers were suspicious of everyone, and quite right too. They worried people.

I went up to the perfectly ordinary front door, and knocked

politely. A concealed sliding panel opened, and a pair of scowling eyes studied me silently. I gave them the password I'd received on the phone, and that was enough to gain me entry. The sliding panel shut, and the door opened just enough to let me in. I had to turn sideways to squeeze through, and the door was immediately slammed and locked behind me.

The security man leaned over me. He was as big as a wardrobe, with muscles on his muscles. I could tell this because he was entirely naked, apart from enough steel piercings in painful places to make him a danger to be near during thunderstorms. He wanted me to take my clothes off too (house rules), or at the very least submit to a thorough frisking. I gave him my best hard look, and he decided to pass the question upwards. I told him I was here to see the founding quartet, and he raised a pierced eyebrow. I gave him their actual names, which impressed him, and after nodding slowly for a moment, he lumbered off to find them.

I stayed put, by the door. I hadn't been entirely sure what to expect. I mean, I've been around, comes with the job, but the Chelsea Lovers were a whole new area of depravity to me. The entire building had been hollowed out to form one large, open and cavernous room. The Kit Kat Club was lit by rotating coloured lights, from no obvious source, giving the scene a kaleidoscopic, trippy feel. Very fitting for a group whose origins lay in the sixties. Pretty much everywhere I looked there were naked people, or people dressed in the kinds of dramatic fetish gear that makes you look even more naked than naked. Leather and rubber, plastic and liquid latex, collar and chains, spikes and masks and every kind of restraint you'd rather not think about. There were no wallflowers here; everyone was involved with someone or something. They moved smoothly together, across the huge room, flesh rising and falling, skin sliding over sweaty skin. There were no words, only moans and sighs and the sounds of a language older than civilisation. The faces I could see held a self-absorbed, animal look: all wide eyes and bared teeth.

Men and women everywhere, tangled together on the floor, up the walls and on the ceiling, and even floating in mid air. Sex beat on the air in an overpowering presence, hot and sweaty and pumped full of pheromones. I could smell sweat and perfumes and a whole bunch of psychotropic drugs. I wasn't worried. My torc would filter them out. Even quiescent around my throat, my armour still protected me.

So much nakedness, so much sex, so much harnessed passion; but I couldn't say I found it arousing. It was scary. They were working magic here, invoking strange and potent energies, produced by people who had willingly driven themselves out of all control, people who would do anything, receive anything, and not give a damn. There was no love here, no tenderness; nothing but indulgence and transgression.

The wide cavernous room seemed much larger than the building should have been able to contain. This was spatial magic, fuelled by the tantric energies. The room expanded to contain the passion within. The walls, floor and ceiling had taken on a puffy, organic look. All pinks and purples and bloody shades, patterned with long traceries of pulsing veins. The wall nearest me was sweating, as though turned on by the never-ending sex. The Kit Kat Club was alive, and part of the proceedings. Where men and women bumped against the floor or walls or ceiling, they sank into the fleshy embrace as though into the arms of another partner.

I shifted my feet uncomfortably, and the floor beneath me gave subtly, as though I was standing on a waterbed. People were drifting towards me, reaching out with enquiring hands. There was something in their faces that wasn't entirely human; or perhaps more than human. Transformed by an emotion or desire so extreme I had no name for it. I was way out of my depth. So of course I put on my most confident face, and even sneered a little, as though I'd seen it all before and hadn't been impressed then. I glared at anyone who came too close, and they turned away immediately, losing interest.

As my eyes adjusted to the flaring lights and colours, I began to recognise faces in the roiling throng: celebrities, footballers, politicians, even a few respectable businessmen from the City that dear prudish Matthew would probably have been horrified to discover in a place like this. I filed the faces away in my memory, for future thought. And perhaps a little blackmail, if money became tight.

The walking wardrobe returned with the four founding members of the Chelsea Lovers. They strolled with almost supernatural grace through the heaving crowds, which opened before them and closed after them without once stopping or even slowing what they were doing. The four founders walked on air, masters of their own space, touching nothing but each other. Their hands wandered constantly over each other's bare flesh. They sank slowly down to hover before me, and the bouncer went back to his door. The four original Chelsea Lovers: Dave and Annie, Stuart and Lenny. Two men and two women, but far beyond anything so human now; instead they were as alien and *other* as anything I ever encountered from another dimension. They had to be in their late sixties, but they still had the smooth bodies of twenty-year-olds. Perfect as statues, lean and hungry, burning with unnatural energies, sustained by an endless appetite that had nothing to do with food.

They looked much as they must have done when they first met in Chelsea, back in the Swinging Sixties, when London swung like a pendulum. Two young couples, then, out on the town and hungry for new experiences. They found something, or it found them, and they were never the same afterwards. They started their first club in a little place off Carnaby Street, and what they did there shocked even the most hardened souls of the permissive generation. The Chelsea Lovers hadn't seen daylight since. They moved from location to location, known only to those in the know, travelling the secret subterranean routes beneath the city streets, flitting silently through the shadows of undertown, with its ancient Roman arches, where all the bad things congregate, for fun and profit. Nothing ever touched the Chelsea Lovers. Even then, they were far too dangerous.

They stood before me, skin like chalk, eyes like pissholes in the snow. Colourless flyaway hair, purple lips and endless smiles that meant nothing, nothing at all. They were entirely naked, untouched by piercings or tattoos or any such trappings. Such lesser things were not for them. Just hanging on the air before me, silent and inviting, they were still the most blatantly sexual things I had ever seen. They had all the impact of the first nude photos you ever saw, the first object of desire, the first boy or girl you ever wanted, and the first you ever lost. I wanted them and I was afraid of them, and God alone knows what I would have done if my torc hadn't been there to protect me from the worst of their influence.

I knew the four names, but not which was who. I don't think anyone does, any more. Perhaps not even them. One of the women spoke to me. Her voice sounded like she had ice in her veins and a fever in her head.

'What do you want here? What's your pleasure?'

I had to clear my throat before I could speak, and even then my voice wasn't as steady as I would have liked. 'I need to consult your computers. I need information, the kind only you might possess.'

'What do you offer in payment?' said one of the men. His voice was calm, cheerful, confidential, and about as human as a spider scuttling across your arm. 'Information in return, perhaps; or money, or your seed? You'd be surprised what we could make from your seed, freely given.'

'Information,' I said quickly. My mouth was very dry, and my legs were shaking. 'First, a secret location used by a Drood field agent, on the outskirts of London.' And I gave them the address of the garage I'd just abandoned. 'Second, the name of the Drood field agent who's just been declared rogue, and is on the run here in London: Edwin Drood.'

All four of them actually shivered with delight, at the prospect of getting their hands on a new rogue Drood; the first in years. They rose and fell on the air, laughing silently, their chalk-white skin shimmering brightly. If they could seduce and corrupt the rogue to their cause, they would have access to secrets and information no one else had. They commanded me to follow them, and floated off towards the centre of the room, descending slowly until they walked on the bodies that moved unstoppably beneath them. I struggled after them, my feet slipping and sliding on the sweat-covered bodies. I stared straight ahead. You can't keep glancing down and apologising. And finally, in the exact centre of the cavernous room, the four founding Chelsea Lovers impersonally levered people out of the way to reveal a large puckered orifice in the floor. They gestured, and it dilated open, revealing only darkness and a sudden pungent smell on the air, like supercharged cinnamon. One by one the four of them floated down into what lay below the floor, disappearing into darkness, until only I was left hesitating on the rim. In the end, I shrugged and jumped in after them. This was what I'd come for, after all.

And found myself suddenly in a brightly lit, high-tech environment that was the complete antithesis of everything above. It was a circular room barely twenty feet in diameter, crowded with all the latest computer equipment. But the computers had burst open, their silicon contents spilling out like fruiting bodies, spreading themselves up the walls and across the ceiling like silver ivy, even dropping down in encrustations like silicon stalactites. The computers here were living things, growing things, fuelled by the sexual energies from above. Self-centred, self-perpetuating. The air conditioning gusted like heavy breathing, and the monitor screens around me could have been eyes or mouths or other orifices. The four Chelsea Lovers stood together in the middle of it all, looking at me expectantly.

'Word is, there's a traitor inside the Drood family,' I said. 'I want to know everything you know about that.'

They nodded in eerie unison, and one of them ran a hand caressingly over a computer console. It was a slow, sensuous lover's touch. I could feel beads of sweat popping out on my forehead. Normal people weren't supposed to be exposed to things like the Chelsea Lovers. Their very presence was toxic to ordinary humans. The computers hummed thoughtfully to themselves. The Chelsea Lovers stood together, in the same stance, even breathing in unison. Their eyes didn't blink as they considered me. I could feel a presence, a pressure, forming in the room. A desire, a need, a physical imperative . . .

'What's it for?' I said abruptly. 'I mean, all of this. The Chelsea Lovers. The Kit Kat Club. The sex magic and the computers. What's the point of it?'

'Apocalypse,' said one of the women, and they all smiled a little more widely. 'The real sexual revolution, come at last. We want to turn the whole world on. Using sex magic, computer magic, ritual and passion, instinct and logic, flesh and silicon bonded together in unthought-of ways, to work a tidal change in reality itself. We will make the whole world sexual. Fetishise everything in it, the living and unliving, suffusing the whole world with a passion and an appetite that will never end. A great joyous sexual apocalypse, the climax of history. The biggest bang. Endless sensation, endless pleasure . . . And we shall all worship the new flesh, for ever and ever and ever . . .'

She broke off as a face appeared on all the monitor screens at once. The computers had discovered the identity of the new rogue

Drood, and it was me. My face was on every wall, with my real name beneath it. The family had released my true identity to the world. The Chelsea Lovers turned as one to orientate themselves on me. They weren't smiling any more. They each thrust one hand out at me, and sex hit me like a fist. I cried out, convulsing helplessly as passion burned in me like a fever, like the nightmares you have when your temperature rises and your blood boils in your brain. I wanted to go to them, on my hands and knees if necessary, and worship their flesh with my own. I would have begged, would have died, for their lightest touch, for the pleasure of their favour.

But there was still enough Drood training and pride left in me to hold them off, enough for me to be able to subvocalise the Words, and my armour flashed around me, golden and glorious, sealing me off from all attack. I staggered backwards, suddenly myself again, like a man who lurches away from the very edge of a cliff. The Chelsea Lovers cried out in one awful voice, full of rage at the sight of Drood armour. I jumped up, the strength of my legs amplified by my armour, and I went soaring up through the orifice and into the Kit Kat Club above.

I erupted into that fleshy, cavernous place, and people fell back from me, shouting and screaming. I had broken the mood, or the Chelsea Lovers had. I ran for the door, and suddenly in answer to some unheard signal, everyone in the room surged forward to attack me. Blows and kicks came from every direction, though I couldn't feel them through the armour, and naked people grabbed at my arms and legs, trying to pull me down. I ran on, kicking and pushing people out of the way, and none of them could slow or stop me. They clutched at me with endless hands, and crowded in before me, blocking the way to the door with their bare bodies. I focused on moving forwards, not striking out, though every instinct yelled in me to fight. With my armour's strength I could kill these people, and I didn't want to do that. Unlike some of my family, I still believed in (mostly) innocent bystanders.

I could see the door, up ahead. The huge bouncer came forward to stop me, his enormous hands opening and closing eagerly. I hit him once, and he fell backwards, blood flying on the air, to be trampled underfoot by the packed crowds still pressing forward.

Strange forces crackled on the air around me, sex magic and computer energies from the room below, crawling over my armour, trying to force a way in. There were screaming faces around me, clutching at me, wrapping their arms around my legs, reaching down from the ceiling to clatter their hands uselessly against my golden head. Naked men and women crawled over me, slowing me down by sheer weight and press of bodies.

I reached through my armoured side and drew my needle gun. I still had it. Strictly speaking, I should have handed it in to the Armourer, but what with one thing and another I never got round to it. There were only a few needles left. I aimed the gun at the nearest wall, and shot iced holy water into the nearest pulsing vein. The whole room convulsed, like a great fleshy earthquake. Everywhere naked men and women were falling away from me, clutching at their heads, crying out in shock and horror. They forgot about me as the room shook, and I ran for the door.

I pulled the door wide open, and daylight poured in. More screams, as much fear as anger. I looked back. The whole place was convulsing with great cracks opening in the drying-out walls. People dropped out of mid air, as the magics fell apart, no longer sustained by the endless orgy. Men and women cried and howled and hit out at each other. I'd broken the mood. I nodded, satisfied. I might not have learned anything useful here, but at least the word would go out; that even though I no longer had the support of my family, I was still a force to be reckoned with.

CHAPTER NINE
Dream a little dream for me

I went into the Underground and took the Tube to Leicester Square station. No one wanted to sit next to me in the carriage; in fact, people actually got up to move further away. It took me a while to realise I stank of musk from the Kit Kat Club. Still, several women did smile at me. And a couple of men. I finally emerged from the station and wandered up St Martin's Lane. The evening was drawing on, and people were out on the town in happily chattering groups. No one paid me any attention, so I guessed the musk was wearing off in the open air. It felt good to be safely anonymous again.

St Martin's Lane is in a nice enough area: all theatres and restaurants, pleasant stores and businesses. Very civilised, in fact. I followed the curving street around till I came to the next address on my list, the very secret home and lair of the Sceneshifters. Probably the most dangerous group on the scene, in their own small way. And so tricky to deal with that I'd never been allowed to have any direct contact with them, even though they were quite definitely on my patch. The Sceneshifters were the exclusive responsibility of a special group within the family; and I was instructed very firmly to keep my distance.

But; things change.

Essentially, the Sceneshifters work behind the scenes of reality, changing small details here and there, to turn the state of the world to their advantage. There are members of the Drood family whose full-time job it is to detect these changes, and put them back the way they were. We assume we're winning, on the grounds that the Sceneshifters don't actually rule the world yet. As far as we can tell . . .

From the outside, their address looked like any other building, part of a fairly modern row with bright white stone and oversized windows, but there was something about the place ... something that raised the hackles on your neck, and made you disinclined to linger. People passing by increased their pace, and averted their eyes without realising they were doing it. I stood before the main entrance, scowling thoughtfully. A field agent learns to depend on his instincts, and every instinct I had was yelling at me to get the Hell away from this awful place. Just standing there, I felt ... uneasy, disturbed, in peril of both body and soul. As though if I went inside I might see things I couldn't stand to see, learn things I didn't want to know. Even with the torc around my throat, shielding me from outside influence, it took all my will-power to hold my ground.

As I stared intently at the building, refusing to look away, the details began to slip and flow, like a melting painting. As though a top coat was being washed away, revealing the true image beneath. Like the family reports said, the Sceneshifters' headquarters was protected by an uncertainty spell. You had to be certain what you were looking for was there, or it wouldn't be. It all came down to mental discipline. Which would be a shock for certain members of my family, who'd been known to say loudly in classrooms that I didn't possess any.

As I watched, scowling fiercely with concentration, the office building before me faded away like a passing thought to reveal the true structure beneath. An old church, with a massive wood and plaster fronting, an arched doorway and medieval stained-glass windows. It was half the size of the modern buildings towering on either side of it, but there was a basic strength and solidity to the place that was somehow reassuring. My instincts were still prickling, but at least I didn't feel like running any more. I strode up to the front door, and knocked like I had a reason to be there.

When you're dealing with people who change reality on a daily basis, there's not much point in trying to sneak in. They probably knew I was coming to see them before I did. And I certainly wasn't planning on throwing my weight around; there were very definite limits to what my armour could be expected to protect me from. When the door opened, I planned on being extremely polite, and using all the reasonableness at my command. I also planned on smiling a lot, and running like a rabbit if my clothes started changing colour.

The door opened to reveal a cheerful-looking soul, a reassuringly ordinary guy in grubby workman's overalls. He was about my age, a bit scruffy, with a pleasant face and a cigarette in the corner of his mouth that he didn't bother to take out when he was speaking. He nodded easily to me.

'Hello, squire. Looking for the Sceneshifters, are you? Thought so. I'm Bert. I do all the real work around here, while they're off saving the world. Someone has to check the state of the tubing, and mop up the spills. Fancy a nice cup of tea? I've got the kettle on . . . well, suit yourself. Don't say I didn't offer. Come on in, come on in . . . So, You're the new rogue Drood, are you? Edwin Drood? Nice to meet you. Sort of thought you'd be taller, somehow . . . Never mind. Come here looking for sanctuary, have you?'

'News does get around,' I said dryly, as soon as I could get a word in edgeways. I stepped inside the church, and he shut the door behind me. I listened carefully, but I didn't hear him lock it. The interior was typical old-fashioned religious, a bit on the gloomy side, with brightly coloured light streaming in through the stained-glass windows. But there were no pews, no altar, and the only religious symbols were those originally carved into the old stone walls. It might be a church, but clearly no one had worshipped here for some time.

'Oh, we always know what's going on,' Bert said cheerfully. 'We hear everything the moment it happens, and sometimes several months before. I've always said we could make a fortune with a good gossip magazine (very upmarket, nothing sleazy); but I can't even get it on the committee agenda. Got their head in the clouds, that lot. Come to join us, have you, Edwin? You should, you know, we're doing important work here; when we're not having endless arguments about what constitutes a pivotal moment in history, and which way we should tip the balance. I ask you. Who really believes World War Two could be averted by giving Hitler back his missing testicle? Still, tell you what, squire: you come along with me and I'll give you the basic tour while we're waiting for the others to show up. How would that be?'

'Won't the others mind, us starting without them?' I said

cautiously. I wasn't sure what I'd expected to find here, but Bert sure as Hell wasn't it.

'Course they won't mind! You're expected, squire; we've been looking forward to you turning up here. The things we could achieve with a Drood on our side! And we could use some new blood in the group, to be honest. Not to mention someone with a propensity for actually getting things done, instead of sitting around talking about it. I swear we'd be ruling this world by now if the committee could get their heads out of their arses once in a while.'

He headed for the back of the church, his hands in his overall pockets and his cigarette still protruding jauntily from one corner of his mouth. I followed along, keeping a wary eye out for sneak attacks or mutating realities, but it all seemed very calm and peaceful.

'So,' I said casually, 'what is this important work that you're doing here, Bert?'

'We're defeating the Devil, one day at a time.' For the first time Bert sounded entirely serious. 'He rules this world, you know. Not God. He hasn't been in charge for ages. I mean, you only have to look around you to see that for yourself. The world wasn't supposed to be like this. Not this ... mess. We were supposed to live in Paradise. But something happened long ago, and the Devil's been playing games with Humanity ever since, the bastard. Telling us lies, driving us to despair, torturing us every day with false hopes, impossible ambitions, and chances snatched away at the last moment. Why do bad things happen to good people? Why do bad guys thrive? Because the guy in charge gets a kick out of it, that's why. He's making a Hell out of this world, just for the fun of it. Some say the greatest trick the Devil ever pulled was to make us believe love was real ...'

'Oh,' I said. I couldn't think of anything else to say, except perhaps, *Have you stopped taking any medication recently?*

'But, bit by bit, we're changing the world the Devil made,' Bert said cheerfully. 'Rewriting reality and transforming the world into something finer and fairer. We're stealing it back inch by inch, and making it something fit for people to live in. We're all going home, to Paradise. That's why the founding members chose this place for our HQ. Centuries of accumulated faith and sanctity help keep the Devil from noticing we're here.'

'So the Devil hasn't always ruled the world?' I said carefully. 'God was in charge, once?'

'Oh yes ... Word is the Devil snatched control of the world away from God, after he persuaded the Romans to crucify the Christ. The Son of God was never supposed to die! He was supposed to stay with us for ever, teaching us how to live proper lives. But with him gone, the Devil sneaked in and stole creation away from the Creator. And we've been stuck with the bastard ever since. Screwing up everyone's lives, in his own private torture chamber, just for a giggle. This way, squire. Mind the step.'

Bert led me out of the back of the church, and into a large antechamber packed with men and women sitting around long tables. They all wore bright red robes, complete with hoods. They were reading newspapers, magazines and books, and making careful notes in their laptops. A few looked up and nodded to Bert, before returning to their work. All four walls were lined with bookshelves, crammed full of books and bound magazines from floor to ceiling.

'Here is where we study the world,' Bert said grandly. 'Through its media, its history books, and every up-to-date commentary. There's another room where they do nothing but watch every single news channel, all day long. We have to rotate those people on a regular basis, or they start developing conspiracy theories, and next thing you know you've got a schism on your hands. And of course there's our wide-ranging net of supporters and fellow travellers, tucked away in governments and religions and big businesses all across the world, keeping us up to date on what's really going on. If you knew what Bill Gates was planning to do next, you'd shit yourself. We're always looking for that crucial factor, that pivotal moment: when tipping over one small domino will set all the others toppling ...Come on, come on, lots more to see.'

He led the way down a long wooden spiral stairway that creaked alarmingly under our weight and finally gave on to a low-ceilinged stone chamber deep beneath the church, full of bubbling chemical vats almost as tall as I was, and a lot broader. Garishly coloured liquids surged up out of the vats and along through what seemed like miles of thick rubber tubing, stapled to the walls and ceiling. All around there were gauges and valves and wheels and some fairly primitive filtering systems. I'd seen stills that were more complicated.

Bert darted back and forth across the chamber, fussing over the equipment, adjusting a valve here and turning a wheel there. He tapped one gauge with a knuckle, sniffed at the reading, and then turned to smile proudly at me.

'It's a very delicate set-up,' he said, patting a nearby vat affectionately. 'Needs constant monitoring, of course. The founders put all this together, years ago, and they won't let me change anything. Even though they're far too intellectual to actually come down here and get their hands dirty on a regular basis. Not that I want them messing about with things, now that I've got everything running just right.'

He looked at me, inviting me to say something. I hadn't a clue what to say about his precious set-up, so I retreated to something else that had been bothering me.

'If the church's sanctity is enough to hide you from the Devil, why do you need the uncertainty spell as well?'

Bert looked distinctly disappointed in me, but soldiered on with his answer. 'That's not exactly a spell, as such. More what you'd call a side effect, really. Comes from the Red King, down in the dream chamber. Or Professor Redmond, as he was. We call him the Red King after the character in *Alice Through The Looking Glass*. Remember him? He was fast asleep and dreaming, and everyone was afraid to wake him because they believed he was dreaming the world and everything in it. So if he did wake up, they'd all cease to exist. Would you like to meet him? We don't normally show him off to visitors, but then you're special, aren't you?'

I was still trying to form an answer to that one when we were interrupted by the arrival of a man and a woman from the door on the far side of the chamber. They were both wearing the ubiquitous red robes, and they both carried a definite air of authority about them. They were middle-aged, with long aesthetic faces and severe expressions. Bert nodded to them, conspicuously unimpressed.

'Thank you, Bert,' said the man. 'We'll take it from here.' He gave me a cold smile. 'I'm Brother Nathanial, and this is Sister Eliza. Welcome to the Sceneshifters, Edwin Drood.'

I nodded coolly in return. I didn't like his eyes, or hers. They both had that look; that certainty beyond any doubt, inhumanly focused, merciless in their logic. Fanatic's eyes.

'I'm here looking for some answers,' I said.

'Aren't we all?' said Nathanial. 'Come; ask us anything. We shall conceal nothing from you. Bert, there's been a spillage in the secondary systems. If you wouldn't mind . . .'

'All right, all right, I'll go and clean up your mess while you give Edwin the old pep talk.' He nodded easily to me. 'Have fun with the Red King, and his dreams. Don't have nightmares afterwards.' He gave me one last cocky wink, and left the room.

'Marvellous fellow,' said Nathanial. 'An invaluable member of our staff, though I'd never tell him that. He might want paying more. Now then, Edwin; Sister Eliza and I run things here, in as much as anyone does. We like to think of ourselves as a cooperative. Don't expect dear Eliza to say anything. She has no tongue any more. Sometimes the small changes we make have the most unexpected repercussions . . .'

'Bert said something about founding members,' I said, just to be saying something.

'Oh yes, that's us. There were six, originally, but now there are seven. Another side effect . . .'

'How many people are there, in the Sceneshifters?' I said, trying for a question that might possess even a slim chance of having a definite answer.

'Oh, more than you'd think,' said Nathanial, smiling coolly. 'Certainly far more than your family thinks. You'd be surprised, Edwin. Our ranks are growing all the time, as we open people's eyes to the terrible truth. We're the real salvation army, fighting a holy war against the Devil and all his works. Bert has filled you in on the basics, hasn't he? Good, good . . . I think it's time for you to meet the centre of our operations, our very own Red King, Professor Redmond. We're very proud of him. This way, please . . .'

'But there are questions I need to ask you,' I said. 'About my family, and why I was declared a rogue . . .'

'Yes, yes,' said Nathanial. 'All in good time. You really can't appreciate what we're doing here until you've met the Red King.'

He and the silent Sister Eliza ushered me politely but firmly through the maze of chemical vats and looping tubes to a door at the back of the chamber, and then through it into a long stone corridor that stretched away before us, sloping down into the earth. Thick pulsing tubing was stapled to the bare stone walls, while from the ceiling hung a series of electric bulbs. We followed the tubes down the corridor, descending for some time, until I lost track of how deep we were under the church and the London streets. The air was chill and damp, and water ran down the bare stone walls.

'Don't you have any security down here?' I said after a while, to break the silence.

Nathanial shrugged easily. 'The uncertainty effect keeps out the riff-raff, while the church's sanctity hides us from the Devil and his disciples. And the Red King dreams he's safe, so he is.'

'How does this all work?' I said, a little desperately. 'This whole ... sceneshifting business?'

'It's really very simple,' said Nathanial, in that smug kind of way that tells you it isn't going to be at all simple. 'While the Red King sleeps, he dreams. Constantly. And while in that state he is able to see behind the scenes of reality, as it were. How things really work, and how they're put together. We can influence his dreams, and persuade him to make small changes. And the alterations he makes ... there, affects things here. In reality. We only deal in small changes, never big ones, no matter how tempting. They might be noticed by ... You Know Who.

'I often wonder what it is the Professor sees, exactly, in his dreams. We can only guess. And whisper the odd suggestion in his ear. He's in an extremely suggestive state. Though you have to be very careful what you ask for; very specific. Did you know there used to be pyramids in Scotland? Oh yes; a huge tourist attraction, in fact. But the Red King dreamed them away, and now they're gone and no one remembers them but us. Your family missed that one, which I sometimes think is rather a shame ... Still, enough small changes add up; when your family doesn't interfere. We're so glad you've come to join us, Edwin.'

'I haven't decided anything yet,' I said.

'But you will,' said Nathanial. 'You will.'

Sister Eliza chuckled abruptly. The sound she made without a tongue was ugly, disturbing. Even Nathanial flinched a little. The corridor turned around suddenly, and spilled us out into a small stone chamber, barely twelve feet in diameter, gloomily lit just enough to be restful on the eyes. The walls had been roughly painted to resemble night skies, with whorls of stars and a procession of the moon in all its phases. In the centre of the room stood a marble pedestal, and on top of that, held in place by an ornate latticework of copper wire, was a severed human head. Male, middle-aged, slack features. From the ragged stump of the neck, whoever had cut it off hadn't had much practice. Someone had placed a fresh laurel wreath around the heavily lined brow. The head wasn't breathing, but behind the closed eyelids the eyes darted back and forth in the rapid eye movements of the dream state. Around the base of the pedestal someone had drawn a traditional pentagram with mathematical precision. And around that someone had traced a series of ceremonial circles, containing signs and pictograms from half a dozen forgotten cultures. Someone had done their homework.

Nathanial gestured for me to examine the head, so I walked around it to take a look. Thick rubber tubes had been plugged roughly into the back of the man's head, trailing away across the floor and out the door into the corridor, presumably all the way up to the chemical vats. I leaned forward for a better look, and winced at the crude holes where the tubes entered. No surgeon had done this. Someone had just drilled into the skull, and then pushed the tubes through into the exposed brain. I came round to study the face. It didn't look happy or unhappy. If not for the eye movements, I'd never have known it was still alive.

'Why just a head?' I said, finally.

'Well,' said Nathanial, 'it wasn't as if we really needed the rest of him, and keeping a whole body alive and preserved would have added greatly to our expenses. We were quite a small operation, when we started out. Just the Professor, and some of his finest students ... The tubes keep the head going, and the wires trickle a constant slow current across the frontal lobes, ensuring that he remains asleep and deep in the dream state. The tubes feed him certain preservatives, and the necessary drugs. He could last for ever, theoretically. Ah yes, the drugs. We haven't explained about those yet, have we? We're feeding the Professor a rather special cocktail of powerful psychotropic chemicals, everything from acid to taduki to datsura. All according to the Professor's own theories. The drugs push his mind up and out while he dreams, blasting the doors of perception right off their hinges, so he can see what lies behind, and beyond.'

'Who was he?' I said. 'How did he come to this?'

'Well, it was his own idea, originally,' Nathanial said, smiling in a rather self-satisfied way. 'He was our professor at Thames University. Remarkable mind, quite remarkable. He became our leader, our inspiration. He gave us these fascinating lectures, you see, about shamanic drugs, and dream states, and how they could be combined to access different levels of reality. He also talked a lot about something called 'experimenter's intent', where the scientist's intent could actually change the outcome of the experiment he was performing. It wasn't that great a step to combine those ideas.

'The Professor was really quite surprised when we finally went to him, six of his favourite students, and told him we'd found a way to translate his theories into a workable, practical solution to all the world's problems. He was even more surprised when we brought him down here, showed him what we'd done, and explained to him that he had been granted the singular honour of being our Red King. The man who would change the world, and save us from the Devil. In fact, when we told him exactly what we intended to do, he reacted very negatively. Actually started to cry when we showed him the bone saw, and held him down . . .

'But that was long ago. He's done such good work since, sleeping and dreaming for all these years, without interruption. The longer you sleep, you see, the more deeply you dream, and the further the drugs can take you. He dreams very deeply and very powerfully these days. I know he'd be so proud of what we've done with his help.'

'I wouldn't bet on it,' I said. 'After what you did to him, if he ever does wake up, it'll be the end of your world.'

'You don't know him like we did,' said Nathanial. 'He'd understand. He was always telling us it was our duty to go out and change the world. And how we always had to be prepared to make sacrifices for the greater good. And we did. We sacrificed him. You know, we're still struggling to understand the significance of what it is we're doing here. We don't just sit on our laurels, oh no! I sometimes wonder if perhaps the whole world, and everything in it, is only a dream. The Devil's dream. And that's why the Professor is able to access it, and change bits of it. If that is the case, we must be very careful not to disturb the Devil with our changes, in case we wake him ...'

'All right,' I said. 'That's it. You're a loony. You people don't know anything for sure, do you? It's all theories and guesses and half-baked stolen philosophy.'

'We're learning by doing,' said Nathanial, more than a little smugly. 'Because anything has to be better than the world we're forced to live in. That's why you have to join us, Edwin. Because we're not the enemy your family says we are. We're the good guys. We're Humanity's last hope.'

'I don't think so,' I said. 'I've read the family's reports on what you've done and tried to do. The changes you've tried to bring about. Every single one of them was concerned with remaking the world in your image, not God's. Changes to further your beliefs, your wishes, your needs. To make the Sceneshifters powerful and important and a mighty voice in the affairs of Man.'

'Of course,' said Nathanial. 'How else can we bring about real change? Permanent change?'

'Your dreams are so small,' I said. 'So petty. No wonder you never achieved anything that mattered. I'll never join you.'

'Oh, but you will,' said Nathanial. 'In fact, you already have. All the time you were chatting so pleasantly with Bert, we were down here murmuring in the Professor's ear, and the Red King dreamed his little dream and made the change so smoothly you didn't feel it happening. You're one of us, Edwin. You've always been one of us.'

I looked down, and I was wearing a long red robe, just like him. Just like Sister Eliza. Of course I was wearing it. It was the same robe I always wore when I came here, to visit my dear friends in the Sceneshifters. I'd been working for them for years, ever since I first came to London, their very own mole in the Drood family. It was good to be back among my friends, in my old familiar robes, in this familiar place. I smiled at Nathanial and Eliza, and they smiled at me. It was good to be home again.

The only thing that seemed out of place ... was my wristwatch. I looked at it stupidly. Something about it nagged at my mind. Nathanial spoke to me, but I wasn't listening. There was something about the watch, something important, something ... special about it that I was supposed to remember. My torc burned coldly around my throat, as though trying to protect me, though I couldn't think from what. I touched the wristwatch with my right hand, trailing my fingertips across it, ignoring Nathanial's increasingly angry words. The watch the Armourer gave me, before I left The Hall. The reverse watch, that could rewind Time ...

I hit the button, and Time stopped in its tracks and shifted into reverse. Light and sound strobed painfully around me as the watch reversed recent Time, taking me back to just before Nathanial told me I'd been changed. And in that moment, while the future was still pliable and in flux, I drew my Colt Repeater and shot Professor Redmond between the eyes.

The bullet slammed through his head, blowing bits of broken tubing and spattered brains out of the back of his skull. His eyes snapped open, and for the first time in years the Red King was awake at last. His mouth stretched wide in a soundless scream of rage and horror, and it was clear from his face and from his eyes that he knew what had been done to him, and with him. And in the last few moments of his unnaturally extended life, using power brought from some terrible other place, the Professor set himself to wiping out everything that had been done in his name. He looked at Brother Nathanial with his awful eyes, and Nathanial disappeared. Winking out of existence, not real, never had been. Sister Eliza turned to flee, but the Professor looked at her, and she was gone too.

I was already heading out of the door when the dream chamber started to disappear around me. The walls painted to look like the night skies became transparent and faded away, and I could feel the Professor's power following me as I sprinted up the long stone corridor. There was something behind me, but I didn't dare look back. I burst out into the room of chemical vats, and Bert looked round sharply in surprise. He cried out in shock as the great vats began to fade away, but I was already out of the room and scrambling up the spiral staircase. Behind me, Bert's voice cut off abruptly.

The wooden steps began to feel increasingly soft and insubstantial under my feet, but I made it to the top, gasping for breath. I couldn't spare the time it would take to call up my armour, and I didn't believe it could protect me from Professor Redmond's wrath anyway. I kept running, through the library and on into the church. The medieval stained-glass windows had already faded away to ordinary glass. The walls were disappearing too, revealing something behind them too terrible to look at. There were great gaps in the floor, and I jumped desperately over them, racing for the door.

I crashed through and out into the street, panting harshly for breath, and only then turned and looked back. The church was gone; nothing left but a hole between the two modern buildings, like a pulled tooth. The Sceneshifters were gone, never had been. The Red King had woken at last from his long sleep; and he had not woken up in a good mood.

CHAPTER TEN
Cutting out the middle man

My next stop was on Shaftesbury Avenue, deep in the busy heart of London. I was looking for the legendary Middle Man. Shaftesbury Avenue is a long road in two parts, walk one way and all you'll see is posh restaurants, top-rank hotels and theatres with old and even famous names. (Sad to say, one of these venerable establishments currently boasted a large banner proclaiming their next big show: *Jerry Springer The Opera – On Ice*. How are the mighty fallen; but anything to bring in the tourists.) Walk the other way, and it's cheap cafés, betting shops and adult video stores with walk-in knocking shops on the top floor. The kind of place where a card tacked on the door advertises the friendly availability of the lovely Vera. It doesn't tell you that there are in fact three lovely Veras, working eight-hour shifts, which is why the bed is always warm. Not to mention the basement clubs where under-dressed and over made-up hostesses encourage you buy over-priced 'champagne' for the privilege of enjoying their company. Though usually it's only the foreign tourists who fall for that one these days.

I'd never met the Middle Man before, but everyone knew he could be found right in the middle of Shaftesbury Avenue, where good meets bad, and often combines into something deliciously sinful. I was pretty sure the Middle Man would know something useful; if I could get him to talk to me. He had been around, on and off the scene, ever since the sixties, and he knew everybody: good and bad and especially in between. His great skill and passion was in putting people together, for mutual profit. If you were planning a bigger than usual heist, an underground conspiracy or merely plotting to take over the world some day, the Middle Man could put you in contact with every kind of specialist you'd need. He could arrange meetings, put together a team of like-minded professionals, or organise every step of an assassination. For a percentage. He'd never been known to get his hands dirty himself, or take a risk that hadn't been calculated to the smallest degree. Whatever happened, you could be sure there were always more than enough cut-outs in place that nothing ever came back to lodge at his door. Word was the Middle Man was so unbelievably rich these days, after so many industrious years, that he didn't need to do it for the money any more. He did it strictly for the thrill and for the challenge.

You find the Middle Man behind a sleazy, deliberately run-down Thai restaurant. From the outside, it looks decidedly appallingly grimy and off-putting, the kind of place only a truly desperate or naïve tourist would try. In fact, the Thai language above the door supposedly translates as *Piss Off Foreigner And Take Your Stupid-Looking Eyes With You*. I peered in through the fly-specked window, past the indecipherable cardboard menu, and wasn't surprised to find the restaurant was completely empty at a time of the evening when it should have been at its fullest. The rickety tables were covered in Formica, the chairs were cheap plastic and none too clean, and the linoleum floor was unspeakable. Somehow I knew that if you were foolish or brave enough to enter, you'd never get anything you ordered, and if you tried to eat it anyway, the staff would lean out the kitchen door watching you, giggling and elbowing each other and going, *Look! He's actually eating it!*

No one is ever supposed to eat there. It's just a front for the Middle Man. Even the staff send out for takeaways.

I tucked my head down so no one would get a good look at my face, slammed the door open and strode briskly in. I ignored the startled Thai staff and headed straight for the kitchen door at the back. The waiters were too surprised to stop me, only just starting to react as I pushed the door open. I heard their cries behind me as I marched into the kitchen like I'd come to condemn it on health grounds, and then I armoured up, overriding the stealth function. The kitchen staff took one look at me in my golden armour and fell back with shocked cries, like so many startled birds. The waiters burst in after me, having armed themselves with knives and hatchets, only to lurch to a sudden halt as I turned unhurriedly to look at them. My family's reputation goes a very long way. The head waiter put down a butcher's knife, and gestured for everyone else to lower their weapons.

'Sod this for a lark,' he said, in decidedly East End accents. 'Marcus isn't paying us enough to take on a Drood. You want to see the Middle Man, golden boy? Follow me.'

He led me through the surprisingly neat and clean kitchen, while the Thai staff watched me pass with expressions that weren't in the least inscrutable. There are places where looks can kill, but fortunately this wasn't one of them. The head waiter took me out the back of the kitchen and down a long narrow corridor with lighting so subdued it was positively gloomy. The carpet was blood-red, and the deep purple walls pressed in from either side. The only decorations were stuffed and mounted heads of various animals, peering down from everywhere. Big cats and African wildlife, mostly. The eyes in the heads moved slowly to follow me as I passed. Now I'm used to weird shit; I grew up in The Hall, after all. But something about those eyes seriously freaked me out.

'Let me guess,' I said nonchalantly to my guide. 'If I start any trouble, you say the Word and the animals connected to those heads will come suddenly crashing through the walls and have a go at me, right?'

The head waiter looked at me strangely. 'No,' he said. 'They're just conversation pieces. The boss bought them as a job lot, to brighten up the place.'

'Sorry,' I said. 'It's the company I've been keeping recently.'

We reached the end of the corridor, and he knocked briefly on the only door before opening it, and standing back to usher me in. I stepped inside, and he immediately shut the door and retreated up the corridor. I didn't take it personally. The room was more than comfortably large, very luxurious, almost sybaritic. Deep pile carpet, padded furniture, drapes and throw cushions everywhere. More subdued lighting, but upgraded to cosy rather than gloomy. The air was perfumed sweetly with attar, the essence of roses, and a hint of opium. And there on the great circular bed was the Middle Man himself, Marcus Middleton, propped up against half a dozen pillows. He smiled at me in a resigned sort of way, but made no move to rise.

He was wearing green silk pyjamas, stylishly cut, and sipping at a slender flute of champagne. He was also smoking a slim black cigarillo set in an ivory holder. His long slender fingers were set off by jet-black nail polish. He was handsome enough, in an aged and ruined sort of way, with flat black hair, surprisingly subtle make-up, and mild brown eyes that had seen absolutely everything before. He studied me for a moment, and then beckoned me forward with a vague smile and a languid gesture. I moved to stand at the foot of the bed, facing him.

The bed was surrounded by dozens of phones, all in easy reach, in a variety of styles from Victorian Gothic to the frankly futuristic. These were interspersed with a nice collection of crystal balls, magic mirrors and even a scrying pool in a chamber pot. At least, I hoped it was a scrying pool. The Middle Man started to say something, but was interrupted by a sudden ringing from one of his phones.

'Excuse me, dear boy,' he said calmly. 'But I have to get this. Do make yourself comfortable.'

He waved me towards a chair, but I declined, standing facing him with my golden arms folded across my armoured chest. It's hard to look fierce and imposing when you're sitting down, and I needed all the psychological edge I could get. The Middle Man sighed the-atrically, flicked some ash from his cigarillo over the side of the bed, and picked up a seventies trimphone in puke-yellow plastic.

'Oh, hello, Tarquin; what can I do you for? Dwarves ... Really, dear heart, I told you only the week before that there was going to be a shortage ... They're all working on this tacky new fantasy film they're shooting at Elstree Studios. Making good money too, from what I hear. Are you sure you couldn't settle for pixies? I could get you a really nice price on a group booking ... Has to be dwarves. I see. Well, leave it with me, duckie, and I'll see what I can sort out for you.'

He put the trimphone down with a graceful sweeping movement and a swirl of his green silk sleeve, and then looked at me for a long moment, while taking another sip of champagne and a deep drag on the cigarillo. If he was impressed by my armour, he was doing a really good job of hiding it.

'Well hello,' he said finally, favouring me with an arch and decidedly self –satisfied smile. 'And which little Drood are you?'

'I'm Edwin,' I said harshly. 'The new rogue.'

124

'Really? How thrilling . . . It's been such a while since anyone was able to tempt one of you away from the straight and narrow. Can I offer you anything? I have some fine Beluga caviar, or perhaps a little Martian red weed? It's such a smooth smoke . . . No? There must be something I can give you to make you feel more at home and relaxed. How about if I was to call in a pretty Thai lady, or ladyboy?'

'No, no and definitely no,' I said. 'I'm here on business.'

'How very tiresome.' The Middle Man sniffed loudly. 'Typical Drood; you people just don't know how to have fun. I suppose it was too much to hope you might have been thrown out of your nauseatingly self-righteous family for actually developing a few civilised vices. So; what can I do for you, dear boy?'

'You've worked for the Drood family for years, off and on,' I said. 'Helping us locate the right specialist, when needed for certain out of the ordinary operations.'

'Yes, and don't I know it, duckie; your family uses me ruthlessly, and never pays a penny. I do as I'm told, or they'll shut me down. And they're always so terribly rude to me. I don't know why; I merely provide a service. I put people of like minds together for mutual fun and profit. What they do afterwards is no concern of mine.'

'No,' I said. 'You don't care how much trouble and suffering you cause. None of the blood that ends up spilled ever stains your dainty fingers. You make awful things possible, but never take responsibility for your actions.'

'Oh, how *very* tiresome. A philosopher Drood. But still something of a man of action, I hear. It's all over town, what you did to the Chelsea Lovers, the poor dears. It'll take them years to regain the ground you've lost them. Not that I care, of course. I never care; it's bad for the complexion. And I can't help feeling they'd find my little peccadilloes far too bland for their extreme tastes. I never had much time for revolutions anyway, of any stamp. I like the world the way it is.' He reached across his pillows and took a Belgian chocolate from a large open box. He popped it into his mouth, chewed for a moment, and then gestured vaguely at me with one black-nailed hand. 'What exactly did you come here for, dear boy? Do get to the point. I have some important lounging about I should be getting on with.'

'You have contacts inside my family,' I said slowly. 'You must ... hear things. Do you know why I was banished, declared rogue?'

'I'm afraid not, no. Haven't heard a thing, I promise you. The news came out of nowhere, no warning whatsoever. You could have knocked me down with a feather, duckie. *Cover me in chocolate and throw me to the ladyboys*, I thought. *Not dear upright Eddie!* You've established quite a reputation here in the city, these last ten years. Honest, upright, and depressingly incorruptible, I would have said. No wonder your family assembled such an army to attack you on the motorway.'

'It was you,' I said abruptly. 'The penny's just dropped. You organised the attacks on the M4!'

'Well of course, dear boy. Who else? And don't think it was easy, contacting and putting together so many disparate elements, and getting them to play nice with each other for the duration of the attack. I wouldn't have chosen half of them, but my instructions were very specific: all bases were to be covered, scientific and magical. Honestly, the disputes I had over orders of precedence! Half of them wouldn't talk to each other, except through me. I would have had them all attack you at once, get it over with and be sure of killing you ...but no, they had to take their separate turn, to show what they could do ... Why can't people be professional?'

I lowered my arms and took a step forward, and he actually flinched back against his pillows. 'There's something else you haven't been meaning to tell me, isn't there?' I said. 'What is it, Marcus?'

'All right, all right! It's just that ... this particular commission didn't come from your family. As such. It was a private commission, from the Drood Matriarch herself. Dear old Martha, bless her black vindictive little heart. I danced with her, you know, one memorable evening back in the sixties, when Soho was still Soho ... Of course, we were both a lot younger and prettier in those days. Such a glamorous scene ... It was only after the attack on you failed that I got word you'd been officially declared rogue. What did you do to upset her?'

'Didn't she tell you?' I said.

'Didn't tell me one thing more than she absolutely had to, duckie. The hired help, that's all I was. And she wanted the whole package put together impossibly quickly, as well as extremely secretly. Gave me less than twelve hours to get the job done, and then was very rude to me when I tried to explain how difficult that was going to be. The words guts and garters were mentioned, and not in a good way.'

He carried on some more about how over-worked and under-appreciated he was, but I'd stopped listening. Grandmother wanted me dead, and only resorted to declaring me rogue when her assassination attempt failed. And twelve hours ... that had to be significant. What could have happened in that short time frame, to set the Matriarch so fiercely against me? I did a good job at *St Baphomet's*. Did everything I was ordered to do, and got out clean.

'So you don't know anything useful,' I said finally, cutting across his well-rehearsed self-pity.

'I could ask around,' he said, with a vague and very languid gesture. 'But all you'll get at this stage is gossip. Of course, now that you're rogue ... if you were looking for a new role in the world, or a secure position, I'm sure I could find a use for you in my organisation. If only because it would be absolutely killing for me to be able to say, ever so casually at one of my little soirées, that I had my very own Drood on the payroll! I know people who would shit at the very thought! I could be generous to you, Eddie. And what better way to get back at your snotty family?'

'I don't think so,' I said. 'I'm ... otherwise engaged. There are answers out there, and I will find them. Nothing is going to stop me.'

'Of course, of course,' said the Middle Man. He shifted uneasily, disturbed at something he heard in my voice. 'But I'm afraid there's nothing I can do to help you there. Nothing at all. I deal in people, not information. I could put you together with certain specialists, who might be able to assist you in your quest. For a consideration, you understand.'

'How about you help me, in return for my not killing you in horrible and inventive ways?' I said.

He sniffed, and puffed sulkily on his cigarillo. 'Typical Drood. Go ahead; threaten me, bully me, see if I care. Why should you be any different from the rest of your appalling family? No one appreciates what I go through for them. I swear, I'm so delicate these days that I'm not long for this world ...'

I raised a hand in self-defence. 'All right! How about: you help me for the satisfaction of putting one over on the Drood family, who've been using you for years without paying you? Wouldn't you like that?'

He considered me thoughtfully. 'Why should I risk upsetting your very powerful, not to mention vengeful, family ... when I could seriously ingratiate myself with them by handing you over? They might be so grateful they'd finally let me off the hook.'

'You really think they'd do that?' I said. 'The Droods never give up anything they own. And do you think you have any way of making me stay here till they come to collect me?'

'No ... and no,' the Middle Man said sadly. 'So ... run along, dear boy. Don't let me keep you, you're free to go. I never bother with a threat I can't back up.'

'If only everyone was so civilised,' I said gravely.

I was turning to leave when the Middle Man leaned forward suddenly. 'There is someone you could talk to. She knows many things, most of which she's not supposed to. And she has more reason than most to hate your family. The wild witch, Molly Metcalf.'

'Ah,' I said. 'Molly. Yes.'

'Do I detect a problem? You don't sound too enthusiastic.'

'Molly and I have a history,' I said.

The Middle Man laughed, and spread his hands as though embracing the universe. 'Who doesn't, dear boy? It's what makes the world go round!'

I armoured down as I walked out of the Thai café, the living armour melting back into my torc. Never wear the gold in public. I smiled slightly. I might be outcast from my family, and on the run, but I was still following their rules. Behind me, the Thai café staff hurried to lock the door and pull down the blinds. I didn't blame them. I stood outside for a while, thinking, and then looked up suddenly as for the first time I realised how quiet the street was. I looked around me, and there was no one to see anywhere, up or down the street. No traffic, no pedestrians. The busy sounds of the city continued off in the distance, but my little part of it was completely deserted. Which just didn't happen at this time of the evening, unless the whole area had been quietly and efficiently sealed off. And the only people with enough clout to do that, in the very heart of London, were my family.

No one says no to the Droods. So; they'd found me. I looked round sharply as a man came strolling casually out of a side street. A very smart, very smooth man with a familiar face, looking inordinately pleased with himself: Matthew Drood.

His manner was assured, even cocky, but I noticed he came to a halt a respectful distance away from me. He smiled and nodded, and I nodded to him. As far as I could tell, he'd come alone, which worried me. That wasn't family policy, when it came to dealing with a rogue. He seemed to be expecting me to say something, to defend or justify myself, so I just stood there, staring back at him. Matthew frowned slightly, and shot the gleaming white cuffs of his expensive City outfit.

'I knew you'd come here first, Eddie,' he said smugly. 'Simple deduction, old boy. All I had to do was stake the place out, and wait.'

'Actually, this was my third stop,' I said. 'Late as always, Matthew. Why did they choose you for this? Volunteer, did you, to impress the Matriarch? Or maybe Alex? You're not still mad at me over her, are you? It was a long time ago; we were teenagers.'

'Of course I volunteered,' Matthew said angrily. 'You're a disgrace to the family, Eddie. I always said you were no good; and now my judgement has been vindicated.'

'What did they offer you?' I said. 'Really, I'm curious. I mean, you wouldn't have been my first choice to take down a dangerous and experienced rogue. You've never been any good at the physical side of what we do. The old ultra-violence ... Leaning on stuffed shirts in the City is more your level; putting the wind up stockbrokers who've been caught with their hand in the till.'

Matthew glared at me, bright red spots burning on his cheeks. 'Once I've proved myself by bringing you in, they're going to give me your territory and responsibilities as well as my own. I'll be the biggest and best agent in one of the most important cities in the world. The Matriarch gave me her word, personally.'

'She's using you, Matthew, just like she used me.' I felt suddenly tired, worn down. 'She's setting us both up. Can't you see that? She's ready to throw you away, to slow me down till more experienced agents can get here. We can't trust the Matriarch any more, Matthew. She's got her own agenda now.'

Matthew looked at me as though I'd suddenly started speaking in tongues. 'She's . . . the Matriarch. Her word is law. We live and die at her pleasure. That's the way it's always been. And you're a dirty little traitor!'

I looked around me. There was still no sign of any back-up for Matthew. Maybe he really had been the only one close enough . . .

'I don't need any help to take down a traitor like you,' said Matthew.

'I'm not a traitor,' I said, taking a step towards him. He stood his ground.

'You've always been a traitor,' he said, and his smile was cold and unpleasant now. 'To the spirit of what we do. To the duty and traditions of the family. You should never have been allowed so much freedom; see what it's done to you. A mad dog, running loose, that has to be put down for everybody's good.'

I studied him for a moment. There was definitely something, in his voice and in his smile. 'This isn't official, is it?' I said finally. 'That's why you're here without back-up. The family doesn't know anything about this. You're here representing the Matriarch, and no one else. You're not here to bring me back alive, are you, Matthew?'

His smiled broadened. 'What good would that serve?'

'I never liked you,' I said. 'You always were teacher's pet.'

We both armoured up, the living metal leaping into place around us. It was eerie, looking at Matthew in his armour, like a mirror image. I didn't know what weapons he might have, but I didn't think he'd use them, for fear I'd use mine. They'd make the situation too unpredictable. And besides, we were both curious. We wanted to do this the hard way, head to head and hand to hand, because it had been centuries since anyone had tried that. It was very rare for two Droods to fight in the gold. We were never allowed to do it outside training sessions, because it was unthinkable that Drood should fight Drood. There were records of such clashes in the Library, very old records, but they were long on flowery words and short on detail. I wanted to do this, and so did he.

And if we were both doing it for the wrong reasons, there was no one here to stop us.

We sprang forward, golden hands outstretched. Equally motivated, equally fierce, equally determined. We slammed together, and the impact of armour on armour sounded like a great bell ringing in the depths of Hell. We hit each other hard, throwing punch after punch with all our amplified strength behind it, not even bothering to defend ourselves. The awful sound reverberated in the empty street, but neither of us took any hurt. Our armour protected us. The unstoppable force meeting the immovable object. I barely felt the impact of his fists, and I'm certain he didn't feel mine. All we were doing was wearing each other out. We wrestled clumsily for a while, chest to chest, neither of us able to gain an advantage.

Finally I tripped him up, and while he was down I kicked him so hard in the ribs he skidded several yards along the street. I ran after him, and while he was still scrambling to his feet, I grabbed him with both hands, picked him up and threw him at the nearest building. He crashed halfway through the wall, was held in place for a moment while dislodged bricks rained down on his armour. He pulled himself free with hardly an effort, and the wall collapsed behind him. He launched himself at me, completely unphased, and we slammed together again.

We couldn't hurt each other. Matthew pushed me away, reached out and grabbed the steel pole of a street light. He yanked it out of its concrete setting, the jagged end trailing wires and sparks. He wound up and swung the steel pole like a bat, and I couldn't move quickly enough to avoid it. The heavy steel smashed into my ribs, lifted me up off my feet and sent me flying through the air. I hit the ground hard, rolling over and over, and was immediately up on my feet again, unhurt, not even breathing hard.

We went to it again, raging up and down the street, smashing everything we came in contact with except each other. We hit out with everything we could lay our hands on, punched each other through walls, demolishing the street from one end to the other. Buildings collapsed, glass shattered and fires broke out, and we didn't even notice. We fought like gods, trampling heedlessly through the paper and cardboard world of mere mortals.

Finally we ran out of room, and came to the barricade set up at the end of the street. Behind a row of steel posts strung with barbed wire, a group of police stood watching from behind their parked cars. Behind them, a crowd of curious onlookers, drawn by the noise. They watched in dumbstruck horror as Matthew and I went at it hammer and tongs right in front of them, so caught up in the

131

righteous anger of what we were doing that we didn't give a damn about the armour being seen in public.

The police and the onlookers scattered as Matthew and I crashed into and through the barrier, the barbed wire snapping instantly, as insubstantial as fog to our armoured strength. We were outside the exclusion zone now, where everyone could see us, and the screams brought me back to myself. I tried to back off, but Matthew was too far gone to stop. He picked up one of the police cars as though it weighed nothing, and threw it at me. I ducked, and it sailed past me to crash into a storefront. I grabbed a nearby parked car and threw it at Matthew. He stood his ground, and the front half of the car concertinaed as it smashed against his immovable form. It exploded suddenly, into an expanding orange fireball. The closer buildings caught alight, and the air shimmered from the intense heat. And Matthew came walking out of the heart of the fireball, brushing blazing wreckage away from him, entirely unhurt. People were running, screaming hysterically, and the police were on their radios yelling in unmanned voices for armed back-up.

I looked at Matthew, in his gold, and the hairs stood up on the back of my neck. Was this how people had seen me? This terrible, inhuman thing?

While I stood there, frozen by insight, Matthew picked up another car and smashed it down on top of me, catching me off balance and throwing me to the ground. He leaned on the car, trying to pin me down, but I pushed back, and the metal of the car tore like tissue paper under our armoured strength. I rose up through the wreckage of the car, and we threw the broken pieces aside to get at each other again. People were still screaming in the background. They sounded like animals, maddened by something they couldn't comprehend. The fire was spreading. It occurred to me that the family were going to have a Hell of a time hushing this one up.

Matthew charged straight at me. I waited till the last moment, and then sidestepped. He stumbled past me, off balance, one arm out to brace himself against the wall ahead of him. I took out my portable door and slapped it against the brickwork, and he fell through the new opening into the interior of the building. I ripped the door away, trapping him inside. And then I used my armour's might to pull the whole damned building down on top of him.

Ton after ton of brick and stone and concrete and steel came thundering down, piling up on top of Matthew. The ground shook with the impact, and the street filled with smoke. I waited a while, tensed and ready, but nothing happened except for the great pile of rubble slowly settling. I snapped my golden fingers at dear, defeated Matthew. The armour would have protected him even from this, but he'd still be a long while digging himself out. By which time, I fully intended to be long gone.

I took one of the abandoned police cars. The officers had retreated so quickly they'd actually left the keys in the ignition. I drove off, armouring down as I went, turning down a side street as I heard the approaching sirens of fire engines and police cars. I wasn't in the mood for any more confrontations. Soon enough I was back in the main flow of London traffic, driving calmly and carefully, and no one looked at me twice. No one ever looks at a police car unless they have to. I stopped the car as soon as I could, and walked away from it. Once again Shaman Bond was just another face in the crowd, no one special, nothing to look at. My cover identity was the only real protection I had left. No one in the family knew my use-name. They'd never asked. Never cared.

I headed for the Underground again. For better or worse, there was only one person I could go to now, for help and answers. The one person the Matriarch would be sure I'd never approach. The wild witch Molly Metcalf. She shouldn't be too angry at seeing me again. It had been months since we last tried to kill each other.

You know: sometimes I swear the whole universe runs on irony.

CHAPTER ELEVEN
Good golly Miss Molly

You hear a lot of stories about Molly Metcalf. How she once frightened a ghost out of the house it was haunting. How she abducts aliens in order to run strange experiments on them. How she once called up the Devil himself, just to tell him an endless stream of knock-knock jokes. The most disturbing thing about these stories is that far too many of them are true. But that's the wild witch Molly Metcalf for you; free spirit of anarchy, Hawkwind fan and queen of all the wild places. Enemy to the Drood family and everything they stand for.

Somehow I knew this meeting wasn't going to go smoothly.

But there I was, on the run in London and hiding in the Smoke, sticking to the darker and nastier back streets because I couldn't afford to be seen by old friends or enemies. Using the secret short cuts and subterranean ways that normal people never get to know about. Heading reluctantly towards the one remaining person who might be able to find me a way out of the mess I was in. My oldest and fiercest enemy, my opposite in every way; Molly Metcalf. Sweet, petite and overwhelmingly feminine, Molly specialised in forbidden old magics, applied with much passion and not a little lateral thinking.

She once changed the magnetic patterns of force over London, so all the migrating birds would have to pass over the Houses of Parliament, and crap on them. She once worked a subtle magic on certain bed fleas and venereal crabs, making them her eyes and ears so she could spy on the very important personages who patronised a brothel which specialised in the rich and famous. As a result she learned many interesting things, and blackmailed her victims ruthlessly. As much for the fun of it as the money. One of her victims had to stand up in Parliament and recite the whole of *'I'm a little teapot, here's my spout'* during Prime Minister's Question Time before she'd let him off the hook. Given who it was, I quite approved of that one . . .

And, of course, there was the time she bribed a group of disgruntled earth elementals into causing massive earthquakes in the bedrock beneath the British mainland. Apparently she wanted to split the United Kingdom into three separate island states: England and Wales and Scotland. I only just stopped that one in time. And she was an enthusiastic part of the Arcadia Project, a gathering of top-rank magicians dedicated to changing the rules of reality itself, to bring about a new world constructed a lot more to their liking. Fortunately for the world and reality, magicians have the biggest egos outside show business and rarely play well with each other. Half of them ended up turning the other half into various kinds of livestock, and Molly lost her temper and called down a plague of frogs on the lot of them.

People were clearing frogs out of their guttering all over London for weeks after that.

Molly Metcalf resisted authority; any authority. She also hated my guts, with good reason. We'd been on opposite sides of a dozen missions, with me standing for Order and her for Chaos. We'd come close to killing each other several times, and neither of us had failed for want of trying. If I went to her in my armour, wearing the golden face she had every reason to hate, she'd attack me on sight. My only chance to get close to her was as Shaman Bond. Molly knew Shaman, in a friendly if distant way, as just another face on the scene. We'd even had the odd drink together, as part of my cover. I planned to use that, to get a foot in her door.

Molly lived in Ladsbrook Grove, in what had once been quite a trendy area, but had now fallen upon reduced circumstances. Her house was a simple two-up, two-down, in the middle of a long terraced row. From the outside it appeared no different from any of the others; a bit shabby, a bit run down, and in urgent need of a new coat of paint. The street was full of squabbling kids, riding their bikes back and forth, kicking a football around, or just hanging about in the hope something would happen. None of them paid me any attention as I went up to Molly's front door and leaned on the bell.

There were always strangers coming and going on a street like this. There was a long pause, long enough to make me consider ringing again, and then the front door opened enough to allow Molly to peer out.

'Shaman?' she said, in her usual dark and sultry voice. 'What brings you to my door, uninvited? I wasn't aware you even knew where I lived. Not many do, and I've killed most of them. I hate being bothered.'

I gave her my best charming smile. Molly Metcalf looked like a delicate china doll with big bosoms. Bobbed black hair, huge dark eyes, ruby rosebud mouth. She wore a gown of ruffled white silk, possibly to lend a touch of colour to her pale skin. She was beautiful; in an eerie, threatening and utterly disturbing way.

'Sorry to bother you, Molly,' I said, when it became clear the charming smile wasn't having any effect. 'I need to talk to you. About the new rogue Drood, Edwin. I know something about him that I think you need to know. May I come in? It is rather urgent.'

She thought about it for a long moment, studying me with her dark unblinking eyes, but finally nodded and stepped back, opening the door a little wider. I squeezed in past her, and she immediately shut the door behind us, and locked it. I barely noticed. I was standing in a vast forest glade, with my mouth hanging open. I didn't know what I'd expected to find behind the façade, but it sure as hell wasn't this. Molly lived in style.

Towering trees surrounded me on every side, heavy with summer foliage. The clearing rose and fell in grassy mounds, and a nearby waterfall tumbled down a jagged rock face into a wide, crystal-clear pool. Out among the trees, deer watched solemnly from a safe distance, while birds sang sweetly and heavy shafts of golden sunlight dropped down through the overhead canopy. Dappled shadows gave the clearing a drowsy, cosy feel, and the air was thick with the rich, damp and earthy smell of woodland.

Molly ignored me, walking among a small stand of trees. She talked to them in a soft whispered language I'd never heard before, and I swear they bowed their heads to listen. Wide-eyed deer came forward to nuzzle her with their soft mouths, and she rubbed their muzzles with gentle hands. A russet squirrel dropped out of the overhead branches to land lightly on her shoulder. It chattered urgently in her ear, and then looked straight at me.

'Hey, Molly,' it said. 'Who's the rube? New boyfriend? About time; you get really moody when you're not getting your ashes hauled regularly.'

'Not now, dear,' Molly said indulgently. 'Run along and play while I speak to the nice man. And don't eavesdrop or I'll do something unpleasant to your nuts.'

The squirrel pulled a face at her, and leapt back up into the safety of the trees. Molly came unhurriedly to stand before me, beside the pool. I decided not to ask about the talking squirrel. I didn't want to get sidetracked into what promised to be a very long story.

'Talk to me, Shaman Bond,' Molly said. 'Tell me this thing you know. And it had better be good, or there'll be another cute little talking animal in my garden paradise.'

'It's about Edwin Drood,' I said. 'The new rogue. He's in real trouble. Outlawed by his family, forsaken by his friends, all alone and on the run. He has been given good reason to doubt his family, or at least some part of it, and he wants to know the truth. He believes you can tell him things that others couldn't, or wouldn't. In return for your help, he's prepared to offer you the one thing you want more than his head on a spike: a chance to bring down the whole corrupt Drood family.'

'Works for me,' Molly said easily. She sat down on the edge of the pool, and trailed her fingers lazily through the lily pad-covered waters. Fish came to nibble at her fingertips. I stayed on my feet. I would have felt too vulnerable sitting. Molly looked up at me with her dark, thoughtful eyes. 'Where do you fit into this, Shaman? This is way out of your usual league. Why should I believe you when you say these things?'

'Because I'm Edwin Drood,' I said. 'And I always have been.'

I armoured up, the living gold covering me in a moment. Molly scrambled to her feet, glaring at me with wild, dangerous eyes. Her ruby mouth contorted with rage as she raised one hand into a spellcasting position. I made myself stand very still, my arms limp at my sides, my hands conspicuously open and empty. She stood still as a statue, breathing harshly, and then slowly she pulled back from the edge and lowered her threatening hand.

'Take off the armour,' she said harshly. 'I won't talk to you while you're wearing the armour.'

With the armour off, I'd be defenceless. She could kill me, torture me or mindwipe me into her slave; all things she'd threatened to do in the past. But I had come to her, so I had to make the gesture of trust. Of vulnerability. I subvocalised the Words, and braced myself as the living gold disappeared into my torc. Molly looked me over, as though searching for signs of treachery, and I looked back at her as calmly as I could. Molly nodded slowly, and moved a single step closer.

'I heard about what happened, on the motorway. About the things your family sent after you. People all over town are having a hard time believing you fought them off. I mean, no offence, but . . . no one on the scene ever thought you were *that* good. Did one of the Fae really shoot you with an arrow?'

Moving slowly and carefully, I unbuttoned my shirt and pushed it back to show her the arrow wound in my shoulder. Molly took another step forward, to study the healed wound more closely. She didn't touch me, but I could feel her warm breath on my bare skin as she leaned in close. She pulled back again, and met my gaze squarely. She was taller than I remembered, her eyes almost on a level with mine. She smiled suddenly, and it was not a pretty smile.

'So; Drood armour can be breached, after all. That's a thing worth knowing. I could kill you now, Shaman. Edwin.'

'Yes,' I said. 'You could. But you won't.'

'Really? Are you sure about that?'

'No,' I admitted. 'You've never been . . . predictable, Molly. But I'm not your enemy any more. I'm not Drood, I'm rogue. That changes everything.'

'Maybe,' said Molly. 'Convince me, Edwin. I can always kill you later, if I get bored.'

I relaxed a little, and buttoned up my shirt again. Give me an inch, and I can talk anyone into anything. 'You've tried to kill me often enough in the past,' I said. 'Remember the time you blew up the whole Bradbury Building, just to get me? The look on your face when I walked unharmed out of the ruins! I thought you were going to pop an artery.'

Molly nodded, smiling. 'Do you remember the time you stuck

me through the chest with three foot of enchanted steel? Only to discover that like all good magicians, I keep my heart safe and secure somewhere else? I thought you were going to have a fit.'

'We've lived, haven't we?' I said dryly, and she laughed briefly. 'We can work together,' I said. 'We want the same things in this; and who else has shared as much history as we have?'

'That makes sense,' said Molly. 'In a warped kind of way. Who knows us better than our enemies? Though I have to say the Shaman Bond thing came as a bit of a surprise.' She cocked her head on one side, like a bird, considering me. 'Why did you come to me as Shaman? You could have burst in here in your damned armour, safe from all my magics, smashed through my defences and demanded I help you.'

'No, I couldn't,' I said. 'You'd have told me to go to Hell.'

'True, very true. You do know me, Edwin.'

'Please; call me Eddie. And besides, I wanted to make a point. That I would share my secrets with you if you would share yours with me. You know things, Molly, things few other people know; things you're not supposed to know. And there are things I need to know about my family. Things that have been withheld from me.' I looked around. 'And I really would like to know how you got a forest inside your house.'

'Because I am the wild witch! I am the laughter in the woods, the promise of the night, the delight of the soul and the dazzle of the senses. And because I hired a really good interior decorator. You never did appreciate me, Edwin.'

'Eddie, please.'

'Yes . . . You look like an Eddie. Now; if answers are truly what you want, look into my scrying pool. But don't blame me if the truth you learn is a truth you'd rather not know.'

Molly sat down beside her pool again, gathering her long white gown around her, and I crouched cautiously beside her. The whole thing was a scrying pool? It had to be twenty feet across, easy, which would make it hellishly powerful. Molly slapped the flat of her left hand on to the surface of the waters, and the ripples spread out, pushing the lily pads to the borders of the pond. The crystal-clear water shimmered, and then blazed bright as the sun, dazzling my eyes, before clearing abruptly to show me a vision of a man and a woman, in two different rooms, talking on the phone. I leaned forward as I recognised them. The man was the British Prime Minister, the woman was Martha Drood.

'You can see into The Hall?' I said, my voice hardly more than a breath. 'That's not supposed to be possible!'

'It's all right,' said Molly. 'They can't see or hear us. But listen now, and pay attention. You need to hear this.'

'Look, this is your mess!' the Prime Minister was saying angrily. 'Drood agents, in full armour, fighting each other in full view of the public? Thank God the media didn't catch it. Do you even realise what it's going to take to put this right? The rebuilding, the witness intimidation programme, the hush money? All because you couldn't take care of your own dirty work!'

'Stop whining,' said Martha, her voice cold as a slap in the face. 'Damage limitations is one of the few things you're actually good at. Probably because you've had so much experience at it. You will do everything you have to, and you'll do it efficiently and well and very quickly, or I'll have you killed and see if your replacement learns anything from the experience. Remember your place, Prime Minister. I got you elected so you could serve the family's interests, just like your predecessors. The family knows best. Always.'

'All right! All right!' the Prime Minister said defensively. 'I'm on top of this, Matriarch. You don't have anything to worry about.'

'No, I don't,' said Martha. 'But you do.'

Molly took her hand off the water, and the vision disappeared. I looked numbly at Molly. 'How could she speak to him like that? How could he grovel to her? She wouldn't really have hurt him. We don't do things that way. The family serves the Powers That Be; we don't interfere. That's always been our duty and our responsibility. To preserve . . .'

'Poor Eddie,' said Molly. 'You only wanted to know the truth because you didn't know how much it would hurt. Well here it is, so brace yourself. The family isn't what you think it is; and it never was. Only those Droods at the very top of the family tree know what the family is really for. You protect the world, yes, but not for the people . . . for the Establishment. The Droods work to maintain the status quo, keeping everyone calm and controlled, and the people in their proper place. Under the thumbs of those in authority. Droods aren't the world's bodyguards, and never have been, You're enforcers. Bully boys. Hammering down any nail that dares to stick its head above the rest.

'And after centuries of establishing power and control, along with the odd assassination of those in power who wouldn't or couldn't learn to get along, even those who make up the official Establishment have learned to be afraid of your family. Politicians all across the world are only allowed to hold power as long as they answer to Drood authority. Your family, Eddie, are the secret rulers of the world.'

I sat there, shocked into silence. My whole world had just been kicked away from under my feet. Again. I wanted to believe she was lying, but I couldn't. It made too much sense. Too many things I'd seen and heard that I wasn't supposed to, so many hints and whispers on the scene, so many little things that had never added up ... till now. There is a reason why things are the way they are; but it's not a very nice one.

I think I might have swayed, because Molly tossed a handful of icy pond water into my face. 'Don't you dare flake out on me, Eddie! Not when I'm getting to the interesting bit.'

'My family runs the world,' I said numbly, cold water dripping unheeded from my face. 'And I never knew. How could I have been so blind?'

'It's not all bad news,' said Molly. 'There is a Resistance. And I'm part of it.'

I looked at her. 'You? I thought you always said you refused to belong to any group that would accept the likes of you as a member. Especially after what happened last time, with the Arcadia Project. As if that whole plague of frogs thing wasn't bad enough, you ended up pulling that Klan sorcerer's intestines out through his nostrils.'

'He annoyed me,' said Molly. 'And anyway, I work with the Resistance, not for them, as and when it suits me.'

I considered that, not liking the taste. One of the Drood family's greatest fears has always been that another organisation might arise to work against it. An anti-family, as it were. There had been several attempts, down the centuries, but the various bad guys had never been able to find enough things in common to hold them together. They always ended up arguing over ends and means, and matters of

141

precedence, and who exactly was going to be in charge. This led to factions and fighting, and it always ended in tears. Though admittedly it didn't usually involve intestines and nostrils.

'The new cabal is called Manifest Destiny,' said Molly, a little grandly, after it became clear I had nothing to say for the moment. 'They, we, want Humanity to be free from all outside control; by the Droods or anyone else. Free to make its own destiny. The leaders of the cabal have brought together powers from across the whole spectrum of opposition: the Loathly Ones, the Cult of the Crimson Altar, the Dream Meme, Vril Power Inc.; even the Lurkers on the Threshold.'

'Ah,' I said. 'The usual unusual suspects.'

'Well, yes; plus a whole army of powerful and committed fellow travellers. Like me. More than you ever dreamed possible; determined to break the Droods' stranglehold on Humanity, once and for all. Not to gain power for themselves, but to set Humanity free. That's what makes this cabal so different; for the first time it's not about us.'

'This ... cabal,' I said. 'Were they behind recent attacks on my family home?'

Molly shrugged. 'I don't get involved in day-to-day decisions. I told you; I only work with them when I feel like it, on matters of mutual interest.'

'So I suppose you don't know the identity of the traitor in my family, either? Or why I was declared rogue?'

'I know there is a traitor. That's old knowledge. And if it matters, word is he or she approached Manifest Destiny, not the other way round.' She looked at me coolly, almost compassionately. 'Poor little Drood; they've taken away your innocence, and now you have to think for yourself. I don't know why your family threw you to the wolves, Eddie; but I know a few people who might. Why don't you come with me and meet some of my friends and associates? See what they're really like, when you and they aren't busy trying to kill each other. Not all of those condemned by your family are one hundred per cent dyed-in-the-wool bad guys. Even monsters aren't monsters all the time, you know.'

I nodded, too numb to muster any arguments. I wasn't up to speed yet. There was a great hole in my gut where my family used

142

to be, and I hadn't figured out what to fill it with. Molly helped me to my feet, and then let go of my arm immediately. She still wasn't used to being this close to me. She turned abruptly, and headed off deeper into the forest. I hurried after her. We walked together, maintaining a comfortable distance, for quite some time. Wherever this forest was, it wasn't inside her house. The front door must have been spelled to transport me straight here, wherever 'here' was.

I'd just about worked this out when we came to another door, standing on its own, upright and unsupported. Molly stood before it, muttering Words under her breath. I wondered where this door would lead; what charming underworld dive Molly wanted to show me. Café Night, perhaps, where vampires flocked together to feast on willing victims. It started out as a fashionable salon, but of late had lapsed into an S&M parlour. Vampires added whole new shades of meaning to the phrase 'tops and bottoms'. It might be the Black Magicians' Circle, which once upon a time was the place to be, if you worshipped dark forces and could boast your very own demonic familiar. These days it was more of a self-help and support group. The Order of the Beyond was still going strong in marvellous new high-tech premises down on Grafton Way, where people offered themselves as temporary hosts to outer-dimensional beings in return for forbidden and outré knowledge. Of course, conversations in that place did tend towards the seriously weird . . . Molly pushed the door open and stepped through, and I hurried in after her. And then I stopped abruptly, and looked around me.

'Wait a minute! This . . . this is the Wulfshead Club!'

And it was. As big and bold and brassy and hellishly noisy as it always was. Molly looked at me pityingly.

'Of course. Where else? The Wulfshead has always been the hottest spot on the scene. Everyone comes here, good and bad and in between. You never noticed the bad guys because you always mix with your own crowd, and we all mix with ours. That's what makes the Club's truce workable. Come on; come and meet some of my friends. Looks like we have an interesting crowd in tonight.'

I was still dazed, so she grabbed me by the arm and dragged me through the crowd in the direction of the bar. I let her. I felt I could use a whole bunch of very large drinks. Several people nodded to Shaman Bond, and several more nodded to Molly Metcalf. Some of them looked quite surprised and not a little intrigued at seeing the two of us so openly together, but no one said anything. The Wulf-shead crowd understands the need for discretion, and the occasional blind eye. Molly and I ended up at one end of the bar, where the professionally uninterested bartender served us drinks. I had a very large brandy, Molly a southern comfort, and I ended up paying for both. She gestured for certain personages to come and join her, and they drifted warily over.

Subway Sue I already knew. She wandered unseen among passengers using the Underground trains, quietly leeching off a little luck from everyone she brushed up against. Which is why so many people miss their trains, or end up on the wrong platform. To look at her, you'd think she was only one step up from homeless, buried under layers of charity clothes, but that was so no one would notice her. There was always someone willing to pay her good money for the stolen luck she hoarded. On the quiet, Subway Sue lived very well.

Girl Flower was an ancient Welsh elemental, made up of rose petals and owls' claws long and long ago, by an ancient travelling sorcerer who might or might not have been Merlin. The story changed every time she told it. She looked human enough, most of the time. Treat her right, and she'd be soft as rose petals for you. Mistreat or wrong her, and the owls' claws would come out. And then the best you could hope for was when the authorities finally found what was left of you, your relatives would be able to find an undertaker who was really into jigsaw puzzles. Girl Flower had high standards, which was why she was always so very disappointed in men. But she remained optimistic, and the police kept fishing body parts out of the Thames. Girl Flower dressed in bright pastel colours, in gypsy styles, and wore so many bracelets they clattered deafeningly every time she gestured. She'd had one glass of champagne and was already more than a bit tipsy.

Digger Browne was a short, stocky personage in an old-fashioned wrap-around coat with mud stains on the sleeves. He wore heavy woollen gloves when he was out in public to hide his long horny fingernails, made for digging and tearing. He also wore a wide-brimmed hat that hid most of his face in shadow. Digger was a ghoul, and smelt strongly of carrion and recently disturbed earth.

'I'm just a part of nature,' he said easily. 'I take out the trash, clean up the garbage, and generally keep the world tidy. So I enjoy my work; is that a sin? Not everyone has a taste for the kind of work I do, but it has to be done. Someone's got to eat all those bodies. Remember the undertakers' strike, back in the seventies? People couldn't do enough for me then . . .'

And finally, there was Mr Stab. I didn't need to be introduced to him. Everyone knew Mr Stab, if only by reputation; the notorious uncaught serial killer of old London Town. He'd operated under many names, down the long years, and I don't think even he knew for sure exactly how many people he'd murdered since he started out with five unfortunate whores in the East End in 1888. He gained something, some power, from what he did then. A ceremony of blood, he called it, a celebration of slaughter. And now he goes on and on and no one can stop him. He still dressed in the formal dark clothes of his time, when he was just being himself at the Wulfshead, right down to the opera cloak and top hat.

Most of these people knew or at least knew of Shaman Bond, and it came as quite a shock to them when Molly introduced me as Edwin Drood. Subway Sue looked around for the nearest exit, Digger Browne chewed nervously on his finger snack, and Girl Flower giggled at me owlishly over her glass. Mr Stab smiled slowly, showing large blocky teeth stained brown with age.

'So you're Edwin Drood. The man behind the mask. You probably have a body count nearly equal to mine.'

'I kill to put an end to suffering,' I said. 'Not to celebrate it.'

'I serve a purpose, as you do.'

'Don't you dare try to justify yourself to me!' I said, and my voice was cold enough that everyone except Mr Stab fell back a step.

'Why not?' said Mr Stab. 'I am a part of the natural order, just like Mr Browne here. I cull the herd, thin out the weak and helpless, improve the stock. Someone has to do it, if the herd is to stay healthy.'

'You do it because you enjoy it!'

'That too.'

I started to subvocalise the Words that would call up my armour. The only reason I hadn't killed Mr Stab before this was because I'd never known where to look for him. I'd seen some of his victims, or what he'd left of them, and that was enough for me. Molly guessed what I was about to do, grabbed me by the arm and pulled me around to glare right into my face.

'Don't you dare embarrass me in front of my friends!'

'This is a friend? Mr Stab? Do you know how many women like you he's killed?'

'But he's never harmed me, or any of my friends, and he has been there for me when I needed him. Not even monsters are monsters all the time, remember? I've killed, in my time, for what seemed like good reasons, and so have you. You really think the world sees you as any different from him? How many grieving families have you left in your bloody wake, Edwin Drood?'

I took a long, slow breath, and forced myself into a kind of calm. I'd come here looking for answers, and the sort I needed could only be freely given. I nodded jerkily to Molly, and she let go of my arm. We turned back to face the others.

'There's a traitor in my family,' I said stiffly. 'I would be grateful for any information you could give me.'

'How grateful?' said Subway Sue. 'Are we talking serious money?'

'If I had serious money, do you really think I'd be here talking to you?' I said, a bit ungraciously. 'I'm rogue, outcast, outlaw. All I have is what I stand up in.'

'I'm sure we could make some kind of deal,' said Girl Flower, in her breathy voice, batting her eyelashes at me; and then spoiled the mood by giggling.

'There is a traitor at the heart of the Droods,' said Digger Browne. 'That's common knowledge. But I don't think anyone knows who.'

'Lots have people have put forward names,' said Mr Stab. 'But it's all guesswork. Lots of people thought it might be you, Edwin. A field agent operating on his own, far from Drood central control, the only Drood ever to run away from home and not be hunted down like a dog by his family. The only reason everyone didn't think it was you was because that would have been too obvious.'

'And none of you knows why I was made rogue?' I said.

'I've done some work for your family on occasion,' said Digger. 'I'd have sworn you were depressingly squeaky clean, like most of your family. I mean, yes, you run the world and everything, but ...'

'I too have done work for the Droods,' said Mr Stab. He smiled crookedly at me. 'Pretty much everyone here has, at one time or another. It's the Droods' world; we just live in it.'

'We would never deal with filth like you,' I said, but my heart wasn't in it. I didn't know what my family was capable of any more.

'There are many like us,' Molly said carefully. 'Allowed to operate as long as we don't rock the boat too much. As long as we pay tithes, or perform the occasional service for them. Dirty jobs, off-the-book cases; the kind you regular field agents aren't suited for. The kind you were never supposed to know about, because it might stain your precious honour. We've all done the Droods' dirty work. That's why we're all so ready to bring them down.'

My head was spinning. I felt sick. Could I really have spent my whole life supporting a lie? Was there really anything left to me now, except to bring down my own family?

CHAPTER TWELVE

Down, down, deeper and down

There are times in every man's life when the woman you've taken up with suddenly disappears on business of her own, and you're left to make polite conversation with her friends. Personally, I'd rather stick needles in my eyes, but it's one of those things you just have to do. Molly Metcalf produced a one-time-only mobile phone and headed for the women's toilet, so she could reach her contact in Manifest Destiny without being glared at by everyone else in the Club. I approved of her sense of caution. One-time-only phones are phones you can only use once, and then immediately discard and destroy. A call that can't be tapped and a phone that can't be traced. It was good to know Manifest Destiny operated in a professional way. But it did mean I was left alone with Molly's friends, most of whom I would have tried to kill on sight only a few days before. And vice versa, quite probably. So we stood and smiled awkwardly at each other, while the only thing we had in common disappeared into the Ladies'.

'So,' I said finally to the ghoul, Digger Browne, as the least obviously disquieting of the bunch, 'you say you've done work for my family, on occasion?'

He shrugged easily. 'I help out, when called upon to do so. The price of existence, in these hard times. My clan's status is not what it was in the old days, when we had an honourable place in society, cleaning up the mess left behind by man's many battles ... These days, your family only ever call us in to devour those bodies deemed too costly or too dangerous to otherwise dispose of. You know: the kind that might rise again, or regenerate, or melt down into hazardous waste. There's not much a ghoul can't digest. Though admittedly our toilets have to be rather more thorough than most ...'

I raised a hand. 'I think we're rapidly approaching the point of too much information. How do you feel about the Droods? Or this new Resistance group, Manifest Destiny?'

Digger shrugged again. 'The names change, faces come and go, but there's always someone in charge. I've yet to see any hard evidence that Manifest Destiny would be any kinder or more just than the Droods ... But it doesn't really matter to me. Whoever's running things, there will always be work for me and my kind.'

I turned, somewhat reluctantly, to Mr Stab. He was drinking a Perrier water with his little finger crooked, every inch the calm and cultured gentleman. I once helped fish a victim of his out of the Thames, down by Wapping. She'd been gutted, cut open from crotch to throat and all her internal organs removed. He'd done other things to her too, before he finally killed her. The only reason I wasn't tearing him to pieces right now was because it might upset Molly, and I needed her on my side. For now.

'I hear you got shot with an arrow,' he said calmly. 'Right through your celebrated armour.'

'News does travel fast, doesn't it?' I said, careful neither to confirm nor deny. 'But I doubt you've got anything that could touch me.'

'You might be surprised,' said Mr Stab. 'But you really should try and relax, Edwin. You're in no danger from me, as long as you're with Molly. Dear girl. She's an old friend, and I'd hate to upset her.'

'You said you'd done some work for my family,' I said. 'What did you do for the Droods?'

'Sometimes people can't simply be killed,' Mr Stab said smoothly. 'Sometimes it's necessary for them to disappear completely. No trace of what was done to them, or why. No body, no clues, just a gap in the world where someone important used to be. Someone who thought no one could touch them. I've always been able to make people disappear. The world only gets to see a small fraction of my many victims. The ones I want seen, to keep my myth alive ... to maintain my reputation. Vanity, vanity, all is vanity; but my legend is all I have left, and I will not have it tarnished or diminished by my many inferior imitators.'

'How did you get to meet Molly?' I said.

'She tried very hard to kill me,' said Mr Stab, smiling fondly at the memory. 'She was part of a coven in those days, still learning her trade, when I found it necessary to kill one of her witchy friends. After we'd exhausted ourselves trying to kill each other, we fell to talking, and discovered we had more in common than we thought. Certain people we detested, and with good reason. People of power and influence that we couldn't hope to reach on our own, but together . . . Ah, those were happy times, teaching her the ways of slaughter.'

'But did she ever forgive you, for killing her friend?' I said.

'No; but she's a practical soul. She knows that sometimes you have to go along, to get along. I like to think we're friends now. You can't do the things we did, and not grow . . . close. And in the whole of London, she is perhaps the only woman I have no desire to kill. I still remember her friend, whose death brought us together. Her name was Dorothy. A dainty little thing, and she screamed so prettily under my blade . . . Don't, Edwin. Don't even think about calling up your armour. You can't kill me. No one can. That's part of what I bought with what I did in Whitechapel, all those years ago.'

'I'll find a way,' I said. 'If I have to.'

Girl Flower moved quickly in to put a gentle hand on my sleeve. 'Boys, boys . . . lighten up, darlings. We're all friends here, and we are very definitely not at home to Mr Grumpy.' She rubbed her shoulder up against Mr Stab, like an affectionate cat, and he nodded briefly to her before giving his attention to his Perrier water. Girl Flower batted her overlong eyelashes at me, and pouted with her dark, lush mouth. 'Why do men always have to talk about such awful things? Life contains much that is good, and much that is bad, and there's nothing we can do that will change it. So why not choose to celebrate the wonderful things in life? Like me! I am the lovely Girl Flower, created so that men might have the pleasure of adoring me! If they know what's good for them . . . Honestly, darlings, if everyone had sex a lot more often, the world would be a far happier place.' She beamed at me. 'Would you like to undo the buttons on my blouse and play with my boobies, Edwin?'

'You know you shouldn't drink, Flower,' Subway Sue said kindly. 'It goes straight to your petals.' She considered me thoughtfully. 'I have to say, Edwin, you're a more interesting sort than most of the specimens Molly drags in here. For such an intelligent woman, she has remarkably bad taste in men. I can't help thinking the two are probably connected. You should choose men with your heart, not your head. Not that I've had much luck with either approach. Men! If there was an alternative that didn't involve ending up living alone with too many cats, I'd sign up tomorrow.'

There didn't seem any obvious answer to that, so I changed the subject. 'Would I be right in thinking you've also done work for my family?'

'Certainly not!' Subway Sue drew herself up proudly, bristling at the very thought. 'I have my principles, you know.'

Perhaps fortunately, Molly chose that moment to come back and rejoin us, and I turned to her with a certain amount of relief. I've never been very good at talking to a woman's friends. 'Did you get through? Will they see me?'

Molly nodded curtly. 'I had a lot of trouble getting through to anyone that mattered, but once I made it clear I could deliver the new rogue Drood, they couldn't wait for me to bring you in. We can go right now, if you want. The head man himself is waiting to greet you with open arms. They'll offer you anything you want, for the inside secrets of your family and a chance to examine your armour in their laboratories.'

'I don't know that I'm ready to commit myself to their cause, just yet,' I said carefully.

Molly snorted loudly. 'I should think not, in your position. This is a meet and greet, a chance for you and the head man to feel each other out, see if you can work together. But do yourself a favour, Drood; drive a hard bargain. Take them for everything they've got. Because once you've given up your secrets, you can't sell them again.'

'There's more to me than secrets,' I said.

'Good bargaining position,' said Molly.

'If you're going to meet the actual leader of Manifest Destiny, I think I might come along too,' Mr Stab said suddenly. 'Although I have performed some small services for them in the past, in return for very generous recompense, I have to say I'm a trifle irritated that they have never tried to recruit me. I would like to ask them why.'

'If he's going, I'm going too,' said Girl Flower, clapping her soft little hands together delightedly. 'I never get to go anywhere.'

I started to object, but Molly cut me off quickly. 'Oh let them, or they'll both sulk. Besides, it's always easier to negotiate when you've got some serious back-up.'

She had a point. I looked inquiringly at Digger Browne, but he shook his head. 'I'm afraid I have a previous engagement. My family and I are having an old friend for dinner.'

'And you couldn't get me one inch closer to Manifest Destiny if you used a whip and a chair,' Subway Sue said very firmly. 'I don't trust any of these big organisations. There's never any room in them for the private entrepreneur. And anyway, I've heard things about Manifest Destiny ... Yes, yes, I know Molly; you won't hear a word said against them. But I've been around a lot longer than you, and there are those who'll talk to me that won't talk to you. I can't help feeling there's a lot more to Manifest Destiny than bringing down the Droods.' She looked at me with cold, piercing eyes. 'Ask them all the awkward questions, Drood. Make them tell you everything before you give them your trust.'

She turned her back on us, and stalked out of the Wulfshead. Digger Browne shook hands politely with all of us, and followed her out. And Molly Metcalf, Girl Flower, Mr Stab and I went off to see Manifest Destiny. One witch of the wild woods, one elemental of rose petals and owls' claws, one legendary serial killer, and one very confused ex-agent for the good.

Some days you just shouldn't get up in the morning.

We left the Wulfshead Club by a back door I didn't recognise, and ended up in a dimly-lit alley off Denmark Street, deep in the dark heart of Soho. It was late evening now, with the twilight people spilling out on to the streets, rubbing the day's sleep from their eyes. Girding up their weary loins to prey on the sheep, one more time. None of them paid us any attention. We very obviously weren't sheep. Molly strode out into the middle of the empty road and looked around her, scowling.

'What are you looking for?' I said patiently. 'You won't find a taxi in this area, not at this time of night.'

She looked back at me, and sighed heavily. 'All right; lecture mode. Pay attention, Drood, and you might learn something useful. Once upon a time, way back during the most paranoid days of the Cold War, the establishment of that time arranged for the construction of a huge network of bunkers and tunnels deep under the streets of London. A last desperate bolt-hole to which important personages could retreat in the event of a nuclear strike. Presumably so they could continue to rule the radioactive ruins above. I love a government that thinks ahead, don't you? Anyway, this very large bolt-hole was fully equipped and supplied, and very safe and secure. But the Cold War ended, officially, and the network of bunkers and tunnels was declared redundant. Abandoned and left to rot, guarded by a few old Cold Warriors who were also pretty much redundant.

'Manifest Destiny occupies the network now, with, it is said, the winking acknowledgement of the current Powers That Be. Unfortunately, and this is the part you're really going to hate, Edwin, the only way to access this network is via the city sewers. According to my contact, there's a manhole somewhere around here that will let us into the system, so stop standing around like a spare dick at a wedding, and help me find it.'

As it turned out, the manhole was right behind her. None of us said anything. She scowled down at the heavy steel cover, snapped her fingers at it, and the cover shot up into the air as though someone had goosed it. The cover hovered above us in mid air, while we all gathered round the hole and peered dubiously down into it. Molly generated a witchfire, a shimmering silver glow around her left hand, but even that magical light could only show us a series of metal rungs, leading down into the darkness. The smell coming out was pretty ripe, though. We looked at each other, and finally Molly sighed heavily and led the way down into the sewers.

Once we were inside, the manhole cover dropped back into place, sealing us in.

Underground, the smell hit me like a fist in the face. Shocked tears ran down my cheeks as I struggled to breathe only through my mouth. It didn't help. The ladder deposited us in a long dark tunnel with curving walls and an uncomfortably low ceiling. Molly boosted her witchlight, pushing back the dark to give us a better view. The brick walls were slick with damp and slime and filth, and dark, churning waters surged through a deep central channel, thick with refuse and unpleasantly familiar things floating in it. The walkway was only wide enough to accommodate two of us at a time, and the old stone beneath our feet was encrusted with foul matter. It was enough to make you vow never to use a toilet ever again. Girl Flower and Mr Stab appeared entirely unmoved, but Molly was almost gagging from the stench. Two rats floated past us, crouched together on a particularly large … object. That was enough. I started to armour up, to protect myself from plague, but Molly whirled angrily on me.

'Don't!' she said, in a harsh whisper. 'We don't want to attract attention.'

'Attention from whom?' I said, not unreasonably. 'Who else would be dumb enough to come down into the sewers at this time of night?'

'She has a point,' said Girl Flower, glancing nervously about her. 'You do hear stories … Of things that have chosen to live down here, away from the light and the scrutiny of Man. Awful, unpleasant things, darling. Not the sort of people you want to meet.'

'Right,' said Molly. 'I've talked to people who work down here, and they all have stories to share that the civilised world doesn't want to listen to. Not everything that gets flushed is gone for ever. There are things that have learned to thrive in conditions like this, and they're always hungry. Strange fruit grown from rotten branches, monsters grown out of discarded experiments, and some blighted shapes that might have been human, long and long ago. I'll generate a low-level field to protect us from … contamination, but any stronger magic might call them to us.'

'Maybe you should lose the witchlight, then,' said Mr Stab. 'I'm almost sure I have a light about me somewhere …'

'No!' Molly said quickly. 'No flames, or anything that might generate a spark. Methane gas has a tendency to build up in pockets, and you can't detect it through the general nasty ambience. Until it's too late.'

'In the old days,' Mr Stab said conversationally, 'the workers used to bring down canaries in cages. And when the canaries started to smoulder, they knew they were in trouble.'

There was a pause, and then Molly said, 'You're really not helping, you know.'

'Poor little birdies,' said Girl Flower.

Molly conjured up her protective field, incorporating a simple directional spell that manifested as a glowing arrow floating on the air before us. We started off after it, slipping and sliding on the treacherous surface of the walkway. Our shadows leapt around us in the witchlight, huge and menacing. Sudden noises echoed away through the dark tunnels, lingering on long after they should have died away. I kept a watchful eye on every shadowed tunnel we passed, and sometimes I thought I saw twisted, distorted shapes lurching away in the uncertain gloom ahead; but nothing ventured out into the witchlight to confront us.

The smell wasn't getting any easier to take.

There were rats everywhere, scuttling and scurrying, and pausing now and then to bare their yellow teeth at us. Many were bigger by far than any rat had a right to be, and they didn't seem nearly scared enough of us to suit me. I've got a bit of a thing about rats. Most just watched us pass from their holes and lairs, dark beady eyes gleaming malevolently. Molly amused herself by pointing her finger at those who got too close, whereupon they immediately exploded wetly in all directions at once. Girl Flower squeaked loudly every time this happened, and finally stopped to pick up most of a dead rat and hold it close to her bosom.

'Poor little ratty.'

'Oh ick,' said Molly.

'I am flowers, darling,' Girl Flower said stubbornly. 'And all dead things are compost to my pretty petals.'

She slipped the rat carcass inside the front of her dress, and it immediately disappeared. Molly looked at me. 'Think about that, the next time she invites you to unbutton her blouse.'

I looked determinedly in another direction. 'If she starts coughing up owl pellets, she's going back.'

We moved on, into the darkness. Tunnel led to tunnel, twisting and turning deep under London's streets. Others had been here before us, leaving their marks upon the brick walls. Some were hopeful, some were despairing messages to loved ones they never hoped to see again. There were arrows, pointing in varying directions, and even the occasional crude map scratched into the brick. Masonic symbols, odd phrases in old forgotten languages ... I half expected to find Arne Saknussen's initials. Or Cave Carson's. We pressed on, following Molly's glowing arrow. Her protective field kept the filth at bay, even when we occasionally had to wade through the revolting waters to get to another tunnel. Pity it couldn't do anything about the smell.

We stopped abruptly, as Mr Stab broke away from us to study a particular section of brick wall close up. I moved in beside him for a look, but it seemed no different from any other wall we'd passed. The curving surface ran with damp, as though sweating in the uncomfortable heat, and the original colour of the brick was lost under layers of accumulated filth and clumps of bulging white fungus. Mr Stab ran his fingers caressingly over the surface, ignoring the thick residue that appeared on his expensively tailored gloves. My first thought was that it seemed there were definite limits to Molly's protective field, and not to touch *anything* with my hands, but I was quickly distracted by the look on Mr Stab's face. He was smiling, and it wasn't a very nice smile.

'I remember this place,' he said, and something in his soft voice raised the hackles on the back of my neck. 'It's been a long time since I was down here. I think they were still building this section then ... I used to come here all the time, to get away from the bustle and noise of Humanity ... Yes, I remember this place.'

He pressed a particular brick, and it sank inwards with a loud click. Mr Stab put all his weight against the wall, and a large section swung slowly inwards on concealed hinges. Only darkness lay beyond, and silence. Mr Stab gestured sharply for Molly to come forward, and she thrust her illuminated hand into the new opening. We all crowded round, to see what was to be seen, but Mr Stab couldn't wait. He took Molly by the shoulder and urged her inside. They moved forward into the gloom, and Girl Flower and I followed close behind.

There was a room behind the brick wall, a very secret room. I stood still, just inside the entrance, held there by what I saw. I felt appalled, and sickened, and terribly angry. My first thought was that it looked like a ghastly doll's house. The room had been fitted out as an old Victorian parlour. Heavy furniture, thick carpeting, stiff-backed chairs on either side of a long dining table, complete with heavy tablecloth, silver settings and candlesticks. Even framed portraits on the walls.

Dead women sat in the chairs, on either side of the long table, dressed in the fashions of widely varying times, all of the bodies in varying stages of decay. The enclosed setting had preserved them to some degree, but that only added to the horror. The dead women stared across the table at each other. Some had eyes, some did not. Some had faces, some did not. They all carried their death wounds openly, and there were so many of them ... Some had the front of their dresses cut open, revealing bodies that had been hollowed out. A few held tea cups in their clawed hands, as though they were attending some hideous tea party.

'Hi honey,' said Mr Stab. 'I'm home.'

Molly looked back at me. 'I never knew about this, Eddie, I swear.'

I stepped forward, to stand between her and Mr Stab. 'This is sick! Give me one good reason why I shouldn't kill you right now!'

'How many have you killed down the years, young Drood?' said Mr Stab, not even looking at me. He moved slowly down the line of corpses, smiling slightly, trailing his fingers above the bowed heads, not quite touching them. 'Could a room this size contain all those you've cut down? I know; you were only obeying orders. You did what you did out of cold duty; at least I'm honest enough to enjoy what I do.' He leaned over one grey shoulder to peer into a desiccated face. 'I keep stashes of my victims all over London. In my secret hidden places, where no one will ever find them. I like to visit them, and ... play with them. I enjoy the ambience, and the smell ... Like coming home.'

I looked at Molly. Her face was taut and strained, but the illuminated hand she held aloft was still steady. 'What was that you said?' I murmured. 'About monsters not being monsters all the time?'

'I never knew,' she said. 'Never even suspected ...'

'You know nothing about me,' said Mr Stab.

He stood at the far end of the table, tall and proud like a typical Victorian patriarch, his chin held high and his eyes alight with a terrible regard. 'You know nothing about what drives me to do the things I do. Once women fascinated me, and then they horrified me. Teasers, liars, betrayers. I took a proud vengeance upon them, hurting them as I had been hurt, and gained much in return ... But now the only intimacy I can ever know is with my victims. That moment when their eyes meet mine, that little sigh as the blade penetrates, is all I have, now. When I was just beginning, when everyone called me Jack, I had no way of knowing that the immortality I bought would be as an immortal killing machine. Driven to kill and kill, and never know peace or rest. I go on and on, in a world that makes less and less sense to me, and all that is left to me is to take what pleasure I can from my endless work.'

'You can't kill him, Eddie,' Molly said quietly. 'You can't. Not even your armour could undo what he did to himself.'

'What about your magic?' I said.

'Don't ask me that, Eddie. He has been my friend. He has done . . . good things, because I asked him to.'

'Enough to make up for this? And all the other stashes we don't know about?'

'Don't ask me that. Not here.'

Girl Flower floated prettily round the room, bending over withered shoulders to stare into corrupt faces, humming a happy song to herself. 'You shouldn't let this get to you, darlings. All living things have their roots in dead things. It's the way of the world.' She slipped a hand inside her dress, frowned prettily for a moment, and when she brought her hand out again it was piled high with seeds. She walked up and down both sides of the long table, dropping a few seeds into the gaping mouths and empty eye sockets of every corpse. 'Let new life bloom,' she said. 'It's nature's way.'

Mr Stab looked at her, and Girl Flower smiled happily back at him, entirely unafraid. And the man who was once called Jack by a whole horrified city nodded slowly.

'Perhaps I'll come back, in some future time,' he said. 'To see what strange new life has blossomed here.'

I didn't kill him. As an agent in the field, you learn that sometimes you have to settle for little victories.

Mr Stab sealed up his private place, and we moved on through the sewers until finally we came to Manifest Destiny's hidden domain, its underground kingdom. I'd come a long way in search of a credible Resistance to my family's newly exposed tyranny, and it had better not disappoint me. I needed it to be something I could depend on, in this treacherously changing world. I needed it to be a weapon I could throw at the family who'd betrayed me. The entrance point was a huge circular portal of solid steel, set flush with the old brick wall. Four very large and muscular men stood before the portal, in stark black uniforms with discreet silver piping, covering us with heavy automatic weapons as we approached.

'Cold iron,' said Molly, indicating the portal. 'Keeps magic out. They're very security conscious.'

Mr Stab sniffed loudly. 'It would take more than that to keep me out, if I wanted in.'

'Oh, get over your bad self,' said Girl Flower, and Mr Stab surprised us with a brief bark of laughter.

I armoured up as we approached the armed guards. I wasn't ready yet to trust Manifest Destiny with the secret of my Shaman Bond identity. The guards were visibly impressed at the sight of my armour, gleaming golden in the gloom, and they quickly got on their radios to check for instructions from someone higher up. Whatever they heard through their earpieces clearly impressed them even more, and then they couldn't open the portal fast enough for me. I strode up to them as though I expected such treatment as my right, and they fell back, raising their weapons in salute. All except for one, still blocking the way but not looking especially happy about it.

He smiled nervously at my featureless golden mask, his eyes darting back and forth. The lack of eyes on the mask really throws people. The guard swallowed hard. 'Your pardon, sir, sir Drood, but . . . We have orders to admit you, and the witch Molly Metcalf, but no one said anything about your . . . companions. Perhaps they could wait here, while you . . .'

'No,' I said. 'I don't think so. This is Girl Flower and Mr Stab. Upset them at your peril.'

'Get out of my way or I'll fillet you,' said Mr Stab, in his most cold and sepulchral voice. The watching guards retreated even further, one of them making small squeaking noises. The guard before us looked as though he'd like to make some noises of his own. I gestured for him to lead us in, and he nodded jerkily. Molly extinguished her witchfire, and the four of us strode into Manifest Destiny's most secret headquarters as though we were thinking of buying the place. Of course Girl Flower had to spoil the moment by giggling.

A short tunnel led into a vast chamber whose walls and high ceiling were covered entirely with gleaming steel. Presumably originally added to protect against the effects of atomic blast, but useful now to keep magic at bay. No wonder my family had never suspected their existence. You couldn't hope to scry or remote view through this much cold iron. The guard led us on, through more gleaming steel corridors and chambers, and everywhere bristled with urgent efficiency. There were banks of computers and monitor screens, maps and clocks and operations tables, and any amount of cutting-edge communications equipment. It reminded me of the Drood War Room, on a somewhat smaller scale. And everywhere there were tall and splendid men and women, in their black uniforms, sitting at work stations or crowded round tables or just striding back and forth with important messages. The men were all perfect masculine specimens, glowing with health and vitality and purpose. Perfect soldiers. The women were tall and lithe, and just as heavily armed as the men. Valkyries, warrior women. They all nodded respectfully to me as I passed. A few nodded familiarly to Molly. None of them so much as looked directly at Mr Stab or Girl Flower. I glanced across at Molly. She didn't seem very happy.

'Have you ever been here before?' I asked quietly.

'No. I was never important enough to be invited. And I have to say ... it isn't what I thought it would be. I don't like the feel of this place.'

The guide led us on and on, through endless branching corridors, escorting us deeper and deeper into this unexpected labyrinth far below the streets of London. A steel maze, with the head of Manifest Destiny at its unknown heart.

'What do you know about this man we're going to see?' I said quietly to Molly.

'Not much,' she said, just as quietly. 'His name is Truman. Never met him. Don't know anyone who has. You should feel honoured, Eddie.'

'Oh, I do,' I said. 'Really. You have no idea. How did you hook up with these people in the first place?'

'I was recruited four years ago,' said Molly. 'By Solomon Krieg.'

'Now him I have heard of,' I said. 'The Golem with the Atomic Brain, right? A Cold War attempt at combining magic and science, to produce a Cold War Super Soldier. Deadly in his time, and a legend in those secret wars the public never get to hear about; but last I heard, he'd been retired from the field.'

'He was,' Molly said. 'Over ten years ago. His old masters didn't need him any more, but he couldn't be allowed to run loose, so they sent him down here to guard the bunkers. Word is, they locked him in here and then changed all the combinations, just in case. Manifest Destiny found him when they moved in, still standing guard, and Truman took him in and gave him a new purpose. The Golem with the Atomic Brain has a new cause and a new faith, and he'd die for Truman. You can't buy loyalty like that.

'So now Solomon Krieg walks abroad in the world's hidden places, its secret haunts and clubs, recruiting people like me as allies to his new cause. He found me at the Wulfshead. He can be ... very persuasive. And there he is, right ahead, guarding his master's lair.'

Our soldier guide handed us over into Solomon Krieg's care with visible relief and not a little haste, barely managing a sketchy salute before hurrying back to his post at the entrance portal. I studied Krieg openly. A legend in his own right, the most terrible secret weapon the British Secret Service ever produced. The English Assassin, the British Bogeyman; Solomon Krieg had many such names down the years. But there was nothing romantic about the Golem with the Atomic Brain. In his own way, he was almost as disturbing as Mr Stab. A killer with no conscience, no compassion and, many said, no soul. The greatest secret agent of all, because he would do absolutely anything, and never once question his orders. He was a terror weapon from the coldest part of the Cold War, designed to scare the shit out of whoever he was up against.

It was a very cold Cold War. Everyone did terrible things, then.

Krieg was a little over six feet tall, with jet-black hair and pale, colourless skin that contrasted eerily with his black uniform. He was muscular, but not to any unusual extent. That wasn't where his strength came from. Krieg was carved from clay, made flesh with ancient magics, and then supercharged with implanted mechanisms. The best technology of his day. Across his forehead ran a long, deep scar, usually hidden by make-up in the old photos I'd seen. It looked like they'd sawed the top of his head off, popped in their amazing atomic brain, and then jammed the top back on again. It wasn't a subtle age, back then.

Standing before us, calm and collected, his pale face empty of all emotion, Krieg looked dangerous. Like a coiled snake or a crouching tiger, ready to strike out and kill at any moment, without warning. I only had to look at him, and I believed every terrible story I'd heard about him. When he finally did speak, his voice was a harsh whisper; uninflected and uncaring.

'Edwin Drood,' he said, and just hearing my name in such a cold voice was like listening to my own death warrant. 'It is right that you should come to us. Now that you're rogue. You understand what it is, to be betrayed by those you gave your life to. You must meet Mr Truman. He is a man of vision, and destiny. You can trust him.'

'Well,' I said. 'That's good to know. Can my companions come too?'

Solomon Krieg looked them over with his cold, unblinking gaze. 'If they behave themselves. You understand: if they step out of line, I may have to spank them.'

'Go right ahead,' I said. 'I'll hold your coat.'

'Come on, Solomon,' said Molly. 'You must remember me? You were the one who brought me into Manifest Destiny, four years ago. At the Wulfshead. Remember?'

'No,' said Solomon Krieg.

He led us down yet another steel corridor, round a corner and into a simple, private office. And there behind a simple desk sat the head of Manifest Destiny. Leader of the Resistance against the old and mighty power of the Droods. He sat in his swivel chair with his back to us, watching as a dozen monitor screens blazed information at him. From the way he moved his head slowly back and forth, it seemed he was taking it all in; though it was just a babble of mixed-up noise to me. He made us wait a while, to remind us who was in charge here, and then he waved one hand at the screens, and they all shut down at once. He turned slowly round to face us, while Solomon Krieg took up a place at his side. Truman had a broad, kindly face, but that wasn't what I was looking at. I'd seen some strange sights in my time, but what Truman had done to himself was truly extra-ordinary.

Long steel rods thrust out of his shaven head at regular intervals, radiating out for over a foot in length, connected by a wide steel hoop like a great metal halo. The way the skin puckered around the base of the rods suggested they'd been there for some time. The combined weight must have been appalling, but Truman showed no sign of any strain. My first thought was that he'd been in an accident, and this was some kind of head brace, but the pride in his eyes and in his bearing suggested differently.

Look at what I have done to myself, his face said. *Isn't it magnificent?*

'Yes,' he said, in a deep authoritative voice. 'It's all my own work. I drilled the holes in my skull myself, inserted the steel rods one at a time, forcing them a specific distance into my brain, following my own very careful calculations. And then all I had to do was connect them up with a reinforcing ring, and I became the first man to realise the true potential of the human brain. Oh yes, my friends, this crown of thorns serves a definite purpose.'

'Really?' I said. 'I'm so glad to hear that.'

'It arose out of my interest in acupuncture and trepanation,' he said, carrying on with his prepared speech as though he hadn't even heard me, and perhaps he hadn't. 'The rods in my brain activate the energy centres, expand my thoughts, and increase the power of my mind beyond all normal limitations. My brain is now the equal of any computer, able to store incredible amounts of information, make decisions at undreamt-of speed, and multi-task like you wouldn't believe. I hold the entire organisation of Manifest Destiny in my head, down to the smallest detail. Nothing escapes me.

'I can see all the scientific and magical forces at work in the world around me, all the things that are hidden to most mortals. I can see the invisible and intangible threats to the works of Man. And at the same time, I am invisible and invulnerable to those forces who would bring me down, if they could. No magic or science can touch me now.'

I tried to interrupt, but he was on a roll. He must have said this many times before, to new recruits, but I could tell he never got tired of it.

'I created Manifest Destiny through the force of my own will, bringing people to me and convincing them of the need for an organisation like this. People of like mind and true hearts, dedicated body and soul to the good and necessary work before us. Nothing less than freeing Humanity from the ancient yoke of the Droods. Nothing less than setting Mankind free, at last. Every day my agents walk abroad in the world, gathering new allies, sabotaging the Drood infrastructure and clawing the world back from them, inch by inch. We're not strong enough to go head to head with the Droods, not yet. But soon enough, we will be. And then ... we'll see a whole new world, with Mankind no longer held in check by Drood authority; free to make our own destiny at last.'

He leaned forward across his desk, fixing me with his powerful gaze. He was staring right into the golden mask of Drood armour, but it didn't seem to phase him at all. 'Join us, Edwin. You know now that everything your family taught you is a lie. Believe me: it is a far greater honour to free a world than to rule it. With your help, with what you know, and with the secrets of your incredible armour ... there are no limits to what we might achieve! Join us, Edwin. Be my agent. And I will give you a new cause and a new purpose. Just like Solomon here.'

He smiled briefly at the artificial man standing beside him. 'My faithful Solomon. He was a lost soul when I found him. Discarded by his creators, abandoned by those he'd served so faithfully, and for so long. A warrior without a war. I opened his eyes to a new cause, new possibilities, and now he is a part of the greatest and most important army this world has ever known. An organisation dedicated to one end ... setting Mankind free.'

'Tell me,' I said, when he finally paused for breath. 'Did you start getting these ideas before or after you began drilling holes in your head?'

He stared at me blankly for a moment, and Solomon Krieg stirred ominously. And then Truman laughed, a big, open cheerful sound, and Solomon relaxed again. Truman shook his head slowly, still chuckling.

'I know; I do tend to go on a bit once I get started, don't I? But people expect a Big Speech from the Big Man, so ... Damn, it's good to have someone here who isn't intimidated or overawed by me! Do you have any idea how hard it is for me to have a normal conversation around here? It's hard to just chat with other people by the water cooler, when everyone's ready to agree with every word I say, as though it was holy writ ... Come and join us, Edwin, if only so I can have someone around me who isn't afraid to tell me when I'm talking crap.'

He grinned at me, and I couldn't help grinning back. I liked him rather more now, even if I still didn't entirely trust him. First rule of an agent: if something seems too good to be true, it probably is too good to be true. Truman turned his smile on Molly.

'How's my little fellow traveller? Still spreading chaos among our enemies? Good, good . . . You've done well, Molly, in bringing Edwin to me. I know how badly you must have wanted to kill him. I'm not blind to the history you two have. But rest assured, having him here changes everything. The time is coming when we will take Drood Hall by force, and you have my word that you will be with us on that day, and wade in Drood blood up to your ankles.'

'You know what a girl wants to hear,' said Molly.

Truman smiled at Mr Stab and Girl Flower, if a little more distantly. 'Be welcome, my friends. There is good work here for you to take up, should you choose to accept it. If not, go freely and of your own will.' He looked back at me, his smile broadening again. 'Tell me the truth, Edwin. Now that you've seen Manifest Destiny, what do you think of it?'

'You have a very impressive organisation,' I said. 'But doesn't it strike you as just a bit . . . Aryan?'

'Hell, no,' Truman said immediately. 'That was the past. We're only interested in the future. We have military discipline here, because you can't get anything done without it. And everyone is expected to achieve their full potential. But we are all dedicated to the cause first, and ourselves second.'

'I'm still not clear on the philosophy behind your cause,' I said. 'Freedom is a marvellous concept, but a bit nebulous in practice. Overthrowing my family is one thing; but what do you propose to replace them with? What, exactly, is Manifest Destiny for?'

Truman sat back in his chair, and considered me thoughtfully. He wasn't smiling any more. He knew set speeches wouldn't work with me. Tiny sparks manifested briefly among his halo of steel rods, like passing thoughts. When he finally spoke, he chose his words carefully, directing them only at me, ignoring everyone else in his office.

'Man has got soft,' he said flatly. 'Under Drood rule, he's lost his courage and his pride. The Droods have used unfair, non-human advantages to keep us in our place, like sheep. They maintain a bland status quo, that allows alien and magical forces and creatures to run freely in what was always supposed to be our world. Man's world. The Droods' control over us must be broken, by any means necessary, so that these inhuman beings can be driven out of our world and Man can be free to forge his own destiny at last.'

'And yet,' I murmured, 'some of these beings are your allies. The Loathly Ones. The Lurkers on the Threshold. Some might call these beings ... evil. Certainly they have no love for Humanity.'

Truman spread his hands. 'I'm fighting a war, Edwin, against the greatest conspiracy this world has ever known, against a powerful and implacable enemy. I have to take my allies where I can find them. We work together, in common cause, to bring the Droods down. Afterwards ... things will be different.'

I took a step forward, and Solomon Krieg tensed. I leaned over Truman's desk, so he could see his own face reflected in my golden mask.

'If you want me on your side, tell me the truth, Truman. The whole truth. And don't hold anything back. This close, the armour will tell me if you lie, even by omission. Tell me everything; or I walk out of here, right now.'

I was bluffing about my armour being a lie-detector, but he had no way of knowing that. When my armour can do so many amazing things, what's one more? I was gambling that Truman was so desperate to get his hands on my secrets and my armour, that he'd tell me things he wouldn't tell anyone else. Truman smiled slowly, his eyes bright with the glee of someone who knows something you don't know, and can't wait to impress you with it. Once again he spoke only to me, ignoring my allies.

'Why not?' he said. 'I knew you'd be someone I could talk to. Someone I could trust with ... everything. Science came from Man's mind. It is ours. We created it and we control it. Magic ... is a wild thing, unnatural and uncontrollable, and it always has its own agenda. We make use of it when we must, but we can never trust it, or those who use it. When we come to power, science will replace magic. It's the only way Man can be truly independent. The Droods are just our first, and most important, enemy. Once they have been thrown down, we will stamp out every other form of magic, and every magical creature, and Mankind shall be free at last.'

I glanced at Molly. She was shocked silent, her face drained of colour. This was obviously news to her. I laid a golden hand gently on her arm, signalling her to hold in her anger till we'd heard everything. I could tell from Truman's face that there was more to come.

'Eliminate all undesirables?' I said. 'That sounds like a huge undertaking.'

'Oh it is,' said Truman, still smiling. 'But we've made a good start. Would you like to see?'

'Yes,' I said.

'Yes,' said Molly.

Truman chuckled. 'Why not? Let me show you the future, Molly. You'll find it ... educational. Come with me, all of you,' he said, but looking only at me. 'I've waited such a long time for someone I could share this with, Edwin. Someone who'd understand. Come with me, Edwin Drood, and see what Manifest Destiny is All about.'

Solomon Krieg wasn't happy about this, but Truman overruled him, speaking quite sharply in the end. So Krieg led us down into the levels below the bunkers, into caverns they'd carved out of the bedrock themselves, to hold Manifest Destiny's most important secret. Something hidden from the rank and file. Krieg and Truman led the way, and I followed, with Molly and the others behind me. At last we were heading into the true heart of the labyrinth, where the final truth was waiting to be revealed.

We descended down bare stone stairwells, in single file, in silence. Whatever was ahead of us, we could feel it drawing closer; and it felt very cold. Molly stuck close to me, her face a rigid mask. Truman breezed along, happily humming some tune under his breath that made sense only to him.

We finally emerged into a great stone cavern, much of it in darkness. The air was cold and damp, and the smell reminded me of the sewers. It was a sick, rotten smell, full of filth and pain and death. Even Mr Stab wrinkled his nose. None of us said anything. We knew we'd come to a bad place, where bad things happened. Except Truman, who was still humming his happy tune. He turned on all the lights at once with a grand gesture, and the cavern's contents lay illuminated below us. We were standing on a narrow walkway, halfway up the cavern wall, looking down on long rows of cells, each with its own beaten-down inhabitant. It reminded me of Dr Dec's establishment in Harley Street, except there were no cages here.

Only long rows and blocks of concrete stalls, with bare concrete floors and cold iron gates. No beds or chairs, not even straw on the concrete floors; just iron grilles to carry away some of the wastes.

'I didn't know about this,' Molly whispered to me. 'I swear I didn't know about this.'

'Come and see, come and see,' Truman said happily, leading us down from the walkway. We followed him, and he led us gaily along the central aisle, proudly showing off the contents of his cells. The first thing he showed us was a werewolf, in full wolf form. Seven feet from head to tail, with silver-grey fur, it had been spreadeagled on its back on the concrete floor, pinned down with silver spikes through all four limbs, like a specimen laid out on a dissecting board. It whined piteously as we looked in.

'We have to do that,' Truman said. 'Otherwise the brutes gnaw off their own limbs to escape. Animals. Still; they're not here long enough to suffer much.'

All I could see was the basic doggy suffering in the creature's trapped eyes. I had no love for werewolves. I'd seen too many of his kind's half-eaten kills in small towns and villages. But this ... this was no way to treat even a hated enemy.

Further down the row, vampires were nailed to the concrete walls by wooden stakes hammered through their arms and legs. They snapped and snarled at us feebly, all intelligence driven out of their minds by continuous suffering. Then there were elf lords, stripped naked of their usual finery, chained with heavy steel shackles. The iron burned their pale flesh terribly where it touched, charring right down to the bone, but not one of the elves would do anything but sneer at us when we looked in. They still had their pride. Gryphons with their eyes cut out whined pitifully in their cells. They might not be able to see the future any more, but they knew what was coming. There was a unicorn whose wings had been broken, her horn gouged roughly out of her forehead, her glory much diminished. And a water elemental who'd been frozen into an icy statue. Her solid eyes were still horribly aware.

Cold-eyed, cold grey lizard men from the silent subterranean ways under South London, smoke-grey gargoyles snatched from the few churches and cathedrals they still haunted. A clay-skinned bogeyman with both its arms and legs broken, dragging itself back and forth across the concrete floor. And something with the stink of the pit about it. A genuine half-breed, born of a demon's lust. A succubus stores semen from a man she sleeps with, and then changes into its male form, an incubus, and deposits that stolen seed in a receptive woman. The result, a human body with a demon soul. Half of this world, and half of the World Below. They fight for one side or the other, both and neither; and they're not nearly as rare as they ought to be. This half-breed was held in check by a pentagram etched deeply into the concrete floor.

It inclined its head mockingly to Mr Stab, as though acknowledging one of its own kind. It couldn't speak. Someone had cut out its tongue, just in case.

Truman looked at me again and again, waiting for me to say something, but I held myself in check as he showed me horror after horror. Pretty much everything on display here was evil, or had done evil in their time; but nothing to match the cold-blooded evil of what had been done to them here. As a Drood agent, I'd fought and killed many of the things imprisoned here, but that had always been in the heat of battle and the hottest of blood. I'd killed but I'd never tortured, never delighted in the agonies of my enemies. That wasn't the Drood way. We fought the good fight to keep the world safe, and we took pride in doing that work well. But this ... this was an abomination.

The last captive, in the last cell, was Subway Sue. Her ragged clothes were tattered and torn and there was blood on them, and on her face. Someone had beaten the crap out of her. She'd been blindfolded and shackled to the wall of her concrete pen. Molly moved in close to the bars, her face terribly cold, her eyes dangerously angry. I looked at Truman.

'This,' he said proudly, 'is today's batch. Arrogant magical creatures who prey on Humanity, overpowered by the science and stealth of specially trained soldiers. My people are very busy these days, hunting these vermin down and bringing them here for elimination. We can't kill in public, of course; that would draw too much attention. It's better this magical filth don't know we're out there, on their trail ... I wish we could take the time to deal with them properly, give them the kind of death they deserve. Make them suffer as they've made Humanity suffer. But we can't take the risk. So we bring them in until the cells are full, and then we kill them humanely and give their bodies to the cleansing flames. It's a very efficient operation. The ovens never grow cold. Solomon sees to that. One by one, creature by creature, we're winning our world back from the monsters who infect it.'

'There's only one monster here,' said Mr Stab. 'And for once it isn't me. Is there, by any chance, a cell here with my name on it?'

'Not as long as you support the cause,' said Truman, and he actually dropped Mr Stab a roguish wink.

'I know this woman,' said Molly, still staring through the iron bars at Subway Sue. 'She's my friend.'

'She's a leech,' Truman said briskly. 'Stealing good fortune from innocent men and women, and selling it to those who don't deserve it. Just another magical parasite on the human race.'

Molly spun round and glared at him. 'She's my friend!'

Truman wagged a finger at her, like a recalcitrant child. 'Don't look at me like that, little witch. Remember your place. We allow you to use your unnatural gifts on our behalf, and in return you get to be part of the only organisation with a real chance of bringing down the Droods you hate so much. Obey me, and you will be well rewarded in the world that's coming. There will be room for you and your kind in the new order; but only as long as you remember your place.'

'That's the problem with tunnel vision,' said Molly. 'All I could see was the destruction of the Droods you promised. So when I listened to your recruitment speech, I heard what I wanted to hear. But you've opened my eyes at last, Truman.' She turned back to the cell. 'Sue, it's me, Molly. What do you suppose are the chances of the locks on these cells falling open, all at once?'

'Not good,' said Sue, through cracked and swollen lips. 'As long as these cold iron bars hold my magic in check.'

Molly looked at me. I grabbed the steel bars with one golden hand and ripped them right out of their concrete setting. Molly gestured once, and Sue's shackles fell away from her. Sue stood up, stretched painfully, and pulled away her blindfold.

'Bingo,' she said softly. And every lock on every cell fell open.

Truman looked at me, gaping blankly, as I crumpled the steel bars into a ball and dropped it heavily on the ground before him.

'You'll never replace my family,' I said. 'You think too small. And too nasty.'

He turned and ran, yelling for Solomon Krieg to hold us back while he went for reinforcements. The Golem with the Atomic Brain moved quickly to block the way while his master scrambled up the steps to the walkway. All around us, creatures were lurching and spilling out of their pens, free at last. Sirens were blaring in the distance. Molly and Girl Flower helped Subway Sue stumble out of her cell, while Mr Stab and I faced up to Solomon Krieg.

The artificial creature smiled for the first time, and there was no humour in it; only a terrible satisfaction that at last he would get to do what he was made to do. He raised one hand, and a gun muzzle poked out of a slit in his wrist. He sprayed Mr Stab and then me with machine gun fire, but couldn't hurt either of us. Bullets ricocheted harmlessly off my armoured chest, and seemed to pass through Mr Stab as though he was nothing but smoke. Krieg turned his aim on the three women, but I moved quickly to shield them. Krieg raised his other hand, and a hidden flamethrower bathed my armour in liquid fire. The heat was so terrible that even Mr Stab flinched, but I felt nothing.

Solomon Krieg shut off his flames and frowned deeply, as though concentrating on some difficult problem. Fat sparks of static electricity appeared spontaneously around his head, like a halo of electric flies. They spat and crackled, growing fiercer and more powerful, and then struck out at Mr Stab like a hammer blow of unleashed energies. The blast picked him up and threw him twenty feet or more, before slamming him into a concrete wall with devastating force. The whole wall crumbled into ruin under the impact, burying Mr Stab under a pile of rubble. Solomon Krieg, the Golem with the Atomic Brain. He turned to me and I braced myself. Once I would have trusted my armour to protect me even from such an attack as this, but after the incident with the elf lord's arrow I wasn't as confident as I once was. I stood my ground. I was all that stood between the three women and Krieg's atomic blast.

And that was when the escaped prisoners fell upon Krieg, like a pack of howling wolves. Humans and inhumans, demons and creatures of the night, they fell upon their common foe and sought to drag him down through sheer weight of numbers. Claws and fangs tore his colourless flesh, but no blood flowed. Krieg swayed under their attack, but did not fall. He lashed out with his machine-driven arms, throwing dead and broken bodies this way and that with appalling strength, not yielding an inch. More prisoners come running from every direction, desperate for a chance to drag down their hated jailer and executioner.

While Krieg was safely preoccupied, I hurried over to search the rubble for Mr Stab, but he was already rising to his feet, entirely unhurt, fussily brushing dust from his coat and opera cloak. He stooped down to retrieve his top hat, and placed it on his head at a jaunty angle. He might be the worst serial killer in history, but the man had style. He looked around him at the block of concrete pens, and shook his head firmly.

'No. I will not stand for this. I am no stranger to the joys of suffering and slaughter, Edwin, but this . . . There are some things a gentleman just doesn't do.'

And he went with me among the cells, helping release those who couldn't free themselves. The werewolves and the vampires and the like. It went against the grain for me to free such vicious and deadly creatures, after years of hunting them down and killing them, but I couldn't leave them here. For the ovens. As Mr Stab said, some things are just beyond the pale.

We left the demon half-breed where he was, of course. We weren't stupid.

We came back from the concrete pens to find Solomon Krieg still standing, surrounded by the bodies of the dead and the fallen. Girl Flower threw herself at him, screaming something obscene in old Welsh. Atomic forces erupted from the Golem's scarred forehead, hitting Girl Flower and blowing her apart into a shower of rose petals. They churned and circled in mid air, and then transformed, becoming a razorstorm of a thousand cutting owls' claws. They hit Solomon Krieg like a deadly hailstorm, ripping and tearing at his pale flesh, but still he stood his ground and would not fall. I might have admired him, if I hadn't hated him so much. (The ovens never grew cold . . .) The razorstorm finally collapsed, exhausted, and I went forward to do battle with the Golem with the Atomic Brain. I needed to punish someone for what had been done here, and he would do. I try hard, but sometimes I'm not a very nice person.

The creatures of the night fell back as I strode through their midst. They recognised the golden armour. Solomon saw me coming, and smiled again. His face was hanging in tatters from scratched and scored bone after Girl Flower's attack, and one eye was an empty red socket, but still he smiled. He didn't bother with his built-in gun or flamethrower. Just stepped forward and threw a punch with all his mechanised strength behind it. I heard the bones in his hand break as his fist glanced harmlessly from my golden mask. I grabbed his arm with both hands before he could draw it back, and broke it over my knee like a piece of kindling. Bits of shattered tech flew out of the gaping wound. Solomon Krieg grunted, once, but that was all. I let go of his arm and grabbed his head, pulling it down and forwards. He fought me with all his legendary strength, but it wasn't enough. Atomic forces sputtered and shimmered on the air as he struggled to put an attack together. I ripped the top of his head off, tearing along the old scarred fault line on his forehead, and then reached into his head with my other hand and tore his atomic brain out.

I held it in my golden hand for a moment, studying it, that nasty triumph of Cold War technology, and then I dropped it on the ground and stamped on it. The brain shattered into a thousand pieces, and Solomon Krieg's empty body fell twitching to the floor. I walked away, and the creatures of the night fell upon the body, tearing it to pieces in a frenzy of rage and revenge.

And that was when a spatial portal opened in the air before us, and an army of black-uniformed Manifest Destiny soldiers came pouring through, opening fire with automatic weapons the moment they caught sight of us. Bullets ricocheted from my armour, but I couldn't shield everyone. Newly freed prisoners fell screaming and dying around me. I grew golden spikes on my armoured fists and charged into the midst of the coming soldiers. I struck down men and women as they tried their best to kill me, and they did not rise again. But more and more soldiers were spilling out of the portal, their faces alight with the fury of the true fanatic. I broke necks and heads, and threw men and women through the air with deadly force, but still more of them streamed past me like a single rock in a river.

I fought on. It felt good to be striking them down. Manifest Destiny had betrayed me, by not being the hope I'd so desperately needed.

Mr Stab stepped forward to stand at my side, a long scalpel gleaming thirstily in his hand. Nothing the soldiers did could touch him, and he cut down all who came within his reach with an elegant disdain. Standing in the midst of blood and slaughter, he was in his element at last. Creatures of the night, hurt and weakened as they were, fought fiercely with the black-clad soldiers, and everywhere there was blood and screaming. Step by step we slowed the soldiers' advance, and step by step we drove them back. Perhaps because their fanaticism was no match for our fury. We forced our way forwards, over their dead and ours, until finally the surviving soldiers turned and fled back through the spatial portal, and it was shut down from their end.

I stood among the dead, in my blood-spattered armour, and raised one spiked fist in triumph. And all around me the creatures of the night howled their triumph.

Molly yelled my name again and again, until finally I lowered my fist and looked at her. 'Eddie! We have to get out of here! Truman must have emergency contingency plans for a mass breakout, and I really don't think we want to be here when he puts them into effect.'

I nodded, and strode over to her, kicking black-uniformed bodies aside. Blood and gore dripped thickly from my hands as I made the spikes disappear. My breathing slowed, and my head cleared. Mr Stab walked beside me, without a drop of blood on his elegant outfit.

'I know you want Truman dead,' said Molly. 'I do too. But there's no way we can reach him, right now.'

'Agreed,' I said. 'His time will come. Any suggestions on what we do next?'

'I open a spatial portal of my own, and we get the Hell out of here and scatter into the night.'

'Sounds like a plan to me,' I said. 'Where's Girl Flower?'

'Oh, she'll put herself back together again, over the next few days, in some place where she feels safe.' She looked at Mr Stab. 'Can I trust you to look after Sue? I have to stick with the Drood. We have revenges to plan.'

He inclined his head graciously. 'Of course, my dear. She will be safe with me. You have my word on it.'

And strangely enough, I believed him. I didn't think he'd lie to Molly. He offered Subway Sue his arm, and she leaned on it gratefully.

Molly opened a spatial portal, and we rushed the surviving prisoners through it as fast as we could. I kept glancing around, ready for another sneak attack, but it never came. The great cavern remained as silent as a mass grave. In the end, only Molly and I were left.

'So now we have two mortal enemies on our trail,' I said. 'My family, and Manifest Destiny. This day keeps getting better and better. Is there anyone left we can trust?'

'Maybe,' said Molly. 'A few names come to mind. But even if it was just you and me, I wouldn't back down or cry off. I will have justice, even if I have to kill everyone else in the world to get it.'

'You know,' I said. 'You'd have made a good Drood.'

'Now you're just being nasty,' she said.

We left through the portal, back up into the cold, clean air of London town.

CHAPTER THIRTEEN
Sleeping with the enemy

Molly and I emerged from her portal exactly where I'd asked her to drop us off: at Greenwich Docks, just down from that grand old sailing ship, the *Cutty Sark*. It was nearly midnight and the air was deliciously cool and clear after the unhealthy atmosphere of Manifest Destiny's holding pens. Long crimson streaks stained the lightening sky, standing out starkly behind the tall masts of the *Cutty Sark* naval museum. I looked up and down the stone wharf, but the docks were deserted. And quite right too; normal people were tucked up in bed by now, and I had every intention of catching up with them as soon as possible. It had been a long day, what with one thing and another.

'You bring me to the nicest places, Eddie,' said Molly. 'Can I ask what the Hell we're doing here, where even fallen angels would fear to tread without armed bodyguards and a written guarantee of safe passage?'

'Greenwich is really very civilised these days,' I said. 'Practically gentrified, in some places. I keep a barge tethered here, with all the comforts and necessities of home. Another of my safe places, when I need somewhere off the beaten track to hide from everyone, even my own family.'

'They don't know about this barge?'

'They never asked. My family never cared how I did what I did, as long as I did what I was told. This way.'

A few minutes' stroll down the wharf brought us to my barge, the *Lucky Lady*. Just another in a couple of dozen long boats and barges tied up to the wharf. A fairly inexpensive way to live in an expensive part of London. You get a lot of actors here ... The *Lucky Lady* bobbed heavily in the dark, tarry waters, her colours a bright racing red and green, and all her brasswork shining in the amber light of the street lamps. (I have a little brownie creature who comes round every other week, and keeps the old boat spotless in return for my leaving out a bowl of single malt whisky. I believe in upholding the old traditions. Especially when it means I don't have to get down on my hands and knees with the Duraglit. Hate polishing brass.)

I would have preferred to take Molly back to my nice flat in Knightsbridge, but I didn't dare. My family knew about the flat. At best they'd have agents in place, watching and waiting in case I was stupid enough to show my face. At worst, and much more likely, they'd have already torn the flat apart looking for clues or incriminating documents, as to where I was and what I might be doing. I knew the procedure. I'd done it myself often enough. Well, let them look. I never left anything of value in my flat. Or anywhere else, really. A field agent has to be ready to walk away from anything, at a moment's notice, and never look back. We're not allowed to be sentimental, or form attachments. Our only roots are in the family. The family sees to that.

I said as much to Molly, and she nodded.

'They probably smashed up your good stuff, out of spite. I've seen how your family operates. Are you sure there's nothing there they can use to track you? I could find you anywhere, just from holding some object that once belonged to you.'

'Not as long as I wear the torc,' I said. 'My armour shields me from everything.'

I handed Molly on to the deck of my barge, and then stepped lightly down to join her. Molly looked at me thoughtfully.

'Your armour comes from your family. Are you sure they don't have some secret way of finding you through the armour?'

'Positive. That's always been our strength and our weakness. The same armour that makes us so powerful also isolates us from everything else in the world.'

'So you're always alone?'

'Yes. That's why so few Droods can cope, out in the world. Away from the all-embracing arms of the family. Come on, it's cold out here. Let's go below.'

I opened the hatch and down we went, into the sumptuously furnished interior of the *Lucky Lady*. Wherever I live, I like to live well. I won the barge several years back in a poker game with a down-on-his-luck private detective. Poor bugger ended up living in his own office. Served him right for trying to cheat. There's nothing more I enjoy than out-cheating a cheat. I can produce extra aces from places you wouldn't believe.

I bustled around the long living area, lighting the old naval storm lamps and adjusting the wicks, filling the barge's interior with a warm golden glow. Molly oohed and aahed over the luxurious furnishings, and positively cooed over the period details. The *Lucky Lady* has no modern conveniences, no electricity. The whole point of being on the barge was to be cut off from the modern world. (There is a chemical toilet. And a portable CD player. There's no point in being a fanatic about these things.) Finally we both settled ourselves on the comfortably padded chaise longue, and I relaxed for the first time in what seemed like for ever.

'I like your place, Eddie,' said Molly, tucking her legs up under her. 'It's so not you. A bit solitary, though.'

'That's the point,' I said.

She considered me seriously. 'I can't imagine what it must be like for you, to live a life so alone ... so cut off from everything and everyone. Never able to trust anyone who isn't family.'

'Comes with the job,' I said. 'And after growing up in house bursting at the seams with family, I was glad to get away.'

'Has there never been ... anyone else? Anyone who mattered?'

'No. Never. I can't get too close to anyone without telling them what I do. And the family doesn't allow that. Marriage, even ... friendships, only take place at the family's discretion. They have to be approved. Especially for those of us out in the field, and open to the world's temptations. From the moment we're born, and they clap the golden torc around our infant throats, we belong to the family, body and soul. I live alone, wherever I live, and though I may invite people in to visit me, from time to time, they're never allowed to stay. For their own safety.'

'So ... no girlfriends? No significant others? No real friends? What kind of a life is that?'

'A life of service, to a greater cause,' I said. 'That was what I believed. What I'd been taught. How was I to know it was all a lie?'

'Is there anything here to eat and drink?' Molly said, kindly changing the subject. 'I could eat, if you had something.'

'Of course,' I said. 'Let me knock some weevils out of the hardtack.'

I set about organising a basic cold meal out of the tins I keep in stock, and opened the bottle of brandy I keep for medical emergencies. Molly busied herself by looking over my collection of CDs, and making disparaging comments about my taste in music.

'What is this? No Hawkwind, no Motorhead, not even any Meatloaf? Just . . . Judy Collins, Mary Hopkin and Kate Bush.'

'I like female vocalists,' I said, coming in with a tray.

'All right, I'll lend you some of my Within Temptation imports. You'll like them. They're a Dutch band with a magnificent female vocalist. A bit like Abba on crack.'

'Well,' I said. 'There's something to look forward to.'

We attacked our food with good appetite. Molly wolfed hers down, to my quiet approval. I can't stand people who pick at their food. Afterwards we sat together with the brandy warming in our bellies, companionably close, still too buzzed from the day's adrenalin to sleep just yet. So we talked about old times, old cases, where we'd always been on different sides; and doing our best to kill each other, as often as not. There are some things you can only talk about with old enemies. Because you had to be there, to understand.

The Case of the Millennium Upgrade was a classic foul-up, of almost legendary proportions. My family got word that a rather eminent German scientist was about to defect from Vril Inc, in Munich, and come to London to sell the fruits of his research to the highest bidder. That put it in my territory, so I was sent in to make sure that his work went to someone the family approved of. Or shut the scientist down, with extreme prejudice, if he didn't feel like cooperating.

We don't normally get that excited over industrial espionage, but Herr Doktor Herman Koenig worked at the cutting edge of the computer/human mind interface, and had apparently developed a means of direct contact between human thought and computer capacities. Theoretically, this could result in a combination of the two capable of producing a whole far greater than the sum of its parts. An awful lot of people were prepared to pay an awful lot of money for exclusive rights to such a process, so it was up to me to ensure that only the right sort of person got their hands on it. Or make sure no one did. My family can be very dog-in-the-manger about some things.

Doktor Koenig had set up a makeshift laboratory in a disused government think tank, in the old Bradbury Building just down from Centre Point. Breaking in was child's play. I was used to the kind of security that throws a demon from Hell at you if you get it wrong. Electronic locks and motion detectors aren't really in the same league. Herr Doktor hadn't even shelled out for some armed guards, the cheap bastard. Really, some people deserve everything that happens to them.

I let myself into the Bradbury Building lobby a good three hours before the auction was due to start, and made my way easily up through the quiet building. Everyone else had gone home, oblivious to the drama to come. I armoured up, and trotted easily up the forty-four flights of stairs to the Doktor's floor. (Never trust an elevator.) I didn't expect any serious opposition on this case.

I didn't know Molly Metcalf was already in the building.

She'd arrived on the roof via a shielded teleport spell, let herself in and worked her way down. She was there to protect Doktor Koenig from outside interference. Not because she understood anything about the implications of the computer/human mind interface, or would have approved of it if she had, but because she believed passionately in the right of people to improve themselves by any means possible, and thus help free the world from Drood control.

Right, Molly said at this point. *Computers baffle me. I can just about work my e-mail, and that's it. Though I do enjoy surfing dodgy porn sites.*

So; we both burst into the Doktor's lab at the same moment, scaring the Hell out of the guy, and then stopped short to glare at each other. I knew Molly by reputation, and of course she recognised the golden armour at once. We both struck out at each other with every weapon we had, unleashing energies and forces that would have been immediately fatal to anyone but us. Doktor Koenig cried out hysterically in German, and tried to protect his precious equipment with his own body. The whole thing escalated very quickly ... and we brought the house down. The Bradbury Building crumbled and fell apart under the impact of the forces we unleashed, and the whole place collapsed into ruin and rubble. Molly and I came out of it entirely unscathed, of course, but Herr Doktor Koenig was gone, and all his equipment with him. He got blamed for the explosion, but it was hardly my finest hour. Certain people in my family were very scathing.

And that was how I first met the wild witch, Molly Metcalf.

The last mission we butted heads on was the Case of the Pendragon Reborn. It seemed like every precog and medium in the country worth their salt was excitedly reporting the return of the Pendragon; that Arthur had been reincarnated, again, and would soon start to remember who he really was. And so the race was on to find him, with all sides ready to claim him as their own.

And brainwash the poor sod to their particular cause, Molly interrupted.

Well, quite, I said.

Anyway, my family always has the best information, and the Pendragon Reborn was quickly identified as one Paul Anderson, a young advertising executive based in Devon. As it turned out, the only Drood agent in that area was still incapacitated after a very unfortunate incident involving one of the local powers, Joan The Wad, so I was sent down to fill in, on the grounds that I was the only field agent not currently working on a case. The family couldn't teleport me there in case such a magic was detected, and gave away our interest. So I had to take the train down from London to Devon, and it's a Hell of a long journey.

The family wouldn't even spring for a first-class ticket.

But I got to Paul Anderson first, explained the situation as best I could, showed him my armour to prove I wasn't crazy, and persuaded him to come back to The Hall with me, for further testing. Just to make sure he was the Real Deal. (You'd be amazed how many pretenders to the throne turn up every century. And don't even get me started about the bloody Fisher King.) Paul was actually rather relieved. Apparently he'd been having recurring and very vivid dreams of knights in armour clashing bloodily on heaving battlefields, which was a bit disturbing for a young advertising executive with prospects.

And then Molly turned up. Yelled for Paul to get the Hell away

181

from me, called me a liar and a fascist stooge to my face, and then backed Paul up against the wall of his own living room while she hit him with her best arguments. I argued my corner just as fiercely, and soon Molly and I were shouting into each other's faces. Unfortunately, all we succeeded in doing was confusing the crap out of Paul, who yelled for both of us to get out of his house and his life, and never come back. Molly wasn't used to being out-shouted, so she lashed out at Paul with one of her best resolution spells, forcing his inherited core personality to the surface.

And that was when it went to Hell in a hand-cart.

The spell hit something inside Paul Anderson, expanded out of control, and blew up the cottage we were standing in. At first I really thought Molly and I had done it again, but when the smoke cleared the three of us were standing safe and sound in the ruins of the cottage. Me in my armour, Molly inside her protective shield, and Paul Anderson in blackened and tattered clothing but with a whole new look on his face. Molly seized the moment to attack me, determined that the Droods would not control and influence this Pendragon Reborn. I fought back, of course, and while the two of us were distracted, the new Pendragon walked away into the night.

The first hint Molly and I got that something had gone terribly wrong was when the forest on the hill behind the cottage exploded. We stopped trying to kill each other and looked around, and for as far as I could see the whole horizon was on fire as century-old trees burned brightly against the night sky. The flames leapt up high, fierce and malevolent, driven by more than natural forces. Molly and I agreed to a very temporary truce, and went up the hill to see what the Hell was going on. I'll never forget my first sight of the man who had been Paul Anderson, transformed and transfigured, standing laughing in the flames, untouched by the terrible heat, chanting ancient and awful spells in a forgotten tongue.

Turned out the precogs and mediums had only got it half right, at usual. Paul Anderson was a Pendragon Reborn, all right, but not Arthur. Paul was Mordred, son of Arthur, back again to spread his malice in the world.

Molly and I approached him cautiously. We both knew who he was, who he had to be. I was already thinking seriously about calling in reinforcements. If Mordred had come into his full power, he was way out of my league. Fortunately, Molly's spell had brought him back prematurely, and he was still pretty confused. Or he'd never have launched such a basic attack spell at my armour. The armour reflected the spell right back at him, and blew his as yet unprotected human form to pieces. Nothing left of him but bloody gobbets, spread over a wide area.

Molly disappeared while I was organising a force to deal with the forest fire.

And the family were really scathing about this one.

That was pretty much the pattern, down the years. Molly and I would show up to claim some important person or prize, always on different sides of every argument, more than ready to kill each other to prevent the other from getting away with the prize or the person. Sometimes I won, sometimes she did, but I'd say honours were about even, on the whole. I can't say I ever really hated her, and was relieved to discover she felt the same way. It was only ever business for both of us; just the job, nothing personal. Except in a strange way I guess it became personal. There's nothing like repeatedly trying to kill someone to really get to know them, and admire them. To appreciate their qualities.

'How many people have you killed, Eddie?' Molly said finally, hugging her knees to her chest.

I shrugged. The question didn't make me feel uncomfortable, as such. It just wasn't anything I ever thought about. 'I stopped counting years ago. You?'

'Surprisingly few, all things considered. It's a big thing to kill someone. You don't just kill who they are, but everyone they might have become, and everything they might have done.'

'Sometimes that's the point,' I said. It was important to me that she understood. That I was an agent, not an assassin. 'I like to think I've only ever killed in self-defence, or to protect the world. To prevent future suffering or killing. But in the end ... my job was to do whatever my family told me to do. And I did, because I trusted them. If they told me someone needed killing, I always assumed they must have a good reason. In my defence, I would say that mostly they were right, and obviously so. I have killed some really evil bastards, in my time. I could give you names ...'

'I probably already know them,' said Molly. 'You have quite a reputation, Eddie.'

'Yes. I was proud of it, once. But not just as a killer, I hope?'

'Well . . . mostly. You never were the subtlest of agents, Eddie.'

'Lot you know,' I said airily. 'Most of the jobs I did, I was in and out and never left a trace. That's the mark of a good agent; to get the job done, and no one ever knows you were there.'

'If you say so,' said Molly, smiling. 'But . . . did you never question any of your orders? Any of your assignments?'

'Why should I? They were my family. We were raised to fight the good fight, to protect the world, to see ourselves as heroes in the greatest game of all. Family was the one thing you could depend on, in an untrustworthy world. So I killed the people they told me to. And if sometimes I wasn't happy about what I did . . . I learned to live with it.'

'That's why you live alone,' said Molly. 'Apart from family, who could hope to understand the things we do?'

We sat quietly for a while, listening to Enya sing on the portable CD player. From outside came the low murmur of the wind, the sounds of the water and the wharf, and the distant rumble of city traffic. A whole world going on, just as always, not knowing that everything had changed. But that . . . was for tomorrow. I could feel my body slowly relaxing, winding down from a day I thought would never end.

'So,' Molly said finally. 'What do we do next? What can we do next?'

'I don't know,' I said honestly. 'I've learned a lot I didn't know, but not the one thing I needed to know. Why my family threw me to the wolves. Why I've been declared rogue by a family I served faithfully all my life. Why my own grandmother is so determined to see me dead. I must have done *something*, but I'm damned if I know what. I mean, I know now why my family have hung on to power for so long. I know what the Drood family business really is. But it's not like I knew or even suspected any of this before today.'

'Have you considered contacting other members of your family who've gone rogue?' Molly said suddenly. 'Would you like to? I mean, if nothing else they should be able to give you some solid hints on how to hide from your family, how to survive on your own, out in the world.'

I thought about that. I still had a definite distaste for the word *rogue*, even though I was one now. There had always been rogues, throughout family history. Certain individuals who threw off family authority, and ran away into the world. Or had been driven out, for good reason. Their names were struck from the family genealogy, and no one was permitted to mention them, ever again. Even now, back in The Hall, someone was removing all traces of my existence, and everyone who ever knew me would be instructed never to use my name again. Even my Uncle Jack and my Uncle James would go along. For the family. Rogues were worse than treacherous; they were an embarrassment. And so they spent their lives hiding in deep cover, to avoid being hunted down and killed.

'The only rogue I've ever known,' I said slowly, 'was the Bloody Man, Arnold Drood. Evil little shit. You know what he did? With the children? I can't believe how he was able to hide it for so long ... Anyway, the family told me what he'd done and where he was hiding, and I went straight there and killed him.' A horrid thought struck me, and I looked anxiously at Molly. 'They told me ... but was it really true? Did I kill an innocent man?'

'No,' Molly said quickly, patting me comfortingly on the arm. 'Relax, Eddie. He really did do the awful things everyone said he did. Your family weren't the only ones on the Bloody Man's trail. But only one of you could get to him despite his armour.' She considered me thoughtfully for a moment. 'How did you manage to kill him, Eddie?'

'Easy,' I said. 'I cheated. Let's change the subject. Given that I've been such a good soldier for so long, will any of the other rogues agree to talk to me?'

'They'll talk to me,' said Molly. 'I've had dealings with some of them, in my time. Don't look so shocked, Eddie. You're out in the real world now, and we do things differently here. Alliances come and go, and we all deal with whoever we have to, to get things done. I don't have a family to back me up, so I made my own, out of the few people I really trust. I know people everywhere. Also, I know people who know people. In fact, I know of three Drood rogues living in and around London. If I vouch for you, they'll agree to a meeting. Probably.'

'I don't care about just surviving,' I said. 'I won't hide in a hole and pull it in after me, like the other rogues. I need to bring my family down, all the way down, for what they've done. For not being what they said they were. But ... there has to be someone around strong enough to stop Manifest Destiny. Bad as my family are, those bastards are worse. And you can bet the damage we did to them today won't even slow them down. They're big and they're organised and they're rotten to the core. If I do break the Droods' hold on the world, who would be left strong enough to stop Truman from doing the awful things he plans to do, to everyone who's not Manifest Destiny?'

'There is one obvious answer,' Molly said. 'Set them both at each other's throats.'

'No,' I said immediately. 'I won't be responsible for starting a war. Too many innocents would die, caught in the crossfire. And not everyone in my family is dirty. Some of them are good people, fighting the good fight not out of family duty but because they believe it's the right thing to do.'

'If you say so,' said Molly.

It was my turn to consider her thoughtfully. 'I couldn't help noticing, Molly, that you've been very ... reticent, today. Holding back, as it were. None of your usual wild magics, in any of our battles. In fact, you've let me do most of the hard work.'

She grinned. 'I was wondering when you'd notice. I've been watching you in action, Eddie. Seeing what you can do. Trying to get a handle on who you really are. I've hated and fought the Droods most of my life, and with good reason. They killed my parents, when I was just a child.'

'I'm sorry,' I said. 'I didn't know.'

'I never found out why. Droods aren't big on explaining their actions. That's how Truman was able to snare me so easily ... but you were always different, Eddie. I've fought a dozen different Drood agents in my time, but you ... you were the only one who ever fought clean. You've always ... intrigued me, Eddie.'

'I love it when a woman talks dirty,' I said.

We were leaning towards each other when the barge's proximity alarm went off; a silent crimson light that filled the cabin. I gestured urgently for Molly to be quiet, and rose quickly to turn off the CD player. Outside, the wind was howling with a voice not all its own. I turned off the crimson warning light with a sharp gesture, and dropped down beside Molly again. I put my mouth right next to her ear.

'Don't move, don't speak, don't do anything. Something's out there. And my security alarms wouldn't flare up like that unless there was something really nasty in the vicinity.'

'Looking for us?' said Molly, barely breathing the words.

'Seems likely. But it's not my family. That would set off an entirely different alarm.'

'You got any weapons on this boat?'

'No. And no defences either. That's the point of this place; nothing to attract any attention. It's supposed to be right off the map. Nothing for any enemy to detect.'

We listened to the wind raging. The cabin was rising and falling jerkily now, as the waters were disturbed. The temperature dropped sharply. My breath steamed on the air, mixing with Molly's.

'What do you think it is?' Molly whispered.

'Could be any number of really bad things. I've made some serious enemies in my time. Probably think I'm vulnerable, now my family's disowned me.'

'But you've got your armour, and I've got my spells . . .'

'No. If we give away our position we'll have to go on the run again. And I'm running out of safe places to hide. Keep your head down and stay close to me. Being this close to my torc should hide you too.'

We sat silently together as the barge shook and shuddered and the wind howled like a living thing. One by one the storm lamps guttered and went out, so that a darkening gloom filled the cabin, as though there was something close that could not abide light and warmth. I could feel the presence of something horribly *other*, drawing inexorably closer, something fierce and foul, like a thorn in my soul. I was shivering now, and so was Molly, and not just from the bitter cold that penetrated the cabin. Something was looking for us, something dangerous to our bodies and our souls, and it was perilously close. I took Molly in my arms, and she held me tightly.

Whether I held her to bring her closer to the torc or out of a desperate need for human contact, I couldn't say.

I could have armoured up. I was pretty sure my armour would protect me from whatever was outside, but using such a strong magic would have given away my position immediately. And Molly would have been left unprotected.

The presence outside finally moved on, and the night went back to normal. The wind fell away to murmurs, and the barge stopped rocking as the waters stilled. The storm lamps popped back on, one by one, and light and warmth slowly filled the cabin again. Molly started to pull away from me, and I immediately let go of her. She shook her head slowly, and then stretched theatrically.

'God, I'm tired. Don't get any ideas, Eddie. We're allies on this case, nothing more.'

'Of course,' I said. 'I need to get some sleep. Would you like me to fix some hot chocolate before we turn in?'

'Hot chocolate sounds very good,' she said. 'But where, exactly, are we turning in? How many beds do you have here?'

'Just the one,' I said. 'In the bedroom at the far end. You can crash there, and I'll put some blankets on the floor here.'

'My perfect gentle knight,' said Molly, smiling.

I made two mugs of steaming hot chocolate in the tiny galley, and we sat together and talked about nothing in particular for a while. Just winding down, from a long hard day. Finally we both started yawning, Molly's eyelids drooped heavily, and she went to sleep right there on the couch. I rescued the mug from her slowly relaxing fingers, and put it to one side. The sleeping draught I'd put in her mug had worked fine, disguised by the heavy taste of the chocolate. It wasn't that I entirely mistrusted her, but we had tried to kill each other too many times; and I needed to feel safe while I slept.

I picked Molly up and carried her into the small enclosed bedroom at the far end of the barge. I laid her out carefully on the bed, and undid a few buttons at her throat. She moved slowly in her sleep, murmuring like a dreaming child. I started to sort out a few spare blankets to sleep on, but I was too tired. And the bed was plenty big enough for two. I stretched out beside her. Molly was already snoring gently. No doubt she'd have a few harsh words to say when she woke up in the morning ... but that could wait.

My bed fit me like a glove, and sleep had never felt so good.

CHAPTER FOURTEEN
Happy daze

I *was dreaming. A great voice spoke in my mind, saying: I can help you, if only you'll let me. There's no end to the things we might achieve together, you and I. I am the answer to all your questions, and all your problems. Just stop fighting me. I wanted to believe the voice. I really did. But I've never been able to trust anyone apart from me. The family saw to that.*

I woke up with a knife at my throat. Molly was sitting astride my chest, and not in a good way. She was leant over me, the edge of her silver dagger pressing hard enough into my throat to cut the skin. It stung, more irritating than painful, but I could feel a slow trickle of blood coursing down the side of my neck. I decided to lie very still. Molly's face hung above mine, red with rage, but her eyes were cold as ice. Her hand was very steady, for the moment, the razor-sharp edge resting just above my Adam's apple. And I'd been having such a good dream, too. I gave Molly my very best polite smile.

'Good morning, Molly. Sleep well?'

'You drugged me, you bastard! Did you think I wouldn't notice? And you slept in the same bed as me, after all that nonsense about blankets on the floor!'

'Yes,' I said carefully. 'I slept in the same bed as you. Emphasis on the word *slept*. You needed a good night's sleep, and so did I, so I . . . helped things along a little.'

Molly's scowl deepened, becoming actually dangerous. 'You *drugged* me. Do you really expect me to *ever* trust you again, after this? You could have done anything to me while I was asleep!'

'Yes,' I said. 'I could have. But I didn't. Still; you shouldn't take it personally. I was very tired. I'm sure I'll do better next time.'

190

'There won't be a next time, you treacherous little toad,' said Molly. But there might have been a hint of a smile, tucked away in one corner of her mouth. She took her knife away from my throat, and climbed off my chest. I raised one hand to my throat, and then winced as my fingertips came away wet with blood. Molly sniffed loudly as she got up off the bed. 'Don't be such a big baby. You've cut yourself worse shaving. I don't suppose there's a shower anywhere on this boat, is there? I feel really funky after sleeping in my clothes.'

'No shower,' I agreed. 'But you can boil some hot water on the gas cooker, for a wash.'

I started to roll out of bed, and then stopped abruptly, crying out despite myself as a stab of pain filled my shoulder and left arm. It hurt like Hell as I forced myself to sit up, cradling my left arm to my chest. I tried flexing it slowly, and yelped again as a vicious pain flashed all the way from my shoulder to my fingertips. Just bending the elbow felt like someone had stuck a screwdriver into the joint, and twisted it. Even moving my fingers hurt. I looked across at Molly, but she shook her head immediately.

'Nothing to do with me. Let's have a look at your shoulder.'

I couldn't get my shirt off on my own. It hurt too much. Molly had to help me, unbuttoning and then pushing the shirt back, not hurting me more than she had to. I turned my head to inspect my left shoulder. All around the scar tissue left by the healed arrow wound, my skin was swollen and inflamed. Molly leaned in for a closer look, and then pressed the skin here and there with surprisingly gentle fingers. I hissed at the pain, and she nodded slowly.

'Were you injured yesterday, fighting at the holding pens?'

'No,' I said. 'I was in my armour. I can't be hurt while I'm in my armour.'

'The elf-lord's arrow got through,' said Molly, studying the scar tissue thoughtfully.

'Yes, but that was ... extremely unusual. And I already used a med blob to heal the wound.'

'Doesn't seem to have made too good a job of it,' said Molly. She stood back and traced a series of complex symbols on the air, glowing trails following her fingertips to leave behind alien characters, hanging shimmering between us. Molly studied them silently for a while, and then looked back at me as the symbols faded away. I didn't like the expression on her face.

'Good of you to take an interest,' I said, trying to keep it light. 'But if you're about to suggest surgery with that knife of yours, I think I'll pass.'

'You're no use to me as a cripple,' she said. 'Unfortunately, there's nothing I can do for you. The original wound has healed, but it seems the elf's arrow left something behind, after you pulled it out. It's not poison, as such. I could cope with that. But there's something in your body that shouldn't be there. I can't tell what it is, but it's spreading.'

I nodded slowly. 'The arrow came from another dimension,' I said. 'That's the only way it could pierce my armour. I've seen the substance once before, in the Armourer's lab. He called it strange matter.'

'Good name for it,' said Molly. 'My magic can detect it, but not affect it. All I can tell you for sure is that your body doesn't have any defences against it. It's bad now, and it's only going to get worse.'

'Say it,' I said. 'Just say it.'

'I'm sorry, Eddie. This strange matter is eating you alive, inch by inch, and I don't have the first idea on how to stop it.'

'How long?' I said numbly.

'Three, four days, tops.'

'And after that?'

'There isn't anything after that. I'm sorry, Eddie.'

I sat on the edge of the bed, thinking. Not feeling much, not yet. 'I thought I'd have more time,' I said finally. 'To do all the things I need to do. But I suppose . . . it's just another deadline. And I can do deadlines. Help me get my shirt back on.'

It took both of us to get my left arm back into the shirt sleeve, and I made some more noises, even through gritted teeth. I sat quietly as she did up the buttons. I was breathing hard, and I could feel cold sweat drying on my face. But all the time I was thinking, hard. Three days, four tops. The only people who might be able to help me were the doctors back at The Hall. And maybe the Armourer. Uncle Jack. All I knew about strange matter was what he'd told me. That it came from somewhere else, that it had certain useful properties that no one understood, and that it didn't follow any of our rules. But even if I were to go back to The Hall and give myself up, the odds were Grandmother would have given orders for me to be killed on sight.

More than ever, I needed answers. Information. Options. And the only people who might have those . . . were the other rogues.

Molly buttoned up my collar, and wiped the sweat from my face with her handkerchief. I nodded my thanks. I wasn't used to needing help. I wasn't used to hurting. The only way to seriously damage a Drood was to catch him out of his armour, and we're very hard to surprise. I hadn't been really hurt since I was a teenager. Pain and weakness were new things to me, and I hated them. Molly saw some of this in my face, and smiled briefly.

'Welcome to the world the rest of us live in. What do you want to do now, Eddie?'

I stood up carefully. My left arm hung down at my side, quiet as long as I didn't try to use it. I needed to be up and moving, doing . . . something. 'Who's the best rogue to talk to? Who's most likely to know something, about me and my family?'

'That would be Oddly John,' Molly said immediately. 'I've never been able to get much out of him, but I'm pretty sure he knows important things.'

'Is he far from here?'

'Two train journeys.'

'Forget that. Call up another spatial portal.'

'I'm not altogether sure that's wise,' Molly said. 'They're really only for use in emergencies. They take a lot out of me.'

'Could anyone track us through the portal, once we're gone?'

'No. But any number of people would detect a magic like that operating, and come here to check it out.'

'Let them,' I said. 'It doesn't matter. I doubt I'll be coming back here again. We can't afford to travel openly in London any more. By now both my family and Manifest Destiny will have filled the city with agents, looking for us. Tell me about this . . . Oddly John.'

'He lives out in Flitwick,' Molly said, not quite avoiding my eyes. 'Nice little commuter town, some way outside London proper.'

'There's something you're not telling me.'

'There's lots I'm not telling you. But this ... you really need to see this for yourself, Eddie.'

'All right,' I said. 'Let's go.'

The portal dropped us off on top of a grassy hill outside a small town, overlooking an old Georgian manor house set in its own spacious grounds. Birds were singing cheerfully under a bright blue sky and the early morning air was crisp and clear. All very picture postcard, except for the high stone wall surrounding the manor grounds, topped with iron spikes and rolls of barbed wire. The only entrance was through a massive iron gate, heavy enough to stop a tank in its tracks. Beyond the high walls, I could make out people walking back and forth in the grounds. All very peaceful. But even from a distance, the manor house had a dour and forbidding look, and there was something ... wrong, about the people in the grounds. Something about the way they moved, slowly and aimlessly, not interacting with each other. I looked at Molly.

'All right,' I said. 'Spill it. What kind of a place have you brought me to?'

'This is Happy Acres,' Molly said calmly. 'A high security installation for the criminally insane. The locals call it Happy Daze.'

'And our rogue is in there? What is he, crazy?'

'Yes, and no,' said Molly. 'You'll have to see for yourself. Oddly John's position here is ... complicated.'

We started down the hillside, slipping and sliding on grass still wet from the dawn, heading towards the home for the criminally insane. All at once, the heavy iron gate didn't look nearly solid enough. I studied the manor house dubiously, until the rising stone walls shut it off from view. I'd never been to a madhouse before. I wasn't sure what to expect. When Droods go seriously crazy, we kill them. We have to. The armour makes them far too dangerous. Like Arnold Drood, the Bloody Man. I still can't believe that bastard was able to fool us for so long. Molly and I reached the bottom of the hill, and I trailed after her as she headed for the entrance. I wasn't holding back. It was just that Molly knew the way.

'So,' I said. 'Criminally insane. Are we talking ... axe murderers, and the like?'

194

'Oh, at least,' Molly said cheerfully. 'But not to worry; I'm sure everyone will make you feel perfectly at home.'

We stopped outside the iron gate, which seemed even bigger close up. It looked like it had been cast in one piece, with bars so thick you couldn't get a hand around them. Its design was stark and purely functional. It was there to keep the inmates in, nothing more. Molly hit the buzzer set into the stone pillar beside the gate, and after a lengthy pause a heavy-set man in hospital whites came over to glare suspiciously through the gate at us. The leather belt around his waist held a radio, a pepper spray and a long heavy truncheon.

'Hello, George,' Molly said easily. 'Remember me? I'm here to see my Uncle John again. John Stapleton.'

'You know the routine, Molly,' said George, in a surprisingly soft and pleasant voice. 'You have to show me a signed and dated pass from the hospital administration.'

'Oh sure,' said Molly. She held an empty hand up before him, and he leaned forward for a closer look, his lips moving slowly as he read the details on a non-existent pass. He finally nodded, and Molly quickly lowered her hand. George worked an electronic lock on the other side of the gate, and there was the sound of metal bolts disengaging. The gate swung smoothly open on concealed hydraulics, and Molly led the way into the house grounds. The gate swung shut behind us, locking us in with the inmates.

'Shall I call up to the house for an escort to take you the rest of the way?' said George, his hands resting on his belt next to the pepper spray and the truncheon.

'No, that's all right, George,' said Molly. 'I know the way.'

I must have looked a bit disconcerted, because George smiled reassuringly at me. 'First visit? Don't worry. None of the patients will bother you. Stick to the path, and you'll be fine.'

We set off up the wide gravel path. 'What was that bit with the empty hand?' I said.

'Basic illusion spell,' Molly said briskly. 'Lets people see what they expect to see.'

'Uncle John,' I said, with some emphasis. 'And you knew the guard's name. Are you a regular visitor here, by any chance?'

'Spot on, Sherlock. I found out who Oddly John really was by accident, and I've been keeping it to myself ever since. I was hoping

I could use him to dig up some useful dirt on your family. Some secret piece of insider knowledge I could use as a weapon.'

'And?'

She looked at me briefly, her expression unreadable. 'Wait till you meet him. You'll understand then.'

Wide green lawns stretched away to either side of the path, cropped and cultivated to within an inch of their lives. Patients in dressing gowns, with wild hair and empty eyes wandered listlessly back and forth, taking the air. A handful of bored-looking guards in hospital whites were taking a cigarette break by the ornamental fountain. Some of the patients muttered to themselves. Some just made noises. None of them looked like an axe murderer. And none of them even glanced at Molly and me, caught up in their own private worlds.

As Molly and I drew closer to the big house, I realised that all the windows were barred with heavy metal shutters ready to be swung into place. Swivelling exterior cameras watched us approach. The main door looked very solid, and very shut. Molly leaned over the electronic combination lock set into the post by the door, and pecked out four numbers.

'You'd think they'd change the number once in a while,' she said fussily. 'Or at least come up with a decent combination. I mean, it's been four, three, two, one for as long as I've been coming here. So the staff won't have any trouble remembering it in an emergency. Anybody could guess it! Or at least, anyone with the normal number of marbles. I'd write a stern letter to the hospital governors, but you never know. I might need to break in here some day. Or break out.'

The door swung open, revealing a pleasant open lobby. Nice carpeting, comfortable furnishings, plaques and commendations on the walls. The only off note was that the receptionist sat in her own little cubicle, behind heavy reinforced glass. She was a middle-aged, matronly figure in the ubiquitous hospital whites, with an easy welcoming smile. Molly smiled and nodded familiarly back, and the receptionist pushed a guestbook through a narrow slit in the glass for us to sign. After only a moment's pause, I wrote *Mr and Mrs Jones.*

'Oh, that's nice,' the receptionist said cheerfully. 'Makes a change from all the Smiths we get coming here. Most people don't care to use their real names, when they come visiting relations. Just in case someone finds out there's a cannibal in the family. Though of course we're always very careful about things like that. Good to see you back again, Molly. Most people don't like to come to a place like this. We get all the bad ones here: the child killers, the serial rapists, the animal mutilators ... All the patients no one else wants, or can't cope with. We had the Dorset Ripper in here the other week. No trouble at all; sweet as you like.'

'We're here to see my Uncle John,' said Molly, cutting off a monologue that threatened to run and run. 'John Stapleton?'

'Of course you are, dear. Oddly John, we call him. He's never a problem, bless him. Don't know what he did to get sent to a place like this, before my time, but it must have been pretty bad, because there's never any talk of transferring him to a less secure establishment, for all his good behaviour. Remember; always watch your back here, dears. Many of the patients in this place are the last faces a lot of people ever saw. Now, you make yourselves comfortable, and I'll call for an attendant to escort you to the top floor.'

Molly stretched out in a comfortable chair, but I didn't feel like sitting. This was not a comfortable place, for all the trimmings. I looked through an open door into an adjoining parlour, where patients were sitting around in dressing gowns. It wasn't what I'd expected. No dazed souls wandering around, no thrashing figures in straitjackets, no muscular guards hovering ready to beat the crap out of anyone who misbehaved. Instead, just a collection of very ordinary looking people, sitting in chairs, flicking through papers and magazines, or watching morning television shows. The only attendant nurse was sitting at the back, doing *The Times* crossword puzzle. Molly moved in beside me, and I jumped a little despite myself.

'It's all done with kindness these days,' she said quietly. 'The chemical cosh. They're doped to the eyeballs, so they won't cause any trouble or talk back. It's a lot cheaper than restraints. Though you'll notice there are surveillance cameras everywhere, just in case. The real hard cases are kept out of sight, so as not to upset the visitors.'

'That's right,' said our escort, appearing suddenly beside us. Another muscular man in hospital whites, this time with a shaved head and a self-satisfied smirk on his face. He kept one hand on his belt, right next to the truncheon. He didn't offer to shake hands. 'Hi, I'm Tommy. Ask me about anything, I've been here like for ever. It's good money, with lots of vacation time, and the work's not exactly demanding, most of the time. Hardly any excitement, these days. The wonders of modern science: better living through chemistry.' He looked though the door into the parlour, and sniggered openly. 'Look at them. You could set fire to their slippers, and they wouldn't notice. Like your missus said, we keep the real animals downstairs, in the bear pit.' He looked sideways at Molly. 'We had to put your Uncle John down there a few times, when he first came here. He didn't give us any more trouble after that.'

'How is he?' said Molly. 'Is my uncle having one of his good days?'

Tommy shrugged easily. 'Hard to tell, with him. Long as he behaves himself, that's all I care about.' He sniggered again, this time looking at me. 'Oddly John, that's what we call him. He's really not all there, poor bastard. First visit, is it? Don't expect too much from the old man. We keep him well tranked, so he won't go wandering. A lot of them get restless legs.'

'It's nice to know you're taking such good care of my uncle,' said Molly. 'I must be sure to give you a little something before I leave.'

Tommy smiled and nodded, the fool.

He and Molly talked some more, but I stopped listening. I used the Sight the torc gave me to see the lobby as it really was, hidden from merely mortal gaze. There were demons everywhere, scuttling across the ceiling and clinging to the walls, and riding on the backs of the patients. Demons don't cause madness, but they delight in the suffering it causes. Some of the demons had grown fat and distended, like parasites gorged on too much blood. A squat black insect thing squatted at the attendant nurse's feet, like a faithful pet waiting for a treat. Some of the demons realised I could see them. They stirred uneasily, sinking barbed claws and hooks into the patients' backs and shoulders, making it clear they wouldn't give up their victims without a fight. I wanted to kill every demon in the room, rip them off their victims, feel their skulls and carapaces break and shatter under my golden fists; but I couldn't risk making a scene. I needed to see Oddly John. I needed to know what he knew.

I turned my back on the parlour, and shut down my Sight. There's a reason why I don't use it very often. If we could see the world as it truly is, all the time, we couldn't bear to live in it. Not even Droods. Ignorance can be bliss.

I went back to stand with Molly, who immediately sensed my impatience. She stopped pressing the guard for information, and said she'd like to see her uncle now. Tommy shrugged, and led us over to the elevators. And all the time I was thinking, *Three days, four tops.* Part of me wanted to sulk and stamp my feet and shout *Not fair!* But when had my life ever been fair? I couldn't afford to give in to hysterics. Had to stay calm, and focused. Perhaps, at the end, all that would be left to me was to go down fighting, and take as many of my enemies with me as I could.

If so, I couldn't wait to get started.

Tommy took us up to the top floor. The elevator had its own security override lock. I peered unobtrusively over Tommy's shoulder as he punched in the combination. Sure enough, it was 4321. A bunch of determined boy scouts could burgle this place. Probably get a badge, these days.

'Why Oddly John?' I said abruptly. 'What is it that's so ... odd about him?'

Tommy sniggered. I was getting really tired of that sound. 'Because he talks to people that aren't there, and often won't talk to people that are. He sees things no one else can, and talks all kinds of rubbish about it, if you'll let him. Lives in a world of his own, that one. Used to have really bad nightmares, until we increased his medication. To be fair, though, he's never violent; eats his food and never makes a fuss about taking his pills. That's the best kind of patient, in a place like this.'

He led us down to the end of the corridor. Its walls had been painted in pale pastel colours, so as not to over-excite the patients. Motion sensitive cameras followed us the whole way. The door to Oddly John's room stood halfway open. Tommy stood back, and gestured for Molly and I to go in.

'Any problems, there's a big red panic button by the door. Hit that, and I'll come running. Don't be afraid to use it. We had nurse here not long ago, let a guy get too close to her, and he bit half her face off before we could pull him away. We kicked the crap out of him afterwards, but it didn't do her much good. Never came back.

Don't blame her. Heard she got some really decent compensation money, though. Remember; no matter how nice and sweet they are to you, you can't trust any of them. They're sick vicious bastards, or they wouldn't be here. No offence, Molly. You have a nice visit with your Uncle John.'

He ambled away, and Molly and I looked at each other. 'Cheerful fellow,' she said.

'I thought so.'

'I really must remember to give him an appallingly fierce case of haemorrhoids before I leave.'

'I would. Shall we go in?'

We went in. The room seemed pleasant enough. More calming colours on the walls, a comfortable-looking bed and some basic furnishings; all clearly bolted to the floor. Some books on a shelf, flowers in vases and a television in one corner, turned off. The patient was sitting quietly in a chair by the window, looking out through the bars. A frail old man, in a faded dressing gown. He didn't look round as we came in, or react as we approached him. I checked him out briefly with the Sight. He didn't have a demon anywhere on him, but he did have a golden collar round his throat. He was a Drood, all right. I moved round to get a good look at his face, and then gasped and gaped openly.

'What?' said Molly. 'What is it? Do you recognise him?'

'Hell yes,' I said. 'His name isn't John. This is William Dominic Drood. And he's not a rogue; he's listed as missing. The family's been looking for him for years. He used to be head librarian, back at The Hall. One of our very best research scholars. He just ... disappeared one day, and was never seen again. And believe me, we looked really hard for him. He knew all kinds of things, about the family and The Hall, secrets we couldn't afford anyone outside the family to know. But we never found him. His disappearance is one of the great unsolved mysteries of my family. And all these years, he's been ... here?'

I stopped, and looked abruptly at the surveillance camera in the far corner of the room.

'It's all right,' Molly said. 'I hit it with my illusion spell the moment we walked in here. They'll see what they expect to see, nothing more. But it won't last long. So talk to the man. Call him by his right name. I've tried everything I could think of, and never got more than a dozen words out of him. See if you can do any better. But make it quick. Time is not on our side.'

'I know,' I said. 'Trust me, I know.'

I crouched down beside Oddly John's chair. It was easier to think of him that way, mostly because of the really unsettling look in his eyes. Whatever he was seeing out of his window, I was pretty sure I wouldn't see it if I looked out. Or would want to.

'William?' I said. 'William Dominic Drood. Can you hear me?'

He didn't even look round. The sad, lost look on his face didn't change for a moment.

'Try showing him your torc,' Molly said suddenly. 'That might jar something loose.'

I opened the top buttons of my shirt with my right hand only, revealing the golden collar round my throat. I took hold of Oddly John's chin with my hand, and turned his face gently but firmly around to look at me. 'Listen to me, William. I'm Edwin Drood, sent to find you. See my torc. Do you remember me? I used to be in and out of the Library all the time, when I was a kid.'

He looked at the torc, and just like that, he woke up. It was eerie, even shocking, to see a whole new personality flow into his face, like water pouring into a glass. He looked sharp and intelligent, and not in the least mad, or drugged. He jumped out his chair and backed away from me, both hands held out as though to ward me off.

'Is this it?' he said. 'Have you come to kill me at last, for the family?'

'No, no!' I said quickly. 'I mean you no harm. I'm not here for the family. I've been declared rogue, and I don't know why. I was hoping you might have some answers, or at least some advice.'

He calmed down almost immediately, and came back to lower himself into his chair. 'So,' he said finally. 'Eddie Drood. Of course I remember you. Always plaguing me with questions, querying every-thing, borrowing books and never bringing them back. Best student I ever had. And now you're a rogue, in the company of the infamous Molly Metcalf. No offence, my dear.'

'None taken,' said Molly. 'Do you remember me coming here before?'

'I'm afraid not. I don't ... come out much, any more. Unless I absolutely have to. There was some talk of transferring me out of here. I soon put a stop to that.'

'But why?' I said. 'What are you doing here, in a place like this? What happened to you?'

He looked at me sadly. 'I can see the ghosts of everyone you ever killed, Eddie. So many of them ... And there's something inside you, something *other* ... I see so clearly these days, whether I want to or not.' He looked across at Molly, crouching down now on the other side of his chair. 'And you've made so many unfortunate deals, to get the power you wanted. To avenge your poor parents. I can see the chains hanging around you, weighing you down. So much weight to carry, for one so young ...' He looked out of his window again, so he wouldn't have to look at Molly or me any more.

'What do you see out there?' I said.

'All the views from all the other dimensions that intersect with this one. I see a forest of flowers, singing in awful harmonies. I see a great stone honeycomb, a thousand feet high, with people crawling in and out of the stone cells, and scuttling up the walls like insects. I see towers of pure light, and waterfalls of blood, and a cemetery where they rise from their graves to dance in the moonlight.'

I looked across at Molly. 'You think he really sees these things?'

'Who knows?' said Molly. 'He's your family.'

Oddly John looked sharply at me. 'So; you're rogue now. What did you do, Eddie?'

'I don't know! I was hoping you might ...'

'You didn't come here for help,' said Oddly John. 'You came here looking for safety and security, like me. I faked madness to get into this place. Faked the symptoms, faked the paperwork. I was very convincing. I'm safe, here. I'm not locked in; the family's locked out. They'll never find me. They want me dead, you know. Or at least some of them do. Because of what I know. What I found out ...'

'I'm going to bring the family down,' I said. 'Break their hold on the world. Will you help?'

'No!' said Oddly John, suddenly banging his frail fists on the arms of his chair. 'That's not enough! The family must be wiped out, slaughtered to the very last of us. Including you and me. We have to die. The Drood family is vile, evil, utterly corrupt. Because of what we did, and what we are ... There can be no forgiveness for such a sin. Only death can make up for such a crime.' He grabbed my hand in a painfully tight grip. 'Are they still looking for me? After all this time?'

'Yes. Of course. You're very important to the family.'

'They're looking for me because of what I know.' He let go of my hand, and stared out of the window again. 'They'll never stop looking for me.'

'What is it?' said Molly. 'What do you know?'

'Their agents could be anywhere,' Oddly John said craftily. 'Visitors, patients, guards. But they'll never find William Drood, because he's not here. Only Oddly John is here. I hide inside him, so deep no one can see me . . . But you're here. If you found me, so can they!'

He grew really agitated then, whipping his bony head back and forth. It took Molly and me some time to calm him down again, hushing and comforting him like a small child after a nightmare. 'Why does the family want to find you so badly?' I said. 'What is it that you know?'

'I don't know,' Oddly John said miserably. 'I can't remember. I made myself forget, you see. I had to. It was the only way to stay sane . . . I found out something, I know that. I read a book I shouldn't have, a very old book, and it told me something terrible, about the family. About what we really are.'

'I know,' I said. 'It was a shock to me, too, to learn that we're the secret masters of the world.'

'Not that,' Oddly John said scornfully. 'Who cares about that? I could live with that . . . No, this was much worse . . . Sometimes I dream I'm back in The Hall. I walk into the Sanctity, and stand before the Heart . . . and then I wake up screaming. There's something I don't remember, something I mustn't remember, because it's too awful, too terrible to bear. The secret at the heart of the Droods . . . I left The Hall. I ran and I ran and I ran, and finally I came here. I'm safe here. Safe from everything and everyone; even myself. I don't know what's happening out in the world any more, and I don't care. Knowing things doesn't make you happy.'

'No one followed me,' I said. 'No one knows we're here. You're still safe.'

'Bless you, Eddie,' he said. 'I wish there was something I could do for you. But I can't help you. I can't help any of us. We're all damned, you see. Damned because of what we did, and what we are . . .'

And just like that, he went back inside himself again. William Dominic Drood disappeared, and there was only Oddly John. The personality drained out of his face, leaving the empty shell behind, sitting quietly in his chair, looking out through the bars on his window at the things only he could see. Hiding from my family, and from whatever it was he was so desperate not to remember. What could he have discovered, what truth could he have stumbled over, that was so much worse than what I already knew? There was no point in asking Oddly John or William Drood.

If he hadn't been crazy when he came in here, he sure as Hell was now.

CHAPTER FIFTEEN

Chasing Eddie

Back at the top of the grassy hill I turned slowly, looking out over the small town of Flitwick. Picturesque houses, narrow streets, farms and farmlands off in the distance. So very ordinary, so everyday; so unknowing of the terrible things that shared the world with them. Once it was my job to protect people like them from the bad things that hid and lurked in the shadows; but the more I investigated, the deeper I dug, the more I discovered just how deep and dark the shadows really were. And now it seemed my family were looking back at me, out of the shadows. What could William have found out, so terrible he had to wipe it from his mind? If I found out, would I end up having to do the same?

I shivered, standing on the top of a hill in the middle of nowhere, looking out over a world I no longer recognised.

My arm hurt. Even when I was careful not to move it, the damned thing ached like a bad tooth. There was something inside me, eating me alive. Three days, four at the most. And always, this constant pressure of needing to be doing something, anything, so as not to waste a moment of the precious time I had left to me; and yet for all my digging, all my questions, I still had nothing certain to lash out at. I knew the names of my enemies, but not their reasons. I had to think, to plan; and still the clock was ticking, ticking . . . I looked at Molly, standing silently beside me.

'Well,' I said. 'Thank you for bringing me here, Molly. That was seriously depressing. Are there any more bright and helpful fellow rogues you think I ought to meet?'

'I could portal out of here and abandon you, you know,' said Molly.

'You'd miss my sparkling personality.'

'Look, don't knock yourself, Eddie. You got a lot more out of Oddly John than I ever did. And I do have another rogue in mind. Someone who could be very helpful. He knows a lot of things. He's called the Mole.'

'Now there's a name that inspires confidence.'

'Do you want to meet him or not?'

'Does he have three friends called Ratty, Toad and Badger?' I said hopefully.

Molly sighed. 'This is revenge for me introducing you to Mr Stab, isn't it?'

'No, really, I can't wait to meet Mr Mole in his hole.'

She looked at me. 'Your arm's worse, isn't it?'

'Yes. Let's go.'

Molly summoned up another spatial portal, frowning with concentration. The process seemed to take longer this time, and sweat ran freely down her face. The air churned and whirled before us, spinning round and round like water going down a plughole. It plucked us off the hilltop and into itself, and we were off on our travels again.

When Molly and I reappeared, we were standing in a toilet cubicle. It was very cramped. Molly and I were pressed tightly together, face to face. Anywhen else, I might have taken a moment to enjoy it, but unfortunately I had one leg jammed down the toilet bowl.

'Oh shit,' said Molly.

'Don't even go there,' I said, struggling to remove my foot from the bowl. 'Do I take it we're not where we were supposed to be?'

'Of course not! But it could have been worse.'

'Oh *shit*,' I said.

'What?'

'It would appear the previous occupant didn't flush. Would you please breathe in, so I can get my foot out?'

We struggled together for a moment, banging loudly against the sides of the cubicle, and finally I was able to jerk my foot free. The bottom of my trouser leg was soaked, and I didn't want to think what with. I glared at Molly.

'Today started out with a knife at my throat, and yet still has managed to go steadily downhill. Where the Hell are we?'

'Paddington railway station.'

'Really?' I said. 'I remember it as being somewhat bigger.'

'Fool. We're in the ladies' toilet, at Paddington. Which means . . . someone tried to intercept my portal spell.'

Getting out of the cubicle took some cooperation and a certain amount of brute force, as the door opened inwards, but eventually we spilled out into the main toilet area. Half a dozen women stopped adjusting their dress and repairing their make-up to stare at us. Molly glared right back.

'Come on; don't tell me you've never thought about doing it in a cubicle.'

'I feel like such a slut,' I said. 'Promise me you'll spank me when we get home, mistress?'

The women couldn't get out of the toilet fast enough. I grinned at Molly, but she wasn't in the mood.

'All right,' I said. 'On a scale of one to ten, how bad is this?'

'Oh, I think this one goes all the way up to eleven. Someone must have tried to override my spell's coordinates, to make us arrive at a destination of their choosing. Where they could be waiting for us. But, being the happy paranoid little soul that I am, I long ago pre-programmed my spell to be prepared for such an eventuality, and at the first sign of outside tampering drop me off at a pre-designated emergency arrival point.'

'God, I love it when you talk technical.'

'Shut up. I chose this place because a toilet cubicle is one of the few places where you can appear out of nowhere without being noticed. Do I really need to add that I did not have two people in mind when I chose this arrival point?'

'Why Paddington?' I said.

'It's a central London station, with trains always going somewhere. You can pick one at random, hop on and disappear without a trace. Now let's get out of here. The only people powerful enough to intercept a portal spell would have to be major league sorcerers. Which could mean your family.'

'Why not Manifest Destiny?' I said, just to be contrary.

'You heard Truman. They put their faith in science, not magic. My kind are only allowed in as fellow travellers. What interests me is how your family could know that you're travelling with me now.'

I shrugged. 'We probably have agents buried deep within Manifest Destiny. We have people everywhere, in every kind of organisation, so we won't be surprised when they try to start something nasty. How else do you think we know everything that's going on?'

Molly looked at me. 'And you didn't think to tell me this before?'

'Sorry; I thought you knew how my family operates. Besides, I've been distracted. I've had a lot on my mind recently.'

'Is there anything else I ought to know?'

'There's something squelching in my shoe.'

'I should have stabbed you while you were still asleep,' said Molly.

We made our way up and out and on to the Paddington station main concourse. The wide open space was full of people, bustling back and forth as though their lives depended on it, or just standing together like sheep, staring vacantly at the changing displays on the information screens. Train engines roared loudly, people spoke into mobile phones, doing their best to look as though their calls were vitally important, and every now and again the station loudspeakers would blast out some deafening but totally incomprehensible statement.

I relaxed a little. I like crowds. Always somewhere to hide in a crowd. Molly and I pretended to examine the menu on a nearby fast food stall, while taking a surreptitious look around. It seemed normal enough. Two armed policemen wandered by, burdened down with flack jackets and equipment, alert for everyday problems. They weren't interested in Molly and me. They didn't know people like Molly and me even existed, the lucky devils.

'I liked this place a lot better before they gave it a make-over,' I said to Molly. 'There used to be a restaurant here where you could order chilli con carne and chips, and beans and bacon and sausages, and pile it as high as you liked. Now that was a meal and a half. I used to call it the cholesterol special. You could feel your arteries hardening just looking at it.'

Molly regarded me with distaste bordering on disgust. 'I'm amazed your heart didn't explode.'

'I always did like to live dangerously. Speaking of which, don't turn around too quickly but spot the two guys approaching from four o'clock. I think we've been made.'

'Already? Damn.' Molly sneaked a look in the direction I'd indicated. Two men in anonymous dark suits were striding towards us, holding their hands up to their faces and talking to their wrists. Either they had radios up their sleeves or they were Care in the Community. Molly scowled. 'They could be plainclothes policemen ...'

The two men produced automatic weapons from slings under their jackets, and opened fire, actually shooting through the packed crowd to get at us. Men and women crashed to the ground, bleeding and screaming and dying. People were thrown this way and that by the bullets' impact, and one man's head exploded. The woman with him sank to her knees beside his kicking body, howling her grief and horror. People ran screaming in every direction, and dived for what little cover there was. And the two men with automatic weapons ran straight at Molly and me, firing without pause. The armed police came running, and the two men shot them down, hosing them with bullets till they stopped moving.

I ducked behind the fast food stall, and Molly was right there with me. Above us, bowls of soup shattered and blew apart, spraying hot liquid everywhere. The staff inside the stall shrieked and ducked down, their screams almost drowned out by the chaos and the roar of gunfire. The whole stall rocked and shuddered as bullets pounded into it again and again. How many guns did these bastards have? Shouldn't they be running out of ammo by now? I risked a quick peek round the corner of the stall. The two men were coming at us, firing steadily, followed by a dozen more men in dark suits from all across the concourse, running to join them. There were dead bodies everywhere, in spreading pools of blood.

'We can't stay here,' I said to Molly. 'I can armour up, but that won't protect you.'

'I don't need protecting,' said Molly. 'I'll arrange a diversion, and then we both run like hell for the nearest street exit. Sound good to you?'

'Sounds like a plan to me. What kind of diversion?'

'Close your eyes and put your hands over them.'

I did so, and a moment later came an incandescent flare that hurt my eyes even through tightly squeezed eyelids. Raised voices cried out in shock and pain, and Molly grabbed me by the shoulder and hauled me out from behind the bullet-riddled fast food stall. I forced my eyes open as I stumbled after her. Black spots blurred and jumped in my vision, but at least I could see. The armed men were staggering around, tears streaming from half-open eyes, firing their guns at any sudden sound or movement. And since most of the civilians were gone, that mostly meant they were shooting at each other. I could live with that. I passed by one gunman as I followed Molly to the nearest street exit, and I paused just long enough to break his neck with one blow. Never involve civilians in our wars, you bastard.

I would have liked to kill more of them, but there wasn't time. I'm not an assassin, but sometimes the only right thing remaining is to kill the bastards until there aren't any left. I hate it when innocents get caught up in my world. That's why I became an agent in the first place: to protect innocents from what lives in my world.

The gunmen had to be Manifest Destiny. My family would have been more subtle. And, I still believed, more sparing of the innocent. But how had Manifest Destiny found us so quickly? Maybe they had all the railway stations staked out, just in case. Made sense. My bad arm yelled at me as I ran after Molly, and I told it to shut the hell up. I was busy. A few bullets flew past me, not even close. Some of the gunmen were getting their sight back. I could have armoured up, but I couldn't trust the stealth factor to work under these conditions, with so many watching eyes, and I was still reluctant to expose my family's greatest secret to public gaze. Unless I had to.

I caught up with Molly as she stumbled to a halt halfway up the steep slope that led out into the main traffic. We were both breathing hard. Cars and vans roared past unknowing, as though it was just another day. I looked at Molly.

'What do we do now? Hail a taxi?'

'I wouldn't. You can never be sure who the drivers are really working for. I've got a better idea.'

She bent over and hiked up her dress, revealing a dainty silver charm bracelet around her left ankle. She snapped one of the charms free and held it up: a delicate little silver motorcycle. Molly muttered a few Words in a harsh language that must have hurt her throat, and breathed on the charm. It wriggled eerily on her palm, and then leapt off, growing rapidly in mid air until, standing on the slope before us, was a Vincent Black Shadow motorbike. A big beast of a bike, and a classic of its kind. I was impressed.

'I'm impressed,' I said to Molly. 'Really. You have excellent taste in motorcycles. If a tad nostalgic.'

'Don't talk to me about modern bikes,' said Molly. 'No character.'

More bullets flew past us. They were getting closer. I looked back down the slope. Men with guns were staggering in our direction, tears still rolling down their cheeks. Their aim wasn't that accurate yet, but with automatic weapons it didn't need to be.

'Get on the damn bike!' said Molly.

I looked round. The Vincent roared to life as she kick-started it, and then swung on to the leather seat.

'Hold everything,' I said. 'I do not ride pillion.'

'My bike, my ride. Get on.'

'I am not riding pillion! I have my dignity to consider.'

More bullets whined past us. They really were getting closer. Molly smiled sweetly at me.

'You and your dignity can always run alongside if you like, but I am leaving.'

I growled something under my breath, and swung aboard the seat behind her. Molly slammed the Vincent into gear and we shot off up the slope, pursued by bullets, and straight out into the main flow of traffic. Outraged horns and voices greeted us from every side, as we appeared out of nowhere and bullied our way in. Fortunately, the average speed of London traffic is rarely more than about ten miles per hour, in between traffic lights, so we were able to dodge and weave in and around the slower-moving vehicles and build up a healthy speed. I held Molly tightly round the waist with my right arm. I tried to use the left as well, but it was too painful, so I let my forearm rest on Molly's left thigh. She didn't seem to mind. Even tucked in close behind her, the air still hit my face like a slap and tugged at my hair. I put my mouth next to Molly's ear.

'Would it have killed you to conjure up a couple of crash helmets too?'

'Helmets are for sissies!' said Molly, shouting back over the roar of the Vincent's engine. She laughed joyously. 'Hold on, Eddie!'

'I'll bet you're not insured,' I said.

*

We weaved in and out of moving cars as though they were standing still, steadily building up speed. Taxi drivers shouted insults, and shop fronts blurred past on either side. We'd already taken so many turns I hadn't a clue where we were any longer. A big red London bus pulled out in front of us, because London buses don't give way to anything, and my heart practically leapt out of my chest as Molly gunned the throttle and shot us through the narrowing gap like a lemming on amphetamines. I may have screamed, just a little.

'Try and lean with me on the curves, Eddie!' Molly shouted cheerfully. 'It makes manoeuvring so much easier.'

We howled across intersections at scary speeds and treated stop lights with contempt. The bike swayed this way and that, dodging and weaving as it plunged in and out of traffic, slowing for no one. It would have been quite exhilarating, if I'd been driving. As it was, I clung on with my good arm and threw up a series of hopeful prayers to St Christopher, the patron saint of travellers. He's been officially decommissioned these days, but no one asked my permission, so . . .

The first I knew that we were being pursued came when a bullet whined past my ear. I grabbed Molly tightly, and risked a look back. Two big black cars were coming up fast behind us. They must have been really heavily armoured, because they built up speed by just shunting and slamming aside everything in front of them. When there wasn't any room, the big black cars would drive right over whatever was in front of them, crushing the lesser vehicle like a tank. Other cars were driven off the road, or intimidated into taking sudden side turnings they hadn't intended to. The traffic between the black cars and us thinned rapidly out, and men leaned out of the cars' shaded windows to fire automatic weapons at us. Luckily, that's a lot harder than it seems in the movies.

I turned back and yelled into Molly's ear. 'Manifest Destiny, right behind! And they're shooting at us!'

'I had noticed, actually. You sure it's not your family?'

'Positive. They wouldn't use guns. They'd use something much more extreme.'

Molly sent the bike flying around a tight corner, leaning right over. I did my best to help, leaning with her, but it was all I could do to hang on with just the one arm. The ground did look awfully close there for a moment. Molly wrestled the Vincent upright again, and opened the throttle all the way. We roared down the street, flashing in and out of startled cars, sometimes close enough to scrape their paintwork with our wing mirrors, all the time dodging gunfire from behind. They were starting to get our range. I risked another look back, turning right round on the leather seat. The black cars were smashing through everything in their path, ramming cars out of their way. Skidding civilian cars slammed into each other, some overturned, and there were pile-ups the length of the street behind us. The black cars just kept coming, and the bullets got closer and closer, no matter how much we dodged and weaved.

I armoured up. The living metal flowed smoothly over and around me in a moment, sealing me off from a hostile world. Bullets hit my back and ricocheted away. They couldn't touch me or Molly now. The rate of gunfire increased as the black cars drew nearer, bullets spraying across my back, my shoulders and the back of my head. I didn't feel the impact, but I could hear it. Armouring my left arm had made it strong again, if no less painful. I slipped it carefully round Molly's waist, and felt a little more secure.

The Vincent was really hammering along now, the passing world a blur. Molly was laughing out loud, whooping with the joy of speed. I was more concerned about what would happen if one of the bullets happened to hit the Vincent's fuel tank. I mentioned this to Molly.

'Don't worry!' she yelled back. 'This isn't really a motorbike. It just looks like one.'

'Not a real bike? Not a real Vincent Black Shadow?'

'Come on,' said Molly. 'What did you expect from a charm bracelet?'

'Just as long as it doesn't turn back to a pumpkin at midnight . . .'

Molly laughed again, and pushed the bike's speed even harder. I took my right arm away from Molly's waist and drew the Colt Repeater from its shoulder holster. It took me a while, and hurt my shoulder like hell, but I finally wrestled the gun out. I breathed hard for a moment, controlling the pain and bracing myself for what I had to do next. I tightened my hold around Molly's waist with my strengthened left arm, turned around on the seat and looked back at the cars behind me. There were four of them now, with a fifth catching up, ploughing their way through any traffic that didn't get out of their way fast enough. Men were leaning out of the car windows and firing at me with a whole assortment of weapons. One even had a rocket launcher. He fired the thing, and the rocket shot out, slammed into my armoured side and ricocheted away to blow up a Gap store. I hoped there was nobody inside, but I had no way of knowing. Manifest Destiny didn't care who got hurt, or killed. And that was when I decided that just escaping these bastards wasn't good enough.

They were all firing at me now, bullets bouncing off my chest and golden face mask. The bike slammed this way and that as we shot in and out of a traffic jam. The extra pain in my arm made me cry out, and tears ran down my face under the mask. But the Colt Repeater in my right hand was steady as hell when I trained it on the pursuing cars.

I tried shooting out the tyres first. That always worked in the movies. But though I hit every tyre I aimed at, not one of them blew. The armoured cars were running on solid rubber tyres. Manifest Destiny must have seen those movies too. So I aimed at the driver of the nearest car. He laughed at me, through his bullet-proof glass windscreen, right up until the Colt Repeater sent a bullet through the windscreen and blew his head apart. The car swerved wildly, mounted the pavement and rammed through three parking meters before sliding to a halt. I aimed carefully and shot dead the other four drivers, and their cars skidded and crashed and slammed into store fronts.

But more black cars were already joining the chase, screeching round corners from every side street we passed. Soon there were a dozen new cars on our trail, swerving back and forth to make my aiming harder. I kept blowing away their drivers, one at a time. Such aim would have been impossible under normal conditions, but luckily the Colt Repeater did most of the work for me. Thank you, Uncle Jack. Still more cars joined the pursuit, seeming to come from everywhere at once, ploughing through the civilian traffic like it wasn't even there, tossing lighter cars aside or grinding them underneath. There was a chaos of crashed and burning vehicles behind us, for as far back as I could see. Wide-eyed men and women huddled in shop doorways, yelling into mobile phones as we shot past.

The gunfire was constant now, slamming into me and the bike, trying to bring us down with sheer pressure of bullets. Most of

214

them ricocheted away, chewing up storefronts and cutting down pedestrians. Manifest Destiny were using me to kill innocent people. I couldn't let that go on.

A black car came roaring out of a side street and drew alongside us. The man in the back seat shot me in the face at point blank range, crying out angrily as the bullet glanced off the golden mask. They were on my left side, so I couldn't shoot them. I risked letting go of Molly's waist with my left arm, punched through the car's windscreen, pulled the driver out, and threw him into the road ahead. The black car ran over him, skidded away, hit a parked car and flipped end over end before crashing to a halt. I put my aching arm back around Molly's waist.

A police car tried to get involved. It came screaming round a corner, siren blaring, lights flashing. Two of the big black cars closed in on either side of it, and then both drivers jerked their steering wheels over at the same time. The heavily armoured cars crushed the police car between them, crunching up the standard steel chassis like so much tinfoil. The black cars roared on as the police car skidded out of control and smashed through a glass storefront, its siren still wailing forlornly. I felt bad for the cops in the car. The police aren't supposed to get involved in our wars. They're not equipped to deal with the likes of us.

I turned back to yell in Molly's ear. 'There are more cars after us now than when we started! Are we going anywhere in particular?'

'Yes! Away!'

I had to laugh. 'I'm so glad we've got a plan.'

'Anything else, Eddie, only I'm a bit busy at the moment ...'

'Too many civilians are getting hurt! Maybe we should just stop and fight it out.'

'Don't even think that! The odds suck. You can bet the moment we stop moving, they'll have long-range sharp-shooters in place to target us. Your armour can't protect me from that. They'd threaten to kill me, until you agreed to armour down. Then they'd shoot you full of tranks, take you back to headquarters and dissect you alive to get at your family secrets, and the armour in particular. They'd probably do the same to me, for turning traitor on them. I'd rather go down fighting. Or at least escaping.'

'You've really thought this through,' I said.

'Hell,' said Molly. 'It's what I'd do. Now hang on. Our only real hope is to lose these bastards.'

A black car emerged from a side alley and lurched out on to the street ahead of us. It spun around on squealing wheels and came charging straight at us. We were blocked in by cars on either side, with no room to manoeuvre. I could have jumped off. The armour would have protected me. But that would have left Molly on her own . . . I was still trying to figure out what to do when Molly revved the engine for all it was worth and aimed the bike right at the gleaming radiator of the approaching black car. I could hear her chanting something, but the rushing wind ripped her words away. The black car loomed up before us, close enough that I could see the driver laughing at us, and then, at the very last moment, the Vincent rose up into the air and sailed over the top of the car. We landed behind it with only the faintest of bumps and kept on going. I looked back in time to see the Manifest Destiny car smash into another black car that had been following behind us. The two cars slammed together, head to head, and then blew apart with a satisfying large explosion.

I turned back and hugged Molly tightly so I could yell in her ear. 'I didn't know the bike could do that!'

'It can't! But I can. Though not very often, so you'd better hope that doesn't happen again.'

I sent up some more prayers to St Christopher.

Molly swung the bike round a sharp corner, and then hit the brakes so hard it would have knocked the breath out of me if I hadn't been wearing my armour. The street ahead of us was completely empty, cleared of all traffic and pedestrians. The only people who could have arranged that so quickly were my family. And sure enough, there they were. I looked over Molly's shoulder and saw what she had already spotted. Halfway down the street three golden figures stood like statues, the light gleaming brightly on their armour.

I was actually a little flattered. Three field agents, just to bring me in. I had no doubt they could do it. So I put the Colt Repeater away, and hit the stud on my reverse watch. God bless you, Uncle Jack. Time rewound itself, spinning the world back thirty seconds, so that once again Molly and I were approaching the corner. As Molly started to turn, I yelled urgently into her ear, and she brought the bike to a skidding halt, the back wheel sliding back and forth as it locked. We both bailed off the bike, and she said the Words that turned it back into a silver charm. I armoured down, and we both disappeared into the nearest side alley.

The three golden field agents were already sprinting towards us, but a dozen black cars came screeching round the corner. They saw the field agents, and drove their armoured cars right at them, the fools. Molly and I watched from the shadows of the side alley as the first car reached the first agent. He stood his ground, and then slammed his golden fist down on to the black car's bonnet at the very last moment. The whole front of the car compacted, slamming into the ground, the back came up, and the car somersaulted over the agent's head before crashing to the ground behind him.

The second agent launched himself through the windscreen of the next car, killed everyone inside, and burst out the back of the car and on to the bonnet of the car following. The third agent picked up one armoured car and used it to hit another. Black cars screeched to a halt, and men spilled out, firing all kinds of weapons. Soon the whole street was full of men in golden armour doing terrible things to men of ill will.

Made me feel proud to be a Drood.

'Time we were going,' I said quietly to Molly.

'Damn, your people are good,' she said.

We sneaked quietly away, just two more terrified pedestrians fleeing the carnage. I suddenly realised there was blood on Molly's face. It was dripping from her nose, and spilling down her chin from her mouth. She dabbed at it with a small silk square from up her sleeve, but all she succeeded in doing was moving the blood around. I stopped her and took out my own handkerchief. Molly stood quietly and allowed me to mop the blood from her face.

'What happened?' I said. 'Were you hit? Did a bullet get you?'

'No,' said Molly. 'I did this to myself. I told you: spatial portals are serious magic. They take a lot out of me. And then what I did with the bike, on top of that . . . Magic always has to be paid for, one way or another. That's why rituals and preparation are so important; they raise the energies necessary to power the spells I use. So I don't have to draw on the energies of my own body. And I have been doing a lot of quick and dirty magics for you just lately, Eddie.'

'I'm sorry,' I said. 'I didn't know. Didn't realise what I was asking of you. Don't think I don't appreciate it. There. You look better now.'

'Thanks.'

'That's okay. I couldn't have you drawing attention to us, could I?'

'You are such a gentleman.' She looked at me. 'You look . . . pretty shit yourself, Eddie. How's the arm?'

'Worse without the armour.'

'The poison's spreading, isn't it?'

'Yes. The pain's moved out of my shoulder and into my chest as well. Are we far from your next rogue agent?'

'Not too far. I was heading in the right general direction all along. We can walk it from here.'

'Good. Let's go see the Mole in his hole.'

'Funny you should say that,' said Molly.

CHAPTER SIXTEEN
Home alone

I wasn't keen on going back down into the Underground train system again, but Molly insisted. It did seem to me that every time I'd gone underground recently bad things had happened to me. But then, above ground hadn't been that safe either. Molly and I walked back the way we'd come, heading for Blackfriars station, and it was like walking through a war zone. Crashed cars, shops on fire, damage and wreckage everywhere. People stumbled around, dazed and confused, crying and clinging to each other. And bodies, in the road or dragged out on to the pavement from burnt-out premises, sometimes decently draped with a coat, more often not. I felt stunned, sickened. This wasn't supposed to happen. In all the secret wars I ever fought, I never once let them spill over into the real world. I never, ever, let civilians get hurt.

'Stop that,' Molly said quietly. 'None of this was your fault. Manifest Destiny is responsible for what happened here, the bastards.'

'We let them chase us,' I said.

'What was the alternative? Stand our ground and die quickly, if we were lucky? I don't think so. You can't allow yourself to be taken, Eddie. You can't let Manifest Destiny get their hands on a weapon like your armour. And besides; you have to stay free because you know the truth. You have a responsibility to do something, to stop Manifest Destiny and your family from running the world like their own private preserve. You're the only hope these people have.'

'Then they're in serious trouble,' I said, after a while.

'That's better,' said Molly. 'Don't let the bastards grind you down, Eddie.'

*

The entrance to Blackfriars station was crammed with people, refugees hiding from the mayhem on the streets. They were gabbling and yelling at each other, but it was clear none of them had a clue as to what was really going on. Molly and I eased our way through the crowds on the stairs and down towards the escalators. I had been concerned that Manifest Destiny or my family might still have agents in the stations, watching for us, but in a crowd this size Molly and I were just two more people. Even the stalled escalators were full of shocked and baffled people, some of them crying, some of them comforting or being comforted. None of them understood what was happening; only that something much bigger and nastier than them had intruded on their peaceful, everyday lives. The very thing I'd spent my life fighting to prevent.

I felt like I'd failed them; and that mattered much more to me than failing my family ever had.

Down on the crowded platform, Molly and I unobtrusively made our way over to a soft drinks vending machine with an *Out of Order* sign on it. We glanced around to make sure no one was watching, and then I pulled the vending machine forward. It moved smoothly and easily, to show the hidden door in the wall behind it. I had to smile. There are a great many hidden doors in the London Underground, many of them hidden behind *Out of Order* vending machines. It's a secret sign, for those in the know. That's why so many of these machines are always, apparently, out of order. The doors lead to all kinds of interesting places that the general public are much better off not knowing about. Molly muttered a few Words at the concealed door in the wall, and it swung smoothly open before us. Molly and I slipped through into the darkness beyond, and the door quietly shut itself behind us.

Molly summoned up a handful of witchfire, and the shimmering silvery light spat and crackled around her upheld hand. A dark, dank tunnel stretched away before us, curving brick walls and a low ceiling, sloping steadily down into the earth. Molly's witchlight didn't penetrate far into the gloom, and the shadows were very dark.

'Is that glimmer really the best you can do?' I said.

'No. But this is as much as I'm prepared to risk. This isn't a place where you want to attract undue attention.'

'Where exactly are we going? Tell me we're not going down into the sewers again.'

'We're not going down into the sewers again.'

'Oh joy.'

'You're starting to get on my tits, Drood. This tunnel will lead us into the systems beneath the train system. Places left over and abandoned by the railways. Old stations that no one goes to any more, discontinued lines, workings that were never completed. That sort of thing.'

I nodded. I knew where we were, and where we were headed; I just wanted to show Molly that I was back to myself again. I could hear the roar of trains passing by, not that far away. The sound faded as Molly and I headed down the sloping tunnel, and into the dark.

'So,' I said, after a while. 'What do we do if we meet some trolls?'

'I plan on running. Try and keep up.'

'Someone told me they're getting ready to swarm again.'

'Happens every five years, regular as clockwork. The trolls over-populate the tunnels, exhaust the food supply, and eventually the sheer pressure of numbers and hunger forces them up towards the light, and people. So every few years the bounty hunters get to make good money by going down into the tunnels and culling the herd back to an acceptable number.'

'I don't see why we don't just wipe the ugly bastards out,' I said.

'Oh, we can't do that,' said Molly. 'Every species performs a function in nature, even if we can't see what it is. Wipe out the trolls, and something much worse might step forward to fill the gap. Better the ugly bastards you know than the ones you don't.'

We moved from one tunnel to another, and then another, always heading down, deeper into the earth. The air became hot and sweaty, almost humid. We splashed through pools of stagnant water on the floor, and more dripped from the ceiling. Fungi flourished in the hothouse atmosphere, sprouting in thick white clumps where the wall met the floor, and scattered in puffy fleshy masses on the ceiling. Huge mats of green and blue moss covered the walls, two to three inches deep, stretching away for as far as I could see. Long slow ripples moved across the surface of the moss, as though it was disturbed by our presence.

'There are those who say if you eat or smoke the moss, it will grant you visions of things unseen, and other worlds,' said Molly.

'I don't need moss for that,' I said. 'That's business as usual, for me. Have you noticed there aren't any rats down here? Anywhere.'

'Yes,' said Molly. 'I had noticed. The trolls must have eaten them all. And if they've been reduced to eating rats, it can only be because they've already eaten everything else. They must be really close to swarming.'

'Maybe we could come back and see the Mole some other time,' I said.

'You're really quite chicken for a Drood, aren't you?'

'Cautious,' I said. 'I prefer the word "cautious".'

'Look, the authorities are bound to have sent bounty hunters down here by now.'

'Yes,' I said, stopping. 'I think I've found one.'

We both knelt down to study the wreckage of what had once been a human body. It lay spreadeagled on its back, in a pool of blood that had already dried enough to be tacky to the touch. Its leather armour had been torn to ribbons, and the chest had been smashed in, to get at the meat beneath. The arms and legs had been torn off, with only the gnawed bones remaining, lying scattered on the stone floor. The face had been eaten away, right down to the bone, leaving empty eye-sockets and grinning blood-smeared teeth.

'Any idea who it might have been?' I said. The state of the body didn't bother me. I've seen lots of bodies.

'No,' said Molly, scowling. 'The only bounty hunter I know is Janissary Jane, and that isn't her armour.'

'You know Jane?' I said, surprised.

'We've worked a few cases together. I keep telling you, Eddie; the world isn't as neatly divided into black and white as your family wanted you to believe.'

I picked up a machine pistol, lying abandoned not far from the body, and examined it closely. 'Doesn't look like they got a shot off. But where are the rest of the weapons? I can't believe any bounty hunter would go after trolls with just the one gun.'

We looked around, but there was nothing else, on or around the body. Molly and I looked at each other.

'They couldn't have taken them,' said Molly.

'Why not?'

'Trolls are animals! They don't use tools, or weapons.'

'Animals evolve,' I said. 'Particularly under pressure from outside forces. Trolls who've learned to use weapons; now that is seriously scary.'

'We need to get moving,' said Molly, rising to her feet and looking quickly about her. 'Get in to see the Mole and get out again, before the trolls swarm.'

'Relax,' I said. 'They can't touch us. I've got my armour, and you've got your magic.'

'Your armour might protect you from direct attack, but a whole swarm of trolls could knock you on your arse, carry you away to their deep larders and keep you there till you had to come out of your armour. And then ...' We both looked at the half-eaten bounty hunter. 'There's a limit to what I can do with my magic now,' Molly said reluctantly. 'I've used up most of my stored resources. Anything big would wipe me out.'

'You couldn't have mentioned that before we came down here?' I said.

We both looked round sharply. There were sounds in the darkness around us. Molly waved her witchfire back and forth, illuminating the dark mouths of tunnel openings ahead and behind us. From not far away came high-pitched hootings and howlings, and the slow, sharp sound of claws and talons scraping against stone. We looked up and down the tunnel, but the many overlapping echoes made it impossible to tell from which direction any sound was coming. Molly and I stood back to back, breathing heavily. And then from behind us, from back the way we'd come, there was the growing sound of heavy feet on the move, of heavy bodies thundering down the tunnel towards us. Molly sprinted off into the darkness ahead, and I was right behind her.

The deeper we went, the shabbier the tunnels became. The old brick walls began to crack and fall apart. Fungi and moss flourished, hiding human workings under rounded organic shapes. Tunnel openings were interspersed with rough holes smashed through the ancient stonework, dark gaps raw as wounds. Things moved in the darkness, hissing at us as we passed. Molly and I ran on, pushing ourselves as hard as we could, not even glancing into the openings, and behind us came the thunder of the trolls, drawing steadily closer.

I could have armoured up, and left them behind in a moment; but trolls were sensitive to magic. They could have tracked my armour easily, even in complete darkness. Even the small magic of the witchfire was a calculated risk.

'How much further to the Mole?' I said, between panting breaths.

'I'm . . . not exactly sure,' said Molly.

'*What?*'

'Hey, it's been a long time since I was last down here! And I may have got a bit. . . turned around.'

Without slowing my pace, I reached inside my jacket and brought out the emergency compass the Armourer had given me, back at The Hall.

'I know which way is north,' said Molly. 'And it really isn't helping.'

'This particular compass is supposed to show me the best way out of any emergency situation,' I said, trying to hold the thing steady as I ran. The compass needle flicked back and forth, and then settled on north-east, just as a new tunnel opening appeared in that direction. The needle moved to point at the opening. 'This way!' I said.

'Your family always has the best toys,' said Molly, and we plunged into the new tunnel without slowing.

We ran on, following the needle from tunnel to tunnel. The hootings and howlings came from all around us now. The tunnels finally ended in a natural stone chamber, complete with jagged stalactites and stalagmites. Strange mineral traces in the walls picked up the witchfire and glowed brightly, pushing back the dark. The compass needle swung back and forth, as though confused, and I stumbled to a halt while I waited for it to make up its mind. Molly leaned on me, fighting for breath. I wasn't much better off. My arm and shoulder were killing me.

'We're in trouble,' said Molly.

'No, really?' I said. 'You do surprise me. Show us the way to the Mole, you useless piece of crap!' And I slapped the compass a few times, to show it I meant business.

'No,' Molly said. 'I mean, I don't recognise this place at all. I've never been here, on any of my previous trips to the Mole's lair. Are you sure that thing is reliable?'

'Of course,' I lied. The compass needle finally settled for pointing straight ahead. I looked at Molly. 'Ready to run some more?'

She managed a quick grin. 'I find the imminent prospect of being eaten alive tends to concentrate the mind wonderfully.'

'I love it when you talk literary,' I said.

And that was when a whole crowd of trolls burst out of a side tunnel just behind us, fighting and clawing at each other in their eagerness to get at us. Molly and I sprinted off again, following the needle, but neither of us were as fast as we had been. I'd only got one quick glimpse of the trolls behind us, but that was enough. I'd faced trolls before, and they hadn't changed. Trolls are huge, stooped creatures, bone-white in colour, with long lanky frames. Jagged claws on bony hands, vicious talons on elongated feet. Spurs and thorns of bone protrude from their backs, arms and legs. Their heads are long, horse-like, with muzzles crammed full of thick, blocky teeth. Their eyes are big and black and unblinking. They run on all fours, leaning on their knuckles like the great apes. They weren't bothering with the hooting and howling any more, not now they'd found their prey. Instead, from behind us came deep bass coughing sounds, urgent and hungry.

I didn't look back. I knew how fast they could move. And what they would do if they caught us.

They were close, and getting closer. My breath burned in my heaving chest, and my bad arm and shoulder shrieked with pain. I could hear Molly straining for breath beside me. We were slowing down, even though we knew it was death to do so. So I armoured up, grabbed Molly in my strong golden arms, and sprinted through the dark tunnels at supernatural speed. Molly didn't have the breath to make any protest, beyond one surprised squeak, and then she clung tightly to me as I flashed though the labyrinth of tunnels. She held the witchfire out before us, the light reflecting brightly off my golden armour.

The trolls couldn't match my augmented speed, but they didn't give up either. I could still hear them, pounding along behind us. Cracked brick walls flashed past as I sped on, concentrating on the needle of the compass set flush into my golden palm. Molly suddenly cried out and pointed, and I skidded to a halt. Molly wriggled impatiently out of my arms as I set her down, and she ran over to a recess in a stone wall that looked just like all the others to me.

'This is it! This is the place! I recognise it ... The door's right here, Eddie! Right here ... somewhere ...'

She leaned in close, running her hands over the rough stone surface. I couldn't see any door. I turned and looked back the way we'd come. I couldn't see any trolls, but I could hear them coming for us, out of the dark. They sounded really angry. Molly cried out again, and I turned back to see her tracing the outline of a door in the dark grimy stone.

'This is definitely it! Leads straight to the Mole!'

'Then you might want to open it,' I said. 'The trolls will be here any minute.'

'I can't! Only the Mole can open it.'

'Stand aside,' I said. 'I'll smash it in.'

'No you bloody won't,' said Molly, grabbing me by one golden arm and glaring into my mask. 'The Mole values his privacy, and you can bet good money that door is protected by seriously heavy-duty security. You even look at it funny, and it could blow up this whole section. Let me talk to the Mole. There's a speakerphone here somewhere ...' She went back to the stone wall. 'Mole! This is Molly Metcalf; remember me? I got you the complete set of *Desperate Housewives* DVDs ... Look, I've got the new rogue Drood with me, and we really do need to come in and talk with you! Now!'

There was a worryingly long pause. The trolls were getting closer. I could feel the vibrations of their pounding feet through the stone floor. I sealed the compass away inside my armour, and started to reach for the Colt Repeater. The trolls burst out of the tunnel mouth behind us, long spiked arms reaching for us. Molly yelled for me to close my eyes, and I squeezed them shut just in time as she hit the trolls with the same incandescent flare she'd used on Paddington station. The trolls slammed to a halt, falling over each other as they clawed in agony at their blinded, light-sensitive eyes. I stepped forward and killed the first half dozen with my golden fists, smashing in their heavy skulls with my armoured hands. I pushed the bodies back into the tunnel mouth, building a barricade to hold the other trolls back. More of the creatures pushed hard from the other side, and it was all I and my armour could do to hold them back.

'Eddie! The door's open! *Come on!*'

I turned and ran for the narrow dark opening in the wall. Molly was already inside. She pulled me in and slammed the door shut in the trolls' faces, right behind me. The door didn't look like much, but it held firm, despite the pounding of heavy fists on the outside. The trolls hooted and howled, slamming against the closed door in frustrated rage.

'Should we brace ourselves for an explosion?' I said to Molly.

'The Mole knows what's going on now,' she said breathlessly. 'He's expecting us. Eddie, be nice to him. He's not used to visitors.'

I followed Molly down the narrow tunnel, lit by naked electric light bulbs hanging from the ceiling at regular intervals. I reluctantly armoured down. As a rogue himself, the last thing the Mole would want to see was a Drood in full armour coming at him. It did feel good not to be running any more, to get my breath back. I massaged my aching left arm, but it didn't help, so I pushed the pain as far away as I could. I had more important things to think about. If the Mole was as crazy as Oddly John, he'd need careful handling.

The tunnel walls were strung with overlapping layers of multi-coloured electrical cables, interspersed with junction boxes and a whole bunch of technology that baffled me completely. Swivelling security cameras kept track of Molly and me as we made our way down the tunnel, and I did my best to smile back at them in a friendly and distinctly unthreatening manner.

'You've been here before,' I said. 'What's his place like?'

'Ah,' said Molly, carefully not looking at me. 'I haven't actually been here before. Not in person, that is. In fact, I don't know anyone who has. You should be very flattered he let us in. The Mole doesn't normally allow visitors. In fact, he tend to discourage them by killing anyone who turns up.'

'Hold everything,' I said. 'You mean, there was a real chance he might not have opened that door for us? That he might very well have left us out there to die?'

'Well, that was a possibility, yes. But I was pretty sure he'd be so curious about you that he'd let us in. Besides, he sort of likes me.'

'He likes you?'

'No, I mean, he *likes* me.'

'How, if you've never been here before?'

'Oh, I've been in his lair lots of times, just not in the flesh. I've dreamwalked here a dozen times, astral travelling. That's how I knew the way. And we talk on the phone a lot. He can be very chatty, as long as you keep your distance. I really was pretty sure he'd let us in.'

'Because he *likes* you.'

'Yes. I do him favours . . .'

'I'm almost afraid to ask. What kind of favours?'

'I find him these dodgy porn sites on the Net.'

'I was right. I didn't want to know.'

The tunnel opened up abruptly into a huge cavern, carved out of the bedrock deep under London. It was vast, almost overpowering in its scale, but the Mole had clearly had a lot of time to make himself comfortable. The great open floor space was packed with every modern appliance, every conceivable luxury and convenience. There were mountains of piled-up computer equipment. Huge flat plasma screens covered the walls, showing fifty different views at once, with the sound turned off. And in every gap and space there were computer monitors, showing dozens of different sites, all at once. Molly led me through the maze of equipment, into the centre of the Mole's lair, and there in the very heart of the labyrinth sat the Mole himself, in a great, bright red leather swivel chair. He kept his back to us until the very last moment, and then he reluctantly swung the chair around to glare at us. He put up a hand, to stop us coming any closer, and we stopped a good dozen feet away. He looked us over, making no move to rise from his chair to greet us.

I'd expected the Mole to be a dumpy little guy, with squinty eyes behind huge spectacles, and that was exactly what he was. He was very pale, with long fly-away hair around a podgy face, and he blinked and twitched quite a bit. He wore Bermuda shorts, grubby trainers and a T-shirt bearing the legend *Tarzan, Lord Of The Geeks*. He also wore a Buddhist charm on a chain around his neck: the All-Seeing Eye. And above that, the golden collar of the Droods. One plump hand rose to touch it as he looked at me, and the torc around my throat, and finally he relaxed a little. He smiled briefly at me, and nodded to Molly.

'Hello, my dear. So good to see you again. And in person, at last. Yes. But please, both of you; don't come any closer. I'm not used to company any more. No. No. Hello, Edwin. Fellow Drood, fellow rogue. Yes. I don't normally allow visitors. They're too hard on my nerves. But if I can't trust a fellow rogue ... So; welcome to my lair. Edwin, Molly. Yes.'

'Nice chair,' I said, for want of anything else polite and non-threatening to say.

'It is, isn't it?' said the Mole, brightening a little. 'I ordered it specially. Through a whole series of cut-outs. I have to be very careful. The armrests hold coolers for soft drinks. Would you care for one?'

'Not just now,' I said.

'Good, because I'm running a bit short at the moment. I must put a new order in. Yes. I have very good people who smuggle all sorts of things down here to me, for a consideration, but of course it's not easy getting things delivered. You wouldn't believe the lengths I have to go to. No. No. I have to be ... circumspect. About everything. I'm safe here, protected, and I intend to stay safe. Cut off from the world. It isn't only the family who want me dead, after all. Oh no.'

'Really?' I said. 'Who else is after you?'

'Pretty much everybody,' the Mole said sadly. 'I know so many secrets, you see. So many things that some people don't want other people to know. Oh, the things I know! You'd be amazed! Really. Yes.'

'How do you power this equipment?' I asked, genuinely curious.

The Mole shrugged. 'I tap all the energy I need from the Underground. And the city. They don't notice. I have all the utilities down here, and I've never paid a bill. Though I could, if I chose. I'm really quite remarkably wealthy. Oh yes. So, Edwin; you're the new rogue. Let me look at you ... I know you by reputation, of course. The only field agent to keep the family at arm's length for almost ten years. Unprecedented! Always knew it couldn't last ... The family doesn't trust anyone or anything it can't control. I used to be Malcolm Drood, you know.'

He said the name as though he expected me to recognise it, but I didn't. We're a big family. He studied my face intently, and then frowned and pouted as he realised the name meant nothing to me.

'So; I've been erased from the official family history. Scrubbed out. I suspected as much. Yes. You will have been wiped out too by now, Edwin. As far as the next few generations of the family are concerned, you will never have existed. All your history gone, oh yes. Everything you ever did for the family, your battles and successes and achievements, will be parcelled out and attributed to others. To agents who still toe the family line, and bow down to family authority. Matthew will probably get most of it. He always was hard-core family, the humourless little prick. He'll always be a good little soldier . . . Not like us, eh, Edwin? We have minds of our own. Souls of our own. Yes. Yes!'

'Can they really do that?' Molly said to me. 'Write you out of history, as though you never even existed?'

'Of course!' said the Mole. 'It's always been that way. As decided by the higher echelons of the family. Of which I was once a valued member.'

'What is it you do down here, exactly?' I said bluntly. 'And what, if anything, can you do to help me?'

He blinked and twitched at me for a while, not used to being so openly challenged in his own private kingdom. One hand reached for remote controls set into his armrest, and then he pulled the hand away again. He smiled nervously at me, and then at Molly. She gave him her best cheerful reassuring smile, and he calmed down a little.

'I watch the world,' said the Mole, just a little smugly. He turned back and forth in his chair, indicating the many screens with one plump hand. 'Down here I can see everything that goes on, or at least everything that matters. I have hidden cameras in places you wouldn't believe. I spy, I eavesdrop, and I make notes. If you knew what Bill Gates was planning to do next, you'd shit yourselves. Yes. Yes . . . I live on the Net, you know. Studying conspiracy theories, searching for evidence of our family at work, and then passing the information on to whomever I think will make best use of it. Wherever it will do the most good, or the most harm to the family.' He looked at me very solemnly. 'Our family has to be stopped, Edwin. Broken, humbled, brought down. For everything that's been done to you and me, and all the others like us. I belong to a hundred different subversive organisations, under a hundred different identities. Oh yes! Nothing happens, nothing is planned, that I don't get to know about in advance. I need to know everything, to make sense of what's happening in the world. Yes ... A difficult job. An endless job ... But someone's got to do it.'

'Do you by any chance belong to a group called Manifest Destiny?' said Molly.

'Of course. Paranoid, xenophobic and definitely in thrall to the cult of the personality; and downright sloppy when it comes to operations in the field ... But I had great hopes of them originally. I mean, yes, they were and are complete and utter bastards in many ways, but at least they have an organisation that seems capable of taking on the Droods. I support them, from a distance, trying to encourage them into more practical pursuits, on the grounds that anyone who opposes the family deserves supporting. Yes. Would you like to see the battle that's going on between their people and the three Drood field agents in the streets above us?'

'That's still happening?' said Molly.

'Oh yes. Manifest Destiny are throwing everything they've got against the field agents. The poor fools. You'll never bring down the family through direct conflict. No. No ...'

'Show me,' I said.

The Mole worked the remote controls on the arm of his chair, and the biggest plasma screen before us suddenly blared into new life, showing Manifest Destiny forces attacking three golden armoured figures, right out in the open. The depth and definition of the image was outstanding, complete with full stereo sound. It was like being in the thick of the battle. I could almost smell the blood and smoke. Truman must have sent half an army to bring down the Drood field agents who'd dared defy him; and much good it had done him. Armoured cars, armoured soldiers, attack helicopters raining down fire from above ... The street was full of thick black smoke from burning buildings and burnt-out armoured cars, but still the three golden figures moved through the thick of it, untouched.

They slammed through the advancing soldiers with supernatural speed, killing with a touch and moving on. The dead and the dying lay in piles, up and down the street. The golden figures overturned armoured cars with a single heave, moving unscathed through hails of bullets and explosions. A black helicopter came in low for a strafing run, and one golden figure leapt straight up into the air, propelled by the strength in his golden legs. He clung on to the side of the helicopter, ripped the door off with one hand, and disappeared inside. He threw the crew out one at a time, and they fell screaming to their death. The agent stayed on board long enough to aim the crashing helicopter at an armoured vehicle, and then he jumped free at the last moment, landing easily and gracefully as his armoured legs soaked up the impact. Manifest Destiny had every advantage of modern warfare on their side, and it didn't do them a damned bit of good against three Drood field agents.

It almost made me proud to be a Drood, to see so few standing firm against so many. Almost.

'That last one had to be Matthew,' said the Mole. 'Always was a show off.'

'How the Hell are they going to hush this up?' said Molly, staring fascinated at the carnage. 'This much death and destruction, a war zone, right in the middle of London?'

'Do you see any media people present?' said the Mole. 'Any television crews, or news photographers? Any paparazzi, even? No. These days, if it doesn't appear on the television news or in the tabloids, it didn't happen. Any civilian witnesses will have their memories altered, all CCTV footage will disappear, and the damage will be blamed on whatever terrorists are the latest bogeymen. Or perhaps on a gas explosion. Or a plane falling out of the sky. Whatever the family decides. Yes. Oh, stories will get out, they always do. The Net does so love its urban legends. But no one will ever know the truth. The family's had a lot of practice at burying the truth. Oh yes.'

'How are we seeing this?' I said. 'If there aren't any camera crews there . . .'

'I have cameras everywhere, remember?' said the Mole, blinking proudly. 'I can tap into any CCTV, any and all security systems, plus a whole bunch of assorted surveillance technology that my people have planted in unobtrusive places. I have eyes and ears in every major city in the world. Plus all those smaller places that the world doesn't know are important. Though I'm still having trouble getting into Area Fifty-three . . . But nothing happens in London that I don't know about, sooner or later. Oh no . . . I knew you'd come down here looking for me, even before you did. Oh yes! I had plenty of time to think about whether I was going to let you in here, Edwin. It helped that you brought Molly with you. A double agent would never have hooked up with the infamous Molly Metcalf.'

He ignored Molly's bristling, intent on the mayhem filling the big screen. The Manifest Destiny soldiers were in full retreat, pursued by the three field agents. The Mole giggled.

'Good thing I'm recording this. I know people who'll pay good money to see Drood field agents in action. And others who'll pay even more to see Manifest Destiny getting their nasty arses kicked so convincingly. Oh; that reminds me. Excuse me a moment while I make sure the machines are recording my soaps properly. I hate it when I miss an episode because the machines have recorded the wrong channel again.'

He gave his attention to fussing with his remote controls, while Molly and I took the opportunity to move a few steps away and talk quietly with each other. I kept my voice really low. I wouldn't put it past the Mole to bug his own lair; just in case.

'What do you think?' I murmured. 'Can we trust him? I get the feeling he's not too tightly wrapped, to be honest.'

'What did you expect?' said Molly, just as quietly. 'He's lived down here in seclusion for God knows how many years, his only contact with the world what he sees on his screens and hears on the Net. Like Oddly John, if he wasn't crazy when he came down here, he almost certainly is now.'

'But he says he knows things.'

'Oh, he does. But whether they're real things, or helpful things ... it's up to you, Eddie, to get him to tell you what you need to know. I mean, the Mole's a sweetie, but he literally doesn't live in the same world as the rest of us any more.'

'Then why did you bring me down here?' I said, a little tetchily.

'Because the Mole genuinely does know some things that no one else knows.'

'Whispering is very bad manners,' the Mole said loudly. 'And we are not at home to Mister Rude.'

'Sorry,' I said. 'We didn't want to disturb you. I was hoping you might know some things I need to know.'

'Try me,' the Mole said grandly. 'I am wise, and know many things. Yes. Including a whole lot I'm not supposed to know.'

'Do you know why I was declared rogue?' I said flatly. 'Why the Matriarch wants me dead so badly?'

'Ah,' said the Mole, his face dropping. He clasped his podgy hands across his protruding belly. 'I'm not privy to our family's inner workings. Not any more. No. I couldn't even tell you why *I* was made rogue.' He blinked at me sadly through his heavy glasses, and sighed wistfully. 'Back then, I was a respected family scholar. Never been out in the world, never wanted to. I was working on an officially sanctioned history of the family. Full access to the Library, access to all documents, interview anyone I wanted. Lots of fascinating stories ... The next thing I know I'm on the run, with the pack baying at my heels. Luckily I was something of a voyeur, even then.' He sniggered. 'Nothing malicious. Not really. I just liked knowing things ... It paid off, though; I was already out of The Hall with as many valuables as I could stuff into a backpack before they'd officially given the order to detain me. Oh yes ... I went to ground here. I knew about this place. I'm not the first Mole under London, you know. There were others before me, for various reasons. I just built on what they started.

'But I still don't know why I was outlawed. After all my years of digging and probing and listening at electronic keyholes, I'm still no wiser. No. I can only assume ... I must have been on the edge of discovering something really important, some deep, dark family secret that the Droods have to keep hidden at all costs ... I just wish I knew what it was. I'd sell it to everyone, to make the family pay for what they did to me.'

Another dead end. I scowled, thinking. 'That reminds me a lot of what happened to the old librarian,' I said finally.

'Ah, yes,' said the Mole. 'Poor old William. You know about to him?'

'Yes,' I said. 'Molly and I went to visit him this morning. He couldn't tell us much.'

'I'm amazed he told you anything,' said the Mole. 'I've been sending people in to talk to him for years, without success. You must tell me absolutely everything he said to you before you go, so I can record it. Everything, every word. Yes. I'll study the recordings later, see if I can cross-reference any useful connections.'

'Do you know what it was he found out?' I said. 'What it was that drove him crazy? He mentioned the Sanctity, and the Heart ...'

'Did he? Did he now? That is interesting ... Means nothing to me, though. No. I'll have to think about that. Yes. Still, I can't help feeling we're probably better off not knowing. Look what knowing it did to a brilliant mind like his.' The Mole blinked rapidly several times, and then deliberately changed the subject. 'I'm still working on a history of the Drood family. From a safe distance. You'd be surprised how much information there is on the Droods out in the world, where they can't suppress it. Oh yes. I'm constantly finding out all kinds of awful things our family has done, Edwin, down the centuries. Oh, some of the things we're responsible for ... Terrible, terrible things! Yes. Lately I've been concentrating on the real reasons behind certain important and well known operations. For example, Edwin, do you know why our family is so determined to wipe out the Loathly Ones?'

'Well, yes,' I said. 'They eat souls.'

'Apart from that,' said the Mole. 'The family needs to silence them so everyone else won't find out that we were the ones who originally opened the dimensional door and let the Loathly Ones into our reality. We brought them here to act as foot soldiers against Vril Inc, during World War Two. Vril had grown powerful enough under Hitler to pose a real threat to the family. Had their own army and everything. Oh yes, there were a lot of secret wars going on behind and underneath the real conflict that the world never knew about. Anyway, the Loathly Ones did the job all right, but when the time came for them to return to their own dimension, as had been agreed, the Loathly Ones reneged on the deal and refused to go. They liked it here. The feeding was so good. The family's been trying to wipe them out ever since, so no one will ever know we were the ones responsible for inflicting them on the world.'

'Dear God,' I said.

'Oh, that's nothing!' said the Mole, leaning eagerly forward in his chair. 'That's nothing, compared to some of the things I've found out! The family history that you and I were brought up on only records the official version of events, not the failures and foul-ups and the secret deals that went horribly wrong.' The Mole paused, considering. 'I have to say, I still believe that most of what we were taught was true ... as far as it went ... but you have to place it in the context of what it was all for, in the end.'

'So that we could be the secret rulers of the world,' I said.

'Yes,' said the Mole. 'Sometimes I wonder ... if perhaps there's another context, beyond that, that I don't know about yet. Some very secret reason why we have to be the secret rulers of the world, for everyone's good. I'd like to believe that. Yes.'

'Have you found any evidence?' I said.

'No,' the Mole said sadly. 'If only I could access the family Library. All the reserved volumes and the restricted books. Learn the whole true history of the Drood family ... But not even my resources can hack the Drood Library. No. That's why they've always kept everything on paper, because of people like me. And, of course, I've never been able to sneak a single surveillance camera into The Hall. No! No.'

'So you can't tell me anything about why I was outlawed?' I persisted.

'You must know something,' the Mole said sharply. 'It's always knowing things that make you really dangerous to the Droods. Knowing things they don't want anyone else to know. Secrets that have to be kept inside their precious inner circle. The Matriarch, her Council, her favourites ...The ones who really run the world.'

'But I don't know anything!' I said. I could hear the desperation in my voice.

'They think you do,' the Mole said simply.

We both looked round sharply as loud music blasted suddenly through the cavern. It seemed Molly had grown bored and wandered off on her own, while the Mole and I argued over family history. She'd found MTV on one of the screens, and jacked up the volume. '*She Bangs*' by Ricky Martin filled the air, the loud salsa beat echoing back from the stone walls. And Molly danced joyously to the music, stamping her feet and shaking her head and swirling her long dress about her. The Mole and I both watched, too entranced to think of protesting, as the wild witch danced to the music. It felt good to see such a moment of happy innocence in the middle of such dark discussions. Molly understood that life was for living, and living in the moment. Anywhen else I would have joined her, danced with her, but just the thought made my bad arm ache the more fiercely.

236

The song finally finished, and the Mole worked his remote control, cutting off the next number. Molly danced on for a moment, and then strode back to join us. Her face was flushed, her eyes bright and happy.

'Spoilsport!' she said cheerfully to the Mole, and actually leaned over him to kiss him on the cheek. The Mole blushed bright red. Molly looked at me.

'Are we finished here, Eddie?'

'Almost,' I said. I turned back to the Mole. 'What do you know about strange matter?'

'Ah,' said the Mole. 'Yes, yes! I heard about the elf lord's arrow! It punched right through your armour? Interesting ... That was, well, I won't say unprecedented, there are stories, but this is the first authenticated case I've ever encountered. All I can tell you for sure is that strange matter comes from another dimension of reality, where the laws of physics are subtly different. So that things which could never arise naturally here are possible there. Like strange matter, with its amazing unnatural properties.'

'It's inside me,' I said. 'Poisoning me. Killing me. Is there a cure, an antidote? Something I could use to drive it out of me?'

'I don't know,' said the Mole, and I could see it pained him to admit it. 'I'd need to know exactly where it came from. Only the elf lord could tell us that, and elves don't talk to anyone who isn't an elf. I have some indirect contacts. Yes. Give me a few weeks, and I might have something to tell you.'

'I don't have a few weeks,' I said. 'And I'm starting to think that the only place which could help me, the only place with the answers I need, is the Library back at The Hall.'

'They won't help you,' said the Mole.

I smiled unpleasantly. It felt good. 'I wasn't planning on asking them,' I said. 'I was thinking more about breaking into The Hall, ransacking the Library, and taking what I bloody well need. And if that happened to involve beating some answers out of various people, like Grandmother's beloved consort, it would be a pleasant bonus.'

'Now that's more like it!' said Molly, clapping her hands together gleefully. 'Hard-core, Eddie! No one's dared burgle The Hall in generations! Let me come too! Oh please; I promise I'll make a real mess of the place!'

'Edwin, no; don't even think it,' the Mole said urgently. 'You know what kind of security protects The Hall. All the terrible things and forces our family rely on, to protect their privacy. Any safe words you might have known will have been cancelled by now. You don't want to end up as one of the scarecrows, do you?'

'Wait a minute: those are real?' said Molly. 'I thought they were just stories, to scare people off.'

'They're real,' I said. 'I've heard them screaming. My family really is as vicious and vindictive towards uninvited visitors as the stories say we are.' I looked at the Mole. 'You probably know more about The Hall's defences than anyone else who isn't actually an insider. If you were to come with us . . .'

'No! No. I couldn't.'

'Not even for a chance to strike back at the people who ruined your life?'

'You don't understand,' said the broken man who used to be Malcolm Drood. 'I haven't left this place since I first came down here. All those years ago. . . This is the only place where I feel safe. The very thought of leaving here is more than I can bear. You're the first real, in-the-flesh visitors I've allowed in since I first shut the door behind me and sealed myself off from the world.' He managed a small smile. 'You should feel honoured.'

'No company, ever?' said Molly. 'I heard rumours, but I never really thought . . . How do you stand it?'

'Because the alternatives are worse,' said the Mole. 'I live through my screens now, and on the Net. A virtual life, but better than none.'

'All those years,' I said. 'Gathering and collating information, but you've never done anything to expose the truth about our family to any of the world's media. Why not?'

'Because I'm not ready to die yet,' said the Mole.

CHAPTER SEVENTEEN
Time and time again

'So,' I said to the Mole. 'Is there by any chance a back way out of this place? Only I'm really not too keen on fighting my way through tunnels full of seriously pissed-off trolls to get back to Blackfriars station. Which is probably swarming with unfriendly people on the lookout for Molly and me anyway.'

'Of course there's another way out,' said the Mole. 'You don't think I'd allow myself to be trapped anywhere, even in my own lair, do you? I may be paranoid, agoraphobic and unhealthily addicted to e-bay, but I'm not stupid. No. I've always known that one day my many enemies will track me down, and then I will have to leave my comfortable little bolt-hole. Probably running. Yes. So, if you would care to make your way to the rear of the chamber, preferably without knocking against or in any way upsetting my very delicate equipment, you'll find an emergency elevator ready and willing to take you to the surface.'

'Where on the surface?' said Molly.

'Anywhere on the surface,' the Mole said smugly. 'Tell the elevator where you want to go, and it will deliver you there.'

'Anywhere in London?' said Molly.

'Anywhere in the world,' said the Mole. 'You always did think too small, Molly.'

'An elevator to anywhere in the world?' I said. 'How is that even possible?'

The Mole smiled on me pityingly. 'You wouldn't understand, even if I did explain it to you. Let's just say that quantum uncertainty is a wonderful thing, and leave it at that. It was nice to meet you at last, Molly. And you, Edwin. But don't come back. You're too dangerous to have around. Bye-bye. Safe journey. Why are you still here?'

Molly and I took the hint, nodded goodbye, and headed for the back of the cavern. Where there was indeed a perfectly ordinary elevator door, set flush into the black basalt cavern wall. The door was polished steel, and beside it was a big red button, marked Up. I looked at Molly.

'On to the next rogue, I suppose. For want of anything better to do. You do know of another rogue?'

'Of course. Sebastian Drood. He has a nice little place in Knights-bridge, just down the road from you.'

I may have blinked a few times. 'I never knew that.'

'There are a lot of things you don't know and I do,' said Molly. 'You'd be amazed. Sebastian's been around for ages, though he doesn't bother to make the scene much. Likes to be thought of as a gentleman thief, but he's really just a professional burglar with delusions of grandeur.'

'Can't say I know the name,' I said. 'Probably got scrubbed from the family history, like the Mole. And me.'

'Sebastian's a lot older than you,' said Molly. 'And though he's not averse to involving himself in the odd plot or intrigue, he's always been a behind-the-scenes kind of player. A real *let's you and him fight* kind of guy. Never does anything unless there's a profit in there somewhere for him. But he might help you ... just to get back at the family that dared to outlaw him. Sebastian's always been a great one for nursing a grudge.'

She hit the Up button and announced the name of a street in Knightsbridge, and the elevator door hissed open. The interior looked exactly like any other elevator. We stepped inside, and the door shut quickly behind us. There was no control panel and no sensation of upward movement, but a moment later the door opened to reveal a street I recognised, only a few minutes' walk from where I used to live. I stepped outside, and looked around cautiously. There was no sign of any Drood agents. Whatever surveillance there was, was probably concentrated around my old flat in case I was dumb enough to go back there.

The sun was high in the sky. Half a day gone, and damn all to show for it. It was hard to think, to plan properly, under such constant pressure. I looked back at Molly, and wasn't surprised to discover that the elevator door had disappeared behind her.

'How is it you know Sebastian?' I said. 'Have you worked with him too?'

'You have got to be joking,' said Molly, curling her lip. 'I wouldn't touch that man with a disinfected bargepole. He works alone because no one else trusts him. He's a two-faced, treacherous little turd who's screwed over pretty much everyone, at one time or another. However ... he can be the man to go to when you need to get your hands on a certain item that no one else can supply, legally or illegally. Sebastian can get you anything, for the right price, as long as it's firmly understood that there isn't going to be any provenance. Or any protection if the original owner discovers you've got it. You can also be absolutely sure that there won't be any refund if the item in question turns out to be not entirely what you thought it was. It's up to you to be sure before you hand over any money. Buyer beware, and carry a bloody big stick.'

'And this is the man you thought might help me?' I said.

'I'd better phone ahead,' said Molly, producing a bright pink phone with a Hello Kitty face on it. 'Make sure he's in, and that he'll agree to see us.'

'Might not be wise, using my name over a standard phone on an open line,' I said. 'My family have people who listen in on everything.'

'Don't teach your grandmother to throttle chickens,' said Molly. 'I haven't spoken over an open line in years. The angels themselves couldn't listen in on one of my calls without actual divine intervention on their side.'

She moved a few steps away while she punched in the number. I leaned back against an ornamental stone wall, and considered my situation. I wasn't impressed with the two rogues Molly had introduced me to so far. Oddly John had gone mad, and the Mole was well on his way in the same direction. Both of them trapped in prisons of their own making. And this Sebastian sounded like a real scumbag. How could I trust anything a man like that might tell me, even if I could persuade him to talk? But time was pressing, and I had to get answers from somewhere. If nothing else, I was pretty sure I'd know the truth, once I heard it. That I would recognise it, somehow. My left arm hurt like Hell, even though I had my hand tucked into my belt, to carry some of the weight. I massaged the muscles with my other hand, but it didn't help. The pain beat sickly in my left shoulder, and down into my chest. The strange matter was spreading inexorably through my system. Three days, Molly had said. Maybe four. Maybe not. I had to get my answers soon, while they were still some good to me.

Time was against me . . .

Molly turned off her phone and put it away. 'He says he'll see us, but only if we come over right away. It's only a few minutes' walk from here. But Eddie . . . try and be nice to Sebastian. He can be a pain in the arse, but he really does know things no one else does. Is there anything you might know that you could offer him in exchange? Some family secret, perhaps, from after his time? Sebastian loves secrets. He can't sell them on fast enough.'

'I am wise,' I said, 'and know many things. And I shall be perfectly polite to Sebastian. Right up to the point where he refuses to tell me something I need to know, and then I will bounce him off the nearest wall until his eyes change colour. I really feel like beating the snot out of someone obnoxious. It's been that kind of a day. Is any of this going to be a problem for you?'

'Hell,' said Molly. 'I'll hold his arms while you hit him.'

Sebastian turned out to have a magnificently appointed first-floor apartment over a very refined and upmarket antiques shop called *Time Past*. I took a quick peek through the window. The shop was full of that delicate kind of item where, if you have to ask the price, you definitely can't afford it. Molly peered over my shoulder, sniffed dismissively at the lot, and then rang the bell beside the discreet side door. There was a name card beside the bell, and it wasn't anything like Sebastian Drood. After a lengthy pause, while Sebastian checked us out in some unobtrusive and probably highly arcane manner, the side door swung open before us. Inside was a narrow set of stairs, leading up. Narrow enough to ensure that anyone ascending to Sebastian's lair could only do so in single file. Good defensive thinking. Molly went first. I followed after, sneering at the terribly passé hunting prints on the wall.

The stairs ended in another door, solid oak barred with cold iron and silver. It opened by itself as Molly and I approached, and we filed through into the gorgeously laid out apartment beyond. Sebastian was waiting for us. He stood, carefully poised and elegant, in the middle of a bright, spacious living room and waited for us to come to him. Sebastian was tall, handsome and oh so sophisticated. You could tell. He'd put a lot of effort into making sure you could tell. He had to be in his late sixties, but his hair was still jet black, and his face had a certain taut look to it that spoke of frequent face lifts and regular botox injections. He had cold blue eyes, and a smile that came and went so quickly it meant nothing at all. He wore a white roll-necked pullover above casually expensive slacks, together with the kind of hand-made shoes you have to take out a second mortgage to pay for. The roll-neck hid the gold collar around his throat, but I could tell it was there.

'Molly! Eddie!' he said, in the kind of deep rich voice you only get by practising, probably in front of a mirror. 'Do come in. Delighted to see you both.'

He shook us both firmly by the hand, but didn't sit down or invite us to. It seemed we weren't expected to stay that long. Sebastian produced an antique silver snuff box from his pocket, and opened it with a flourish. A hidden mechanism played a tinkly version of 'The British Grenadiers', while Sebastian tapped out two small mounds of dark powdered tobacco on to the back of his hand, and snorted them up one nostril at a time. He then sneezed explosively into a silk handkerchief, before putting it and the snuff box away again. It was a performance designed to impress. If it had been anyone else, I would have applauded.

'That stuff's worse than coke,' said Molly. 'You'll see; one of these days the whole inside of your nose will drop out.'

'I like my vices old-fashioned,' said Sebastian, quite unconcerned. 'I find the qualities of the past so much more satisfying than those of the present. As you can see ...'

He indicated the contents of his apartment with a graceful wave of one long-fingered hand. It was sumptuously appointed, every item of the highest quality. Upon the waxed and polished bare board floor stood antique furnishings from a dozen different periods, carefully arranged and presented so the different styles wouldn't clash. Original paintings on the walls, each carefully illuminated by concealed track lighting. Plus a handful of Victorian pen and ink erotica, ranging from the cheerfully vulgar to the actually appalling. There was even a glass and diamond chandelier hanging from the ceiling. And yet for all the effort that had gone into it, I couldn't help thinking Sebastian's living room looked more like a showcase than a room where someone actually lived.

'Very nice,' said Molly. 'Very ... you. Is that antiques shop downstairs yours as well?'

'Oh, of course. It makes for good cover when I want to bring in something new I've just ... acquired. I have this delightful young lady who runs the shop for me. Charming little filly. She's really a golem with a concealing glamour spell, but the customers never seem to notice. Now then, Eddie; let us talk business.'

'Yes,' I said. 'Let's.'

He looked me over as though I was something he was considering buying, probably against his better judgement. 'So, you're the latest rogue. Old goodie two-shoes Eddie, no less. The whole area's been full of family looking for you. I've hardly dared step outside my flat. I was actually quite shocked when I heard the news. I'd gone to such pains to hide my presence from you all these years ... and now you're an official disgrace, just like me. Do you know why I left the family, Eddie?'

'No,' I said. 'But I'm sure you're about to tell me.'

Molly hit me in the ribs with her elbow, but Sebastian didn't notice. He had a story to tell, and nothing short of an appearance by Death herself was going to stop him.

'The family sent me out into the world to be their agent,' he said grandly. 'But I decided I liked the world much more than I liked the family. Never any room in the family for personal ambition or advancement, or the acquisition of lovely things. So I walked away, disappeared behind the scenes, and set about using the torc for my own purposes. To enrich my life, and make it so much more comfortable. And I have! I have become quite extraordinarily successful at my chosen profession, as one of the most admired gentleman thieves in London. It could have been the world, but I do so hate to travel.

'With the help of my armour, I can break into any establishment and walk off with anything I take a fancy to. And I do. Alarms and security mean nothing to me, when I'm in my armour. I come and I go and I take what I will, and no one ever knows anything about it until it's far too late. Scotland Yard, baffled again! I have the very best antique furniture, everything from a Louis Quinze chair to a Hepplewhite sideboard. Famous paintings, in their original frames! Whatever catches my eye. Nothing is safe from me.

'You know how I track it down? I simply make it my business to patronise the best auctions, and make a note of who buys what. There are those who hide behind anonymous bids, but auction house security is a joke to such as us, Eddie. All the lovely things in this flat originally belonged to someone else, who couldn't hold on to them. Probably didn't appreciate them, anyway. Not nearly as much as I do. I'm sure the pretty things are much happier here, with me.'

'Wait a minute!' Molly stalked over to a side table and snatched up a stylised statuette of a black cat. 'This is mine, you bastard! I always wondered what happened to it. This is the Manx Cat of Bubastis! I went through all manner of Hells to get my hands on this, and then it disappeared from my old place four years ago!'

'Really?' said Sebastian airily. 'I honestly don't remember where I acquired that particular piece.'

'It's mine!' said Molly, dangerously.

'It's only yours if you can hang on to it, Molly dear. But if you're going to make such a fuss about it . . .'

'This leaves here with me,' said Molly, striding back to my side with the Manx Cat firmly in her grasp. 'And if I hear one word of objection from you, Sebastian, I'll rip your nipples off.'

'Dear Molly,' said Sebastian. 'Gracious as ever.'

'I thought we were going to be polite,' I said, amused.

'You be polite,' she growled. 'He wouldn't believe it if it came from me. The Manx Cat has power I invested in it long ago. It can restore a lot of the energies I've been using up recently. Though it'll take a while.'

I turned my attention back to Sebastian, who didn't seem in the least put out by Molly's actions. 'How have you stayed hidden from the family for so long?' I said. 'Hell, how did you stay hidden from me?'

'Oh, I'm pretty sure the family has always known roughly where I am,' he said. 'But they know better than to rock the boat. You see, some years ago I took the precaution of leaving certain very detailed information packs with a number of journalists, and other interested parties, all over the world. In well-sealed caskets, set to open automatically in the event of my death. Even our family couldn't be sure they'd got all of them, so they leave me alone. In fact, they'd do well to insure that nothing ever happens to me.'

'How very ... practical,' I said. 'But you could still die in an accident. What then?'

He shrugged. 'If I'm dead, I won't care. I'm sure the family will think of something. They always do.' He looked at me thoughtfully. 'I really don't think I can help you, Eddie. Whatever it is you want, I can't supply it. The family is very upset with you, and I don't care to get caught in the middle. I only look out for myself, these days. And before you ask; no, I have no idea why you were made rogue. I have no contact with anyone inside the family. I don't even speak to the other rogues. You're wasting both our time by being here.'

'Then why did you agree to see me?' I said, feeling a slow, hot anger build within me. 'I don't *have* time to waste.'

He sneered at me. 'I always wondered if you'd be the one they sent to kill me. If they ever did find a way to dismantle my little safeguards. You killed poor Arnold, after all, and you did live just up the road from me.'

'How did you kill the Bloody Man, Eddie?' said Molly. 'I mean, I thought the armour made all you Droods invulnerable.'

'Only when we're wearing it,' I said. 'I staked him out, learned his routine, and then shot him through the head from a safe distance using a rifle with a telescopic sight. He never knew I was there, never got the chance to armour up. Very effective, if not especially honourable. But I was a lot younger then, and he was the Bloody Man. You don't take chances with a man like that.'

Sebastian smiled. 'Funny you should say that, Edwin.'

There was a sudden sting in my neck, even as I heard the window glass beside me shatter. I started to turn. I thought, *I've been shot.* And then my legs were buckling, and I sank very slowly to my knees. I put my hand up to my neck, and it seemed to take for ever to get there. Sound slowed and my vision blurred, as though I was underwater. My numbing fingers found a feathered dart in the side of my neck, just above the torc, and I pulled it out with the last of my strength. *Tranquilliser dart*, I thought, and the words seemed to echo round and round inside my head. I tried to call up my armour, but my thoughts were already too dulled to concentrate on the activating Words. I slumped to the floor, hitting it in a boneless heap, and I didn't even feel the impact.

This happened in a few seconds. Molly threw herself down beside me, below the shattered window, out of the line of sight for any more darts. She put her hands on either side of my face, and muttered urgently under her breath. I could feel her touch when I couldn't feel anything else, and then I felt subtle magics flowing into me, fighting off the effects of the tranquilliser drug. My body was still numb, still helpless, but my thoughts slowly began to clear. Molly glared up at Sebastian.

'You bastard! You sold us out!'

'Of course,' he said smoothly, giving all his attention to the adjusting of a cuff. 'It's what I do. Rest assured, I got a very good price. For both of you. A certain Mr Truman of Manifest Destiny was very pleased to learn exactly where and when he could be sure of finding you. I was on the phone to him the moment I stopped talking to you. And then all I had to do was keep you entertained here until his people could get into position.'

The door burst in, and a dozen armed men streamed into the apartment, all of them in familiar black uniforms. They looked quickly around to make sure the place was secure, their guns constantly trained on Molly and me. She stayed very still. I twitched my fingers, ever so slightly. Molly's magics were fighting off the drug, but only very slowly. I looked at the guns, and wondered why they weren't already shooting. I would have. One of the men knelt down beside me, checked the sluggish pulse in my neck and then stood up again, satisfied. He yelled out of the open door, and his group commander sauntered in. And if I hadn't been so tranked, I would have yelled out, in shock and anger.

I knew the group commander. She wore battered old army fatigues, still stiff with dried black blood from fighting in a Hell dimension. She wore her black hair cropped short, so enemies couldn't grab at it during close combat. Her scarred face was no longer pretty, and her bare muscular arms were scarred too. I knew all these things about her because I knew her. She was Janissary Jane; an old friend and colleague, to Molly and to me. Except it wasn't her. Not really. Around her neck she wore a Kandarian amulet on a chain, and that meant this was really my old adversary Archie Leech.

Archie Leech, serial possessor, occupying another stolen body. Only this time he'd taken someone who mattered to me, no doubt in revenge for what I'd done to him in that cellar under Harley Street. Archie/Jane swaggered forward into Sebastian's apartment and grinned down at me, proudly waggling the gun she'd used to shoot me. And then she shot Sebastian in the neck with another tranquilliser dart. Sebastian crashed to the floor, thrashed awkwardly for a moment and then was still, an almost comical look of shock on his face. I would have laughed, if I could. The betrayer betrayed. Archie strolled over to him, his exaggerated masculine movements out of place in Jane's body.

'You really should have seen that one coming, Sebastian. You got soft, living on your own. Playing at being the gentlemen thief. Got cocky, thinking no one could touch you. You should have realised two Droods were always going to be worth more than one.' She turned abruptly back to look down on me, and smiled happily. 'How do you like my new body, Eddie? I thought I'd slip into something a little more comfortable, this time. You know I hate it when you destroy my bodies before I'm finished with them. Before I've squeezed every last bit of fun out of them. So this time I went out of my way to take a friend of yours, just to prove that I'll always be able to hurt you so much more than you can hurt me.'

She kicked me in the ribs a couple of times, to make his point. The force of the blows was enough to lift me up off the floor, but I hardly felt them. My hands and my feet were tingling, and my face wasn't as numb as it had been, but that was all. Molly's magic was working. My head was clearing fast. I probably could have armoured up, but I didn't want to risk it, not yet. Not with so many guns trained on Molly as well as me. So I lay still, watching and listening and biding my time. Molly stayed down beside me, also keeping very still, giving Archie no reason to trank her too.

'What happens now?' she said, her voice carefully calm and non-threatening.

'I deliver the three of you to Mr Truman,' said Archie. 'My current and very generous employer. He can't wait to get his hands on two Droods, and their torcs. I understand he has a whole team of surgeons standing by, ready to take his two new prizes apart one piece at a time until they find out exactly what it is about a Drood and his torc that's so special. A very slow, very painful process, I should think. Maybe Mr Truman will let me watch, if I ask nicely. Apparently he was impressed by what three armoured agents were able to do to the well-trained and expensive army he threw at them. He can't wait till he's able to put a torc around the neck of every Manifest Destiny soldier, and then turn them loose on the world. I do so admire a man with ambition . . .'

'He won't learn a thing from vivisection,' Molly said flatly. 'Except to remember what happened to the goose that laid golden eggs.'

Archie shrugged with Jane's shoulders. 'I don't think he cares that much. He just needs someone to take out his rage on. He really is very upset at what those three Droods did to his fine army. You should have heard him! I suggested he kill Eddie and Sebastian and bring them back as zombies. Then he'd have two Droods with torcs who'd do anything he told them to. But apparently that wasn't enough for him. The Droods have torcs, so he has to have them too. It's a parity thing. But you shouldn't feel left out, Molly; I gather he has quite detailed plans for you, too. He keeps special torture cells for those of his own people who turn on him.'

Strength flooded suddenly through me, as Molly's magics stamped out the last of the drug's effects. Sensation flooded back through every part of me, and my thoughts were clear and sharp. I looked up at Molly, caught her eye and mouthed the word *Now*. She grinned back at me, and lashed out at the watching armed men with a simple tangle spell. All twelve of them crashed to the floor at once, their muscles spasming helplessly as witchy lightning crawled over them, spitting and crackling. The spell hit Archie Leech too, but she staggered backwards, fighting it with the strength the amulet gave him.

I was already on my feet, heading for Archie. And thinking desperately on how to stop him without damaging or even killing Janissary Jane. I'd had to kill Archie's last host body to stop him, but I couldn't do that here. No more dead innocents on my watch. Unfortunately that gave him the advantage. He wouldn't care what happened to Jane's body; he could always jump to another. I slammed into Archie's stolen body just as she shrugged off the last of the tangle spell, and the two of us hit the floor together. The gun flew from Archie's hand, and she struggled fiercely under me, fighting to draw the knife at her belt.

I grabbed the Kandarian amulet in both my hands. It tried to evade me, twisting this way and that, but at such close quarters there was nowhere for it to go. I closed both my hands around the awful thing, squeezing them tightly shut, and the amulet burned my palms with a cold fiercer than any heat. I subvocalised my activating Words, and the golden armour flowed around me in a moment, even as Archie finally got her knife free and thrust it at my ribs. The heavy steel blade slammed and shattered against my armour, even as the living metal flowed over both my hands and what they contained. The Kandarian amulet was now inside my armour with me, sealed off and insulated from the rest of the world. And that was all it took to sever Archie's connection to the amulet.

I rolled away from Archie as he screamed like a damned soul, Jane's body thrashing and kicking as his possessing spirit lost its hold on her, and she forced him out. Archie had nowhere to go; his original body had been destroyed long ago. I used my Sight, and saw Archie's real shape superimposed over Jane's, just for a moment. And then his soul fell away from the world, howling horribly, summoned at last to the Hell that had been waiting for him for so long. I turned off my Sight. I didn't want to see what was waiting for him.

Janissary Jane lay unconscious on the floor, twitching and shuddering. Physically exhausted and in psychic shock, probably. But she'd recover. She was a fighter, and had known worse in her time.

The Kandarian amulet writhed inside my enclosing hands like a living thing, burning colder than the fiercest winter. A coldness of the heart, and of the soul. I could feel its presence inside the armour with me, fighting to impose its will on mine. The armour couldn't protect me while the amulet was inside it. I seemed to hear a dark inhuman chorus of voices, drawing slowly closer: *Join us. Join us.* Just the sound sickened me, as though something had trailed slime across my mind. I armoured down, and the moment the living metal disappeared from my hands I threw the nasty thing away from me.

The amulet skidded across the floor and Sebastian snapped out of his apparent stupor, rolled to one side and snatched it up. He scrambled to his feet, smiling terribly as he clutched his prize to his heart. 'You're not the only one who can play possum, Eddie; I protected myself against all poisons years ago. And now ... I have power beyond dreams. Because if you haven't got the balls to use this, Eddie, I have. I shall enjoy hundreds of bodies, young bodies, and live lifetimes.'

'Throw it away,' I said, rising slowly to my feet. 'It'll destroy you.'

'Like that fool, Archie Leech? I don't think so. I can control it.'

'No one can control it,' I said. 'It corrupts. That's what it does. You'll end up like Archie: the spiritual rapist.'

'I need a new body,' said Sebastian. 'This one's getting old. It's slower, and it lets me down. People like me shouldn't have to grow old. Not when we enjoy life so much. Appreciate its pleasures and its qualities. It isn't right that someone like me should die just because an old body is wearing out.' He smiled at me, and it wasn't his smile, not any more. 'Maybe I'll take your body, Eddie, for a little test drive. See what it can do. And maybe I'll do awful, awful things with your body; just for the fun of it.'

Molly hit him over the head from behind with the Manx Cat statuette, and he crumpled to the floor, unconscious. He'd been so taken up in taunting me he never noticed Molly sneaking up behind him. The Manx Cat cracked into pieces, crumbled, and fell apart. Molly looked at me, shrugged and smiled, and brushed the last few bits off her hands. The Kandarian amulet had spilled out of Sebastian's hand as he collapsed, and now it lay on the floor between us. Such a small thing, to be so evil. I stepped forward and stamped on it, and the ancient stone crumbled into dust under my heel.

But with the Manx Cat shattered, the power sustaining Molly's tangle spell was gone too, and the dozen black-uniformed men scrambled to their feet again, raising their guns. Mad as hell at being taken out so easily, they opened fire on Molly. The bullets hit her again and again, sending her staggering backwards under the repeated impacts. Blood spurted from dozens of wounds, snapping her head back and forth, and she couldn't get enough breath to scream. Finally the men stopped firing, and Molly fell, as though that was all that had been holding her up. I fell to my knees beside her and grabbed her hand. She tried to say something to me, blood gushing and spraying painfully from her mouth, and all I could do was hold her hand until at last the life went out of her eyes. I looked up at the armed men, and they fell back a step, afraid of whatever it was they saw in my face.

But I wasn't going to kill them. That wasn't enough.

I finally thought to hit the button on my reverse watch, and rewind time. I'd almost left it too long. The watch didn't want to take me far enough back, but I hit it again and again and again, until finally it took me to the point where the armed men were starting to train their guns on Molly. I threw myself in front of her, between her and the bullets, armouring up as I went. The living metal swept over me even as the bullets flew through the air; and fast as the bullets were, the armour was faster. Every single shot that would have killed Molly ricocheted off me instead.

I threw myself upon the armed men, beat the crap out of them and tossed them around the room for a while, until Molly finally stepped in and stopped me. Not for their sake, but for mine. She knew I'd feel bad afterwards if I killed them. I armoured down, and smiled tremulously at her. I'd come so close to losing her.

'I'm a witch,' Molly said slowly, holding my eyes with hers. 'I see things, and remember things, that others can't. I remember lying on that floor, dying . . . and then you rewrote history, changed the world itself, to save me. And risked your own life doing it. You couldn't have been sure the armour would cover you in time to save you from their guns. Why would you do that, risk that, to save me?'

'Because I had to,' I said.

'Eddie . . .' she said.

'Molly . . .' I said.

'Oh God,' said Molly. 'Are we having a romantic moment?'

We looked at each other; and it would be hard to say which of us was more appalled at the thought.

CHAPTER EIGHTEEN
Gone fishing, on golden pool

'I've made a decision,' I said to Molly.

'Good for you,' said Molly.

'I've decided I don't want to meet any more rogues,' I said. 'Not if they're going to be like the ones I've already met. I mean, one crazy, one shut in and one moral cripple? Is that the kind of future I've got to look forward to, if by some miracle I survive the next few days?'

'Probably,' said Molly. 'If you give up, like they did. They were afraid to do anything that mattered. How about you?'

'I'm going home,' I said. And just like that, I was certain. 'It's all that's left to me. I'm going back to The Hall, and the Library, and my back-stabbing family. Because they're the only ones I can be sure have the answers I need.'

'Good for you!' said Molly. 'I'm coming too!'

'No, you're bloody not,' I said. 'This is going to be difficult enough, without having to look after you as well.'

'I do not need looking after,' said Molly, her face clouding up dangerously.

'You could die in a hundred ways just trying to get on to The Hall's grounds,' I said, trying hard to sound reasonable. 'My family is protected in ways even I don't like to think about sometimes.'

'If you think I'm going to miss out on an opportunity to stick it to the Droods where they live, you've got another think coming. I've dreamed of revenge like this! Usually after eating cheese. I'm going with you, and you can't stop me!'

'Will you please keep the noise down?' growled Janissary Jane. She sat up slowly, wincing and groaning, and then peered blearily about her, taking in the unconscious Manifest Destiny soldiers piled up around her. 'Must have been a Hell of a party ... Shaman? That you? Where the Hell am I? And what have I been doing? It feels like someone took a dump in my head.'

'You were possessed by Archie Leech,' I said, helping her to her feet. 'I drove his spirit out of your body, and then destroyed it. He won't be coming back. Ever.'

'Leech? That rat turd? He must have sneaked in while my defences were down. Hold everything. You destroyed him? No offence, Shaman, I mean, well done and thanks for everything and all that, but I never really saw you as being in Archie Leech's league.'

'Yeah, well, that's because he isn't Shaman Bond,' said Molly. 'He's been fooling us all for years with that mild-mannered reporter shit.'

'Molly? You're here too?' Janissary Jane squeezed her eyes shut, and shook her head slowly. It didn't seem to help. 'Well if he isn't Shaman Bond, who the Hell is he?'

'There's no easy way to say this,' I said. 'I'm a Drood, Jane. Eddie Drood, field agent, at your service. Only I'm not an agent for the family any more. They made me rogue, so I'm on the run from everyone.'

'I go to fight in the Hell dimensions for one lousy month, and the whole world stops making sense while I'm gone.' Janissary Jane studied me suspiciously. 'You're a Drood, Shaman? You? Bloody good disguise ... Eddie. You two-faced little shit. Wait a minute, I'm still catching up here. You're a rogue? What did you do?'

'I don't know. But my family wants me dead. That's why Archie came after me.' I thought it best to keep the explanations simple, for the moment. And I didn't think I'd tell her that Archie had targeted her specifically, just to get back at me. I could do later. From a safe distance.

'At least you killed the bastard,' Janissary Jane growled, running her hands over herself vaguely, as though checking for signs of recent interference. 'I'll bet you didn't even take the time to torture him properly first, did you? No, I thought not. So, Eddie: why are we all here, who are those sleeping beauties and why are you hanging out with the infamous Molly Metcalf?'

'If I hear one more person use that word ...' Molly said ominously.

'You mutilate a few cattle, abduct a few aliens, and you get a reputation ...'

'Let us please not go there,' I said quickly. 'Jane, Molly and I are working together, for the moment. On matters of mutual interest.'

'Like what?' said Janissary Jane. 'What could you two possibly have in common?'

'We're going to his old family home to take names and kick arse,' Molly said happily. 'And possibly burn the place to the ground while we're at it.'

'You're not much of a one for keeping secrets, are you?' I said.

'You want to break into The Hall?' said Janissary Jane. 'Better you than me. I've been to Hell and back so many times they made me a special visa, and I still wouldn't go anywhere near The Hall. You couldn't bust through their defences with a tactical nuke. The Chinese tried, in sixty-four.'

'Nineteen sixty-five, actually,' I said.

'Shut up, Eddie, I'm on a roll,' said Janissary Jane. 'The point is, The Hall has serious defences. A hundred different ways to kill your intruder, all of them quite spectacularly vicious and nasty.'

'Indeed,' I said. 'Spot on, in fact.'

'So what you need,' said Janissary Jane, 'is a skeleton key.'

Molly and I looked at each other. 'What?' I said.

'You need something to get you through The Hall's defences without them kicking off on you. Something that'll let you sneak through.'

'No, hold everything,' I said. 'There's no such thing. The whole point to my family's many and varied protections is that there are no weak points, no possibilities for overrides. My family has spent generations designing and improving on their defences, including multiple redundancies and a quite appalling attention to increasingly nasty details. It has to be that way, or our enemies would have wiped us out long ago. We have a lot of enemies.'

And then I broke off, as a new wave of pain shot through me. It stabbed through my shoulder as though I'd just been shot again, a pain so bad it made me cry out despite myself, and then it slammed down through the whole of my left side. It hurt so badly I couldn't breathe, couldn't think. I staggered and would have fallen, if Molly and Janissary Jane hadn't been there to grab me from both sides.

255

'Shaman? What is it? Molly, what's wrong with him?'

'Elf lord shot him with an arrow made of strange matter,' said Molly. 'The stuff's still in his system, poisoning him. Eddie, can you hear me? Eddie?'

'I'm all right,' I said, or thought I said.

'Jesus, he looks bad,' said Janissary Jane. 'Should we get him to a healer? I know some good people, ask no questions.'

'It wouldn't help,' Molly said flatly.

'Oh,' Janissary Jane said quietly. 'Like that, is it?' And after a moment, she said, 'Bloody elves. Vicious little turds. Okay, strange matter ... nasty stuff, yes, other dimensional ... Really bad mojo, when you can get your hands on it, which mostly you can't. Never dealt with the stuff myself, but I know a man who has. Word is, he can even supply it direct from the source, on occasion.'

I forced strength back into my legs until they straightened and could hold me up again, and then I forced my head up to look at Janissary Jane. 'Who?' I said.

'I think you need to lie down, Shaman. I mean Eddie.'

'Haven't got the time. I'll lie down when I'm dead.' I breathed deeply, fighting down the pain and pushing it away through sheer force of will. I gently eased my arms out of Molly and Janissary Jane's grip, and they immediately stepped back to give me some room, keeping a watchful eye on me. I could feel cold sweat drying on my face, but my thoughts were clear again. 'Jane, who do you know that knows about strange matter?'

'The Blue Fairy.'

'What?' said Molly. 'Him? The man's a major league piss artist! Never met a bottle of booze he didn't like!'

'I saw him sober once,' I said. 'He looked *awful.*'

Janissary Jane sighed loudly. 'You of all people should know enough to look past the surface. You do know why he's called the Blue Fairy, don't you?'

'Well, yes,' I said. 'Because he's gay.'

'No! I mean, yes he's gay, but that's not where the name originally came from. It's because he's half elf.'

'Oh come on!' said Molly. 'Are we talking about the same guy? That useless little tit who's always sponging drinks at the Wulfshead?'

'He can't be half elf,' I said. 'Elves never breed outside their own kind. It's their strongest taboo, utterly forbidden.'

'There's always a few who move to a different drummer,' said Janissary Jane. 'The elves have a special name for those who indulge outside the permitted gene pool. They call them perverts.'

Molly smirked. 'You mean they're *humosexuals*?'

'Please,' I said. 'Let us not go there.'

'The point,' Janissary Jane said firmly, 'is that the Blue Fairy has some elf abilities, and even a few direct contacts within the Fae. I would be prepared to bet you good money that he was the one who supplied your elf lord with the strange matter to make his arrow. So he might be the man to go to for a cure. Certainly he knows more about strange matter than anyone else I know.'

'All right,' I said. I was feeling better, for the moment. 'Any idea of where he's hiding out at the moment? I lost track of him when he went to ground after the unfortunate incident with the kobold in Leicester Square. Though what they ever saw in each other . . .'

'He moved around a lot after that,' said Janissary Jane. 'And he went downhill rapidly. He didn't want any of his old friends to see what he'd been reduced to.'

'Hell, we wouldn't have cared,' said Molly.

'No, you probably wouldn't,' said Janissary Jane. 'But he did. The point is, I know where to find him. I throw him the odd commission now and again, for old times' sake. If you want, I can take you to him.'

'I want,' I said. 'But we can't go gallivanting across London in plain sight, not while Manifest Destiny are after me. That's who the sleeping beauties belong to, by the way.'

'You've got them mad at you as well?' said Janissary Jane. 'Good for you! You continue to rise in my estimation, Eddie. Can't stand these amateur night wannabe soldiers, in their pretty new uniforms. They give real mercenaries a bad name. Probably crap their pants and then run a mile if you dropped them into a real war zone; crying for their mummies all the way.'

'Could we at least make an effort to stick to the subject?' I said, just a little plaintively. 'The point is, it's not safe for Molly and me to travel openly across London, and she's all out of spatial portals.'

'Well, how did I get here?' Janissary Jane said reasonably. 'How did the Manifest Destiny arseholes get here? They must have had transport, right?'

We moved over to the shattered window and looked out. In the street below were three large black cars, parked in a row, that looked very familiar to me. I couldn't help but grin.

'Perfect,' said Molly. 'Look, they even have tinted windows so no one can see in! No one's going to pay any attention to just another Manifest Destiny car out on patrol.'

'All right,' I said. 'Let's go and give the Blue Fairy his wake-up call.'

Molly insisted we take a little time to leave a suitably insulting message for whoever came to retrieve the unconscious Manifest Destiny soldiers. So she and Janissary Jane pulled down their trousers and underwear, commenting in loud and very unfair ways as they went along, and arranged the unconscious men in an erotic daisy chain. Then they stood back to admire their work, and giggled a lot. Never let them give you to the women.

'I'd love to see them try and explain this to their superior officers when they turn up,' Molly said happily, and Janissary Jane nodded solemnly.

While they were busy, I had my own ideas for a little useful mischief. I picked up Sebastian's stylised Edwardian telephone, and phoned home. As always, they picked up on the first ring, and a familiar voice answered. One I'd never expected to talk to again.

'Hello, Penny,' I said. 'Guess who?'

There was a sharp intake of breath at the other end, and then Penny's well-trained professionalism quickly reasserted itself. 'Hello, Eddie. Where are you calling from?'

'Trace the line,' I said. 'By the time you can get here I'll be long gone. But you'll still find something interesting waiting for you. Now put me through to the Matriarch.'

'You know I can't do that, Eddie. You've been officially declared rogue. I'm sure it's all a terrible mistake. Tell me where you are, and I'll send someone to pick you up.'

'I want to talk to the Matriarch.'

'She doesn't want to talk to you, Eddie.'

'Of course she does. That's why she's listening in. Talk to me, Grandmother, and I'll tell you about Sebastian.'

'I'm here, Edwin,' said Martha Drood. I could hear the difference on the line as she went to secure mode. She knew we were about to discuss things that Penny wasn't cleared to know. Even though Penny was officially cleared to know everything.

'Hello, Grandmother,' I said, after a pause. We both sounded so very civilised, as though this was just a little family tiff, nothing that couldn't be settled over a nice cup of tea. 'How does it feel, Martha, to be talking to a dead man? How did it feel to order the death of your own grandson?'

'The family comes first, Edwin, you know that.' The Matriarch's voice was calm and even. 'I will always do what is necessary to protect the family. All you had to do was die; and you couldn't even get that right, could you?'

'I would have died for you, for the family,' I said, holding the phone so tightly my hands hurt. 'If you'd given me a good reason, if you'd trusted me enough to explain. I love the family, in my own way. But not any more. You made me rogue, so rogue I'll be.'

'Why did you call, Edwin? What do you want?'

'To tell you about Sebastian. Who is currently very unconscious, in his flat. If you were to send some people here, they could collect him while he's helpless. And then you wouldn't have to worry about those information parcels he's been holding over your heads. You see my war is with you, Grandmother. Not with the family.'

'I am the family. I am the Matriarch.'

'Not for much longer,' I said. 'I've been digging up your nasty little secrets, and I'm really very angry with you, Grandmother. For what's been done, in the family name. I'm coming home, and not as the prodigal son. I'm coming home for the truth, even if I have to tear the family apart to get it. See you soon, Grandmother.'

I hung up, and then stood there for a moment. My hands were shaking. If I hadn't already known I was dying, I'd probably have been scared. I looked around for Molly and Janissary Jane. They'd only just remembered to go through the pile of discarded trousers, looking for car keys.

'Time to get moving, ladies. The family will be here soon.'

'Okay,' said Molly. 'I think we've done about as much damage here as we can.'

Janissary Jane drove the big black car through the streets of London, because she knew the way and because she had the car keys and refused to give them up. Molly sat in the back seat with me, arms tightly folded, sulking. She was never comfortable unless she was in charge. Janissary Jane drove far too fast and manoeuvred aggressively at all times, to keep our cover, she said, but finally we arrived at Wimbledon, still in one piece. Most people only associate the name with tennis, but these days the area is eighty per cent immigrant population, and a thriving small business community. Brightly coloured posters in the shop windows advertised unusual goods in Indian and Pakistani, and here and there blue-skinned nautch dancers gyrated down the street to electric sitar music. Our black car with its impenetrable tinted windows drew many cool and thoughtful glances as we glided smoothly through the narrow streets. Eventually Janissary Jane drew up outside a hole in-the-wall off licence, the kind of place that's open twenty-four hours a day and there's always a sale going on. We got out of the car, and Molly and I looked inquiringly at Janissary Jane.

'The Blue Fairy has a bed-sitting room above the off licence,' she said. 'Brace yourselves. He's not very house proud, these days. And we'll have to go through the shop to get to the flat, so remember we're here to see Mr Blue.'

'Why . . . here?' I said.

'Would you look for him here?' said Janissary Jane, and I had to nod. She had a point.

Janissary Jane led the way into the off licence. The walls were stacked from floor to ceiling with every kind of booze under the sun, many of them boasting labels I didn't recognise. The middle-aged Pakistani behind the counter greeted us cheerfully, nodding quickly when he heard we were here to see Mr Blue.

'Of course, indeed. Hello, Miss Jane; it is very good to see you again. Mr Blue is indeed upstairs, and at home; you go right up. He is resting, I believe, and a bit under the weather. I am sure it will do him good to have some friendly company.'

He showed us through to the back, still smiling. We ascended some dimly lit stairs to the next floor, and found a door with the right name next to a bell push. The door was standing slightly ajar. Not a good sign. I drew my Colt Repeater, Janissary Jane her two punch daggers, and Molly made her witch knife appear out of nowhere. I gestured for Janissary Jane and Molly to stick behind me. They ignored me, pressing silently forward, and I sighed. Janissary Jane pushed the door slowly inwards. It didn't make a sound. The room beyond was dark and shadowy, even though it was still afternoon. We slipped inside one at a time, prepared for the worst, but nothing could have prepared us for what we encountered.

The room was a mess. A real mess. The kind of mess you have to work at. My first thought was that the sitting room had been turned over by professionals looking for something, but it quickly became clear that no self-respecting professional agent would sully his hands on the general filth of this place. Grime and slime fought it out for most of the surfaces, what could be seen of the carpet was stained a dozen colours, and junk and debris formed a layer on the floor so thick we had to kick our way through it. Old clothes had piled up in the corner, perhaps for washing but more likely for burning, and takeaway food cartons clung stickily to each other. Something crunched wetly under my foot, and I really hoped it was just a cockroach. The curtains weren't drawn, but the window glass was so thickly smeared over that the afternoon light had to fight its way through.

Empty bottles stood on every surface, mostly Indian Pale Ale and Bombay Gin. There were pill bottles, and not the kind you get on prescription. Crinkled tin foil, for chasing the dragon. And half a dozen syringes, with a cigarette lighter standing by to sterilise the needles. The only thing left after this was drinking methylated spirits straight from the bottle in a cardboard box on the Charing Cross embankment. Assuming the Blue Fairy lived that long.

We moved around the sitting room as quietly as we could. No sign of any bad guys, and I was beginning to wonder if we were looking for a corpse rather than a person. I pushed open the bedroom door, and there was the Blue Fairy, lying face down on his bed. Snoring gently and making mouth noises in his sleep. We all relaxed a little, and put away our weapons. The Blue Fairy was wearing nothing but a pair of boxers, well past their sell-by date, and a charm bracelet around his left ankle. Janissary Jane and Molly and I had a brief but animated discussion over who was going to have to actually touch him long enough to turn him over. We played a few quick games of paper, scissors, stone, and I lost. I still think they cheated somehow. I took a firm hold of the Blue Fairy's surprisingly hairy shoulder, turned him over and yelled his name right into his face. I then backed quickly away as he sat bolt upright in bed, hacking and coughing.

'All right, all right, I'm awake! Lay off the rough stuff, I'm delicate. Especially first thing in the morning.'

'It's afternoon,' I said.

'To you, maybe. For me it's the beginning of a new day and I really wish it wasn't. You'll have to excuse me, the old grey matter is never at its best first thing, at least until I've had a few cups of coffee and a ciggy. Now, who are you, what are you, and why are you persecuting a poor fairy at this ungodly hour? I didn't order out again, did I? I could have sworn the escort agency said my credit wasn't any good any more, the bastards.'

He squeezed his eyes shut, coughed up half a lung, and then stared at me blearily. His eyes widened as he finally got a good look at me, and then he scooted back across the crumpled bedsheets, holding up his hands defensively, until he crashed into the headboard and couldn't go any further. He tried to smile, but couldn't pull it off convincingly.

'Eddie! It's you! If I'd known you were coming, I'd have tidied up, made a bit of an effort ... help yourself to anything you like, make yourself at home ... Oh God, Eddie, don't kill me, please! I'm no threat to you!'

'Interesting,' I said. 'You should only know me as Shaman Bond. But you know my real name. How is that, Blue?'

'I can see your torc,' he said, blinking rapidly. 'I'm half elf, you know. Of course you know. You Droods know everything. And I have been known to do the odd job for your family, on occasion. I have to. They give me money. Don't kill me, Eddie, please. They made me do it!'

'All right, Eddie, lay off him,' said Janissary Jane, moving forward to stand beside me. 'Hello, Blue. It's me, Jane. You've got yourself into some real trouble this time, haven't you? Even I may not be able to get you out of this one. What exactly did you do for the Droods that you're so ashamed of?'

'Ah, Jane,' said the Blue Fairy, calming down a little. 'And Molly, too. How nice. Welcome to my humble abode. Excuse the mess, but I live here. And I can't seem to work up the enthusiasm to give a damn any more. Terribly lax of me, I know, but that's life, these days. My life, anyway. Still, I'm glad you're here. If one is about to die horribly, it is marginally better to do it in the company of one's friends. Could you perhaps persuade your friend the assassin to let me put some clothes on? I really would prefer not to meet my maker wearing only my underwear.'

'Get dressed,' I said, amused despite myself. 'I'm not here to kill you, Blue. Just to ask you some questions.'

'Wait till you hear the answers,' said the Blue Fairy.

We backed away from the bed, and he levered himself off the slumping mattress and pulled on a battered old silk wrap. He ran his hands through his thinning hair, took a cigarette from the pack by the bed, lit it with a fingertip, and took a deep drag. He then had another long coughing fit, accompanied by really horrible noises, and sat down on the bed again, his face grey and sweaty. He was carrying too much weight, and it showed in the jowls and puffy cheeks. His face had an unhealthy sheen, and his eyes were seriously bloodshot. The word was he'd been quite a dandy in his time, back in the heady days of glam rock, but he hadn't aged well. The Blue Fairy had lived not wisely but too well. He might have been a personage to be reckoned with once, but that was long ago. But if he really had done half the things he was supposed to have done, in and out of bed, it was a wonder he was still here at all. Presumably even half-elves are very hard to kill.

'God, you're a mess, Blue,' said Janissary Jane. 'You look worse than your sitting room, and that's saying something.'

'I know, I know,' said Blue, drawing on his cigarette again, and stifling another coughing fit through sheer effort of will. 'Think of me as a work in progress. I keep hoping if I drink enough, or ingest enough things that are bad for me, I won't have to wake up again to this awful room, this awful life. This hole that I dug for myself, this burrow I have crawled into ... But I always do. It's hard to kill an elf, even when he's cooperating as hard as he can. Even a half-elf. Bless dear old Daddy and his rampant gonads.'

'For someone so determined to die, you seemed very concerned about me being here to kill you,' I said.

'I would prefer to go with some dignity,' said the Blue Fairy. 'Not kicking and screaming all the way, as you reduce me to small bloody pieces. I know how you Droods operate.'

'But why do you want to die?' said Molly. 'If you don't like your life, change it, turn it around. There's still time.'

The Blue Fairy smiled fondly at her. 'Ah, there speaks the innocence and optimism of youth. When life seems full of promise, and possibilities. But no one loves a fairy when he's fifty. They want their magic from a younger bit of stuff. And my magic, sad to say, is not what it was. It faded, along with my good looks ... which were magnificent, once upon a time. I was invited to all the very best parties, you know. Mixed with the celebs, had my face in the glossies every week. But alas, we half-elves bloom early and fade fast. Daddy dearest's energies were never meant to be contained in a mostly human form. The candle that burns twice as fast turns out not to be much of a bargain, in the end.

'Now I'm no longer good looking enough to hang on to the pretty boys and pretty things that alone make life worth living. Sweet young things do still turn up in my bed, but only when I pay them. And the fortunes I once had, that I thought would last for ever, are gone, long gone. On this ... and that. I never worried about money, until I didn't have it any more. Which is why I have to take whatever work I can get. Even the jobs I know will come back to haunt me afterwards.'

'What have you done, Blue?' I said.

He looked at me pleadingly. 'I didn't have any choice. One of your people turned up here, quite unexpectedly. I didn't think the Droods even knew I existed any more, let alone where to find me. But he had work for me, and the money was good. Very good. And the threat behind it was very real. You don't say no to a Drood. And since all he wanted was a little strange matter I didn't see the harm. Acquiring unusual objects from other dimensions is one of the few things I'm still good at. It's in the genes, you see. I got some strange matter for your family's Armourer once, some years back, and it must have been on file somewhere, because when they wanted some more they came to me.'

'Who did they send?' I said.

'Matthew,' said the Blue Fairy. 'They always send Matthew when they're not prepared to take *Go to Hell* for an answer.'

'Of course,' I said. 'It would have to be Matthew. He'd do anything for the family. Go on, Blue.'

The Blue Fairy blinked nervously at me, picking up on the coldness in my voice. He stubbed out the last inch of his cigarette on the bedside table, and tried to sit up straight, clasping his hands together in his lap so they wouldn't shake.

'Well,' he said, 'I went fishing. That's what I do. Drop a line into the other realms and see what I can hook. Strange matter isn't easy to find. I call it that because I haven't a clue what it is, or what it's for. It's organic . . . maybe alive, maybe not, and it has some . . . quite unique properties. Fishing the dimensions can be very dangerous, you know. You never can tell when you'll hook something big and nasty by mistake, and then up it comes through the planes, mad as Hell and looking for revenge. But I got Matthew what he wanted, and he paid me in cash, right there on the spot. Good money. Far too much, for someone in my reduced circumstances. That was when I started to get suspicious.

'But I didn't do anything. I had new booze to drink and new drugs to take, and . . . he was a Drood, after all. You don't mess with the Droods. Then I heard you'd been ambushed by an elf lord, with an arrow made of strange matter, hired by the Droods . . . and I knew. I felt bad, Eddie, really I did. I've always known you were a Drood; you can't hide a torc from elf eyes. And we'd had some good times together, in the old Wulfshead. You bought me drinks and listened to me talk, and you never laughed at me. So after I heard what had happened I waited for you to come looking for me. And here you are. But you're not here to kill me, are you? You want something.'

'The strange matter's still in my body,' I said. 'And it's killing me. Can you get me a cure?'

'No,' said the Blue Fairy, meeting my eyes steadily. 'It doesn't work that way. I need to know exactly what I'm looking for when I go fishing, or I can't find it. And I don't know nearly enough about strange matter to have any idea of what its counterpart might be.

I'm sorry, Eddie, really I am. I didn't know what they were going to do!'

'Would it have made any difference if you had?' I said.

'Probably not,' he admitted. 'It was very good money.'

'How would you like a chance to redeem yourself?' said Molly. 'How would you like to go fishing for something for us?'

'What did you have in mind?' said the Blue Fairy.

'We need a skeleton key, to get us past The Hall's defences,' I said. 'Is there such a thing?'

He smiled suddenly. 'Oh yes. There is. I've waited years for someone to come and ask me. It's really very simple. Quite elegant, actually. But are you sure you want to do this, Eddie? Once word gets out that the Drood's defences have been breached . . .'

'Let it,' I said. 'Let the whole family crash and burn, if that's what it takes to get to the truth.'

We went out into the sitting room. The Blue Fairy dug through a pile of debris and came up with a very ordinary looking fishing rod and reel. The kind of thing people use when they go fishing for recreation, rather than competitive sport. The Blue Fairy then produced a knife out of nowhere, pulled up the left sleeve of his dressing gown, and made a shallow incision just above the wrist. I could see a whole series of scars reaching up his arm to the elbow, some old and some not, from where he'd done this before. Golden blood welled up from the cut, and he held his arm out over the space he'd cleared on the floor before him. The blood dripped down to form a golden pool. When it was about three or four inches in diameter, the Blue Fairy pressed his fingers against the cut, muttered under his breath and the wound healed over immediately, leaving another scar on his arm.

The Blue Fairy pulled his sleeve down again, not looking at the three of us watching, and snapped out half a dozen words in old elvish. I caught some of it, but his accent was unfamiliar. The pool on the floor blazed suddenly with a golden light, and spread out on the floor until it was almost a yard in diameter. It didn't look like a pool of liquid any more. Looking into it was like staring into a deep well that kept getting deeper the longer you looked. I felt like I was off balance, and might fall. I grabbed Molly's arm for support just as she grabbed mine. We both smiled at each other, a little shame-facedly. Janissary Jane didn't look into the pool. She kept all her attention on the Blue Fairy. And she had both her punch daggers at the ready.

The Blue Fairy took up his fishing rod, checked the hook was secure and the line was running smoothly, and then dropped his line into the glowing golden pool. The hook disappeared, followed by more and more line as the Blue Fairy kept feeding it in.

'How far down does it go?' said Molly.

'All the way,' said the Blue Fairy.

'Some questions you just know you're not going to get an answer that helps,' said Molly.

'Elf blood has many useful properties,' the Blue Fairy said calmly. 'Even diluted, degraded blood like mine. All elves have an in-built talent for travelling. They can walk sideways from the sun, access other planes of existence, enter dimensions you and even I couldn't conceive of, let alone operate in. But the blood itself is enough to open doors, and allow me to go fishing ... Sometimes for the fun of it, fishing at random for whatever's there, sometimes to order, for a price. If I concentrate hard enough, I can find pretty much anything ... and what you need, Eddie, is a Confusulum.'

'A *what*?' I said.

'A Confusulum,' the Blue Fairy said patiently. 'Don't ask me what it is, because I've no idea. That's the point. It doesn't actually change anything, just confuses the Hell out of everyone. It works on the uncertainty principle, that nothing is necessarily what or where it seems to be. I found the first one years ago, quite by accident, and it scared the crap out of me. Everyone needs some certainties in their life. I threw it back in, but something about it stuck in my mind. The Drood's family defences are based around certainties: friend or foe, permitted entry or not, that sort of thing. But the Confusulum will take those certainties out of the equation. The Hall's defences will be so confused they won't know whether they're operating or not, whether you're permitted entry or not; even whether you're actually there or not. They'll be so confused you'll be able to walk right through them, while they're still struggling to make up their minds. By the time anyone at The Hall notices that their defences have just had a major nervous breakdown, you'll be in.

'The Confusulum isn't one hundred per cent guaranteed; its uncertainty even applies to its own nature. So there's no telling exactly what its effects will be, or how long they'll last. But since I'm the only one ever to encounter a Confusulum, you can be sure your family have no specific defences against it.'

He fished randomly for a while, getting himself in the mood, and Molly and Jane and I sat more or less patiently around the golden pool, watching. I was having trouble getting used to the idea that I could be going home so soon, and that my family's notorious protections could be brushed aside so easily. And all because of a little man in a bed-sitting room, nursing a grudge and waiting to be asked.

The first thing he pulled out of the pool was a seven-league boot with a hole in its soul, followed by a small black lacquered puzzle box, a stuffed moomintroll and a statue of a black bird. The Blue Fairy threw them all back, and then stared into the pool with a look of fierce concentration on his face. His eyes bulged, and his lips drew back from his gritted teeth in a fixed snarl. Beads of sweat popped out all over his straining face. His line jerked suddenly, sending slow ripples across the surface of the glowing pool. The Blue Fairy let out a long breath, and began to slowly reel his line back in. He took his time, keeping a light but constant pressure on the line, staring so intently he wasn't even breathing any more. And finally he brought something up out of the golden pool.

I couldn't tell you what it was, exactly. It clung to the hook, writhing and twisting like a living thing, even though I knew on some deep instinctive level that it wasn't alive and never could be. It changed size and colour, shape and texture, from moment to moment; its dimensions snapping in and out and back and forth. It looked like the things you see out of the corners of your eyes when you've just woken up and you're still half asleep.

'Quick!' said the Blue Fairy, his face contorted with concentration. 'I brought it here for you, Eddie, so it's up to you to give it a shape in this dimension. Impose a single nature on it, so it can survive here. The link you make will mean it will serve you, and only you. But do it quickly, before it becomes something we can't bear to see with only human eyes.'

I concentrated on the first image that came to me. It just popped into my head: a simple circular badge I'd seen in an old head shop

268

in Denmark Street years ago; a white badge bearing the legend *Go Lemmings Go*. And just like that, the twisting unnerving thing on the hook was gone, and the badge was resting on the palm of my hand. It looked and felt perfectly normal, perfectly innocent. I pinned it carefully on the lapel of my jacket

'All the things you could have chosen,' said Molly. 'Everything from Excalibur to the Holy Hand Grenade of Saint Antioch, and you had to choose *that*. The workings of your mind remain a complete mystery, Eddie.'

'That's the nicest thing you've ever said to me,' I said, and we both smiled.

'By any chance, are the two of you an item?' Janissary Jane said suddenly.

'We haven't decided yet,' I said.

'We're working on it,' said Molly.

'We're ... partners, on this particular enterprise.'

'Partners in crime.'

'Or possibly a suicide pact.'

'You two deserve each other,' said Janissary Jane, shaking her head.

None of us had noticed that the Blue Fairy had inadvertently allowed his line to drop back into the glowing pool. He cried out abruptly as something below grabbed the hook and tugged hard on the line. The Blue Fairy was almost pulled forward, and the line whirred through the reel until it ran out. The Blue Fairy was jerked forward again, but hung on grimly.

'What have you got?' I said. 'What were you concentrating on?'

'I wasn't thinking about anything! I didn't catch this; it caught me!'

I hit the button on my reverse watch, and nothing happened. I hit the button again, and still nothing. I shook my wrist vigorously.

'Oh shit,' I said.

'It sounds so much more helpless when he says it,' said Janissary Jane.

'He's had a lot of practice recently,' said Molly. 'What's wrong, Eddie?'

'I appear to have broken the reverse watch,' I said. 'Or exhausted its batteries, or whatever the Hell the damn thing runs on. I think I asked too much of it when I forced it to save you.'

'So it's my fault?' said Molly.

'Always,' I said, smiling.

We looked on as the Blue Fairy wrestled with the fishing rod, the taut line jerking back and forth across the pool. It snapped abruptly, and the Blue Fairy stumbled back. And something huge and long and inhumanly strong burst up out of the golden pool, reaching for him. It was a single tentacle, dark purple in colour and lined with rows of suckers full of grinding teeth. More and more of it came up out of the pool, snapping back and forth.

'Get out of here!' yelled the Blue Fairy. 'I'll handle this!'

'Don't be a damned fool!' Janissary Jane yelled back at him. 'You can't deal with this on your own!'

'It came through my blood,' the Blue Fairy said grimly. 'So only I can put it back down. Go. You've got things to do. Things that matter. This is my business. No damned thing from the vasty deeps is going to get the better of me in my own home! Will you all please get the Hell out of here, so I can concentrate? And Eddie, make your family pay! For what they did to you, and what they did to me.'

More and more of the tentacle was forcing its way into the room, yards and yards of it, straining against the edges of the pool that contained it. The Blue Fairy threw his fishing rod aside and sketched ancient signs and sigils on the air with dancing hands, leaving bright incandescent trails on the air. He was chanting in elvish, in a form so old I couldn't follow one word in ten. Magic spat and crackled around him, and for the first time he was smiling. A cold, inhuman smile.

Molly and Janissary Jane and I left him there, standing on the edge of the golden pool, defying the monstrous thing that had come fishing for him. I left him there because I had important things to do, and because ... it was the only gift I could give him, for his help. A chance to stand alone against a fearsome foe, and either win back his pride or gain the good death he craved. I looked back at him, one last time, before I closed the door. He stood tall and proud, and powerful in his magic; and for the first time it wasn't difficult at all to see the elf in him.

CHAPTER NINETEEN
You can go home again (provided you carry a really big stick)

Molly and Janissary Jane and I stood in the street outside the off licence, looking up at the Blue Fairy's window. The vivid flashes of light had stopped, and it had gone very quiet. People passed by, paying us no attention. Thinking this was just another day, no different than any other. They didn't know there was another world, a more dangerous world, if they would only stop and look. Molly and Janissary Jane and I looked up at a silent, empty window and finally turned away.

'Should we . . .?' said Molly.

'No,' said Janissary Jane. 'Either way, it's over. Finished.'

'It's time to go home,' I said. 'For I have promises to keep, and miles to go before I sleep.'

'I love it when you talk literary,' said Molly.

'Eddie,' Janissary Jane said. 'I'm sorry, but I'm not going with you. I know my limitations. Fighting demons in Hell dimensions is one thing, taking on your family in the seat of their power . . . that's way out of my league. I'd just get in your way. So I think I'll sit this one out, if that's all right with you.'

'It's all right, Jane,' I said. 'I understand. Trust me; if I didn't have to do this, I wouldn't be doing it either.' I looked at Molly. 'You don't have to, Molly. My family probably doesn't even know you're involved. You could still walk away. I'd understand.'

'Hell with that,' Molly said cheerfully. 'I've been dreaming of sticking it to the Droods where they live for years. Besides, you wouldn't last ten minutes without me to back you up, and you know it.'

'Thank you, Molly,' I said. 'That means a lot to me.'

'Just promise me one thing,' she said. She held my gaze with hers,

271

fierce and demanding. 'Promise me that we're going back to tear the place down. Promise me you won't go soft, and beg them to take you back.'

'Not a chance in Hell,' I said, meeting her gaze. 'This isn't about what my family did to me any more. It's about what they've done to everyone.'

'You've come a long way, Eddie,' said Molly. 'I wish ... I could do something to help you. To save you, from what's inside you. All those years I spent trying to kill you, and now something else is beating me to it. I would save you if I could, Eddie. You do know that?'

'I know,' I said. 'But I've lived more this last day with you than in all those years on my own.'

'Oh, get a room, you two,' said Janissary Jane. 'I'm out of here before you start comparing favourite poems.'

'We are not an item!' said Molly.

'Definitely not,' I said.

'Yeah, right,' said Janissary Jane. 'I'll take the black car, and visit my local union branch. See if I can organise some direct action against Manifest Destiny, for allowing Archie Leech to use me as a weapon in their fight. The Mercenaries' Guild looks after its own. And we've always come down very hard on unfair competition from amateurs. If secret societies want to build up their own private armies, they should come to us. And pay the going rate. So ... Eddie, Molly. This is goodbye. Good luck, guys. You're going to need it. And Eddie, thank you. For saving me from Leech. You could have destroyed my body and got rid of him that way. It's what most people would have done.'

'I'm not most people,' I said.

'Got that right,' said Molly.

We all laughed a little, and then Janissary Jane turned and walked away, without looking back. She's always been a sentimental sort, for a mercenary. Molly and I watched her drive away in the big black car, and then we stood together on the pavement outside the off licence, and looked at each other. I really didn't know what to say to her. Were we an item? Were we ... a couple? This was all new to me. Unfamiliar territory. I admired Molly. Liked her, respected her, enjoyed her company ... and I risked my life to save hers without even thinking about it. Could this be love, come to me late in life and unexpected? The family allows its agents to have friends, even lovers, but never loves. Marriages are decided by the family. It's another way of controlling us. Love is something that comes afterwards, if you're lucky. Duty and family must always come first.

Because we protect the world. I'd kill them, for that lie.

And because I of all people know my family aren't fit to rule the world. They had to be stopped, brought down and humbled. While I was still strong enough to do it. I might not be able to save myself, but I could save the world. One last time.

'I know what you're thinking,' said Molly.

'Rather doubt that,' I said.

'Let's say I'm as much in the dark as you are,' said Molly, her hand resting gently on my right arm. 'You're a good man, Eddie. I think I could become very fond of you . . . in time. But we don't have much time, do we? So let's do what we have to, and worry about other things afterwards. If there is an afterwards.' She smiled suddenly. 'Hell, your family will probably kill us both anyway. So let's concentrate on what we're going to do next.'

'Yes,' I said. 'Let's do that.'

'Starting with that thing on your lapel,' said Molly, leaning in close for a better look at the badge. 'The Confusulum. Any idea how you work it?'

I frowned, peering down at the badge. 'The Blue Fairy didn't say. And there wasn't exactly an opportunity to ask for an instruction manual.' I tapped the badge with a fingertip. 'Hello? Is there anyone in there?'

And just like that, I made contact with *something*. Not with my mind; more like with my soul. I could feel something, inside my head and inside my heart; not human, not in any way human, but large and laughing, playful and curious. The Confusulum found everything marvellously funny, from this fascinating new world it was in to its own form and nature. It was alive and not alive, more than alive . . . As much a force and a purpose as a person. This new world, and the people in it, were a fascinating novelty to the Confusulum, to be enjoyed and played with for a while. Until it got bored. The Confusulum would serve me for as long as it remained amused, and then it would go somewhere else and do something else. It tried to show me what, but I couldn't understand or appreciate any of it. The Confusulum laughed again, like a child playing with a brand-new toy, and broke the contact. I looked at Molly.

'Well?' she said.

'I think it'll do whatever we want,' I said cautiously. 'It's ... very strange. I don't know if it'll confuse our enemies, but it baffles the Hell out of me.'

Molly sniffed. 'Should have given it to me. I'd soon teach it to sit up and beg. I'm used to dealing with magical items with a mind of their own. You have to show them who's boss.'

'Oh, I'm pretty sure it knows who's boss,' I said.

'Look, can it help us with our most urgent problem? Namely: how we're supposed to get to The Hall? The usual and unusual ways out of London are bound to be closely monitored now, either by your family or Manifest Destiny, and I don't have nearly enough energy left in me to summon a spatial portal. If only I hadn't had to smash the Manx Cat to save your life. I could have drawn a lot of power from that statue.'

'So this is my fault, then?'

'Everything is your fault, Drood, until proven otherwise.'

'All right,' I said, patiently. 'Let's start with that. Confusulum; can you help Molly get her power back?'

Oh sure! Said a happy voice in my ear. *Easy peasy!*

The badge on my lapel pulsed with an otherworldly light, and all around us the world became uncertain. The Confusulum exerted its unique nature, and confused the issue so much that the universe itself wasn't sure whether Molly had her power or not. It was as though someone had nudged the universe in the ribs, so that it skipped a beat, and just like that ... the world was subtly different. Magic spat and crackled on the air around Molly as power surged through her, and she laughed aloud with sheer exhilaration. She swept her hands back and forth, and shimmering trails of energy followed her hands. Molly's face was flushed with an almost sexual excitement, and she looked incredibly alive, full to bursting with the energies of the wild woods.

I thought she'd never looked more beautiful.

(There were side effects to the change. Posters in the shop windows were suddenly different colours, or had different names.

274

Red roses bloomed in the gutters. And a sheep walked solemnly backwards down the street.)

'Damn!' Molly said, grinning from ear to ear. 'This is amazing! I feel like I could take on the whole damned world and make it cry like a baby! You want a spatial portal, Eddie? I could transport this whole street from one end of the country to the other!'

'Actually, I think that might be a bit conspicuous,' I said, in what I hoped was a calm, reasonable and very soothing voice. 'And anyway, we can't risk using a spatial portal to get us to The Hall. My family's defences would detect that. No, our only chance is to sneak in and take my family by surprise.'

'You said you wanted to bring your family down!'

'I do, I do! But even with you back at your best, there's still no way we can hope to go head to head with my family and survive. You know that, Molly.'

She scowled. 'All right, maybe I do. So how are we going to get to The Hall?'

'We use the Confusulum,' I said. 'If it can confuse the whole universe about whether you have magic, it can confuse the world about where we really are. Right, badge?'

Oh sure! No problem! I live to confuse the issue! You know, you think very clearly for a three-dimensional entity!

So, the Confusulum exerted itself, the world threw up its hands and said *Oh have it your way then,* and Molly and I appeared just inside The Hall's grounds. Vast grassy lawns stretched away before us, with the house looming on the horizon. It was early evening now, the light already going out of the day. The sky was full of lowering clouds, and the air was hot and heavy. I looked quickly around, but there didn't seem to be anyone about. I was half crouching, tense with anticipation for alarms going off and defences activating, but every-thing seemed calm and quiet, the peace of the evening undisturbed except for the singing of a few drowsy birds and the whickering of the unicorns in their stables. The peace didn't fool me. The Hall and its grounds were seriously protected, at all times, by quite appallingly vicious scientific and magical means. All of which, it seemed, were currently utterly bewildered by the Confusulum. I straightened up and nodded slowly.

I'd come home.

'Stick close to me,' I said to Molly. 'The family can't remote view me while I wear the torc, and as long as you're right beside me it should protect you too.'

'I can protect myself,' Molly said automatically. She was staring about her with wide eyes and a disbelieving smile. 'Oh Eddie, you should have told me. This place is fabulous! I mean, the size of these grounds . . . you could land an airplane on lawns this size! And you've got fountains, and your own lake . . . and swans! Oooh, I love swans!'

'Me too,' I said. 'Delicious.'

'Barbarian! Are those peacocks over there?'

'Yes. Try not to set them off. They can make more noise than the alarms.'

'I always figured you guys lived well, but this is incredible. I know some landed gentry who don't have it as good as this!'

'Welcome to my home,' I said. 'One day, absolutely none of this will be mine.'

Molly looked at me. 'Why drop us off here, so far from The Hall? Why not arrive somewhere useful, inside the house?'

'Because that would have set off alarms,' I said. 'Even the Confusulum couldn't handle the kind of security my family has set up throughout The Hall. The kind of alarms primed to go off if they're even suspicious, or have a bad dream. The defences out here are more straightforward; on/off, kill/don't kill, that sort of thing. Child's play for the Confusulum.'

Molly grinned cheerfully. 'If I'd known burgling The Hall was this easy, I'd have done it years ago.'

We moved cautiously forward across the lawns, towards the house. We stayed off the gravel path, far too noisy, and we gave the peacocks plenty of room. A few sounded off, but no one in the house would give their plaintive cries any attention. Molly and I actually covered quite a distance before half a dozen robot guns rose suddenly up out of the ground from their hidden silos. Big, ugly brutal weapons, they swivelled back and forth as their fire computers struggled to target the intruders whose proximity had set them off. Molly and I stood very still, while I rested one hand on the badge at my lapel. The Confusulum did its thing, and the guns swivelled jerkily back and forth, increasingly confused and upset by conflicting impulses. So in the end, the stupid things decided that since they were the only things moving, they must be the intruders. And they shot the Hell out of each other. Muzzles roared, bullets flew, and one by one the robot guns exploded messily in bursts of fire and smoke. None of the bullets came anywhere near Molly or me.

'So much for sneaking in,' said Molly, as the last echoes of gunfire died away.

'Shut up and run,' I said.

We sprinted forward across the lawns. Lights were coming on inside The Hall. I had no doubt people would be crowding round their security monitors, trying to figure out what was happening. Hopefully the Confusulum would keep them guessing for a while. The robot guns had been known to malfunction before; they were one of Alistair's ideas.

'Up ahead,' said Molly. 'What are those ugly looking things?'

'Oh shit,' I said.

'I really hate it when you say that.'

'Stick really close to me, okay?'

Two of the gryphons came lumbering across the grass towards us, great lumpy things with grey scaly bodies and long morose faces. They were the only ones who looked forward to intruders, because they got to eat them. The Confusulum had to be having some effect on them, or they would have foreseen our coming and warned the house. But this close, the simple creatures believed what their senses were telling them, no matter how confused they might feel. I waited till they were almost upon us, and then sank down on to my haunches and spoke easily to them, calm and friendly, letting them remember my voice as they got my scent. They approached me slowly, gave me a good sniff all over, and then nuzzled my hands with their soft mouths. They blinked suspiciously at Molly, but I kept talking sooth-ingly to them, keeping their attention on me. They sat down and leaned their great weight against me, making happy snuffling sounds.

'Those things smell really horrible,' said Molly.

'Hush,' I said. 'You'll hurt their feelings. They're gryphons. Better than guard dogs because they can actually see the near future. Usually. But because they never met a piece of carrion they didn't want to roll in, they're never allowed inside the house. I always felt sorry for them when I was a kid; left out here alone in all weathers. So I used to sneak out at night and feed them bits of offal and stuff from the kitchens. It seems they remember me.'

'You soppy old softy, you,' said Molly. She reached cautiously over and scratched one of the gryphons behind its long pointed ear, and it snuffled loudly in gratitude.

'Down!' I said suddenly.

Molly and I crouched down with the gryphons, just a grey silhouette in the growing dusk, while I watched the Serjeant-At-Arms stalk out of The Hall's main front entrance. He looked around the grounds, taking his time, but his gaze swept over Molly and me and the gryphons without slowing. Of course he wouldn't believe the guns blowing each other up was a malfunction. He lived to defend The Hall. More members of the family poured out of the entrance behind him, and the Serjeant directed them this way and that with curt instructions. They swarmed around the exterior of the house, looking for signs of an attack or a break in, while others fanned out across the grounds. A few even took off from the landing pads on the roof in those clumsy old Da Vinci helicopter chairs that the Armourer's been trying to get the bugs out of for years. Rather them than me. They roared by overhead, spotlights stabbing down through the gathering gloom.

I hadn't expected such a dramatic response to a single incident. Presumably everyone was still on edge after the attack on the Heart. Or perhaps it was because I'd phoned and told them I was coming home . . . I liked to think so.

'You had to tell them you were coming,' said Molly.

'The grounds' defences have been activated,' I said, to avoid answering her. 'But as long as the Confusulum's operating, they shouldn't be able to lock on to us.'

'Why are they carrying weapons?' Molly said suddenly. 'I thought you people mostly relied on your armour?'

'Mostly, yes. But recently there've been some serious attacks on The Hall. Really nasty ones. No one feels like taking chances any more.'

'Attacks?' said Molly. 'By anyone I might know?'

'We don't know who's behind them,' I said. 'And if my family doesn't know, no one knows. But that's why they're pulling out all the stops. The very thing I'd hoped to avoid, by sneaking in. Bloody Alistair and his stupid bloody robot guns.'

'Should we leave?' said Molly. 'Maybe come back later?'

'We don't have the time,' I said. 'For better or worse, this is the only chance we'll get. You still game?'

'Always,' she said, grinning. 'Let's go start some trouble.'

'Let's,' I said, grinning back at her.

We gave the gryphons a few last pats, and then pushed them firmly away and sprinted across the open lawns towards the house. In the growing dusk, we should be just two more moving figures. If the family were bracing themselves for an attack by the kind of thing that had broken into the Sanctity, they shouldn't be looking for merely human targets. I could feel the grounds' defences trying to kick in; all the hidden trapdoors and deadly weapons, all the scientific and magical devices in their underground silos, but none of them could lock on to Molly or me as long as we were protected by the Confusulum. Force shields snapped on and off around us, magical energies manifested and dispersed in a moment, and none of them could touch us. The grounds' defences were baffled. But there were still far too many people around, too many Droods between us and The Hall. Someone would be bound to challenge us soon.

'We need a diversion,' I said to Molly. 'Something big and dramatic, to draw people away from the front of the house.'

'No problem,' said Molly, breathing a little hard from the running. 'Watch this.'

She muttered under her breath, gestured sharply, and suddenly a huge dragon was hovering over The Hall. A massive creature with a long, golden-scaled body and vast, flapping membranous wings. It shrieked horribly as it descended on The Hall, a horrid horned head thrusting forward on the end of a snake-like neck. It was impossibly big, half the size of the house, and it tore enormous holes in the outer wall of the East Wing with casual blows from its clawed hands. It breathed fire across the landing pads on the roof, sweeping away the vehicles there in one great blast of flames. It screamed in triumph, and slammed into The Hall with one shoulder, so hard the whole building shook.

'Will that do?' said Molly.

'Where the Hell did you find a dragon that size?' I said. 'I am officially impressed, Molly. Honest. But that is my home, and I would rather like to have some of it left at the end of the day! Does the word *overkill* ring any bells with you? Are you sure you can even control it?'

'Of course,' said Molly. 'I once took a thorn out of its paw. Relax, Eddie, it's not a real dragon. Just another charm off my bracelet.'

'So the damage it's doing to The Hall isn't real either?'

Molly frowned. 'Well, yes and no.'

'Let's get inside quick,' I said. 'Before the family works out what's happening.'

Most of the family had gone round to the back of the house by now, to deal with the most obvious threat, leaving the front of The Hall undefended. Only open lawns between me and the front entrance. And then the scarecrows appeared out of nowhere, blinking in to block my way; first one, then two, and finally an even dozen. I grabbed Molly by the arm, and we skidded to a halt well short of them. They moved stiffly to take up defensive positions between us and the front entrance, their gloved hands stiff as claws. Unnaturally still, impossibly strong. Twelve scarecrows come down off their crosses, wearing battered clothes from various periods all the way back to the seventeenth century. The Drood family's most hated enemies, made over into scarecrows to guard The Hall they'd threatened. Just because we could. The scarecrows' faces were weatherbeaten, taut, brown as parchment, and as brittle. Tufts of straw protruded from the ears and from the mouths, but their eyes remained, still alive, endlessly suffering.

'Are those the . . .?' said Molly.

'Yes,' I said. 'Someone in The Hall has panicked, and let the scarecrows loose. Our fiercest enemies, defeated and put to use. Their bodies hollowed out and filled with straw while they were still alive, and then bound by unbreakable pacts to defend The Hall, to their destruction if necessary. Not dead, any of them. They couldn't still suffer if we let them die. If you listen in on the right supernatural frequency, you can hear them screaming.'

'Oh my God,' said Molly. 'That's Laura Lye, the water elemental assassin, the one they called the Liquidator. And that's Mad Frankie Phantasm. I always wondered what happened to them.'

'No one attacks the family where we live and gets away with it,'

I said. 'We take that personally. And we always did like a splash of irony with our revenge. So now you know what waits for us, if we get this wrong.'

'Why isn't the Confusulum dealing with them?' said Molly.

'Good question. I think ... because the scarecrows exist on the border between life and death, neither one nor the other. Their nature is already so confused the Confusulum probably couldn't make it worse if it tried.'

'Are we in trouble here?' Molly said carefully.

'Absolutely,' I said. 'Because of what they are, and what was done to them, the scarecrows can't be hurt, stopped or turned aside.'

'So what do we do?'

'We take them down hard,' I said. 'Because in the end they're just scarecrows, while we're Eddie Drood and Molly Metcalf.'

'Damn right,' said Molly.

I armoured up, the living metal sweeping over me, and I went forward to meet the scarecrows as they lurched forward. The golden armour made me strong again, despite the pain stabbing through all of my left side now. I slammed into the first scarecrow, and tore it apart with brute armoured force. I ripped its arms off, smashed in its chest and then tore the head off its shoulders and threw it away. The other scarecrows crowded around me, beating at me with their stone-hard fists, pulling at my shoulders, but even their unnatural strength was no match for my armour.

(It was never intended that they should be able to take down a Drood. We never take the chance that our own weapons might be used against us.)

They pulled at my golden legs, trying to overturn me, pressing in from all sides, but I stood firm, and would not fall. I tore them apart, limb from limb, and no blood ever flowed, just more straw sticking out of ragged sockets. I ripped their hollow bodies apart, throwing the pieces this way and that. Heads rolled across the grass, the eyes still alive, still suffering and hating.

When this was over, the family would put them back together again. No rest for those who dared to be wicked against us.

Molly took out her fair share of the scarecrows. She hit them with the four elements, all at once. Hurricane winds whipped up out of nowhere, picked up the scarecrows, threw them high into the sky and then slammed them to the ground again. Sudden downpours targeted individual scarecrows and soaked them so heavily they could hardly move. Others burst into flames that burned so fiercely the straw-filled bodies were consumed in seconds. And finally the earth itself cracked open, swallowed up all the scarecrows left standing, and then slammed itself together again, trapping the scarecrows underground. Molly looked around her and nodded once, satisfied.

'Damn; we're good.'

'Yes,' I said. 'We are.'

I could have used the Confusulum to interrupt the forces that kept the scarecrows going. I could have used it to free the trapped spirits from their scarecrow bodies. But I didn't. Because they had attacked my family where we live; and we never forgive that.

We were almost at The Hall when a voice in my ear suddenly said, *Sorry! That's it! Business calls and I have to be going! It was fun; we must do this again some time!* I looked down, and the badge on my lapel was gone. Just like that, the Confusulum had abandoned me. About to enter the centre of my family's power, Molly and I were on our own. Which . . . was typical of the way my life had been going recently. I decided not to tell Molly. It would only upset her.

I strode up to the main front entrance, pushed open the door with a flourish and strode on into the hallway beyond. Molly couldn't wait to get in, actually pushing past me in her eagerness. I shut the door behind us, and the background roar of my family fighting the dragon was immediately shut off. Inside the house everything was quiet and peaceful, just like always. The slow ticking of old clocks, the smell of beeswax and polish and dust. Home. And then the Serjeant-At-Arms stepped out of his security alcove to confront me, and I remembered why I'd been so happy to leave in the first place. He stood solidly before me, blocking my way, stiff and formal as always in his old-fashioned butler's outfit. The man who had always been so much more than merely a butler. I stood very still. I was wearing my armour. I looked like any other Drood. There was a chance . . .

'I know it's you, Edwin,' said the Serjeant. 'I've been waiting here for you. You always were sloppy, undisciplined. When the defences in the ground couldn't lock on to anyone, I knew it had to be you. Always the lateral thinker, the sneak, skulking in the shadows. And your companion is the infamous Molly Metcalf? Didn't take you long to fall into bad company. I always knew you were no good, Edwin. Even when you were a boy.'

I armoured down, to face him. I wanted him to be able to see my face. 'I haven't been a boy for a long time, Serjeant. I'm not afraid of you any more. You see this man, Molly? He made my life miserable when I was a child. He made all our lives miserable. Nothing we did as children was ever good enough for him. You see, all adult members of the family can override the collars of the children. So they can discipline us, control us ... Punish us. We're a very old family, very old-fashioned, and we never did believe in sparing the rod. And this man loved to punish children. For any reason, or none. Just because he could. We all lived in fear of the Serjeant-At-Arms when we were kids.'

'It was for your own good,' the Serjeant said calmly. 'You had to learn. And you were always so very slow to learn, Edwin.'

I armoured up again, and held up my fist. Golden spikes rose out of the heavy knuckles. 'Step aside, Serjeant. I'm not going to be stopped this time.'

'It's not too late,' said the Serjeant. 'You could still surrender. Submit to family discipline. Make atonement for your crimes.'

'I never committed any crimes! Never! But the family has.'

The Serjeant sighed. 'You never listen, and you never learn. Loose your armour, Edwin. Or I'll make your companion suffer.'

He pulled weapons out of the air. His singular talent, given to him so that he could protect The Hall. A gun appeared in one hand, a flame-thrower in the other. He aimed them at Molly, and I lunged forward to protect her. Bullets hammered against my armoured chest and ricocheted away, but the flames swept past me to threaten Molly ... only to turn aside at the last moment, deflected by Molly's magic. She jabbed out a hand at the Serjeant, and he staggered backwards from the unseen impact. Molly laughed at him.

'My companion can look after herself,' I said to the Serjeant.

'Damn right,' said Molly.

The Serjeant started to subvocalise the Words that would call up his armour. He should have done that the moment he recognised me, but in his pride he still saw me as a child to be chastised. But even as he started the Words, Molly hit him with a rain of rats. They

283

fell on him out of nowhere, streams of big black rats swarming all over him, clawing and biting. He cried out in shock and pain, slapping at the rats and trying to shake them off, unable to concentrate long enough to say the Words that would have brought his armour to protect him. He staggered back and forth, beating at the rats with his bare hands. One sank its teeth deep into his palm and hung there, kicking and wriggling as he tried in vain to shake it off. Another ripped at his ear. Blood ran down his face as they tore open his scalp.

I would have liked to stand around for a while and watch him suffer, but I didn't have the time. So I stepped forward and punched him out. The strength behind the golden fist almost took his head off, and he crashed to the floor, barely twitching. Molly disappeared the rats with a gesture. I stood over the Serjeant-At-Arms, looking down at him, and it felt good, so good, to have finally avenged myself for years of pain and scorn. He didn't look nearly as big as I remembered him. He was still conscious, just.

'How many children did you whip for running in the hallways?' I said. 'How many did you flog for being late, or not being where they should be? For answering back? For daring to have minds and hopes and dreams of their own?'

The Serjeant stirred painfully, blood running out of the corner of his torn mouth as he smiled. 'It's a hard world, boy. Had to toughen you up, so you could survive it. You learned your lessons well, Edwin. Proud of you, boy.'

'We were children!' I said, but he was unconscious, and couldn't hear me any more.

'Your family do love their mind games, don't they?' said Molly.

'Not now, ' I said. 'Please.'

I stepped into the Serjeant's security alcove, and opened the emergency alarms locker. It was keyed to open to anyone wearing a torc. I looked at the switches set out before me, grinned, and then hit every single one of them. Interior alarms, exterior alarms, fire, flood, witchcraft and Luddites. (Some of our alarms go way back.) Bells and sirens went off throughout The Hall, ringing and howling and clanging in an ungodly cacophony of noise. Lights flared and flashed, emergency doors slammed shut, steel grilles came crashing down, and members of the family ran madly this way and that, driven mad by the whooping alarms. I always said we needed more emergency drills.

I walked confidently through the hallways and corridors with Molly at my side. People rushed by, shouting and gesturing, but none of them paid me any attention. To them I was just another Drood, anonymous in my armour. And if Molly was with me, well she must be an authorised guest. In an emergency, people only have time to see what they expect to see.

I led Molly deeper into The Hall, and she oohed and aahed as she took in all the luxurious furnishings, the portraits and paintings, the statues and works of art, and the other marvellous loot my family has acquired down the centuries. I grew up with it, so I still mostly took it for granted and I had to smile as Molly went ecstatic and rapturous over this rare piece or that. I actually had to drag her away from a few things she wanted to examine more closely. We had to keep moving; time was not on our side. Molly pouted rebelliously, but she understood.

'Colour me major impressed,' she said. 'I'd heard stories about this place, but I had no idea. There are things here they haven't got in museums! Paintings by major artists that aren't in any of the catalogues! So many beautiful things … and probably wasted on you, you philistine. No wonder Sebastian had such excellent taste. I'm not leaving here without stuffing a few things in a bag.'

'Later,' I said. 'We have to get to the Armoury.'

'Why?'

'Because there's something there I need. Something I can use to bring the house down.'

The Armoury should have been closed, shut down, sealed and guarded, according to the emergency protocols. I'd half expected to have to fight my way through armed guards and force the blast-proof doors open with my armoured strength. Or have Molly use her magics. But in the end the heavy doors stood wide open, entirely unguarded, which was unheard of. I edged over to the blast-proof doors, and peered cautiously through into the Armoury. It gave every indication of being deserted. I insisted on going in first, and Molly made her disapproval clear by crowding close behind, almost stepping on my heels.

The cellars were deserted, the work stations shut down. The quiet was eerie. None of the usual fires or explosions or sudden surprised cursings. One man was waiting for us, sitting at ease in his favourite chair right in the middle of everything. He watched, smiling wryly, as Molly and I cautiously approached him. A tall, middle-aged man with a bald pate and tufty white eyebrows, wearing a stained white lab coat over a T-shirt bearing the legend *Guns Don't Kill People – Unless You Aim Them Properly*. The Armourer. My Uncle Jack. I should have known he would stand his ground when everyone else had fled.

'Hello, Eddie,' he said calmly. 'I've been expecting you.'

He held up something in his right hand. A simple clicker, in the shape of a small green frog. He snapped it once, and my armour went back into my collar, just like that. I gaped at the Armourer, shocked speechless, and he laughed softly.

'A little toy I put together long ago, and kept for myself. After all, you never know when it might come in handy ... When I heard all the alarms go off at once, I knew it had to be you, Eddie. You always did have a taste for the dramatic. Why did you come back? You know it's death for you to be here, now you're rogue. And why have you brought one of your oldest enemies into the most confidential part of The Hall?'

'I'm not sure who the enemy really is any more, Uncle Jack,' I said. 'You know Molly Metcalf?'

'Of course I know who she is, boy. I know all the names that matter. I was an agent in the field for twenty years, and I still leaf through the reports. How else would I know what to design for agents today? What is the infamous Molly Metcalf doing here with you, Eddie?'

'Why does everyone keep using that word?' said Molly. 'I am not infamous!'

'She's with me,' I said.

The Armourer smiled suddenly. 'Oh, it's like that, is it? Well, it's about time.' He grinned charmingly at Molly. 'Delighted to meet you, my dear. I'm afraid I only know you by reputation; and quite a fearsome reputation it is.'

'I earned it,' said Molly. 'Though I've always preferred to think of myself as a fun person.'

'Did you really turn the whole Berkshire Hunt into foxes for forty-eight hours?'

'Of course,' said Molly. 'I thought it might give them a little insight.'

'Good for you, girl,' said the Armourer. 'Never did approve of fox hunting. Barbarous sport, mostly followed these days by inbred aristos and nouveau riche arriviste arseholes. So, Eddie, you finally brought a girlfriend home to meet the family. I was beginning to worry about you.'

'She is not my . . . well . . .' I said. 'We're working on what we are.'

'Right,' said Molly. 'It's . . . complicated.'

'How do you feel about him, Molly?' said the Armourer, leaning forward.

'I'm fond of him,' she said thoughtfully. 'Like a big shaggy dog no one wants that's come in out of the rain, and you haven't the heart to drive out again.'

The Armourer winked at me. 'She's crazy about you, kid.'

'Woof, woof,' I said.

'Now then, lad,' said the Armourer, briskly back to business. 'What the Hell are you doing here? And whatever possessed you to phone ahead? The Matriarch went mad. She's been beside herself, issuing orders for you to be killed on sight. I'm committing treason against the family just for talking to you like this.' He sniffed loudly. 'Like that's going to stop me. I've never needed someone else to tell me what's in the family's best interests. If you ask me, Mother's not all there these days. But even so, you can't expect me to actually assist you in . . . whatever you came here for. You should never have come back, Eddie. What did you think you'd find here, for God's sake?'

'Armourer,' I said. 'I came here looking for the truth. Just like you always taught me, Uncle Jack.'

He sighed heavily, and clicked his green frog again. 'Oh, all right; there's your armour back. I know I'm going to regret this. I always was too soft-hearted for my own good. Why did you come here, Eddie? What do you want from me?'

'I need to discover the real reason why I was made rogue,' I said slowly. 'I was never a traitor to the family, Uncle Jack. You know that.'

'Yes,' the Armourer admitted. 'I know that. Anyone else I might have believed, but not you, Eddie. You were always so honest and open about your doubts ... I couldn't believe it when they told me. Wouldn't believe it till they ordered me to shut up and do as I was bid. Something's happening in the family, Eddie, that I don't understand. Factions, in-fighting, deep divisions over arguments I can't even follow ... And now different parts of the family are actually keeping secrets from each other. I'm being deliberately kept out of the loop, as well; and that's never happened before. Mother would never have permitted it ... she always used to trust my judgement. But things have changed dramatically in the years since you left, Eddie; and not for the better. Do I really need to tell you that stepping down as Armourer in favour of dear little Alexandra wasn't my idea? Thought not.'

'I need your help, Uncle Jack,' I said. 'I need you to trust me.'

'I'm really not going to like this, am I?' He rose to his feet, and clapped me on the shoulder. 'You'll probably do less damage if I help you. Look, if you want answers you need the Library. Everything's in there, somewhere.' He fished a key ring out of his pocket and took off one small key. He handed it to me. 'The library will have gone into automatic shutdown once the alarms started, but that key will open all the doors for you. Take good care of it, Eddie; I want it back. Now get the Hell out of here before someone comes in and catches me talking to you.'

'Thanks for the key,' I said. 'But I need something else from you.'

'Oh yes, of course! Molly's a delightful young lady, Eddie. You have my blessing.'

'Not that! Well, thanks for that, but ... I need something from the Armoury. To be exact, I need something from the Armageddon Codex.'

The Armourer stopped smiling. 'You want me to give you one of the forbidden weapons?'

'Yes. I need Oath Breaker.'

He looked at me for a long moment, and his gaze was very cold. 'Why in the name of the good God would you want that awful thing?'

'There's something rotten at the heart of the family,' I said, meeting his gaze steadily. 'You know that as well as I do. I need the one weapon no member of the family can hope to stand against. The one weapon they won't even think of challenging. It's the only way I can be sure of avoiding bloodshed, Uncle Jack.'

'No, boy,' the Armourer said flatly. 'You're asking too much.'

'He has to,' said Molly. 'He doesn't have time to be subtle. He was shot with an arrow made of strange matter. It's in his system, poisoning him.'

The Armourer looked at me sharply. 'Is this true, Eddie?'

I nodded stiffly. 'Punched right through my armour. I thought I'd healed the wound with a med blob, but the strange matter's still in me. And it's spreading.'

'Dear God . . . How long have you got, Eddie?'

'Three days,' I said. 'Maybe less.'

'Oh my dear boy . . . I heard about the arrow, but I never knew . . . Strange matter. Cursed stuff. I destroyed the only samples I had. Let me call up some old notes, see what I can do . . . there must be something . . . '

'I don't have the time, Uncle Jack,' I said. 'That's why I have to do this quickly, and that's why I need Oath Breaker. You have my word I won't do anything with it that would hurt the family.'

'I don't know . . .' said the Armourer.

'I do,' said a harsh, cold and very familiar voice behind me. 'You get nothing, traitor; except what's coming to you.'

We all looked round, and there stood Alexandra, tall and proud as ever. She was dressed in black and carrying something awful in her hands. Molly started towards her, and I grabbed her arm and held her back. The Armourer grabbed her other arm.

'Don't move, Molly,' he said quietly. 'She's holding one of our most dangerous weapons. She's holding Torc Cutter.'

'What the Hell's that?' said Molly, but she didn't try to fight us.

'What it sounds like,' I said. 'Hello, Alexandra. You're looking . . . very yourself. What are you doing with Torc Cutter?'

'I took it out of the security locker, just for you, Eddie,' she said. Her voice was almost teasing, but she wasn't smiling, and her eyes were very cold. 'Time's up, Eddie. Game over.'

'Would someone please tell me why everyone's acting so dramatic?' said Molly.

'The shears she's holding are the only thing that can sever a

Drood's torc,' the Armourer said. 'It breaks the life-long connection between a Drood and his armour. The operation is always fatal. Torc Cutter is a very ancient weapon, older than family history. It's only ever supposed to be used as a last resort, to bring down a rogue who threatens the whole family when all else has failed. It hasn't been used in centuries.'

'It looks like gardening shears,' said Molly, and she had a point. Torc Cutter was made of black iron, not steel, and looked like what it was: a simple cutting tool. Bleak and functional, to any Drood it was ugly with vicious significance. One of the few things absolutely guaranteed to kill a Drood. I stood very still, and made sure Molly did too. Alexandra wouldn't hesitate to use Torc Cutter. It occurred to me that I wasn't entirely sure why she hadn't already used it. I would have. Perhaps ... there was just a chance that part of her wanted me to talk her out of using it. We had been close, once.

'Don't do this, Alex,' I said carefully. 'You know this is all bullshit. You know I could never be a traitor. You were the one who knew me best.'

'I thought I did,' she said. 'But then you went away; and you didn't take me with you.'

'I did ask,' I said.

'You knew I couldn't go! I had to make a new life for myself, here at The Hall. A life in which I have become very powerful, Eddie. And you are most definitely a traitor, to the true spirit of the family. You're a threat to the family's future, Eddie. And I can't, I won't, allow that.'

She stepped forward, raising Torc Cutter, and the Armourer snapped out a single Word. The ugly black shears jumped out of Alexandra's hands, and into the Armourer's. She looked at him with something like shock, as he stuffed the shears carelessly into his coat pocket, smiling smugly.

'I put a Safe Word into everything that passes through my lab, in case they should fall into the wrong hands. And all the most deadly weapons have passed through the Armoury recently, thanks to the Matriarch's instructions. Mother always was a little paranoid, and luckily she passed a healthy dose of it on to her children.' He took a needle gun out of his other pocket and shot Alexandra in the throat.

She just had time to slap a hand to her neck, and then she crumpled to the floor, out like a light. The Armourer blew imaginary smoke off the barrel of his gun, and put it away again. 'I always keep that handy, for when my lab assistants get a bit over-excited. She'll sleep for an hour or so. Put her somewhere comfortable, Eddie, while I go and get the key for the Codex.'

'Then you'll help me?' I said.

'Yes. I won't let you die with a traitor's name hanging over you. I can do that much for you. Besides, if Alexandra's running around armed with Torc Cutter, God alone knows what else is out there. You're going to need Oath Breaker.'

'I promise I'll return it safely,' I said.

'Too bloody right you will,' said the Armourer. 'Don't make me come after you, Eddie. I know some dirty tricks you never dreamed of in all your years in the field.'

'I always wondered why your old files were blocked,' I said.

Molly and I propped Alexandra up in a corner. She muttered querulously in her sleep and Molly looked down at her.

'Would she really have killed you with that thing?'

'Probably,' I said.

'Want me to kick her while she's down?'

'No. I don't do that.'

'Wimp.' She looked at me, consideringly. 'So; this Alexandra was once a flame of yours?'

'A long time ago,' I said. 'When we were both a lot younger. She wasn't always like this, you know. You're not jealous, are you?'

'Me? No! Why would I be jealous? I've had lots of boyfriends in my time. Dozens!'

'They probably didn't appreciate you like I do,' I said.

The family keeps the Armageddon Codex in a pocket dimension, for extra security. Only the Armourer, and his designated successor, can even approach it, let alone access it. The Codex contains the family's most powerful weapons, too dangerous to be used unless reality itself is under threat. Normally you have to fill out reams of paperwork before you're even allowed to approach the Matriarch with a request. The Armourer was trusting me a lot, to let me take Oath Breaker. He wouldn't do that, for all his sympathy, unless he was already convinced that there was something seriously wrong with the family.

To get to the Armageddon Codex, you have to pass through the Lion's Jaws. At the very back of what used to be the old wine cellars, before they were converted into the present Armoury, there is a giant stone carving of a lion's head, complete with mane. Perfect in every detail, twenty feet tall and almost as wide, carved out of the dark, blue-veined stone that makes up the cellar's furthest reaches. The Lion's eyes seem to glare, the mouth seems to snarl, and the whole thing looks like life itself frozen in stone. As though waiting to pounce, if it could only force the rest of its body through the stone wall that held it. Not surprisingly, Molly fell in love with it at first sight and stood before the stone face, running her hands over the detailed carving and cooing delightedly.

The Armourer stepped up to the Lion's snarling mouth and slipped a long brass key into a hole in the mouth that I couldn't see. He turned the key twice, subvocalising a whole series of Words, and then withdrew the key and stepped smartly back as the Lion's Jaws grated slowly open. The upper lip rose steadily, operated by some hidden mechanism, revealing huge jagged teeth, above and below. The Jaws continued to open, until the Lion's mouth gaped wide, revealing a tunnel big enough to walk through without having to duck your head. The throat of the Lion, that led to the Armageddon Codex.

'Is it ... alive?' Molly murmured.

'We don't think so, but no one knows for sure,' I said. 'It's as old as the house. Maybe older. The family might have made it, or just made use of it. Legend has it that if you pass through the Lion's Jaws, you must be pure of heart and pure of purpose, or the Jaws will close on you.'

'And then?' said Molly.

'Have you never seen anyone eaten by a stone head?' said the Armourer.

'I did, once,' I said. 'I was down in Cornwall ...'

'I was speaking rhetorically!' snapped the Armourer. 'I'm sorry, Molly, my dear, he always was terribly literal, even as a child.'

'You mean it really does eat people?' said Molly. 'If they're not ... pure in heart?'

'Oh yes,' I said.

'Think I'll wait out here,' said Molly.

'Relax,' said the Armourer. 'It's a story we tell the children, to stop them from messing around with the Jaws. The crafty little buggers are always getting into things they're not supposed to. Trust me, Molly; you'll be perfectly safe, as long as you're with us. Just as well, really. I haven't been pure in heart since I was ten years old, with my first erection.'

He waggled his bushy eyebrows at her, and Molly smiled dutifully. She still stood very close to me as we followed the Armourer through the Lion's Jaws and down its throat into the Armageddon Codex. Which turned out to be another stone cavern, but with terrible weapons hanging in rows upon the stone walls, like ornaments in Hell. Some hung on plaques, others stood in special niches carved from the bare stone. None of them was identified; either you knew what they were and what they could do, or you had no business touching them. I knew some of the weapons by sight and reputation, from my extensive reading in the Library.

There was Sunwrack, for putting out the stars, one at a time. Beside it was the Juggernaut Jumpsuit. And there the Time Hammer, for changing the past through brute force.

The Armourer noted me looking at the Hammer, and nodded quickly. 'Studying that gave me the idea for the reverse watch I gave you, Eddie. A lot of thought went into that. I hope you're taking good care of it.'

I nodded absently, still fascinated by the terrible weapons arrayed before me, things I'd never dreamed I might some day see in person. There was Winter's Sorrow, a simple crystal ball full of swirling snowflakes. It might have been a paperweight or a child's toy. But break the crystal, and it would unleash the Fimbulwinter: an endless season of cold and ice all across the world, for ever and ever and ever. Molly reached out a hand to touch it, saying '*Oh cute!*' And the Armourer and I both yelled at her and dragged her away. We sent her back to stand at the entrance, and she went, sulking. And then, finally, there was Oath Breaker.

It wasn't much to look at. A long stick of ironwood, deeply carved with prehuman symbols. An ancient weapon, older than Torc Cutter, older than family history. Older than the family, probably. We have no idea who created it, or why. Perhaps those people used it, and that's why there's no record of them anywhere. The Armourer finally reached out with a steady hand, and took the stick down. He grimaced, as though the touch of it was disturbing to him. He hefted it in his hand once, and then turned abruptly and gave it to me. I accepted it gingerly. It felt ... heavy, weighed down with spiritual weight, rather than physical. A burden to the body, and to the soul.

Because of what it was, and what it could do.

'But ... it's just a stick,' said Molly. She'd sneaked forward to join us again. 'Is that it? I mean, is that all of it? Does it change into something else, if you strike it on the ground? Or do you plan to beat people over the head with it?'

'This is Oath Breaker,' I said. My mouth was very dry, even while my hands were sweating. 'It undoes all agreements, all bonds. Right down to the atomic level, if necessary.'

'All right,' said Molly. 'Now you're scaring me.'

'Good,' I said. 'Because it scares the crap out of me. Armourer, give Molly Torc Cutter. Just in case.'

'Go to the Library,' said the Armourer. 'And learn what you need to know. I'll keep an eye on Alexandra. But don't take too long, Eddie. Those alarms and excursions you set off won't fool people for ever.'

'I know, Uncle Jack.'

'The family ... isn't what it was, Eddie. Part of me wishes I could go with you when you leave. But someone has to stay and fight for the soul of the family. For the sake of the Droods, and the world.'

CHAPTER TWENTY
Getting to the heart of the matter

'Uh oh,' said Molly.

I looked at her. 'This isn't going to be good news, is it?'

'The dragon charm just reappeared on my bracelet. Which means someone in your family finally rubbed two brain cells together, realised a dragon that big couldn't possibly be real and worked a simple dispersion spell on it. My little diversion is now officially at an end.'

'They'll head straight back into The Hall,' I said, frowning. 'To find out what the dragon was diverting them from. So any minute now, the whole place will be swarming with really pissed-off Droods looking for someone to take it out on . . . Time we were going, Molly. It was good to see you again, Uncle Jack.'

'How far is it to the Library?' said Molly, practical as always.

'Too far,' said the Armourer. 'You're not even in the right wing.'

'No problem,' said Molly. 'I'll call up a spatial portal, take us right there.'

'No, you won't,' the Armourer said flatly. 'The Hall's inner defences don't permit teleports, magical or scientific, for security reasons. Even I couldn't produce anything powerful enough to break through The Hall's defences.' He stopped and scowled thoughtfully. 'Not unless I can persuade the Council to fund my black hole research after all.'

'If we could please stick to the subject,' I said.

'There must be some way we can get to the Library without being spotted,' said Molly. 'How about an illusion spell? I could whip up something simple, make us look like someone else? Or an aversion spell. Make everyone look everywhere except at us?'

'Wouldn't work,' I said, 'Our torcs alert us to that kind of spell automatically. They'd fire up their Sight and look right through them.'

'When in doubt, keep it simple,' said the Armourer, a little smugly. He produced two battered old lab coats from a nearby locker, and thrust them at us. 'Put these on. Anyone you meet will look at the coats, not your faces. The family's used to my lab assistants turning up everywhere, and getting under their feet. Keep your heads down and keep moving, and you'll be fine. Damn, I'm good ...'

Molly and I slipped the lab coats on. They were both covered with an assortment of quite appalling stains, not to mention rips, cuts and in my case one really serious-looking bite mark. Molly's came right down to her ankles; but I had enough sense not to smile.

'My coat smells funny,' she said, glaring at me mutinously.

'Be grateful,' I said. 'Mine smells downright disgusting.'

I turned to the Armourer and we shook hands, a bit awkwardly. It wasn't something we did, as a rule. But we both knew we might not get a chance to do it again.

'Goodbye, Eddie,' the Armourer said, meeting my gaze squarely. 'I wish ... there was more I could do for you.'

'You've already done far more than I had any right to expect,' I said. 'Goodbye, Uncle Jack.'

He smiled at Molly and shook her hand too. 'I'm glad Eddie's taste in women has finally improved. It was a pleasure to meet you, Molly. Now get out there, and give them all Hell.'

'Damn right,' said Molly.

Molly and I left the Armoury, and carefully shut the blast-proof doors behind us. No point in advertising that the Armoury had been left open to casual visitors. I couldn't allow the Armourer to come to harm for helping me. I could already hear my family coursing through the outer sections of The Hall, searching for intruders. They were drawing steadily closer, shouting instructions and findings and comments back and forth, in loud and excited voices. It sounded like the whole damned family had been mobilised. The Matriarch wasn't taking any chances. The lab coats would get us past a few people, but not crowds like these ... All it would take was a moment of recognition, one raised voice ...

Fortunately, there was another option. Just, not a very nice one.

'When I was a kid,' I said conversationally to Molly, as we hurried down an empty corridor, 'I worked out various ways of getting round The Hall without being seen. Because if you got caught in places where you weren't supposed to be, you got punished. Often severely punished. But luckily The Hall is very old, and down the years certain useful hidden doors and secret passages became lost, forgotten, displaced. And because I did a lot of reading in the Library, especially in sections I wasn't supposed to have access to, I was able to turn up certain old books describing the exact locations of these very useful short cuts.

'There are doors that can take you from one room to another, from one wing to another, without having to cross the intervening space. There are narrow passages within thick hollow walls that used to be part of the old central heating and ventilation processes. There's a trapdoor in the basement that opens out into the attic, and some rooms that are only there on certain dates. I must have used them all, at one time or another, in my never-ending quest to discover things I wasn't supposed to know about.'

'Didn't your family ever suspect?' said Molly.

'Oh, sure. Finding these old passages is a sort of rite of passage for young Droods; tacitly permitted, if not actually encouraged. The family likes to see initiative in its children. As long as they follow the accepted rules and traditions. But I found some very odd ways that no one else even dreamed existed, and I never told anyone. I needed something that was mine, back then, and not the family's.'

'Am I to take it that you know a short cut to the Library?' said Molly.

'Yes. There's an opening into a crawlspace within the wall, not far from here.'

'Then why didn't you say so before?'

'Well,' I said.

'There's bad news, isn't there? Somehow I just know there's bad news.'

'It's dangerous,' I said.

'How dangerous?'

'The crawlspace is... inhabited. You see; The Hall has to put its electrical cables and gas pipes and so on somewhere out of sight, but for security purposes they can't just be hidden away inside the walls;

they have to be protected. Against sabotage, and the like. So our crawlspaces and hidden maintenance areas are located in attached pocket dimensions. Like the Armageddon Codex and the Lion's Jaws, but on a much smaller and less dramatic scale. And a lot easier for people to get into, obviously. Anyway, some of these pocket dimensions have been around so long they've acquired their own inhabitants. Things that wandered in and ... mutated. Or evolved.'

'What ... exactly inhabits this particular crawlspace?' said Molly.

'Spiders.' I said unhappily. 'Big spiders. And I mean really big spiders, things the size of your head! Plus a whole bunch of other really nasty creepy-crawly things that the spiders feed on.'

'Spiders don't bother me,' said Molly. 'That's more a boy thing. It's slugs that weird me out. And snails. Do you know how snails have sex?'

'These spiders will bother you,' I said firmly, refusing to be side-tracked. 'Hopefully they're not actually as big and nasty as my childhood memories insist, because there's no way of avoiding them. Their webs are everywhere. I still have nightmares, sometimes, about the times they chased me through the crawlspace with their scuttling legs and glowing eyes.'

'Then why did you keep using that particular short cut?' said Molly.

'Because I've never let anything stop me from doing what I need to do,' I said. 'Not even my own fear. Perhaps especially not that.'

'And there's no other way of getting to the Library?'

'Not safely.'

Molly sniffed. 'You have a really weird idea of what's safe and what's not, Drood.'

I led her down a shadowy corridor, past a long row of tall standing vases from the third Ming dynasty, and then past a glass display case full of exquisite Venetian glass until I came to a wood-panelled wall that stretched away into the distance. I had to keep pulling Molly along, as she got distracted by so much wealth within easy snatching distance. I counted off the panels until I came to a particular carved wooden rose motif, and then I turned it left and right the correct number of times until the primitive combination lock reluctantly fell into place. The rose clicked loudly, and a panel in the wall slid jerkily open. The ancient mechanism must have been wearing out.

Beyond the panel and inside the wall, there was only darkness.

The opening that had been more than ample for a child was only just big enough to let Molly and I squeeze through. We crouched down before the opening, and peered into the darkness. A slow cold breeze came out of the dark, carrying a dry, dusty smell. Molly wrinkled her nose, but said nothing. Thick strands of cobweb hung down inside the opening, swaying heavily on the breeze. There was no sign that anybody had been in the crawlspace for years. I listened quietly, gesturing sharply for Molly to keep still when she fidgeted. I couldn't hear anything. For the moment. I took a deep breath, braced myself, and then squeezed quickly through the cramped opening, before I could change my mind. Molly followed me in and the wooden panel slid jerkily back into place.

The darkness was absolute. Molly quickly conjured up a handful of her trademark witchfire, and the shimmering silver light showed us a narrow stone tunnel, the bare grey walls all but buried under accumulated layers of colour-coded wiring, cables, and copper and brass tubing. Thick mats of webbing crawled across the surface of both walls. I grimaced despite myself, even though I was careful not to touch or disturb any of it. Molly's witchlight showed the tunnel stretching away before us, but if there was a ceiling the light couldn't reach high enough to find it. A thick streamer of webbing blew away from one wall, carried on the gusting breeze, and I flinched away from it.

'You big baby,' said Molly, grinning broadly.

'Isn't that a slug by your foot?' I said, and grinned as Molly made a loud eeking noise.

I led the way down the tunnel. Pride would allow no less. The floor was thick with undisturbed dust. Even the smallest sounds we made seemed to echo on for ever; the only sounds in that endless eerie silence. The tunnel steadily widened, until it seemed the size of a room, and then a hall, and then abruptly it widened out still further until I could no longer tell how big a space we were moving in. I stuck close to the right-hand wall, its familiar man-made cables and piping a comfort to me. Until they became so thickly buried under webbing I could no longer see them clearly.

Molly boosted her witchlight as much as possible, but the light didn't travel far. Beyond a certain point, the darkness just seemed to soak it up. There was a feeling of space . . . stretching away, endlessly. We walked and walked, and the journey was as bad as I remembered. Perhaps more so; I kept coming across suddenly familiar details that I hadn't let myself remember. Like the hollow husks of really big insects and beetles, scattered across the floor, their insides chewed out. And the thick strands of webbing that hung down from somewhere high above us, twitching and twisting even though the breeze was no longer blowing. I was amazed I'd found the courage to come this way, back when I was a kid. But thinking of the Serjeant-At-Arms' punishments had made it easy. I was far more scared of him than I ever was of giant spiders. Even though I was pretty sure he wouldn't have actually killed me.

There were noises, out in the dark. Scuttling, scurrying noises. Molly and I stopped short, and looked around us. Molly held her handful of light up high, but it didn't help. Soft, wet sounds came from behind and up ahead, along with slow scraping sounds, like claws on stone.

'Okay,' said Molly. 'This is seriously creeping me out.'

'Are you sure you can't make any more light?' I said. 'I don't think they like the light.'

'I'm giving it all I've got,' snapped Molly, sounding a bit strained. 'Something in this pocket dimension of yours doesn't like light. It's all I can do to maintain what I've got. How much further to the Library?'

'Still some way yet,' I said. 'If I'm remembering correctly. Follow me, hurry as much as you can, but don't run. They chase anything that runs. I found that out the hard way.'

We moved on, striding quickly through the dark. The webbing hanging down from above was getting thicker, heavier, like hanging curtains of dirty gauze. I ducked around them, careful not to let any of them touch me. They were stirring restlessly now, twitching as though disturbed from a long sleep. And always there were the noises, out in the dark, slowly but steadily closing in on us. Molly and I moved as quickly as we could without actually running. We were both breathing hard.

We almost ran straight into the massive web that blocked our way, its silver-grey threads only showing up in the witchlight at the very last moment. It hung unsupported on the air before us, huge and intricate, radiating away beyond the limits of the witchlight. It would take a spider the size of a bus to spin a web that size. Or an awful lot of smaller spiders, working together. I wasn't sure which thought was the most disturbing. It very definitely hadn't been here the last time I came this way.

'That is a big web,' said Molly. 'Still, I've got some shears and you've got a bloody big stick. Do we smash our way through?'

'Can't help feeling that's a bad idea,' I said. 'But we don't have any choice. We have to go on.'

'Look,' said Molly. 'If you're really that worried, armour up.'

'I can't,' I said. 'The rules of reality work differently here. The armour won't come. I found that out the hard way, too.'

'Now he tells me,' said Molly. 'Okay, it's time to squeeze one out or get off the pot. We can't go back, so . . . burn, baby, burn!'

She thrust her handful of witchfire into the nearest clump of threads, and they caught alight immediately, burning with a fierce blue light. The fires shot up and along the trembling threads, spreading quickly across the huge cobweb. And in this new, revealing light, Molly and I could at last see what it was that had been following us all this time. We were surrounded by an army of spiders, thousands of them, stretching away for as far as the light carried, and probably beyond. And they were really big spiders. Black furry bodies the size of my head, many-jointed legs a yard or more long, clusters of eyes that glowed like precious jewels. And heavy mouth parts that clacked viciously together, drooling a thick saliva.

'Run,' I said.

Molly and I burst through the burning remains of the web, slapping aside the entangling threads. The spiders came after us like a great black wave, silent except for the pattering of their many legs on the dusty stone floor. This close, I could smell them: a sour, bitter smell, like acid and spoiled meat. Something else I'd made myself forget, down the years. Molly and I sprinted through the dark, pushing ourselves as hard as we could. Horrid pain slammed through the whole of my left side with every step, forcing tortured sounds past my clenched teeth. So much tension and exercise must be spreading the strange matter further through my system. I managed a small smile, at the thought of the spiders behind me.

Hope I poison you, you bastards . . .

I could feel myself slowing. Molly was leaving me behind as she kept up a pace I could no longer match. I could have called to her, but I didn't. One of us had to get out. She looked back anyway, realised she was getting too far ahead, and dropped back to grab me by the arm and urge me on. Thank God she grabbed my good arm. A spider came sailing through the air towards me on the end of a long streamer of webbing, like a big, black hairy balloon. I lashed out with Oath Breaker, and the heavy ironwood stick struck the giant spider right among its eyes. The body exploded in a wet splatter of flying innards. More spiders came sailing out of the darkness. I struck about me with Oath Breaker, killing everything I hit. Molly threw handfuls of witchfire this way and that, and burning spider bodies fell out of the air.

We ran on, not as swiftly as before, our feet squelching heavily through pulped spider remains on the floor, sometimes still shuddering and twitching. The spiders were swarming close behind us now, almost on our heels. I thought longingly about the Colt Repeater in its shoulder holster; but in the time it would take me to stop and wrestle the gun out of the holster, the spiders would be over me. So I kept going, fighting for breath, crying out at the pain within me, lashing increasingly wildly about me with Oath Breaker, which seemed to grow heavier with every blow.

The exit from the crawlspace wasn't far, I was sure. I was almost sure.

We slowed still more, exhausted by the long day, and the spiders caught us up and swarmed over us, clawing and biting. Molly and I stumbled on, crying out in pain and shock and disgust. I pulped their soft squishy bodies with my bare hands, thrusting Oath Breaker through my belt. Molly brushed the spiders away with her handful of witchfire, and the burning bodies fell away from her to skitter madly back and forth on the floor, blazing brightly in the dark. But there were always more, climbing over us, dropping out of the air. Both Molly and I were yelling out loud as we beat the things away. More scurried around our moving feet, darting up our legs or trying to trip us, but they were too light and flimsy, for all their size. We crushed them underfoot and stumbled on.

Until finally I saw, in the flickering witchlight, a familiar sight up ahead. The exit panel for the crawlspace, leading back into The Hall.

Into light and warmth and sanity. I could see it, light from outside shining brightly past its edges, clear as day in the endless crawlspace dark.

I pointed it out to Molly, and we found a few last vestiges of strength to hurry us on. The panel slid jerkily open as we approached, activated by our presence, and then stuck halfway. Just long enough to scare me with the thought that the ancient mechanism had broken down, and then it started moving again, spilling painfully bright light into the darkness.

I pushed Molly through the narrow gap and forced myself through behind her. I spun round and twisted the carved wooden rose on the wall, and the panel closed itself with a series of heavy, slow jerks. One last giant spider forced its way through after us, rearing up, only to collapse and die on the floor, its long multi-jointed legs scrabbling weakly. The oversized thing couldn't exist in our reality. The spiders that still clung to Molly and me slowly fell away, also dying. They scuttled weakly across the waxed and polished floor, trying to get back to the safety of the dark, but we stamped on them, pulling them under our feet. They would have died anyway, but we needed to kill them.

Even dead, some of the spiders clung to Molly and me, their clawed and barbed legs embedded in our torn and bloody clothing and in our flesh. We took it in turns to pull the nasty things off us, flinching at every touch, until it was over. We were both dead tired, breathing so harshly it hurt, our hearts pounding in our chests, bloodied and aching from a hundred cuts and bites. We stumbled away from the dead spiders, and held each other tightly, shuddering and shaking and making quiet shocked noises. We clung to each other like children newly wakened from a bad dream, and it would have been hard to say who was comforting whom. Finally we let go, and stood back. Too embarrassed to look at each other, for a while; partly because neither of us was used to being weak, but mostly because of the unexpected depth of our emotions.

'All right,' said Molly, her voice nearly back to normal. 'I admit it: those were really big spiders.'

'Persistent little bastards, weren't they?' I said, trying for a light touch, and only just missing it.

'You're hurt,' said Molly.

'So are you.'

Somehow she found the strength for a quick healing spell, enough to heal our bites and close over the scratches. I can't say it made me feel any better, but I acted as though it did. She didn't need to know about the spreading pains in my left side. Three days, maybe four? I didn't think so.

'I know where we are,' I said. 'The Library's only a few minutes away.'

'Then let's go,' said Molly. 'But this Library of yours had better be worth the trip, Drood.'

I had to smile.

We trotted down the corridor, glad to be back in our own comfortable world again. The light was clear and warm, and The Hall was full of human sights and scents. For the first time in a long time, I was glad to be home. It felt as though I'd spent years in the crawlspace dark. How did I ever stand it, as a child? Maybe it was because I could run faster, back then.

Molly and I rounded a corner, and half a dozen members of my family came strolling down the corridor towards us, chattering animatedly about the false dragon's attack. All kinds of names came up as possible suspects, but none of them so much as mentioned me. I didn't know whether to feel relieved or insulted. They glanced briefly in our direction and then, just as the Armourer said, they looked away again the moment they took in our lab coats. To be on the safe side, I'd already buried my face in my hands, as though I'd been injured. Molly caught on immediately, and half supported me as we passed the other Droods.

'It's your own fault!' she said loudly. 'I've no sympathy for you. How can anyone mistake gunpowder for snuff?'

'My nose,' I moaned. 'Did anyone find my nose?'

The other Droods laughed briefly, and kept going. Another lab mishap, nothing to see, keep moving. Molly and I kept up the act until we were safely round the next corner, and there was the Library, right before us. No one else was around. I tried the doors, but they were locked, as expected. Still no one standing guard, though. Everyone must have run outside, to get a look at the dragon. Very sloppy security, entirely unprofessional and bad discipline. What was the family coming to? No doubt the Serjeant-At-Arms would have a thing or two to say, when he finally woke up. I used the key the Armourer had given me, and the doors swung open at a touch. I ushered Molly in, and quickly closed and locked the doors behind us. I didn't want to be disturbed. I didn't know how long this was going to take.

The Library appeared to be completely deserted. I called out a few times, and no one emerged from the towering stacks to hush me. Molly stared about her, gaping openly. I nodded, understanding. The sheer size of the place always hit new visitors hard.

'Welcome to the Drood family Library,' I said grandly. 'No shouting, no running between the stacks, no peeing in the shallow end. And no, it isn't as big as it looks; it's bigger. Takes up the whole lower floor of this wing. The whole world is in here, somewhere. If you can find it.'

'It's ... huge,' Molly said finally. 'How *do* you find anything in here?'

'Mostly we don't,' I had to admit. 'William was the last librarian to try and put together an official index, and most of his papers disappeared with him. We're always adding books, losing books and mis-filing them. At least the sections are clearly marked.'

'You look for family history,' said Molly, pulling herself together and putting on her most efficient manner. 'I'm going to work my way through the medical section. There must be something here I can use to help you. Even if it's only to slow down the progress of the strange matter till we can get you to someone who can help you.'

'Molly ...'

'No, Eddie. I don't want to hear it. I'm not giving up, and neither should you. I won't let you die. Not when you risked your life to save me. I can't ... There has to be someone out there who can put you right! Hell, if all else fails, I know people who can bring you back from the dead as a zombie!'

'Thanks for the thought,' I said. 'Medical section is down there; twenty stacks along, third right, then follow the ...'

'Oh Hell,' said Molly. 'I never was any good at directions. I'd better use a locator spell, or we'll be here all night.' She pulled a pendulum on a silver wire out of a hidden pocket, and set it spinning. The pendulum slammed to a halt pointing right at me. Molly frowned. 'That's . . . interesting. It's reading a power source on you, and it's not Oath Breaker. In fact, I'm picking up quite a lot of undischarged magic still attached to the key the Armourer gave you.'

She put the pendulum away as I pulled out the key and looked at it. The Armourer had made a point of giving me the key, even though he had to know I could just armour up and kick the doors in. Was the key a clue of some kind? To some secret he couldn't quite bring himself to say in person? I studied the key with my Sight, and there was a second spell written on it, so clearly even I could tell what it was. A spell to work a hidden lock, to open a hidden door. Here; in the Library? There'd never been even a whisper about a secret door in the Library . . .

I turned the key back and forth, and the spell flared up briefly when it pointed in one particular direction. I followed the key through the stacks, Molly trotting along at my side, until finally we came to the picture on the south-west wall.

It was the only painting in the Library. A huge piece, a good eight feet tall and five wide, contained in a silver frame. It was centuries old, older than The Hall itself, some said; artist unknown. The painting depicted another library, whose many shelves were packed with massive leather-bound volumes and parchment scrolls tied with colourful ribbons. There were no people in the painting, no symbolic objects, no obvious arrangement of important items. No meaning, no message. Molly and I stood before the painting, considering it.

'I'm no expert,' said Molly, 'But that is a seriously boring painting. Is it significant to the family?'

'Sort of,' I said. 'This picture shows the Old Library the original repository of Drood knowledge. In this first Library was held all the early history of the Droods, perhaps even knowledge of our true beginnings, long lost to us. You see, the Old Library was destroyed, in a fire set by our enemies. One of our greatest tragedies. The whole house burned down with the Library, which is why the family moved here, in the time of King Henry the Fifth. This picture is all that remains from that time, to remind us of what we lost.'

'There's something weird about this painting,' Molly said slowly. 'I can feel magic in it. In the frame and the canvas, in the paint and the very brush strokes. Can you feel it?'

I studied the painting closely with my Sight, holding the key tightly in my hand, and the whole portrait seemed to blaze with an inner light. And finally I noticed something I'd never seen before. There was a small, carefully disguised keyhole in the silver frame, hidden away in some ornate scrollwork. I pointed it out to Molly, and then slowly eased the Armourer's key into the hole. It fit perfectly. I turned the key, and just like that the whole picture came alive. I wasn't looking at a painting any more, but a scene from life, an opening into another place. A doorway into the Old Library. I took Molly by the hand, and together we stepped through.

The Old Library wasn't lost, wasn't gone; just hidden in plain sight. Hanging in front of our eyes for all these years. The Old Library; real and intact, its ancient history and knowledge preserved after all. (*Preserved for who? No. Think about that later.*) I stood very still, just inside the doorway, looking about me. The Old Library stretched away in every direction, endless towering stacks and shelves packed with books and manuscripts and scrolls, for as far as the eye could see, in every direction. I looked behind me, and beyond the open space of the doorway I could see more stacks, more shelves.

I walked slowly forward down the aisle before me, almost numb with shock. The greatest tragedy in my family's history was a lie. I shouldn't have been surprised, after everything else I'd learned, but to deliberately conceal so much knowledge, so much wisdom . . . was a sin almost beyond understanding. I took down some of the over-sized books, handling them very carefully, and opened them. The leather bindings creaked noisily, and the pages seemed to exhale dust and ancient smells. They were handwritten, illuminated manuscripts, the kind monks laboured over for years. Latin mostly, some ancient Greek. Other tongues, equally old or obscure. There were palimpsests and parchments, and piles of scrolls, some so delicate looking I didn't want even to breathe too heavily near them.

'There's some kind of magic suppressor field operating in here,' Molly said suddenly. 'I can feel it.'

'I'm not surprised,' I said absently, absorbed in a scroll concerning King Harold and the Soul of Albion. 'Must be a security measure, to protect the contents.'

'I could probably force through a few small magics, if necessary,' said Molly. 'If we have to defend ourselves.'

'Will you relax?' I said. 'We're the only ones in here.'

I rolled the scroll up again, retied the ribbon and carefully put it back in its place. The answer to my earlier thought was clear. The only people who could have hidden the Old Library like this ... were the inner circle of the Droods. The Matriarch, her Council, and her favourites. Our history and true beginnings weren't lost, weren't destroyed; they were deliberately hidden away from the rest of us, for the benefit of the chosen few. But what could be here, so important, so dangerous, that it had to be hidden away? That they couldn't, or wouldn't, share with the rest of us? I moved on through the stacks, opening books and scrolls at random, almost drunk on the prospect of so many answers to so many questions, and all mine for the taking. (*Maybe that's why they kept it for themselves ... so they could feel like this.*) As I moved deeper into the stacks, I discovered histories written in languages no one had used for centuries; works put down on parchment and tanned hide by the Saxons, the Celts, the Angles and the Danes and the Norse. And other tongues, so old nobody had spoken them aloud in centuries.

'All this was here,' I said finally. 'And I never knew it. My family's true heritage, stolen away from us by those we were always taught to trust and revere. This should have been made freely available to us. We have a right to know where we came from! Who our ancestors were, what they did and why they did it. It makes me wonder what other secrets the inner circle have been hiding from the rest of us; from the rank and file, and all the good little soldiers who went out to fight and die for the honour of the family ... We've reached the end of the trail, Molly. The answer is here; I know it.'

'The answer?' Molly said carefully. 'Which particular answer is that, Eddie?'

'To how it started! Where we came from. Where the armour came from. How we became Droods.' I looked at Molly. 'I did wonder, sometimes, if maybe my ancestors made some kind of deal with the Devil.'

'No,' Molly said immediately. 'If that was the case, I would have known.'

I decided I wouldn't ask. This was no time to get distracted. I looked around, using my Sight. A complex latticework of protective spells lay over everything, some of them quite impressively strong. And nasty. Some books and scrolls shone brightly on their shelves, radiating strange energies. And one blazed like a beacon, full of ancient power. It turned out to be a simple scroll, inked on roughly tanned animal hide. The outer markings were in a language I didn't even recognise. Molly crowded in close beside me.

'Any idea what that is?'

'The answer,' I said.

'Well, yes, but apart from that. . .'

'Only one way to find out,' I said, and touched the wax seals holding the scroll closed with Oath Breaker. The activating Words popped into my mind, from the old ironwood staff itself, and as I said them, one by one, the protections around the scroll shattered and disappeared. I unrolled it, very carefully, and the dark ink on the interior stood out clearly against the coffee-coloured hide. The text was Druidic, from Roman times. Which was unusual in itself, because Druidic learning was strictly an oral tradition, passed down mouth to mouth from generation to generation. Never written down, in case it might fall into the hands of enemies. But they'd made an example for this; and I could see why.

'It's Latin,' said Molly, peering curiously over my shoulder. 'Strange dialect. Something about a bargain.'

'You read Latin?' I said, unable to keep the surprise out of my voice.

She glared at me. 'I may not have had the benefits of your private education, but I know a thing or two. You can't work any of the major magics without at least a working knowledge of Latin. Most of the old pacts and bindings are written in it. What we're looking at here is a spell. A spell to reveal hidden truths ... about the beginnings of the Drood family! You were right, Eddie: it is the answer. So, do we use the spell? Right here and now?'

'Of course,' I said. 'We might not get another chance.'

'Is this something you need to do alone?' said Molly. 'I mean, I'd understand if you . . .'

'No,' I said immediately. 'We've come this far together; it's only right we go the last mile together too.'

So we both spoke the spell in unison, chanting the ancient Latin aloud, and the world we knew blew away on a wave of wild magic, as the spell gave us a vision of time past.

We were not there. We saw and heard everything, but we were not present. This was the past and we had no place in it, except as observers.

Before us lay old Britain. The Romans called it the Tin Islands, because that was all we had that interested them. The land of the Britons: a savage place, when we all lived in the forests, in the wild woods, in the dark places the Romans dared not follow us. The vision shifted and changed, showing us sights charged with meaning and significance. We watched, and learned.

In this time, Drood history began. Fierce men in ragged furs, with blue woad daubed on their snarling faces, ran howling through the trees. My ancestors, the Druids. So fierce, so savage, they shocked even the hardened Roman Legionnaires. They fought; tribes against armies, bronze against steel. And yet at first the Druids won, forcing the invading Romans back to their waiting ships, and then slaughtering them in the shallows until it seemed the whole ocean ran red with their blood. The survivors sailed away; but they came back. The Romans came again, and again, until finally they triumphed; through steel and tactics and weight of numbers. Because they were an army, and we were just scattered tribes who often hated each other as much as the invaders.

The Romans feared the Druid priests most of all, and wiped them out, destroying their spoken knowledge and traditions, along with their savage religion. And so it might have gone ... until the Heart came, and everything changed.

It did not fall from the sky, as the official story says. It did not fall like an angel from heaven, or a meteor from outer space. It downloaded itself from another dimension; a different kind of reality. Imposing itself upon our world through an act of sheer will. The impact of its arrival killed every living thing in the vicinity, and flattened the trees for miles around. The ground shook for days, and strange bright lights and energies burned in the skies. But the Druids, though sensibly cautious, were scared of nothing, and sent emissaries to the Heart.

Those Druids would become the very first Droods.

They walked among fallen trees for mile after mile, and though they saw wonders and horrors, and living things twisted and mutated by the terrible energies released through the Heart's arrival, they did not stop or turn aside. They were shamans, whose job it was to defend and protect the tribe from outside threats. And finally they came to the great clearing of dead and blasted earth in which the Heart lay: a diamond as big as a hill, brilliant and beautiful; and alive. It spoke to the Druid shamans who came to it, and they worshipped it as a sign from the gods, or perhaps even one of the gods themselves.

The Heart was quite content for them to do this. It was lost and far from home, and weakened by its long journey. It had come to our world fleeing something else. Something the Heart was still very much afraid of. So it proposed a bargain to the Druid shamans. It would make them powerful, make them as gods among their own kind, and in return they would revere and protect the Heart against all enemies. In this world . . . and without.

The Heart gave the Druids their living armour, and they became more than men.

Originally, the shamans only used the armour to protect the tribes against the dark powers and forces of evil, who walked more openly in the world in those days. But the armour made these Droods very powerful, and all power tends to corrupt . . . The greatest threat to the tribes were the invading Romans, but the shamans were wise enough to know that not even the golden armour could hold off the Roman armies for ever. So they went to the Romans, and made a deal. Rome would rule . . . through the Droods. And thus the tribes would be protected from the worst of Rome's power. When, five centuries later, the Roman Empire finally declined and fell, and Roman authority left Britain, the Droods just kept going. Operating secretly, to protect the tribes from threats, from without . . . and within.

But what was the armour, this glorious golden living metal? Where did it come from? And what price did the Heart demand, to make those first few Droods so much more than human?

A Drood stood before the Heart, presenting a pair of twin babies to the massive diamond. One of the babies was snatched out of the Drood's arms by an unseen force, and it hung on the air before the Heart, kicking and screaming. And then it was suddenly sucked into the Heart's shining surface, and disappeared inside. Its screams cut off abruptly. And around the neck of the baby still held by the Drood, a shining golden   collar appeared. The vision showed other sacrifices, other sights, down many years, until the secret of the family's armour was plain.

All the Druids exposed to the energies of the Heart underwent predetermined genetic changes, and from that point on all Drood children were born as identical twins. Soon after birth, one child was given to the Heart, which absorbed its body and its soul so the surviving twin might wear the golden armour, and serve the family. When I wore the living metal, I was surrounding myself with all that was left of my sacrificed twin. The brother I never knew. Every time I armoured up, I was wearing my brother like a second skin.

How many memories wiped, to hide the truth? How many twins, had been sacrificed to the Heart down the long centuries? How many innocent children denied their chance at life, so the Droods could be more than human?

The vision showed us more. It got worse.

As more and more babies were given to the Heart, the other-dimensional being grew brighter, stronger. The souls of the sacrificed children were held and sealed within the Heart, trapped there to generate the power that created our armour, that powered our magics and our sciences, that made our family strong.

I felt sick. Soiled. I had been brought up to revere and protect the Heart in its Sanctity, without ever knowing what it really was. An eater of souls. Like those disgusting entities the Loathly Ones, but on a far greater scale. All those babies ... all those generations of trapped souls, denied an afterlife, condemned to never-ending existence within the Heart, to make it powerful. Did they know? Were they aware, in there? Did they suffer endlessly? Were they screaming behind the gleaming facets of that massive diamond?

The vision ended, and Molly and I fell back into our bodies. We looked at each other, shocked speechless. I'd never felt so angry in my life. I rolled the scroll up, very carefully, retied the ribbons and set it back on its shelf. I couldn't risk it being damaged. It was evidence, of a crime. My anger burned cold within me, and I had never felt so focused, so determined. Molly reached out to me, and then stopped at the last moment. As though I might have burned her fingers. I don't think she liked what she saw in my face, in my eyes.

'Eddie ...'

'It's all right,' I said, though something in my voice made her flinch. 'I've always known my family was rotten to the heart.'

I didn't hear anything, didn't see anything, but suddenly I knew that he was there, standing behind me. And since I'm not easy to sneak up on, I knew who it was, who it had to be. I turned slowly, and there he was, with a gun pointed at me. Molly turned too, and then instinctively moved a little closer to me. The Matriarch had sent the greatest field agent of all to deal with me.

'Hello, Uncle James,' I said.

He nodded, not smiling, tall and dark and handsome as ever, splendidly elegant in a formal tuxedo, the gun seeming almost out of place in his hand, as it covered Molly and me. He might have just come from a cocktail party, or an ambassador's ball. Some important occasion, where the high and the mighty gathered to discuss the matters that mattered. Uncle James was always at home in the very best circles, when he wasn't chasing the scum of the earth through back-street bars or hidden lairs, the Amazonian rain forests or the darkest canyons of the urban jungle.

'Hello, Eddie,' he said, and his voice didn't sound at all strained. 'You never would obey, even as a child. I told you not to come back here. Told you I'd have to kill you if we ever met again. And yet here you are, and here I am. So . . . Aren't you at least going to introduce me to your young lady?'

'Heavens,' I said. 'What was I thinking? Uncle James, this is Molly Metcalf, the witch of the wild woods. Molly, this is my Uncle James. Better known in disreputable circles as the Grey Fox.'

'Really?' said Molly. '*The* Grey Fox? Damn! Eddie, you never told me the legendary Grey Fox was your uncle! It's an honour to meet you, sir. Really. I've followed your career for years; from a distance, of course. You took on the Unholy Inspectres, the Bloody Beast of Bodmin Moor, and the Murder Mystics . . .'

'Not that last one,' Uncle James said graciously. 'My brother Jack took down the Murder Mystics. He never did get the renown he deserved.'

'You have a gun,' I said. 'You could have shot me in the back the moment you walked in here, before I even knew you'd found me. It would have been the sensible thing to do, before I could armour up.'

'Yes,' he said easily. 'I could have killed you, and your young lady, but I didn't. I needed to talk to you first, Eddie. I know you've opened the scroll, said the Words, seen the vision. When you broke the seals it set off a silent alarm, and we knew it had to be you. So I said I'd come down here and take care of things. How did you break the seal, Eddie?'

'I have Oath Breaker,' I said, and showed him the ironwood staff.

'So you do. You've been to see Jack, haven't you? He always was the soft-hearted one. I shall have to have words with him later. Put the staff down on the floor, Eddie. Very carefully.'

I crouched down, laid the stick on the floor, and then straightened up again, never once taking my eyes off Uncle James.

'Who sent you?' I said. 'The Council, or the Matriarch? How deep does the rot go?'

'The Council and the Matriarch,' said Uncle James. 'You've pissed off pretty much everybody, Eddie.'

'Do you know the secret of the scroll?' I said. 'The truth behind the armour, and the Heart?'

'Of course I know. It's the first thing they tell you, when you join the Council.'

I raised an eyebrow. 'I wasn't aware serving field agents were allowed to serve on the Council.'

'Exceptions are made for exceptional people,' said James. He wasn't boasting, just stating a fact.

'What did you do,' I said, 'when you found out about the children who've been sacrificed, so we could become what we are?'

'Oh, I was shocked,' said Uncle James. 'Horrified. But I got over it. Just as you will, in time. The original bargain was made in a simpler, more savage time, by savage people. But the family has become too important, too necessary to risk undoing the bargain. We don't only protect the tribe any more; we protect Humanity. We have a duty, a responsibility, to stand between them and the forces of darkness that they must never know about. And the secret is part of the burden we have to bear, so we can do the things that have to be done.'

'Like ruling the world, from behind the scenes?' said Molly. 'Like stamping down hard on anyone or anything that doesn't fit your narrow criteria of what's acceptable?'

'Getting upset won't change anything,' said Uncle James, still looking only at me. 'It won't bring back your twin brother, or mine. They died so we could wear the armour, so we could be a force for good in a world that needs us now more than ever. We can't tell everyone in the family, Eddie; you must know that. Most of them have no idea what it's like out in the world. They wouldn't understand how necessary some things can be. That's why only the Matriarch and the Council know: those of us who've proven our worth through long service to the family. And the world. We bear the burden of the truth, so others don't have to. So we can go on saving the world every day.'

'That's it?' I said. 'The end justifies the means? Come on, Uncle James, you can do better than that.'

'I insisted they send me down here,' Uncle James said urgently. 'Because I'm the only one who wouldn't shoot you on sight. I needed to talk to you, Eddie, make you understand. I don't want to have to kill you, not when you could still do so much for the family. You have so much potential ... and you remind me so much of your mother.'

'Don't go there,' I said, and I could hear how cold my voice was.

He didn't flinch. 'My sister was one of the best field agents of her generation,' said Uncle James. 'Only makes sense that her son would be special too. I raised you, Eddie. Taught you everything I knew. I always saw you as the son I never had.'

'You raised me to know right from wrong,' I said. 'To fight evil wherever I found it. That's what I'm doing, Uncle James.'

'We keep the world safe,' Uncle James said, almost pleadingly. 'We protect Humanity from the forces that would destroy them if we weren't there.'

'You are one of the forces that would destroy us,' said Molly.

Uncle James still ignored her, concentrating only on me. 'Someone has to be in charge, Eddie. You can't trust politicians to do what's right, not when it's always so much easier to do what's expedient. Do you have any idea how many wars we've prevented, down the centuries, by working behind the scenes? How many world wars that never happened thanks to us? There have been times when the family was all that stood between Humanity and utter extinction.

Our record may not be perfect, but the world would have been a far worse place without us.'

'You don't know that,' said Molly. 'Not for sure. Who can say what kind of a world we might have made for ourselves, if we'd been forced to make our own mistakes and learn from them?'

'We've been a force for good,' said Uncle James, holding my gaze with his.

'Yes,' I said. 'On the whole, I believe we have. But the price is too high. You can't be just a little bit corrupt, Uncle James. Maybe that's why we went from serving and protecting the world to running it.'

'Please,' he said. 'Surrender. Don't make me kill you, Eddie. We can still work this out. It's not too late. I'll speak for you, before the Council. Your grandmother isn't a monster, Eddie. If she can find a way to save you, she will. You know she will.'

'I can't let this go on,' I said. 'Not now that I know. I'm here to set the world free, Uncle James. To tear off their shackles, and let them run. We were meant to be the world's shepherds, not their jailors. We've become the very thing we were raised to fight. The family must fall, for what it's done to the world, and itself; and to me. No more lies, Uncle James. No more dead babies. No more Droods walking around unknowing in the living skins of their murdered twins. This should be between you and me, Uncle James. Will you let Molly go? If she agreed to just walk away?'

'I'm sorry,' he said, and he sounded as though he meant it. 'You know I can't let her leave, Eddie. Not now she knows the secret. If she stands with you, she dies with you. But if you were to come back into the family, perhaps something could be arranged As your wife, she'd be family too.'

'Wait a minute!' said Molly.

'Be quiet, child,' said Uncle James. 'I'm trying to save your life. The two of you could never leave The Hall again, Eddie, but you could still live long, useful, productive lives here.'

'Serving the family,' I said.

'Yes.'

'Work for the Droods?' said Molly. 'Screw that shit. I'd rather die. No offence, Eddie.'

'I have to do what's right,' I said. 'I have to fight evil wherever I find it. Just like you taught me, Uncle James.'

'Eddie . . .' he said, taking a step forward.

'I'm sorry.'

'So am I.' Uncle James sighed heavily, but his voice was calm and his eyes were so cold as to seem almost disinterested. 'Don't bother armouring up, Eddie. This gun came from the Armourer, long ago. He made me some special armour-piercing bullets, out of strange matter. They'll punch through your armour, like the arrow on the motorway.'

'You knew about the ambush!' I said, almost surprised to find I could still feel shocked after so many secrets. 'That's how you were able to teleport to me so easily. Did you know the arrow would leave some of itself in my body, poisoning me, killing me by inches?'

'No!' Uncle James said quickly. 'It was supposed to be a clean kill. They promised me it would be quick, or I would never have agreed. You weren't supposed to suffer . . . You were supposed to die valiantly on the motorway, facing the family's fiercest enemies. It seems I taught you better than I realised. I am proud of you, Eddie. And I promise it will be a clean kill, this time. For you and your young lady.'

'Like Hell,' said Molly.

All the time Uncle James had been talking so passionately, concentrating his attention on me, I'd been quietly aware of Molly subvocalising Words of Power, a trick she'd learned from me, struggling to raise enough power to force one good spell through the security measures suppressing magic in the Old Library. And now the spell activated, opening one small spatial portal right beside Uncle James's hand. It sucked the gun out of his grasp, and started to pull his arm in too before the security measures reasserted themselves and shut the portal down. It snapped out of existence, and Molly almost collapsed, exhausted by the strain. She grabbed at a heavy book stack to support herself, and grinned at me.

'There you go, Eddie! Even playing field. Now kick his self-righteous, hypocritical arse!'

Uncle James looked at his empty gun hand as though he couldn't quite believe it, and then he looked at me. I smiled, and suddenly so did he. That old familiar devil-take-the-hindmost grin.

'All right, Eddie. Let's do it. Show me how much you've learned.'

'You always were a big drama queen, Uncle James,' I said.

317

We armoured up, the living golden metal enclosing both of us in a moment. The terrible pain in my left side was immediately muted, and I didn't realise how bad it had got until it wasn't there any more. The golden armour made me strong and powerful again. My dead brother made me strong ... but I couldn't think about that now ... I had to concentrate everything I had on Uncle James, or he would kill me. He was, after all, the most proficient and deadly field agent the family had ever produced.

But he'd never had to face someone like me. A semi-rogue who'd learned his best tricks outside the family. Tempered in the fires of two appalling days, made stronger than ever before by what I'd had to do, to survive. And Uncle James didn't have my outrage, my anger, my righteous cause. No; he'd never met a Drood like me.

We circled each other slowly, warily, gleaming golden and glorious in the muted light of the Old Library. I didn't know what weapons he might have, under his armour, but the odds were he wouldn't dare use them, for fear of damaging the Old Library. A few sparks in the wrong place could cause a terrible fire ... And all I had left was the Colt Repeater, its everyday bullets useless against his armour. So it came down to him and me, one to one, man to man.

I grew heavy spikes on the knuckles of my golden hands. Uncle James grew long slender blades out of his. The edges looked very sharp. I'd never known a Drood who could do that with his armour before, but the Grey Fox always was the best of us. Champion of a thousand undisputed victories against the forces of evil. He knew tricks no one else did, learned the hard way in thirty years of fighting in dirty secret wars. Deep down ... I knew I couldn't beat him. But I had to try. If only to buy Molly a chance to escape, and take the truth with her. Uncle James stood between us and the only exit, the painting's frame that led into the main Library. So I had to drive him back, drive him away, fight him to a standstill; die on my feet if that was what it took to buy Molly her chance.

My one advantage over the Grey Fox. I was already dying. So I had nothing to lose.

I surged forward, driven by all the supernatural strength and speed my armour could produce; and still Uncle James was ready for me. He side-stepped gracefully and his right-hand sword came sweeping round, the supernaturally sharp edge slicing through the armour over my right side. My armour healed itself immediately, closing the cut, but I wasn't so lucky. Pain flared across my ribs, and I could feel thick blood coursing down my side, under my armour. I'd never felt that before. I charged Uncle James again and again, knowing my only hope was to get in close and grapple with him; and every time he avoided me like a toreador with a bull, his impossibly sharp blades cutting through my golden armour again and again, cutting me, hurting me, slowing me down through accumulated shock and blood loss. The Grey Fox circled me, staying carefully out of my reach, watching for the first sign of weakness, so he could move in for the kill.

So I gave him a sign. I pretended to stumble, almost going down on one knee, and he came gliding in, smooth as any dancer. Only to find me waiting for him. I lunged forward, forcing him backwards, off balance. He quickly got his feet back under him again and straightened up, but by that time I had both my hands round his throat, my golden fingers pressing down on his golden throat. I concentrated, and grew sharp barbs on the insides of my fingers, digging them deep into the living metal round his neck. And Uncle James couldn't grab my wrists to force my hands away, without giving up his swords.

He drew back his right arm and slammed his sword forward, with all his armour's strength behind it. The golden blade punched through the armour over my left side, through me and out of my back. The pain was horrific. I cried out, and there was blood in my mouth. It coursed down my chin, under my golden mask. I almost passed out. I probably would have, if I hadn't been so angry.

I clung on to his throat with both hands, searching desperately for some last trick I could use against him; and that was when I remembered how I'd once fused both my hands together, to contain and seal off Archie Leech's Kandarian amulet. If I could fuse my armour together, why not mine and Uncle James's? Just for a moment. Just long enough to do what I had to do. I concentrated, focusing all my will power, sweat running down my face under my mask, and the living metal around his throat yielded to my greater will; my greater fury. His armour fused with mine, and suddenly my bare hands were around his bare throat, and I bore down hard.

He struggled fiercely, not understanding what was happening, throwing me this way and that by sheer brute strength, but I wouldn't let go. He pulled his right hand back, jerking the sword blade out of me, and I cried out again as I felt things break and tear within me, but still I wouldn't let go. Not even when he ran me through again, and again, sinking the blade deep in my guts and twisting it back and forth.

He was weakening fast, but so was I, and God alone knows what might have happened if not for Molly.

We'd been so caught up in ourselves, fighting face to golden face, that we'd both lost track of Molly Metcalf. She came up behind Uncle James, in his blind spot, and she had Torc Cutter in her hands. She jammed the ugly shears up against the back of his neck, yelled the activating Words, and cut through his armour, right where his collar should be. Uncle James screamed once, like a soul newly damned to Hell, and then his armour disappeared all in a moment, and his whole body went limp in my hands. It took me a moment to realise what had happened, and a moment more to armour down and unclench my hands from around his throat, but finally I let go. His body fell to the floor and did not move again. I sat down suddenly beside him, my legs giving way. I hurt so badly I could hardly breathe. There was blood all over me. My Uncle James was dead. I wanted to hold him in my arms, tell him I was sorry, but my arms wouldn't work. I would have cried, but somehow ... I was too tired. Too deathly tired.

Molly crouched down beside me, and put her arm across my shoulders. 'I had to do it,' she said. 'He could still have won. And he would have killed you, Eddie.'

'Of course he would,' I said. 'He was the Grey Fox. He was the best. He knew the mission always comes first.'

'I killed him,' said Molly. 'So you wouldn't have to.'

'I know,' I said. 'That was kind of you. But ... he was my dad, in every way that mattered. The one Drood I always loved and admired. The man I most wanted to be.'

I cried then, and Molly did her best to comfort me. After a while, she retrieved Oath Breaker from where I'd left it, and hauled me back up on to my feet so she could half lead, half carry me out of the Old Library, back through the painting into the main Library again. Blood poured down my sides with every movement, my face was slick with sweat, and my hands hung numbly at my side. Away from the Old Library's magic suppressor field, she was able to run a whole bunch of healing spells over me, but though she closed my wounds and stopped the bleeding, I couldn't say I felt any better.

'It's the strange matter in you,' she said finally, frowning. 'It's interfering with my magics. I've stabilised you, but that's about all I can do for you.'

'That's all right,' I said, smiling at her. It didn't feel like much of a smile, but I did my best. 'It doesn't matter, Molly. I'm dying anyway. And none of that three or four days shit, either. Just ... hold me together long enough for me to do what I need to do.'

'What *can* we do?' Molly said desperately. 'Against something like the Heart?'

'You have Torc Cutter, and I have Oath Breaker,' I said. 'I'm going to destroy the Heart, and bring the whole damned family down.'

'Because they betrayed you,' said Molly.

'Because they lied,' I said. 'They lied to all of us. About who we are, and what we are. We were never the heroes of our story. All along, we were the real Bad Guys.'

CHAPTER TWENTY-ONE
A family at war

There was only one way to fatally weaken the family. To break their hold on the world. Take away the power that made them strong, made them untouchable; their glorious golden armour. And the only way to do that was to destroy the source of the armour; the Heart. Only a few days ago I would have found that unthinkable; hell, I'd risked my life to defend the damned thing from outside attack. But step by painful step I had been driven to this place, this moment, forced to turn away from everything I'd been taught and brought up to believe in. All that was left to me now was to destroy the one thing I was raised to revere and protect above everything else. The rotten, corrupt, lying Heart of the Droods.

Life's a bitch, sometimes.

I hefted Oath Breaker in my hand. Only a stick, really, a long wooden cane carved with symbols I couldn't read. It didn't look like much, to destroy an invader from another dimension and bring an end to centuries of lies. But as with so many other things where my family was concerned, appearances were deceiving. I only had to glance at Oath Breaker with my Sight to see a power so great, so terrible, I had to look away or it would blast the eyes from my head. Oath Breaker was ancient and awful, made when the world was young, specifically to undo things that could not be allowed to exist. There were stories that said Oath Breaker had thrown down cities and continents, in its time, and killed old gods so thoroughly that no one remembered their names any more.

It occurred to me that by destroying the source of the family's armour, I might be signing my own death warrant. And that of everyone else in my family. I'd seen Torc Cutter kill my Uncle James, by severing his collar. It could be that no Drood would survive if I took the armour away. But I'd come too far now to even consider turning back. The family that had bowed down to the Heart's murderous demands for so long, that had chosen to rule Humanity instead of protect it, that had embraced the ruthless aims of Zero Tolerance was not a family I recognised any more. I had to save the family's honour, or put it out of its misery for ever.

And what the Hell; I was dying anyway.

At least with the Heart destroyed, there was a chance that the sacrificed souls trapped inside the massive diamond would be freed at last, to pass on to the afterlife denied them for so long. Perhaps they would speak for me at the Gates of Heaven or Hell and ask that I not be judged too harshly for my crimes and sins. That I had done at least one good thing in my life.

'The only way to use Oath Breaker,' I said to Molly. 'Is up close and personal. That means we have to get into the Sanctity, the most closely guarded chamber in The Hall, and stand before the Heart itself.'

'Hold everything,' said Molly. 'Even assuming we can get there, which I'm not, but for the sake of argument: isn't there the smallest possibility that destroying an alien life form like the Heart could be extremely bloody dangerous? I mean, you use an unknown weapon like Oath Breaker on an unknown other-dimensional thing like the Heart, and God alone knows what kind of forces and energies might be released. You could blow up the whole house. Hell, you might even blow up the whole country.'

'Why think so small?' I said. 'We might blow up the whole world. But you know what, Molly? I don't care any more. This is something I have to do, and it's something I'm going to do. Whatever the cost. You don't have to come with me if you don't want to . . .'

'Oh, screw that,' Molly said briskly. 'I didn't come this far to miss out on seeing the Droods' power broken, once and for all. This is what I signed on for, Eddie, and don't you forget it. To have my revenge on the family who murdered my parents.'

'The family killed my parents too,' I said. 'Though they would never admit it. So I suppose this is my revenge too.'

'Besides,' said Molly. 'You'd probably mess it up on your own anyway. You need me, Eddie.'

I smiled at her. 'Thank you,' I said. 'For everything.'

'Wouldn't have missed it for the world,' she said, and smiled back at me.

'We've come a long way together,' I said. 'All those years we wasted, trying to kill each other . . .'

'Don't get sloppy and sentimental on me now, Eddie. We have things to do. Maybe later there will be time for . . . other things.'

'If there is a later.'

'Oh, look on the bright side; the odds are your family will kill us long before we get anywhere near the Heart.'

We laughed quietly together, and then I took her in my arms and held her close. I couldn't hold her tightly, it hurt my left side too much, but she understood. She held me like I was the most precious thing in her life, that might crack and break if handled too roughly, and buried her face in my shoulder. We stood like that for some time, and then we made ourselves let go. It was all the time we could allow ourselves. We kissed, quickly, and then we stepped back and took on our professional aspects again. The rogue Drood and the wild witch, determined to do or die and probably both.

'So,' said Molly, entirely business-like. 'Do you know of another short cut that can take us from here to the Sanctity? Preferably one that doesn't involve being chased by a bunch of hungry spiders with severe glandular problems?'

'Unfortunately, no,' I said. 'The Sanctity is sealed off from the rest of The Hall by powerful forces. Partly to protect the Heart from outside attack, and partly to protect the family from the Heart's various emissions and energies. You can only access the Sanctity by approaching it via the single officially authorised route. Anything else will trigger The Hall's internal security responses . . . and we really don't want to do that. If you thought the defences in the grounds were bad, they're nothing compared to what's inside The Hall. Death could be the kindest thing that would happen to us.'

'God, you're depressing to be around sometimes,' said Molly. 'Surely the official route will be heavily guarded by now?'

'Of course. And don't call me . . .'

'Don't you dare.'

'Sorry. Imminent death and danger always brings out my flippant side. No, we're going to have to fight our way through a whole army of armoured Droods, just to get to the Sanctity.'

Molly produced Torc Cutter from a hidden pocket in her dress, and scowled darkly at the ugly shears. 'They'll probably pack the corridors with cannon fodder. All the inexperienced, expendable Droods. It's what I'd do. How many more of your family are you prepared to see die, Eddie?'

'There's already been one death in the family too many. There has to be another way.'

Molly waited patiently while I thought fiercely, coming up with plan after plan, and turning them all down. The family had had centuries to concoct counters to every possible way of taking the corridors by storm. The corridors . . . I looked at Molly, and grinned suddenly.

'When I'm in the armour, I'm stronger, faster, more powerful. Stronger by far than the fragile world I move in. So why walk along the corridors, going this way and that to reach my destination, when there's a much quicker way? Why not walk in a straight line to the Sanctity, smashing my way through everything in my path?'

'Sounds like a plan to me,' said Molly, her eyes sparkling.

I slipped Oath Breaker through my back belt, and armoured up. My Sight showed me the straight line I needed, from where I was to where the Sanctity was. I turned to the wood-panelled wall on my left, and punched a great jagged hole through the heavy teak. I pulled my golden hand back, and a whole panel came away. I stuck both hands into the gap, and tore the wall apart with my the armour's strength. The dense wood ripped and tore as though it was paper. Molly jumped up and down, cheering and clapping her hands together delightedly. I forced my way through the wall and into the room beyond, and Molly hurried through after me.

The room was full of couches and settees and love-seats, in various periods and styles, all of them pleasantly comfortable and cosy. A perfect place to relax and indulge in quiet contemplation. I strode across the room, kicking the heavy furniture out of my way, headed for the next wall. Molly followed behind, murmuring *Typical man* . . . just loudly enough for me to hear. And then the door burst open, and a dozen armoured Droods charged into the room, splintering the doorframe as they all tried to squeeze through at once. It was obvious from their haste and clumsiness, as well as the haphazard way they grouped themselves before me, that none of them had any combat experience. Probably just house Droods, pressed into service. Thrown into my path to slow me down, until more experienced fighters could get to me. Poor bastards. More innocents, sacrificed for the family good. I studied them as they fanned nervously out into a semicircle before me, gleaming and golden, and then stood there facing me. Clearly none of them wanted to be the one to make the first move.

'Get out of my way,' I said, and it wasn't difficult to sound cold and nasty and dangerous.

Give them credit, none of them backed off. One Drood actually managed a step forward. From his voice he was young, but even though he had to be sacred shitless his tone was firm and steady.

'We can't let you pass. You're rogue. We fight for the honour of the family.'

'So do I,' I said. 'If you only knew. Stand aside. You know you can't stop me. I'm field trained.'

The young Drood didn't move. 'Anything, for the family.'

I nodded slowly, understanding, acknowledging them. 'Of course. Whatever happens, I'm proud of all of you.'

I charged forward and slammed the young Drood out of my way with a single backhand that lifted him up off his feet and sent him flying across the room. The other Droods hesitated, frozen where they were by uncertainty and shock, and then I was in and among them. Even house Droods have to go through basic training when they're kids, but most never raise a hand in anger in their lives, in armour or out of it. They never stood a chance. I knocked them down and kicked them away, picked them up and threw them this way and that. They couldn't be hurt inside their armour, but it knocked the pepper out of them. A few tried to make a fight out of it, coming at me with wildly swinging fists. I picked them up and threw them at walls, and they crashed right through the woodwork. Molly used her magic to collapse the walls on top of them, pinning them down with the weight of the wreckage. They'd dig themselves out eventually, but by then we'd be long gone.

I smashed through the opposite wall and into the next room, and then the next wall and the next room, or the next corridor, on and on, heading always in a straight line through the structure of The Hall. At least the Sanctity was in the central building, and not one of the other wings, or it could have taken me hours. Walls that had stood for centuries fell under my armoured strength and cold, cold anger, and though more Droods came to meet me, in armour and out, and with all kinds of weapons, none of them came close to stopping me.

Occasionally the odds would get a bit heavy, as family members filled a room before me, but still none of them had field experience, and it was child's play to out-think and out-manoeuvre them. I could have killed so many of them, but I didn't. It wasn't necessary. Sometimes I fooled them into fighting each other; one golden form looks much like another. Sometimes I buried them under piles of furniture or wrapped them in precious tapestries they didn't dare tear. Once Molly stopped an entire crowd by threatening to overturn a glass display case full of delicate china, and a dozen voices cried out in horrified protest.

'Those pieces are irreplaceable!' cried an anguished voice, as Molly tilted the case slowly so the china pieces slid jerkily across the shelves. 'They're priceless! Historical treasures!'

'Then why are you hoarding them for yourselves?' snapped Molly. 'Why aren't they in a museum, so everyone can enjoy them? Back the Hell off, or I'll create a china jigsaw like you've never seen!'

'We're backing, we're backing!' cried the Droods. 'Barbarian! Philistine!'

They got out of our way in a hurry. Molly and I picked up the display case and carried it across the room, and the Droods scattered before us, crying out piteously for us to be more careful. I smashed a hole in the wall and stepped through, and Molly dragged the case into position to block the hole. Secure in the knowledge that the Droods would spend ages carefully moving the case aside, so as not to risk damaging the contents.

More Droods in the corridor beyond. And these at least had seen some training. They held themselves well, all ten of them, fanning out so as not to bunch up and make an easy target. I didn't waste time talking to them. I concentrated, applying what I'd learned from James, and grew supernaturally sharp claws on my golden hands.

First thing a field agent learns; any trick is a fair trick if it means you win and they lose. I took them down, one by one, fighting hand to hand. My claws ripped through their armour, and they cried out in shock as well as pain. Their flesh was torn and they bled inside their armour, and that had never happened before. Some turned and ran. The rest fell back, scattering, and Molly and I went straight through them.

A few saw Molly as an easier target. They went for her, reaching out with their golden hands, and she laughed in their featureless faces. She conjured up a howling stormwind that bellowed down the narrow corridor, picking them up and carrying them away, tumbling helplessly end over end like discarded toys, the whole length of the corridor.

The remaining Droods tackled me at once, knocking me off balance, and then piling on top of me as I crashed to the floor, trying to pin me down with the sheer weight of armoured bodies. Good tactic. Probably would have worked against anyone who wasn't field trained, and used to thinking around corners. I cracked open the floor beneath us with one sharp blow from a golden elbow, and our combined weight collapsed the floor. A great hole opened up and we fell through, the other Droods kicking and screaming and grabbing at each other, all the way down into the room below. I, of course, just grabbed the side of the hole with one hand, and pulled myself up and out. The Droods below were so inexperienced it probably wouldn't even occur to them that they could use the armoured power of their legs to jump back up again. Or at least, not until Molly and I had already moved on.

The next room was a trap.

I recognised the place the moment I entered it. The room was called Time Out, and it was full of ornate clocks and timepieces from across the centuries, covering all four walls with everything from water clocks to atomic devices, and the various forms of clockwork in between. I never did like Time Out; always struck me as a sinister place, when I was young. Full of the ticking of a million mad clocks. In this room Time itself could be slowed down, extended. A day could pass in here, between the tick and tock of a clock outside. Time Out was originally put together in the nineteenth century, to make possible the observation of certain delicate scientific and magical experiments, but these days it was mostly used by students, revising and cramming for an imminent exam.

I knew something was wrong before I was halfway across the room. The heavy ticks and tocks around me had taken on a strange dying fall, and the air was thick as syrup. I looked back at Molly, still stuck in the hole in the wall I'd made, her movements little more than a snail's pace. There was nothing wrong with her. It was the room. Time was slowing down, trapping me here like an insect in amber. Like a prisoner in a cell with invisible, intangible bars. I could cross the room in a few seconds, only to find that days had passed outside it, and the whole family waiting to meet me.

I raised my Sight, and the air seemed to shimmer around me, thick with slowly congealing forces. It wasn't something I could fight with my armour. All its strength and speed meant nothing, next to the slow inexorable power of Time. From all around me came the slowing remorseless ticking of the million mad clocks, nailing me down, pinning me in place like an insect on display, transfixed on a spike.

I lashed out at the grandfather clock next to me, and the heavy wooden case exploded under the impact. I ripped out the chains and the pendulum and threw them aside, and the great old clock was silenced. And Time's growing hold on me seemed to hesitate ... I grabbed a seventeenth-century carriage clock and crushed it in my golden hand, and cogs and pinwheels flew out of it. Time's hold slipped away from me, just a little. I could feel it. I laughed aloud and rampaged round the room, smashing the clocks, destroying everything I could lay my hands on, until Molly was suddenly striding across the room towards me, demanding to know what the Hell I was doing. She hadn't noticed anything. I stopped, breathing hard, and looked around me. The room was a mess. And Time moved normally on its way, ticking and tocking as though nothing had happened. I shook my head at Molly, and headed for the far wall.

I smashed through the wall as though it was cardboard, and stepped through into the corridor beyond. My feet shot out from under me, and suddenly I was plummeting the length of the hallway, scrabbling frantically for handholds on the walls as they rushed past me.

Someone had changed the direction of gravity, so that the wall at the far end of the long hallway was now the floor, and the two walls the sides of a long drop. I fell all the way to the bottom, tumbling helplessly, until the far wall came flying up towards me like a fly-swatter. I tucked myself up into a ball, got my feet underneath me, and used my armoured legs to soak up the impact as I hit.

Luckily, it was a really solid wall. Old stone, thick and sturdy. I hit hard, and the stone cracked from top to bottom, but it held. I took a moment to get my breath back. The hallway stretched end-lessly above me, the walls like mountainsides. I could see Molly way above me, looking out of the hole I'd made in the wall, peering anxiously down at me. I yelled at her to stay put. I thought hard, as my heart rate slowed reluctantly back to something like normal. The family had to know the fall alone wouldn't be enough to kill me. This was another delaying tactic. It was all they had.

I forced myself up out of the broken stone wall, damaging it still further, and looked up at Molly. 'Stay put! I'll climb up to you!'

'I could retrieve you with my magic!' she yelled. 'Maybe even undo the gravity inversion!'

She really did look a long way off. Maybe someone was messing about with space here, as well as gravity. Or were they connected anyway? It was a long time since my old science classes.

'No!' I yelled back. 'Don't do anything! Your magic could set off The Hall's inner defences!'

'You mean this isn't . . .'

'Hell, no! This is just some crafty little bugger showing off his lateral thinking.'

I punched a hole in the left-hand wall that used to be the floor, carefully pulled my golden hand back out again, and then made another hole. I kept on punching holes until I had enough hand and foot-holds to get started, and then I climbed up the wall, heading back to Molly. I picked up speed as I got the hang of it and had a rhythm going, and soon I was scuttling up the wall like a giant spider. (I winced as the thought occurred to me, and pushed it firmly away.) I soon reached the hole in the wall where Molly was waiting, and she helped pull me back through. We both looked down at the long drop between us, and the wall opposite.

'Now what?' said Molly.

'When in doubt, brute force and ignorance,' I said. 'Climb on my back.'

She gave me hard look, but finally did so, holding on tightly as I walked back across the room we'd just come through. Then I took a good run up to get some speed going, jumped through the hole, across the gap, and smashed through the far wall into the room opposite. Molly jumped down from me, slapping dust and splinters from her hair and shoulders.

'I don't want to have to do that again, *ever*,' she said firmly. 'Next time, I'll fly us across.'

I looked at her. 'I didn't know you could fly.'

'Lot of things you don't know about me. You should see what I can do with a ping-pong ball.'

I looked around the room, and once again I recognised it. I always thought of the long, narrow chamber as the Souvenir Room. It was crammed full of old trophies and mementoes, and a whole bunch of basically interesting old stuff that my various ancestors had brought back from their travels around the world. Books and maps, objects and artefacts, and some odd and obscure items that presumably meant something to someone once, but whose stories were now lost and forgotten. To a young Drood like me, they were all wonderfully interesting and fascinating, with their hints of a much bigger world outside The Hall. I spent a lot of time here as a child, leafing through the books and playing with the pieces. At least partly because I knew I wasn't supposed to. I was still fond of a lot of the exhibits, so I was careful not to break anything else as I made my way across the room. I pointed out a few of my favourites to Molly.

'That's the skull of a Vodyanoi from pre-Soviet Russia. Those are genuine Thuggee strangling cords from the Hindu Kush. That lumpy looking hairy thing is a badly stuffed Chupacabras, from Chile. Which if anything smells worse dead than it does when it's alive. And the intricate carvings in that cabinet are scrimshaw, carved from the bones of a great white whale.'

'You should charge admittance to The Hall,' said Molly. 'You could make a fortune out of the summer trade.'

The door ahead of us slammed open and my grandmother, Martha Drood, the family Matriarch herself, strode into the room to face me, accompanied as always by her consort, Alistair. I stopped abruptly, facing them, and they stopped where they were, maintaining a cautious distance. Molly moved in close beside me, reassuring and supporting me with her presence. I was glad she was there. Even after all that had happened, after all I'd discovered ... Martha was still the Matriarch, the will and authority of the Droods. And once I would have died rather than fail her.

The Matriarch wasn't wearing her armour. That might have come across as an admission of weakness, and Martha's arrogance would never allow her to see me as a serious threat. For a rogue to triumph against the will of the family was unthinkable.

So I armoured down too. Just to show my contempt.

'Hello, Grandmother,' I said. 'Alistair. How did you know where to find me?'

Alistair smirked. 'Intercepting your path wasn't exactly difficult, Edwin. All we had to do was follow the wreckage and destruction, draw a straight line to the Sanctity, and then get here ahead of you.'

'You always were very direct, even as a child,' said the Matriarch. 'That's why I chose this room, for our ... little chat. The number of times I had to send someone to drag you out of here, because you weren't where you were supposed to be ... You always were such a disappointment to me, Edwin.'

Molly looked at me. 'It's your family, Edwin. How do you want to handle this?'

'Very carefully,' I said. 'My grandmother wouldn't be in here, facing me without serious back-up, unless she was confident she had some really nasty cards to play.'

'This is the Drood Matriarch?' said Molly. 'Well, colour me impressed. The queen bitch of the family that runs the whole world. Hatchet-faced old cow, isn't she?'

The Matriarch ignored her, fixing me with her cold gaze. 'Where is James?' she said harshly. 'What did you do to James?'

'I ... killed him, Grandmother,' I said.

She cried out briefly then; a lost, devastated sound. She crumpled as though I'd hit her, and might have fallen if Alistair hadn't been there to hold her up. She pressed her face against his chest, eyes squeezed shut to keep the tears from falling. Alistair glared at me over her bent head. I wanted to see her suffer, for what she'd done to me, to all of us, even Uncle James; but in the end it was disturbing and even sad to see such a legendary façade crack and fall apart, right in front of me. I'd never seen her show any honest emotion in public before.

'You killed my son,' she said finally, pushing herself away from Alistair. 'My son, your uncle . . . he was the best of us! How could you, Edwin?'

'You sent him to his death, Grandmother,' I said steadily. 'Just like you tried to send me to mine on the motorway. Remember?'

I stepped forward to confront her with the other things I had to say, but to my surprise Alistair stepped forward to face me, putting himself between his wife and the rogue who threatened her. He stood tall and proud, doing his best to stare me down, and it occurred to me that for the first time he actually looked like a Drood.

'Get out of my way, Alistair,' I said.

'No.' His voice was high but steady. He had no authority, no power, and he knew it, but in his refusal to remove himself from the line of fire he had a kind of dignity, at last. 'I won't let you hurt her any more.'

'I don't want to hurt her,' I said, almost tiredly. 'I don't want to hurt anyone. That's not why I came back. But I have something important to do, and not much time to do it in. Take her away, Alistair.'

'No. This ends here.'

'I have Oath Breaker,' I said. 'And Molly has Torc Cutter. Even the Grey Fox couldn't stand against that.'

'You used Torc Cutter on your own uncle?' Alistair looked at me with horror. 'Dear God. What have you become, Edwin?'

'I don't know,' I said honestly. 'Awake, perhaps; to all the lies and betrayals . . . It's time to cut the rotten heart out of the family.'

'I have a weapon too,' Alistair said abruptly, and just like that there was an old-fashioned pistol in his right hand. It would have looked primitive, even pathetic, if I hadn't recognised it. If I hadn't known it for what it was. Alistair nodded grimly, seeing the knowledge in my face. Even Martha was shaken out of her grief by the sight of the gun.

'Alistair! Wherever did you get that? You can't use it! I forbid it!'

'I'll do whatever I have to, to protect you, Martha.' Alistair was looking at me, but the gun was trained steadily on Molly. 'You stand very still, Edwin. Or I'll hurt your woman, as you've hurt mine. I know none of you ever really thought of me as one of the family. Never thought I had it in me, to fight the good fight like the rest of you. But I love this family, and all it stands for; just as I've always loved you, Martha. And this is where I prove it.'

'Please, Alistair,' said Martha, trying for a calm and reasonable voice. 'Put away the gun. Let me handle this.'

'How can you love the family?' I said to Alistair. 'Knowing what you do, about the Heart? About the price we pay to be what we are?'

He frowned, suddenly uncertain. 'Martha? What's he talking about?'

I looked at Martha. 'He doesn't know, does he, Grandmother? You never told him. Never told him why he can't wear the golden torc.'

'He's not part of the Council,' she said dully. 'He never needed to know, so I never told him. It would have been ... cruel. You always were too soft-hearted, Alistair.'

'Not here, not now,' he said. 'Not when he dares to threaten you, and the whole family. You do know what this gun is, don't you, Edwin? Of course you do. Why don't you tell your little witch friend what it is?'

'Yes, Eddie,' said Molly. 'You know I hate to be left out of things.'

'That ... is a Salem Special,' I said. 'It's a witch-killer. It shoots flames summoned up from Hell itself. Or so the records say. No one's used the awful thing in centuries.' I glared at Alistair. 'I can't believe you're even thinking of using a Salem Special. You put your soul at risk just by handling it.'

'It'll stop you, and that's all that matters,' he said. He smiled briefly, nervously. 'Fight fire with fire, eh? Oh, I know it won't hurt you, Eddie. You'll get your armour up in time to protect you. But it'll do terrible things to your pretty girlfriend ... So you're going to stand very still, Edwin; until the rest of the family get here, take your weapons away and put you under arrest. Or I'll burn your woman alive before your eyes.'

'Don't be a fool, Alistair!' snapped the Matriarch, some of her old authority returning. 'You're not a field agent! I protected you from that!'

'I never asked you to protect me, Martha.'

'He'll kill you!'

'You never did have any faith in me,' said Alistair. 'But this is where I prove you wrong. You thought you could stop him with your authority, thought you could intimidate him into giving up. I never believed that. He was never intimidated by authority in his life. But look at him now. Look at him! Afraid to move a muscle, because of me!'

He took his eyes off me to glare at her, and that was all I needed. In the moment when he was distracted, I whipped Oath Breaker out from under my belt and brought in round in a swift ranging arc. He started to turn back, raising the Salem Special, but the long ironwood staff undid the binding seals on the ancient pistol, and it exploded, all its stored Hellfire bursting out at once. Supernaturally bright flames consumed Alistair's hand and arm, burning the meat down to the bone in seconds. The stench of brimstone and burnt flesh filled the air. Alistair fell back, howling and shrieking. He flapped his arm wildly, as though he could shake off the flames. What remained of his right hand fell away as the Hellfire consumed the small connecting bones in his wrist. It fell to the floor, still wrapped around what was left of the Salem Special.

Alistair screamed horribly as the flames leapt up to take a hold of his right shoulder. Martha beat at the flames with her bare hands, crying out at the pain, but still trying to help. I armoured up and moved quickly forward to smother the flames with my golden hands, but even though they couldn't burn me, I couldn't beat them out. In the end, Molly stepped forward, reeled off some Latin, and the flames disappeared in a moment. Alistair's cries fell away to shocked moans, and he sat down suddenly on the floor, looking dully at what little was left of his right arm. Martha sat there with him, holding him in her arms, trying to comfort him. I armoured down, and looked at Molly.

'Those were Hellfires ... how did you ...'

'Please,' she said. 'Remember who you're talking to.'

Alistair's moans stopped as he finally, mercifully, passed out. Less than half of his upper right arm remained, charred down to the blackened bone. It would have to be removed; it would never heal. Martha rocked him back and forth, crooning to him like a sleeping child. She was crying. I'd never seen her cry before. I tried to feel sorry for Alistair, but this was what he would have done to my Molly, if I hadn't stopped him.

'Martha . . .' I said.

'Don't. Don't pretend you care, you unnatural child.'

'So many tears,' I said. 'For Uncle James, for Alistair. But how many tears would you have shed over my death, Grandmother, if I had died on that motorway? Or if Uncle James had killed me, like you ordered? Did you cry over my twin brother, when he was sacrificed to the Heart? He was your grandson too. How did you choose between us? Flip a coin, perhaps? Or did you leave it up to the Heart, so you wouldn't have to feel accountable?'

But she wasn't listening. All she cared about was her Alistair, and what I'd done to him. Molly gently pulled me away.

'We have to go, Eddie. Others will be coming. You know that.'

I let her lead the way to the far end of the room. I had always thought it would turn out that Alistair was the traitor within the family. Because he never was one of us, really. I wanted it to be him. But in the end . . . he fought well and valiantly, to protect the woman he loved from my anger. I admired him. The poor damned fool. I didn't need to smash through the far wall. Just open the door, and step through into the next room, leaving Martha and Alistair behind.

The next room was huge: gleaming white tiles on the walls, and hygienically clean surfaces, packed full of assorted computers and other advanced technology in a hermetically controlled environment. A whole room full of machines to monitor and regulate conditions inside the Sanctity. They protected the Heart from outside influences, and protected those who lived in The Hall from the various disruptive energies and dangerous forces that emanated from the Heart. Normally there'd be half a hundred technicians scattered across the massive room, carefully tending the equipment and making constant small but necessary changes and adjustments to the Sanctity's delicate balance . . . but the place was deserted. Presumably they'd been evacuated, once it was clear I was coming here. I threaded my way through the bulky machinery, heading for the door at the other end of the room. Beyond that door lay the Sanctity, and the Heart, and my revenge.

Molly and I were almost there when the door suddenly opened, and Matthew and Alexandra stepped through. I stopped abruptly, and Molly moved in close beside me again. Matthew looked sharp and smooth, as always; the family's blue-eyed boy in his immaculate Armani suit. He smiled dazzlingly at me. Alexandra's smile was cold, and so were her eyes. I nodded briefly to them both, doing my best to look entirely unimpressed.

'Matthew,' I said. 'I should have known you'd turn up. You never could bear to miss out on anything important. But I honestly can't say I was expecting to see you again, Alex.'

'You of all people should know I don't give up that easily.' Alexandra's voice was sharp, and pointed. 'And you really should have expected to see Matty and me here, together, at the last. But then, you never were very quick at figuring out what was really going on, were you?'

I frowned, first at her, then at Matthew. There was something about their smiles, their easy confidence, their air of *I know something you don't know*. I'd missed something. And I couldn't afford to make mistakes, not when I was this close to the Heart, and its destruction ... What could I have missed? Neither Matthew nor Alexandra was wearing their armour, even though they both had good reason to see me as a threat. Something significant was happening here. I could feel it. They had to be planning something ... I risked a quick glance with my Sight. Both Matthew and Alexandra were carrying concealed weapons, radiating enormous amounts of power, but so were Molly and I. I checked the room around us. No booby traps, no hidden assassins. Just Matthew and Alexandra with their cold, calculating smiles. I looked straight at Alexandra.

'What did you do to the Armourer, Alex?'

She shrugged easily. 'You didn't really think I could be taken easily, did you? I maintain a constantly updated protection against all forms of poison. Basic security measure. And he really should have known better than to turn his back on me ... But he'd got old and soft, like so many of the family today. We're going to change all that.'

And with that *we* the penny finally dropped. 'You, and Matthew

... you're part of the Zero Tolerance faction! The hard-core family fanatics who want to change everything! Kill all the bad guys, and to hell with the consequences!'

'Yes,' said Matthew. 'That's us. Only we prefer to call ourselves Manifest Destiny.'

I must have made a shocked sound. Their smiles widened, and Molly grabbed on to my good arm and hung on tightly. Perhaps she thought I'd attack them. I was too stunned. Matthew and Alexandra laughed at the expressions on our faces.

'Truman only thinks he runs things,' Alexandra said lightly. 'But he's just our front, our public face, so the rest of the world won't realise that the Droods are actually bankrolling and running Manifest Destiny, for our own reasons. Until it's too late.'

'But ... you fought their troops,' I said to Matthew. 'I saw you, in London ...'

He shrugged. 'A necessary deception. And occasionally, the troops have to be put in their place. It keeps Truman from getting too uppity if we slap him down hard now and again.'

'Working behind the scenes has always been the Drood way,' said Alexandra. 'Kingmakers, rather than Kings. Zero Tolerance is the only way forward for the Droods, Eddie. The family's got very old-fashioned, very set in its ways; and far too complacent. Too content with the way things are in the world. Most of the younger generations follow us now, impatient to change the world for the better, instead of risking their lives to maintain the status quo. And after all, why should they? Look around you. The status quo sucks. It's time we took the lead, stamped out the bad guys, once and for all, and make a better world for everyone.'

'But who gets to decide what's better?' I said. 'The Droods? Manifest Destiny? You?'

'The family will decide,' said Matthew. 'And who better? We're the only ones who know what's really going on in the world.'

'I thought you of all people would understand, Eddie,' said Alexandra. 'You were always the great rebel, the renowned free-thinker of the family. You opened my eyes. Showed me there was more to life than duty and responsibility. After you left, I waited and waited for you to do ... something. But you settled for being just another field agent. Such a disappointment.'

'Funny, Alex,' I said. 'That's what I was thinking about you. I thought you were smarter than this. Matthew, he's always been out for himself, but you . . . You've become the very thing this family has always stood against. Another would-be dictator, with delusions of grandeur.'

'Oh, they're not delusions,' said Matthew. 'Not any more. We have followers, weapons, and far-reaching plans. It is our time, our destiny. Tomorrow belongs to us.'

'The family's spent too long at war with the supernatural,' Alexandra said briskly. 'Spending our lives in their countless secret wars. The time has come to put an end to the wars: by winning. We will wipe out everything that isn't human, isn't natural. No more magics, only dependable, rational science. We'll make the world a cleaner, simpler place. A human world, where human destiny is controlled only by humans.'

'No more magic?' said Molly. 'No more miracles, no more winged unicorns, no more dancing on moonbeams or laughter in the wild woods?'

'Oh, we'll probably keep a few of you around,' said Matthew. 'As pets.'

'With the Drood family in charge,' said Molly.

'Of course,' said Alexandra. 'No more hiding our light in the shadows, doing good from a distance. We've earned our time in the spotlight. We've been planning this for so long . . . Only you came so terribly close to derailing everything, Eddie.'

'I did?' I said. 'How very like me.'

'We were the ones who found and reprogrammed the Karma Catechist,' said Matthew. 'We planned to use his accumulated knowledge in the coming war. Only the process went wrong. He'd been through so many hands, you see, down the years. So many different groups with their different views and aims. I have to tell you, Eddie, the inside of his head was a real mess. So we slipped the poor fellow into Saint Baphomet's, very secretly, to be repaired. By certain medical experts sympathetic to the cause of Manifest Destiny.'

'And then you came along,' said Alexandra. 'What were you doing in his room anyway, Eddie? It wasn't part of your mission. You weren't even supposed to be on his floor! But you never could be trusted to just do the job . . . We couldn't risk what he might have told you, about us and our plans. He knew our names, knew everything. And we knew you wouldn't go along with what we'd worked so hard to bring about . . . So we whispered in the Matriarch's ear, told her you deliberately murdered the Karma Catechist because *you* were a part of Manifest Destiny. It really wasn't that difficult to convince her. You always were the black sheep of the family. A rogue in all but name. We persuaded her that you were a clear and present danger to the family, and Eddie . . . she signed your death warrant without even hesitating. Terrible old woman.'

Matthew grinned broadly. 'We always knew the way to power was through her. So we cultivated her. Fed her paranoia. We might not have been Council members, but we were her favourites for years, and she kept nothing from us.'

'He never told me anything,' I said harshly. 'The Karma Catechist. He killed himself first. This . . . everything that's happened . . . it was completely unnecessary. All for nothing.'

Alexandra shrugged. 'We gave him the poison tooth, and programmed him to use it if he felt at all compromised. Perhaps we shouldn't have given him such a hair trigger on the thing. But it doesn't make any difference. You've actually been very useful to us, Eddie. You made such a wonderfully visible scapegoat, holding the family's attention while we quietly put our plans into operation.'

'We would have had to destabilise and weaken the family first anyway, before we could take control,' said Matthew. 'But now you've done that for us! You've demoralised the family, taken out most of their heavy hitters, and destroyed the Matriarch by destroying her beloved Alistair. James is dead, Jack is dead . . .'

'You killed him? You killed the Armourer?' I said to Alexandra, shocked, and she winced at what she heard in my voice.

'He was in the way,' she said. 'He should have retired long ago.'

'I'll see you burn in Hell for that,' I said, and my voice was cold enough to throw both of them for a moment.

'You always were a sentimental soul,' said Alexandra.

'Right now, there's a power vacuum at the heart of the family,' said Matthew. 'And who better to step into the breach than the Matriarch's acknowledged favourites? Especially when we have such a large and determined popular following within the family.'

'The Council won't know what's hit it,' said Alexandra. 'Until it's far, far too late.'

'Do you know about the Heart?' I said. 'The bargain that was made, and the price we're still paying, for our armour and our power?'

'Oh, that,' said Matthew. 'The Matriarch told us about it, long ago. She didn't believe in keeping secrets from her beloved favourites. It was a bit of an eye-opener, I'll admit, but as Lexxy said there's no room for sentimentality in a family that's going places. We have a world to put to rights. What are a few lives, in the face of that? It's just . . . the way things are.'

'You can't take the moral high ground with innocent blood on your hands,' I said.

'Watch us,' said Alexandra.

'Or not, as you please,' said Matthew. 'It's really up to you, Eddie. Surrender to us, and serve Manifest Destiny (after a suitable amount of brain-washing and reprogramming, of course), or die, right here and now.'

I laughed in his face. 'The Armourer opened the Armageddon Codex for me. I have Oath Breaker.'

Alexandra and Matthew looked at each other sharply, their confidence shaken for the first time. This hadn't been part of their plan. But they still didn't believe they could fail, after coming this far, and they stared at me haughtily.

'That wooden stick is the mighty and legendary Oath Breaker?' said Matthew. 'I don't think so.'

'You wouldn't have the balls to use Oath Breaker,' said Alexandra. 'It's too big, too powerful, for a little man like you.'

'We have weapons,' Matthew said grandly. 'Real weapons. Terrible weapons! And the will to use them.'

Alexandra held up her right hand, and suddenly there was a long scalpel in it, shining supernaturally bright. 'This is Dissector, the ultimate scalpel created by the ultimate surgeon, Baron Von Frankenstein. It can cut through anything, neat as you like. It can cut you open, and reduce you to your component parts, with just a thought. You even touch that nasty old staff, Eddie, and I'll take your hand off at the wrist. Or maybe I'll cut your little witch's throat.'

'You're really starting to get on my tits,' said Molly.

'You always were a vindictive soul, Alex,' I said.

'And I have Dominator,' said Matthew, more than a little grandly. He snapped his fingers imperiously, and a laurel wreath fashioned from pure silver appeared on his head. 'With this, my thoughts become your thoughts, your wishes become my wishes. I'll enjoy seeing you kneel to me, Eddie.'

'Really?' I said. 'I always heard your tastes went the other way.'

'Surrender or die,' Alexandra said sharply. 'No more talking. Your precious Uncle Jack isn't here to save you with his Safe Words this time.'

Matthew chuckled nastily. A halo of psychic energies was already forming round his head.

I concentrated on Alexandra, trying to reach her with the sincerity in my voice. 'Don't do this, Alex. For old times' sake ... for what we used to be to each other ... You mustn't do this. It's not worthy of you, or the family.'

'What do you know about the family?' she said flatly. 'You haven't been a part of it for ten years. I don't know that you ever were, really. Always had to go your own way, live your own life, leaving the rest of us to struggle on under the yoke ... until we found our own way out ... And how can you talk about the family being worthy, when you know the secret of the Heart? The deal with the devil our ancestors made so long ago? We're not what we thought we were, Eddie. Never were. It was all a lie. Manifest Destiny is the only truth.'

'You can't use forbidden weapons, forbidden methods, to save the world,' I said. 'You'll destroy it, trying to make it over into what you want it to be.'

'So what?' she said. 'What has the world ever done for us, except lie to us? Better to die free, than to live a lie one day longer. We're going to make the world make sense, whether it wants to or not, whatever the price. This is our time, our destiny, and nothing can stop us.'

'Wrong, as usual,' said a familiar voice behind me.

We looked round sharply, and there was the Armourer, Uncle Jack himself, standing swaying on his own two feet. He wore a simple breastplate of an unfamiliar crimson metal over his lab coat. Caked blood had dried down one side of his face from a vicious scalp wound on his bald pate. He nodded briefly to me and Molly, and then grinned nastily at Matthew and Alexandra. And as they stood there gaping at him, he spoke two Safe Words in a language I didn't recognise, and Dissector vanished from Alexandra's hand as Dominator vanished from Matthew's brow. They both jumped, startled, and looked at the Armourer with wide, wild eyes.

'I thought you were dead!' Alexandra said loudly. 'Damn you, why aren't you dead?'

The Armourer sniffed. 'I was a field agent for twenty years, remember? I don't die that easily, girl.'

'We have other weapons,' said Matthew, too loudly. 'There's a whole army on its way here, armed to the teeth!'

'See this breastplate?' said the Armourer. 'This is the Juggernaut Jumpsuit. Yes, that one, from the Codex. Bring on your weapons, and your army. It won't do you any good. Eddie, you go on, boy. You've got work to do.'

'Listen,' said Alexandra. 'Hear those running feet? That's our reinforcements. Dozens of them. You can't stop us all, old man.'

And that was when the ghost of old Jacob Drood appeared. Out of his chapel at last, for the first time he looked truly frightening. We shrank from him as he manifested on the air before us, in a rush of air cold as death itself. He didn't look like a grumpy old ancestor any more, he looked like what he was: a dead man hanging on to existence through a terrible act of will. A stark, spectral figure, more a presence than a person, his face was all hollows and shadows, his eyes burning with unearthly fires. Just looking at him froze the blood in my veins, and closed a cold hand around my heart. We were in the presence of death now, stark and awful and utterly unrelenting.

Time for me to take a hand, said the ghost of old Jacob, in a harsh and terrible voice that resonated inside my head. *This is what I've been waiting for, all these years. Even though I often forgot, for years at a time, still I hung on, just for this. Bring on your army, Matthew and Alexandra, and I will show them the awful things I've learned to do since I died.* He looked at me, and I flinched despite myself. *Go to the Heart, Eddie. That's where the answers are. And do . . . what you have to do.*

Jacob and the Armourer headed towards Matthew and Alexandra, and they backed quickly away, leaving open the way to the Sanctity door. Molly and I hurried forward. A door to our right burst open, and a whole crowd of armoured Droods rushed in. They saw the Armourer, and the terrible ghost of old Jacob, and stumbled to a halt. Molly and I opened the door to the Sanctity and rushed in, pulling the door shut behind us.

And as the door closed, the screaming began.

CHAPTER TWENTY-TWO
Heart breaker

Standing there in the Sanctity, with the door slamming shut behind me, I felt like a vandal breaking into a cathedral. The Heart blazed before me, shining like the sun, so bright I had to force myself to look at it. A single massive, magnificent diamond, so big it filled most of the huge chamber my family had built to contain and protect it, all those centuries ago. Merely standing in the presence of the Heart took my breath away, made me feel small and insignificant in its presence. But I didn't believe that any more. I knew better now. I glared into the light, refusing to look away or bow my head, even as the simmering light seemed to blaze right through me, seeing everything in my mind and in my soul.

The feeling of awe snapped off, just like that. The light was as bright, the Heart was as huge, but its presence wasn't overpowering any more. It was just a really big diamond. I heard Molly make a soft, relaxed sound at my side, as she felt the sudden change too, and I started guiltily as I realised I'd forgotten she was even there. The Heart's presence could do that to you. Molly and I advanced slowly on the Heart until we were almost close enough to touch it. The curving side of the diamond rose up before us like a multi-faceted cliff face; but there was no trace of our reflections. The light blazing from inside the Heart overpowered everything else. I could feel the light on my skin, crawling slightly, like diving into an icy cold pond. And for the first time I got the impression that the Heart knew I was there, knew why I had come; and that it was looking directly at me.

'Hello, Eddie,' said the Heart. Its voice was warm and friendly, male and female, and it seemed to come from everywhere at once. 'Normally I take great pains to maintain a suitably spiritual and refined atmosphere in here, manipulating the emotions of all who come before me so as to keep everyone in a properly respectful attitude. But there's no point with you, is there? You know my secret, and you came here for the truth. Poor boy. As if your little mind could contain or appreciate all my truths.'

'You can talk?' I said. A bit obvious, I know, but I was honestly shocked. The Heart had never spoken to any Drood that I knew of; not since it made the original bargain with my Druid ancestors.

'Are you really so surprised to find that I'm a living, thinking thing?' said the Heart. 'Not all intelligence is based in meat.'

'Did you really come here from another dimension?' said Molly, to make it clear she wasn't being left out of anything.

'From a higher dimension,' said the Heart. 'What can I say? I always did have a thing for slumming.'

'Why have you never spoken before?' I said.

'I have,' said the Heart. 'But only to the ruling Matriarch of your tribe. By long tradition, each Matriarch has to agree to continue our long-standing bargain. Bind her family to me, body and soul. And in return, I grant you a morsel of my power. I only speak to you now, Eddie, because you carry Oath Breaker. Nasty little thing. I've been trying to persuade your family to get rid of it for generations.'

'Because it could destroy you,' said Molly.

'Of course,' said the Heart.

'Why did you come here?' I said harshly. I was so close to answers now, I could barely stand it. I wanted to know everything. I'd come so far, lost so much, and I could feel Death herself tapping on my shoulder as the strange matter moved through me ... but whatever happened here, I was determined to know the truth at last. 'You were on the run, weren't you? Being chased across the dimensions by something that scared you. So what did you do that you had to download yourself into this small, primitive dimension?'

'I was only having fun,' said the Heart. Its voice had changed subtly. It still sounded warm and friendly and ingratiating, but underneath it sounded like pulling the wings of flies or stamping on butterflies. 'I like to play. And if sometimes I play a little too roughly and break my toys, well ... there are always more toys.'

'Toys?' I said. 'Is that what we are to you?'

'What else could you be? Such limited, short-lived things; you flicker in and out so fast I can hardly keep track of you. I have lived for millennia!'

'And you can't think of anything better to do than play with toys?' said Molly.

'To be loved and worshipped and obeyed without question,' said the Heart. 'What could be more important than that?'

'And if your toys ever dare to rebel?' I said.

'Then I crush them,' said the Heart. 'Toys must know their place. That's why I allowed you in here, Eddie. I made you what you are. I gave you the gift of my golden collar, and you wore it for years like the good doggy you are. But it's still my collar.'

The torc around my neck burned icy cold as the golden living metal swept over and around me in a moment, even though I hadn't called it. The armour enclosed me like a prison cell, insulating me from the world and holding me helpless within. I said the activating Words, again and again, but nothing happened. I strained my arms and legs against the encasing metal, but the armour held me still. I wasn't in control any more. The Heart was. I was just a gleaming golden puppet now, with a man trapped inside it.

'Kill the woman,' the Heart said happily, greedily, and the armour moved to obey, advancing on Molly despite everything I could do to stop it.

Molly called out to me as the armour closed in on her, but she couldn't hear my answer. And since the Heart took up most of the space in the Sanctity, there wasn't anywhere for her to go. She backed away around the perimeter of the great chamber, trying to keep a safe distance between her and the advancing armour. There were two exits out of the Sanctity, but she had to know the armour would be upon her before she could even open a door. I was screaming the activating Words now, and screaming at Molly to get away, but none of it got past the featureless golden mask that covered my face.

Molly realised she couldn't reach me, and stood her ground. Her face became calm, and coldly resolved. She conjured up a roaring stormwind that came howling in out of nowhere, sweeping the air before it like a battering ram. It tried to pick me up and blow me away, but my armour grew heavy spikes out of the bottom of its golden feet, and anchored itself to the wooden floor. The wind battered harmlessly against my golden exterior, failed to find any purchase, and dropped away to nothing. The armour took a step forward.

Molly conjured up handfuls of Hellfire, and threw them at me. Flames from the deepest part of the Pit, designed to sear both body and soul, and still they couldn't touch me through the golden armour. The flames scoured and blackened the floor around me, and the air shimmered in a vicious heat haze, but I felt nothing. The armour took another step forward.

Monsters appeared out of nowhere to block my path. Huge, awful creatures, with armoured hides and lashing barbed tentacles and wide, snapping mouths full of razor teeth. But the armour walked right through the illusions, to get to Molly. She backed away, dismissing the illusions with a wave of her hand, and conjured up a bottomless pit between her and me. The effort brought beads of sweat to her face. The armour leaped easily over the gap, propelled by the unnatural strength of its armoured legs. Molly called up a shimmering screen of pure magic, to stand between her and me. It snapped and crackled on the air, supported by her iron will. The armour placed a single golden hand against the screen and pushed, slowly, remorselessly, with all the armour's boundless strength behind it.

Until the screen shattered and broke and disappeared, and Molly fell back, crying out in shock and pain. Because in the end Molly was human, and the armour wasn't.

Molly was clearly exhausted now, all her inner resources drained. She stumbled backwards, away from me, clinging to the wall for support, and the armour went after her. Its deadly golden hands stretched out towards her, and there wasn't a damned thing I could do to stop it.

'Eddie,' said Molly, in a voice trying hard to be calm and steady, 'I hope you can hear me in there. I know this . . . isn't you. I've done all I can. It's up to you to stop the armour now. But if you can't . . . I want you to know I understand. I understand it won't be you, doing it. So don't blame yourself. Just . . . find a way to make the Heart pay. Goodbye, Eddie. My one true love.'

I couldn't even answer her.

I'd exhausted my strength, fighting helplessly inside the armour. Setting my human strength against its inhuman power. I couldn't move any part of me, except as the armour moved me. It was like having my hand disobey me, pick up a weapon and commit murder, while I could only watch and scream helplessly at it to stop. It didn't help that so much stress had weakened my defences, and the strange matter had flooded into all of my body now. I could feel it, pulsing within me. The pain was sickening, and I was so weak I would probably have fallen if the armour hadn't been holding me up. I was so tired. I'd fought for so long, refusing to give in, and all for nothing.

And then a little voice at the back of my head said: *Then stop fighting, you idiot.* The voice didn't sound anything like mine. It didn't sound like the Heart's, either. So I took a gamble, and stopped fighting.

I let the weakness flood through me, taking the strength from my arms and legs. I stopped resisting, and let the strange matter do what it would. I gave up ... and the armour lurched to a sudden halt. Its golden hands stopped a few inches short of Molly's throat, and then slowly and ponderously the armour sank to its knees before her. Because the torc was linked to me, body and soul; and even the Heart couldn't break that link. The armour is only ever as strong as the man within, and this man ... had nothing left. The golden living metal rippled over my skin, struggling to obey the Heart's orders, but it was overridden by my stubborn weakness, backed by the strange matter's presence in my body. A small amount of control came back to me, and I slowly forced the golden metal away from my face, so Molly could see and hear me. She crouched down before me, and I think she could see death in my face. She started to cry.

'Sorry, Molly,' I said. 'But this is as far as I go. We always knew I probably wouldn't get to see the end of the story ... The strange matter's all through me now. Only one thing left you can do for me. Quickly, before the Heart finds a way to force control of the armour away from me. Take Torc Cutter and cut the torc around my neck. That destroys the armour. It won't be able to hurt you. Then take Oath Breaker, and smash that smug talking diamond into a million pieces.'

'I can't do that, Eddie! It'll kill you!'

'I'm dying anyway! Do it, Molly. Please. Protect yourself. At least this way ... my death will have some meaning. Some purpose.'

'Eddie ...'

349

'If you love me, kill me. Because I'd rather die than see you hurt.'

'I wish things could have been different.'

'Me too. Goodbye, Molly. My one true love.'

I lowered my head, showing her my neck. Already my movements were getting stiff, as the Heart fought to regain control. Molly produced the ugly black shears, and set them against the side of my golden neck. Somewhere in the background the Heart was shouting orders, but neither of us was listening. Molly forced the shears together, and the black blades cut through my torc. My armour disappeared in a moment, and the two halves of my golden collar fell to the floor.

And I laughed out loud as new strength flooded through me.

I rose to my feet, still laughing, and lifted Molly up with me as she stared blankly into my face. She started to laugh herself, from sheer relief. I took her in my arms and held her close, and she held me, and I felt strong and well and at peace at last. Molly and I clung on to each other for what seemed like for ever, and it felt good, so good to be alive. Finally we let go, and stood back and looked into each other's faces.

'Eddie, you're alive. . .'

'I know! Isn't it great?'

'How . . . Eddie, there's a collar around your throat. And it's silver.'

'I know,' I said. 'It's the strange matter. Apparently there's been something of a misunderstanding.'

'To put it mildly,' said a new voice. 'I was beginning to think I'd never get through to you in time.'

The voice was large and powerful and very sane, and it thundered through the Sanctity. It emanated from me, but it wasn't me speaking. The Heart cried out in rage and despair, but it sounded like a very small thing compared to the new voice. The strange matter, speaking through me.

'Time for the truth at last,' it said. 'Know now the true history of that foul and evil creature you know as the Heart. Criminal. Sinner. Thief. Coward. Murderer. It came here because it was running scared. Because it knew I was close behind it, coming to capture it and take it back to where it came from, for judgement and punishment. For all the awful things it has done, in so many dimensions. The Heart has been on the run for millennia, passing through dimension after dimension, and preying on whatever it found there.

'I . . . am the shaman of my tribe, much like your Druid ancestors. We protect the innocent and punish the guilty, and we never give up.

'I'd almost lost track of the Heart. The trail had gone cold, and I had searched so many places. And then a small opening appeared, between the dimensions. It was like nothing I'd ever seen before: vague and unfocused, quite primitive really. It was the Blue Fairy, using his gift at random to go fishing and see what he might find. Intrigued, I allowed him to catch a small piece of myself, and take it through into his primitive backwater dimension. And there was the Heart! Hidden away, in the back of beyond where no one would think to look. I could sense its presence, but its exact location was hidden from me. So I manipulated the Blue Fairy into passing the small piece of me on to the most powerful group in this dimension: the Drood family. And sure enough, once I was brought here I was able to locate the Heart. Unfortunately, there wasn't enough of me to break through the defences your family had put in place around the Heart.

'So I waited. And soon enough the Blue Fairy went fishing again, and I allowed him to catch more of me. And then I manipulated him, and the Drood traitors, and finally the elf lord, all so that he would fire an arrow of me into you, Eddie. So that you could bring me here, into the presence of the Heart. Inside all its protections. I never meant to cause you such pain, Eddie. The suffering and weakness were caused by my strange matter clashing with the Heart's collar. What you might call a short circuit. The human body was never meant to contain such diametrically opposed other-dimensional materials.'

'Why didn't I die when Molly cut the torc from me?' I said.

'Droods only die when separated from their torcs because that's what the Heart wanted,' said the voice. 'It couldn't risk any of its toys getting loose. But that's over now. The Heart can't hurt you any more, Eddie. Not while I'm here to protect you. And it won't be able to hurt your family either, once it's been destroyed. And though I've chased the Heart for so very long I think it's your privilege to put an end to the it, Eddie. If you want to.'

351

'I want to,' I said, and I drew Oath Breaker from my belt and turned to face the Heart.

'You can't do this!' it screamed. 'I made you what you are! I made your family powerful! I put you in charge of this stupid little world! You don't dare hurt me! I'm your god!'

'Bad god,' I said.

I raised Oath Breaker over my head, and brought it smashing down on the huge diamond. The ancient weapon took on its simple brutal aspect, and undid the forces that bound the other-dimensional being together. The Heart screamed shrilly, its light flaring in great staccato pulses, and then the massive diamond exploded soundlessly. It shattered, into millions of lifeless fragments, falling to the floor like sand, until nothing was left of the Heart. There hadn't been much to it. It was hollow, all along.

And with the Heart finally destroyed, the souls that had been trapped within itself for so long were finally set free. They manifested briefly on the still air of the Sanctity, one after another, flashing on and off, countless shimmering forms exploding like so many soundless fireworks in one last display of joy at their freedom, before finally passing on to whatever comes next. Molly cried out in delight, clapping her hands together.

And at the very end, one small soul came to me. My twin. My brother. He hung on the air before me, a baby only a few days old, and then he expanded suddenly into adult form; my size, my age. He looked . . . like the face I see in the mirror every day, only without the lines driven into it by pain, and loss, and duty. My brother considered me for a long moment, and then he smiled at me, and winked, and was gone.

And that was that.

Epilogue

With the Heart gone, the Sanctity didn't feel like the Sanctity any more. It felt like the quiet after the explosion, the calm after the storm, the incredible peace of waking up and knowing that the nightmare is finally over. The Sanctity was just an empty room now, wide and echoing, with a layer of sand on the floor. The dragon was dead; but I didn't feel like a dragon-slayer.

'How are you, Eddie?' said Molly.

'Pretty good,' I said. 'The pain is gone, the weakness is gone, I'm back to normal again.'

'No, Eddie,' she said gently. 'How do you *feel?*'

'I don't know,' I said. 'Numb. Lost . . . I used to know what I was, what my life was about. Then that was taken away from me. I used to have a family, and that's gone too. All gone . . .'

'You still have me,' said Molly.

'Do I?'

She put her hands on my shoulders, pulled me in close and kissed me. 'Try and get rid of me, idiot.'

'So,' I said, after a while. 'The Heart's dead. What do we do now?'

'You mean for an encore?' said Molly. 'Haven't you done enough?'

The door behind us swung open, and we both spun round, ready to defend ourselves, but it was only the Armourer and the ghost of old Jacob. Molly and I relaxed as they came over to join us. The Armourer's face was still half buried under dried blood, but he looked a lot steadier on his feet. Jacob had resumed his grumpy old ghost form, with garish Hawaiian shorts and a grubby T-shirt bearing the legend *Dead men Don't Eat Quiche.*

'Eddie, my boy,' said the Armourer. 'Are you okay? We heard all kinds of noises from in here, but we couldn't get in till now. Not even Casper the Unfriendly Ghost here. And what the Hell happened to the Heart?'

'Look down,' I said. 'You're standing in what's left of it.'

He looked down, winced, and then shook his head. 'So that's what Oath Breaker does. I always wondered.'

'Here,' I said, handing the ironwood staff to him. 'The sooner this is back in the Armageddon Codex, the safer we'll all be. Molly, give him Torc Cutter.'

'Oh poo,' said Molly, pouting. 'I was hoping to keep it as a souvenir.'

The Armourer gave her one of his hard looks, and she handed the shears over without another word.

'So,' I said, 'that's it, at last. All over. Someone lead me to a comfortable chair and place a nice cup of tea in my hand. It's been a busy few days . . . but at least it's finished now.'

'You have got to be joking,' the Armourer said sternly. 'After the damage you've done here, you think you can sit back and take it easy? You've done more in one evening to bring the Drood family to its knees than centuries of enemy action. It's up to you to save the family, Eddie. You can't leave a job half done. You brought the family down; only you can raise it up again.'

'To Hell with that!' Molly said sharply. 'This is what I lived for: to see the high and mighty Droods humbled and forced to their knees, made to live down here in the dirt with the rest of us. Don't listen to him, Eddie. You've taken the Droods' foot off the neck of everyone in the world. We're free at last!'

'Free?' I said, reluctantly. 'No, Molly. It's not that simple, and it never was. Truman's Manifest Destiny is still out there, remember? Free from Drood influence and control, and still determined to wipe out everything that doesn't fit their narrow definition of normal, and human. Who's going to stop them, if not the family? And then there are the other dark forces, only kept in check by fear of what the family would do if they ever got out of hand . . . There has to be another power in place to stop the forces of darkness from over-running the world. But, if there has to be a Drood family, it's going to be a new kind of family.'

'Now you're talking,' said Jacob. 'Always knew you were destined for great things, Eddie. Even if I couldn't remember why.'

354

I considered him thoughtfully. 'You just remembered you were only hanging about here in order to help me destroy the Heart . . . So, and don't take this the wrong way, why are you still here?'

He gave me his usual shifty grin, and shrugged vaguely. Little bubbles of blue-grey ectoplasm jumped up from his shoulders before slowly settling back into him again. 'Guess I've got used to it here. And besides, I am curious to see what's going to happen next. I haven't had so much fun since the Great Gender Swap of 1741. We never did find out who was behind that.'

'I don't see Alexandra, or Matthew,' I said. 'What have you done with them, Jacob?'

He met my gaze easily, and for a moment something of his old terrifying self surfaced in his gaze. 'They won't be coming back. Ever.'

'Don't ask,' the Armourer said stiffly. 'Trust me; you really don't want to know.'

'Poor Alex,' I said, and I meant it.

'What was this Alex person to you, anyway?' said Molly.

'It was more what she might have been,' I said. 'If things had gone differently.'

'Oh,' said Molly. 'Yeah. I've had lots of relationships like that.'

I looked at her for a moment. 'I won't ask,' I said finally.

'Best not to,' she agreed.

And then, finally, I looked at the Armourer, my Uncle Jack, and said the one thing I'd been putting off, the one thing I knew I'd have to say the moment I saw him coming through the door. 'I'm sorry, Uncle Jack. I'm really sorry, but . . . Uncle James is dead.'

'I know,' said the Armourer. 'You couldn't have done anything else, Eddie. James wouldn't have given you any other choice. For him, the family always came first. And he never could say no to Mother.'

'He was supposed to kill me on the motorway,' I said. 'But he let me go. Gave me a chance . . . made all this possible.'

'Good for him,' said the Armourer. 'Maybe he was growing up, at last. So, the Grey Fox is dead . . . Good bartenders and bad women will be weeping bitter tears in bars all around the world, once word gets out.'

There was no point in telling him that Molly had actually killed my Uncle James. The family was going to have enough problems accepting her as it was.

Jacob fixed me with a firm look. 'You have to address the family, Eddie. Here, now! Explain to them what's been going on. They need to know the truth. I'll summon them and you can tell them what needs to be done, to put the family back together again.'

'What?' I said. 'I don't know what to tell them!'

'You'll think of something,' said the Armourer. 'You have to take charge, Eddie. Push change through, before the old guard take control again.'

'Wait a minute!' I said quickly. 'I never even wanted to be a regular part of the family, let alone tell them how to run things! I ran away from this family the first chance I got, remember?'

'Well you can't run away this time,' said the Armourer. 'Not after the trouble you've caused. You've smashed our defences, wrecked The Hall, demoralised the family fighters, destroyed the Heart and taken away everyone's torcs! You have a duty to undo the damage you've done.'

'But . . .' I said.

'Only you can tell them the truth,' said Jacob.

'It's what your Uncle James would have wanted,' the Armourer said solemnly.

I glared at him. 'I never knew you were so proficient at emotional blackmail.'

He grinned. 'Runs in the family.'

And then we winced and shuddered as Jacob took on his deathly aspect again. His spectral presence filled the chamber, cold and distant and only remotely human; powerful beyond imagination now that he was no longer bound by life's limitations. His voice spread out through The Hall, ordering every member of the family to attend the Sanctity. Right now, no omissions, no excuses. I only caught the edges of the ghostly summons, and that was still enough to make me sway on my feet. The sheer power in Jacob's voice was like nothing in this world. No one in the family would dare disobey.

And soon enough they came streaming through the great double doors and into the huge empty chamber of the Sanctity; in ones and twos, and then in groups, and finally in crowds, until there was a steady flow of bewildered Droods, pressing in through the two doorways. Many of them were still wide-eyed with shock from the sudden loss of their torcs. For the first time in their lives they felt utterly defenceless, and vulnerable, and they were desperate for answers and reassurances. They came in gabbling and shouting, only to subside instantly into murmurs and mutterings once they saw who was waiting for them. The family rogue, the family ghost, the bloodied Armourer and the infamous Molly Metcalf. Whatever answers were coming, they clearly weren't going to be very reassuring. Still they kept streaming into the Sanctity, house Droods and security Droods, researchers and planners and house staff, and every other member of the family. Right down to some toddlers and babies carried in their parents' arms.

'Make a start,' the Armourer said to me. 'Before people start getting crushed in the pack.'

I looked at Molly, and she conjured up an invisible platform for the four of us to stand on, and then raised it several feet into the air, so everyone could see and hear me.

'It helps that they have to look up to us,' she muttered in my ear. 'Gives us the psychological edge. Now go on, promise them bread and circuses or something.'

'Speaking of edges,' said the Armourer, a little testily, 'could you perhaps put some colour into the edges of this damned platform, so some of us can see where the bloody things are? It's a long way to fall, and some of us are feeling a bit fragile at the moment.'

The edges of the platform glared suddenly silver. They were a lot closer than I'd realised.

The chamber was now packed to bursting, with more faces peering in through the open doors. The muttering kept threatening to break out into something more, but didn't, because any time someone started to raise their voice they found Jacob glaring at them, and then they got tongue-tied and went off the idea. The crowd went completely silent as the Matriarch finally arrived, pushing her way through the crowd. Everyone made as much room for her as they could, to let her pass. She reached the front of the crowd, and glared up at me on my platform. Instead of Alistair, at her side stood the Serjeant-At-Arms. His face was bruised and swollen, but his gaze was as cold and direct as ever. I nodded to the Matriarch.

'Hello, Grandmother. How's Alistair?'

'Alive. Barely. He's in the infirmary. They're trying to save his face.'

'He surprised me,' I said, aware everyone in the Sanctity was hanging on our every word. 'He was a good man, and true, at the end.'

'I've always known that,' said the Matriarch. 'He served the family. Not like you. What have you done to us, Edwin? *Where are our torcs? Where is the Heart?*'

'That's what you're here for,' I said. 'To hear the truth, at last.' I looked out over the crowd, at the confused, frightened, desperate faces. 'You're here to learn the truth about everything that's happened. Everything that's been hidden from you, down all the centuries of this family's existence. The secrets only a Drood can tell you.'

'We know you,' said a female voice from deep in the crowd. 'But what's the infamous Molly Metcalf doing up there with you?'

There was a general murmur of agreement, quickly cut off as Molly snapped her fingers, and the woman squeaked loudly as her clothes suddenly disappeared. Molly smiled sweetly.

'Any more questions? I love answering questions from the crowd.'

And while the crowd was quiet, I told them everything.

I explained to them what the Heart really was, and the true nature of the bargain that had given us our torcs. There were shocked cries and gasps, but no one challenged me. I told them how the bargain had to be confirmed by every new Matriarch, and every eye in the chamber went to Martha Drood. She ignored them, glaring coldly up at me. I explained how I'd destroyed the Heart, and why they hadn't died when their torcs disappeared. And then I told them the final awful secret of the Droods, known only to the inner circle. That we were not the secret defenders of Humanity, but their secret rulers.

I think there would have been a riot then, as various factions in the family shouted and pushed at each other, but Jacob rose suddenly up into the air, and took on his spectral aspect again. The temperature in the Sanctity plummeted, and we all shuddered, and not just from the cold. Death was in the chamber, and looking right at us. Jacob glared about him with no longer human eyes, and everyone went very quiet and very still, not wanting to draw his attention. Jacob sank slowly back on to the platform, and resumed his usual form.

From the silence, one voice rose. The Matriarch cursed me, naming me traitor to the family, calling me a fool and a liar and an enemy of everything the Droods stood for. She said I was no grandson of hers, and called on every Drood present to rise up, drag me down and kill me. Her voice rose and rose, shrill with fury and hysteria, spittle flying from her mouth, until suddenly the Serjeant-At-Arms dropped a hand on her shoulder, and gave her a good shake. Her voice cut off abruptly, and she looked at him, shocked. The Serjeant let go of her, and turned his back on her to address the crowd.

'You all know me,' he said, and his familiar harsh voice held everyone's attention. 'You know what I stand for. And I tell you; Edwin has earned the right to be heard. He's the truest son this family ever had. Go on, boy. Tell them what they need to know.'

'Thanks,' I said. 'I still hate your guts, mind.'

'Goes with the job,' he said, entirely unconcerned. 'Get on with it.'

So I told them the rest: how I'd been falsely outlawed by the zero tolerance faction, who were secretly running Manifest Destiny. That really put the cat among the pigeons. They knew about Truman, and what his people stood for.

'We've been lied to,' I said finally, tiredly. 'We're not who we thought we were. We aren't the good guys, and haven't been for centuries. But we can be; we can be what we were meant to be. If you're prepared to fight for it.'

The men and women before me didn't look much like fighters at the moment. Most of them appeared pretty shell-shocked, as though someone had just punched them in the gut, after hearing so many unpleasant and unsuspected truths one after the other. They looked at each other uncertainly, and then back at me, until finally a voice at the back of the crowd said:

'What do you want us to do?'

'I want us to do what we were born to do! I want us to be what we were always supposed to be: shamans to the tribe, protecting people from the evil forces that threaten them! Only now the tribe is Humanity, and we have to be warriors of the world, fighting the good fight; not for ourselves, but because it's the right thing to do! We have to earn the right to be proud to be Droods again!'

'But . . . how can we fight, without our torcs?' said another voice.

I smiled, and let one hand rise to the silver torc at my throat. 'The Heart is gone, but fortunately I've found a new sponsor for the family.' And I subvocalised: *Show them, strange matter.*

The new armour flowed over me in a moment, encasing me completely in shining silver. The crowd cried out, some even applauded. A great voice spoke to them then, the strange matter addressing the family through me, its voice full of peace and calm and good fellowship.

'Long and long have I pursued the creature you knew as the Heart, across all the many dimensions, to punish it for its terrible crimes. Now it is gone, I will stay here to help undo the evil it did. I will be your new protector; and there shall be torcs for all.'

'How long do you plan on sticking around?' said a practical voice.

'Until I've taught you how to be strong, without armour,' said the voice. 'You have no idea of your true potential.'

There was a lot more murmuring in the crowd about that.

'But what price do we have to pay, for this new armour?' said another voice in the crowd. 'The Heart wanted our children. Our unknown brothers and sisters. What do you want?'

'Just to help,' said the voice. 'That's my job. And you've already paid me, by destroying the Heart. You have no idea how long I've spent chasing that damned thing. I'm glad it's finally over ... I'm entitled to some leave, so I think I'll spend it here. Just for a few millennia. Fascinating dimension, fascinating people. You're really going to have to tell me more about this sex thing you do ...'

'Later,' I said quickly, subvocalising. 'You know, I can't keep calling you strange matter. Don't you have a name I can use?'

'How about Ethel?' said the voice in my head. 'That's a good name.'

'We'll discuss that later, too,' I said. 'Now get this armour off me, please.'

'Oh, sure.'

The silver armour disappeared back into my torc, and I looked out over the family. 'Follow me, and you'll all have armour again. And we will be ... what the family was supposed to be before we lost our way.'

'Under your leadership?' the Matriarch said loudly, her voice harsh and unforgiving.

'Not if I have anything to say about it,' I said. 'Never wanted that. Too much like hard work.' There were a few chuckles from the crowd. 'No, we've had enough leaders; they can't be trusted. You agreed to the Heart's bargain, Grandmother; generations of Matriarchs, agreeing to the slaughter of generations of children.'

'We had no choice!' she said fiercely. 'We had to be strong, to fight the forces of darkness!'

'You always had a choice,' I said. 'We never did. We never agreed to the sacrifice of our brothers and sisters, Grandmother.'

And there must have been something in my voice, because she looked away, and did not answer.

'I suggest an elected Council,' I said to the crowd. 'You can sort out the rules. Except that current members of the Council must be banned. They were part of the conspiracy. Part of the lies. I'll see things through the transition, and then ... I'm out of here. Back to being a field agent again. That's where I belong.'

'If you're planning to run out on the family, why should we listen to you?' said a female voice, only to duck her head down as Molly looked at her thoughtfully.

'I'm not leaving the family,' I said firmly. 'Just going back to doing what I do best. Kicking the bad guys' arses, and making them cry like babies. Manifest Destiny's still out there, and the other monsters who'd attack us in a minute if they thought we were weak.'

'We are weak!' said the Matriarch. 'You've shown them our defences can be broken!'

'We became weak under you, because you allowed the family to split into factions,' I said, and once again she looked away. 'We have to be strong, united. Shepherds to the flock, not wolves. Hell, if fighting evil was easy, everyone would be doing it. But don't worry, Grandmother; from now on there will be no more fanatics. Just men and women of good will. And anyone who can't or won't go along with that can hit the road. Without torcs.'

The Armourer stepped forward. 'This is Edwin Drood. He took on the whole family, and won. Who better to lead us? To make us strong again? To make us what we were always supposed to be? I am the Armourer, and he has my support.'

'And mine,' said the ghost of old Jacob.

'And mine,' said the Serjeant-At-Arms.

The crowd looked at the Matriarch. She gazed slowly around her, taking in what she saw in their faces, and finally her proud shoulders slumped and she turned away.

'I'm tired,' she said. 'And Alistair needs me. Do what you want. You will anyway.'

She turned her back on me and walked off through the crowd, pushing out blindly with her hands, and again the people opened up to let her pass. No one said anything, no one jeered. She was the Matriarch. And even after all that had happened, after all she'd done, to me and so many others, it still hurt me to see her humbled and broken. She was my grandmother, and she always gave me the best toys at Christmas when I was little, and nursed me when I was sick.

'Edwin leads us now!' said the Armourer, grabbing my hand and holding it over my head like a prizefighter. 'The greatest field agent of all time! The truest, bravest son this family ever had! Edwin! Edwin!'

The crowd took up the chant, yelling my name, working themselves into a frenzy as the great chamber filled with the sound of the family cheering me, over and over. I found it a bit scary. I'd never wanted to lead the family, but it seemed I wasn't being given any choice. So, I'd stick around for a while. Do what I could. And run away again, first chance I got. I eased my arm out of the Armourer's grasp, turned to Molly, and grinned at her.

'It's been a crazy few days, hasn't it?' I said. I had to raise my voice, to be heard over the din of the crowd. 'Who would have thought we'd end up here, eh?'

'I'm glad for you, Eddie. But where do I fit into all this?'

'Wherever you want. The family is going to have to reach out to many of those who were once our enemies. I've seen for myself that the distance between us and the bad guys isn't as clear and distinct as I was brought up to believe. We have to learn to work together, against the real threats. Like Manifest Destiny. And who better than you, to be our emissary?'

She smiled. 'That the only reason you want me to stick around?'

'No,' I said. 'I need you here because . . . I need you.'

'So,' she said. 'We are having a relationship, after all?'

'Looks that way,' I said.

And that's how I ended up running the family business. It's a strange old world, sometimes.

SHAMAN BOND WILL RETURN
IN
Daemons are Forever